DUST DEVILS

Dust Devils

Journeys in the Vanishing American West

Dayton Lummis

SUNSTONE
PRESS

SANTA FE

Book and cover design by Vicki Ahl

Sunstone books may be purchased for educational, business, or sales promotional
use. For information please write: Special Markets Department, Sunstone Press,
P.O. Box 2321, Santa Fe, New Mexico 87504-2321.

Library of Congress Cataloging-in-Publication Data:

Lummis, Dayton.
  Dust devils : journeys in the vanishing American West / by Dayton Lummis.
    p. cm.
  ISBN 978-0-86534-483-9 (pbk. : alk. paper)
  1. West (U.S.)--Fiction. I. Title.

PS3612.U48D87 2007
813'.6--dc22

                                                                    2006101860

WWW.SUNSTONEPRESS.COM
SUNSTONE PRESS / POST OFFICE BOX 2321 / SANTA FE, NM 87504-2321 /USA
(505) 988-4418 / ORDERS ONLY (800) 243-5644 / FAX (505) 988-1025

To my mother, Dorothy L. Lummis (1912–1997),
who loved the West.
She was lassoed by a cowboy in Cody, Wyoming,
in 1926. But she slipped the rope!

and

In memory of "Old Mr. Moore"
1947–2004

"Hawks belong with hawks,
and sparrows with sparrows . . ."

As a hawk I soared
across the West, the old,
honest, workingman's West,
free and alone, watching
changes that disturb the
quiet solitude of purpose.

Desert and rimrock country
suit me best, where one can
see for miles, where trouble
blows in the dust-devils
three miles high.

Then, even echoes die away;
"Cowboy," "Dr. Avis" and the
others always knew—the Abyss
of History is deep enough
to hold us all.

CONTENTS

PREFACE

Some years back I had the idea of writing a novel, a semi-autobiographical novel based on my experiences in the West and the characters I have known. I even started the book—but produced only one page. This is it:

In a bar in Bisbee, Arizona, down near the border with Old Mexico, two men,one pushing 70, the other in his 30s, sat at a table drinking beer. They seemed chance companions, men who did not know each other very well, wanderers whose paths just happened to bring them both to Bisbee, a day or two or three ago. The mood was solemn.

"I'm kinda burned out," the older man said. "Used up jest about all the energy a man's given for one lifetime. I'm jest coastin' these days." He finished his beer and put the bottle down on the table, sharp! The younger man drank from his bottle, made no comment. The older man continued. "I'm goin' up north, away from all this desert country. To the North Country, where it rains and it's green. Where I'm from. There comes a time when a man decides to go home. You understand?"

The younger man nodded silently, staring at his beer. He pulled out his wallet. From it he extracted five crisp $100 bills, U.S., and placed them on the table. "Will this get you there?" he asked. The older man looked at the money but made no move to pick it up. "Yes, it would," he said. "But I don't need it. I can git there on my own."

Smiling grimly, the younger man said, "Take it. You've earned it, and more. I owe . . ." His voice trailed off. He tapped his fingers on the table.

"So—owe," the older man said, getting up.

He walked outside to his truck. He stood beside it for a moment.

A warm wind was blowing from the south, out of Mexico. The street-lights of Bisbee were still the yellow incandescent ones, from an earlier time. The man stood there, looking at the soft light on the old buildings, the shadows and the great darkness beyond. Then he got in his truck, started it, and drove out of town. North. He was headed north, where it rained and was green. Where he was from.

I was going to call my book "Dust Devils," because I had always been fascinated by those swirling funnels of dust and debris that whirled across the desert and then were suddenly gone. Used themselves up, ran out of energy, one might say. Very Western, I thought.

Yet that single page was as far as my novel ever got. Over days that stretched into weeks, then months, then years, I would from time to time ponder those few words, wondering where I meant them to be going. I guess I saw myself as the older man, that sort of character. And the younger man? Well, he was a Hollywood hustler, a burned-out screenwriter desperately seeking some new idea to revive his career. What he was trying to pay for was three nights over beer, pumping the old man about his life, his Western experiences. On the table was a tape recorder. To the younger man, the three nights of talk were a treasure trove, to be worked into plots, scenarios, scripts. He thought that by paying $500 he was buying the rights to all this.

I am not from Hollywood—although I do have memories of Hollywood when it was different, in the 1950s, even then a place of manipulation and backstabbing. It was Samuel Goldwyn, I think, who advised a young man new to Hollywood, "Son, the most important thing in this town is sincerity. If you can fake that, you've got it made!"

Nor am I from the North Country—unless you count New York City, where I was born, or Pennsylvania, where I grew up, as the North Country. The pull of my life was always westward—Malibu, Santa Monica, Lake Tahoe, San Francisco, Colorado Springs, Cripple Creek, Bisbee, eastern Oregon, central Nevada, the East Mojave desert. And now Santa Fe.

Nor am I that older man in the bar, although much of him is in me. I understand what he was saying to that younger man, who was grasping, grasping for one more con to peddle in L.A., in Hollywood, in the Golden State, in California. Thinking that $500 could cover it, or if not $500, then maybe a grand, before his dwindling funds ran out, and also his last chance to make it back to Hollywood. The tape recorder, the money on the table—$500 for a life!

I still think that the novel's one page was onto something. But maybe I should just tell my own story, exactly as it happened.

PART I
WESTWARD

The First Time

Train slowing and creaking
in a sudden rainstorm
after the gleaming rush across
flat sun-washed Colorado grasslands,
the long climb through
rock walls of Raton Pass,
the first piñons and adobe buildings,
signs of another culture.
All the way from Chicago
the stern, ordered, rich farmlands
giving way to a wilder,
more open, less structured
sense of space,
the growing influence of mountains,
things breaking up into a jumbled
unplowed, untrodden landscape,
ragged, distant, hard-to-get-to
places with unfamiliar names.
They are still there, shrinking,
being discovered, exploited, taken over;
here and there
some of the mystery remains,
glimpses of various seasons
when the light is just so
and no one is around,
in the great silence broken
by sudden winds blowing from
lost years drifting like dust
from some long-ago vehicle
on a forgotten nowhere road.

1

El Rancho Piedra Gorda

The front porch of the restored cabin at *El Rancho Piedra Gorda*
was as restful as any place in the world.

When I read about the big Malibu fire in the spring of 1993 I just knew it had swept over my father's old place, El Rancho Piedra Gorda as he called it—Big Rock Ranch. I wrote to a neighbor, George Green, and asked him to go up there and have a look around. I was not surprised to get his card: "Nothing remains of the barn or cabin, just piles of ashes."

Some time later I drove over to Santa Monica from Santa Fe and took my usual accommodations at the Embassy Hotel Apartments, my father's last dwelling place. Then I went to Malibu, armed with a camera to record "the final chapter." Nearing Big Rock Canyon I recalled my first time on that route, and how little traffic there was along the coast back then. Living back in the mountains, in primitive circumstances, apart from "regular folks" in nice houses on tree-lined streets—that was where my penchant for lonely travels in remote parts of the West was born.

My father had tried to steer me away from my early fascination with the vast empty spaces. He said there was no future in them, only loneliness. But that was what attracted me. He wanted to see me oriented toward a normal life, a dignified profession, a nice wife and family, security—the white-picket-fence syndrome. All of which were things that he had never had. He viewed the West in terms of various failure—abandoned towns, dried-up wells, dead cows, dust storms, hobos and drifters. His was a Great Depression, Dust Bowl, mentality. Those were the times that formed him.

All the while that my father was wanting normality for me he lived alone at an isolated little ranch at the end of a dirt road in the mountains outside Los Angeles, with no hot water or toilet. He kept a scraggly old dog and fed a visiting coyote; and bobcats and occasional mountain lions prowled around. He was some form of hermit, with an on-and-off connection with the real world —increasingly off as the years went by. I remember our excursions to town for showers at the YMCA and meals in "workingman's restaurants," as my father called them.

At one of them the proprietor asked my father if he was a fireman, because of the blue denim "chore coat" from Sears that he was wearing. "No," my father said. "I have a small place up in the hills." As if that explained everything. The man nodded, wiping the counter, looking at us. I imagined he was thinking, "Another Okie, come out here in the '30s from some Dust Bowl place, got hold of some hardscrabble land back in the hills, real cheap, gets by. A man with his kid, eking out a living. The old man looks kinda worn-out, that thin, gaunt look—and that beard! Maybe the kid'll do better, there's more opportunities now.

But you never know. Sometimes these kids take after the old man, in their loner, redneck ways." I could almost hear the man thinking those things.

"Dessert, gents?" the man asked.

"No," my father said, laying a few bills on the counter. "We'll be on our way."

A small place up in the hills—that was the long and short of it. Okies we were not, but that is how the proprietor of that old-time Western cafe saw us. He had seen plenty of Okies, coming and going. An old man and his boy, living somewhere up in "the hills." There were lots of isolated shacks and hardscrabble ranches in the Southern California hills in those days, in the 1950s, and lots of Okies inhabiting them, scratching out livings.

My father worried about me always wanting to be alone with him in wild country, with no other human intrusion. He worried about my outbursts when people happened along, reminding me that we did not have these quiet places all to ourselves, that others liked to enjoy them also. But I felt the West was all mine, and did not want to share it. My father even considered "counseling" for me, but did not know quite what or where. Finally he decided my anti-social tendencies were something I would grow out of. Like he had grown out of his? He suggested various "social activities" to divert me from my fascination with lonely places. But generally we followed routines that kept us isolated from the mainstream of society.

I remember trips to town with my father, looking at the houses on the tree-lined streets, feeling both perplexed and envious. It seemed we were always on the outside looking in. But that's where we chose to be. I would ponder this on the way back, as we climbed ever higher into the dark mountains on the winding, narrow road. And finally atop the oak-studded mesa, we would see the porch light down in the draw, the outline of the cabin. My father was always glad to get back. At first sight of the little light he would say, "Well, there it is—home. It ain't much, but it's ours."

Resources at the ranch were always stretched thin. I was admonished to make things last. Not to waste precious water from the small well in the canyon, to turn off the tap while brushing my teeth. Years later, still following the same procedures, I would think back to *Piedra Gorda*, my father always worrying about the well running dry. And it did from time to time. Eventually my father installed a large tank, which he filled during the wet winter, when the well was productive.

He lived almost 20 years on the ranch. But near the end of his life he lived in a small apartment he called "a room." Once while I was there a telephone solicitor called. "No, no—you got the wrong person," my father said, winking at me." I'm just an old guy in a room, on the way out."

Almost all his final dreams were about the ranch. The chores that consumed so much of his time. The abundant wildlife that he appreciated so much. Old Spike the dog, who was bitten many times by rattlesnakes and then seemed "rejuvenated" afterward. The winter storms in the night, when my father would get up and put on his rain gear, rubber boots and slicker, and go out to "push the water around," as he put it, to save the cabin from sudden rushes down the canyon.

On the ranch he was really in touch with the elements. I remember him listening to the dry winds rising in the nights, the horses nervous out in the corral, then saying, "I don't like this, don't like it at all. Things could burn." And burn they did—twice! Both times, however, his house was saved by backfiring. But in the second fire the guest cabin, the one I had lived in, was destroyed. The cabin was insured, but rather than replacing it he decided to build a proper barn, with living quarters on the second level. The new barn was Eastern-style, with a silo, or turret. It was a handsome, even artistic, structure, but it seemed wrong for that Western setting. Still, with this final touch, the ranch had been transformed into a "minor showplace"—nothing fancy, but reflecting pride and purpose. It was hard to remember the hardscrabble environment it once had been.

My father himself even allowed as to how there was some improvement. He had vastly improved the orchards, and in good years with plenty of water, the fruit trees flourished. He had run irrigation lines all around, and kept the wild grass neatly mowed with his tractor. He built a fine corral for boarding horses. He even built a "gingerbread" doghouse for Spike, who rarely went into it, and an elaborate playhouse in the limbs of one of the biggest old live oaks, for the enjoyment of the children from the houses sprouting up on the mesa above the ranch.

These children liked to come down and visit, because my father and the ranch were so different from the antiseptic suburban environment they inhabited. Some parents would occasionally drop by, and my father, "the old guy with a beard," became a mentor to men who wanted to learn about the area and do rough work on their places. He would lend tools and give advice. It was obvious, though, that the ranch was becoming an oddity, surrounded by expensive mini-estates whose occupants had less and less fondness for "that little rural outpost" at the end of that disreputable street, still a private road, narrow, unpaved and rutted.

Fortunately, the ranch backed up against steep mountains, which maintained some sense of privacy. I know my father longed for the days when he had all that country to himself, and the taxes were minimal. I remember how uncomfortable he became when the first house was going up, about a mile away, built slowly on weekends by the owners, a couple named Stone, from Canada. My father was very uneasy about that intrusion, though he did say, "Stone is a good, solid man." He started taking the long way over the mesa to avoid seeing the new house. The pavement ended at the top of Big Rock Drive, then the dirt road split into two routes, the longer one much the rougher and more difficult to navigate in the thick fogs that often hung over the mesa.

I always sensed my father's feeling of satisfaction as the little light on the front of the cabin came into view through the oaks. He would slow his old truck—he had owned a succession of impractical vehicles that boiled over coming up the hill and were generally not suited to the task—to savor the scene. I felt his sense of ownership, his modest pride in the place. Old Spike would greet us hysterically, leaping in the air, "like a flea," my father said. The familiar routines of a place, all his, or ours. "Home—it ain't much, but it's ours." That phrase has stayed with me through all these many years. I can hear it now.

Living with the elements as he did, my father came to understand and predict the weather. Outside the kitchen door was a large antique thermometer, the kind stores used to give away for advertising. He would study it and say things like, "It always rains when it is 59 degrees." Evidently at that temperature something happened to the Pacific moisture rolling into the mountains. The winter storms that blew in always seemed to hit the ranch with particular force. My father had a special "rainy day" outfit that he wore into Santa Monica for the mail, lunch and errands. His blue jeans were tucked into knee-high black rubber boots, and he wore a dark blue trenchcoat. A black turtleneck sweater and a blue captain's hat completed the outfit. Once in a great while there was snow at the ranch's 1,200-foot altitude, but it almost always melted the same day. Still, to see the place white with snow was to be in another world.

Santa Monica, the old, unpretentious Santa Monica that I remember from those days, always had its eccentrics who were known about town. "Characters," they used to be called. Some were merely individualists and some were unhinged. All were harmless as far as anyone could tell. Among the characters that I remember are "Cowboy," so named because of his resemblance to Buffalo Bill and his big straw hat; "The Bouncer," a muscular man in his 30s who walked around bouncing a rubber ball and talking to himself; and David, a little Jewish man from Chicago who was always bundled up as for winter, and was perhaps the only Jewish member of the KKK. Today Santa Monica is so filled with freaks and weirdos that eccentricity no longer has much relevance.

I suppose my father was considered one of the Santa Monica characters, with his beard, his denim outfit and his always-present captain's hat. More than a few people around town called him "Captain," and some Hispanic workers addressed him as *Señor Capitan,* respectfully. From time to time hippie—or beatniks, as I suppose they were called then—would come up to him and ask how they could get a job on a ship. My father would always reply, "I have no idea—I've never been on one." He had an old leather briefcase that he took with him to the post office, to collect the mail from Box 1091. The briefcase accompanied him on his rounds, and was part of the outfit.

For several years he owned a low-slung, bright red 1939 Ford "hot rod" truck that he purchased from one of the local Malibu lads. He bought it not for its racy appearance, nor for the souped-up Oldsmobile engine. Rather, he needed a truck for the ranch, and this one—before the advent of small foreign pickups—was the only one he could find that would fit under the barn door opening. The truck attracted much attention on the Pacific Coast Highway and the streets of Santa Monica. Unfortunately, it was highly impractical. It guzzled gas and frequently needed repairs. Most automotive shops did not want to deal with such a hybrid vehicle, but my father heard of a place in West L.A. that specialized in such work. It was owned by a young Japanese-American. The first time my father went there, on a wet afternoon in his "rainy day" outfit, the Japanese fellow came up from under the hood of a car and took a long look at the red '39 Ford truck with two chrome exhaust stacks running up the sides, and at its driver. Then he smiled and stepped toward my father with his arms held wide. "I *know* you!" he exclaimed. "You Nazi U-boat captain!" Startled, my father replied, "No, No!" The man smiled even more broadly. "Yes, yes, yes!" It was his idea of a joke. My father was not amused, but the guy sure could fix the truck.

Coming back late one night in that truck, we caught a glimpse of a bobcat in the headlights. "He's a big one!" my father said as the cat loped into the tall grass and was gone. "I bet that's what's been getting the cats around the ranch. They know the coyotes, keep safe from them most of the time. But the bobcat, maybe they think he's a cousin but don't realize that their cousin will kill them." Then he went on about the coyotes, said he heard them so close they sounded like they were right outside his window at night, cavorting in the orchard. "I can tell by the pitch of their barking when they are after a deer," he said. "They get in a frenzy, the barking is higher-pitched. One night I heard them after a deer up the canyon in back. Finally I heard the deer shrieking. It sounded just like a woman screaming. Horrible! Next morning I went up the canyon and found what was left of the deer, torn apart. That's life in the mountains."

He told of another time, during his first years at the ranch, a hot night when he was unable to sleep and lay awake listening to the owls. Suddenly he heard muffled voices near the guest cabin. He crept out and turned on the very powerful hand-held spotlight he kept by the door. Three young men in T-shirts and jeans stood frozen in the light. "Don't shoot!" came a frightened voice. Of course they assumed my father had a gun, which indeed he did, grabbed from its mount on the door. One young man said they had been "hiking" in the mountains and had gotten lost. Could my father direct them to the Coast Highway? That he did, and when they were on their way he called the sheriff, on his newly installed telephone. Deputies apprehended them halfway down Big Rock Drive. They had escaped from the detention camp on the other side of Saddle Peak.

After that he always slept with his pistol by the bed. He felt a certain vulnerability out there alone at the end of a dirt road—and this was in the quiet years before things started to go wild around Los Angeles. Before he got the telephone, he said, he felt pretty alone at times, particularly during storms, when he would walk from small room to small room, the dog following, knowing that something was not right. The phone made him feel "more connected," he said. I still remember the numbers he had, first Malibu 2856, then Globe 6-2856. I looked up that second one in an old Malibu directory that I still have, the 1951 edition.

How strange it all seems, the scenes and people depicted in that old directory. Some of the men in it tried to get my father involved in the Lions Club, but he would have none of it. Finally they gave up and left him alone in the hills. Except for Pierce Sherman, the real-estate agent who sold my father the ranch. Sherman was from an old Los Angeles family, knew about Charles F. Lummis, our distant relative and famous Western writer, and kept up a sort of friendship, stopping by to visit from time to time. We liked Pierce Sherman. He reminded us of a simpler world.

My father was an oddball, as am I, I suppose. Both of us never took too well to society, though we could when we made the effort, which was rarely. He lived to be almost 85. I doubt I will make it that far. He said he had had enough of the changing West, did not like the "New West," with its endless recreation. He liked "real Americans," the Gary Cooper type: quiet, competent men not afraid of hard work, who got things done without a lot of yakking.

My father—who also bore the name Dayton, and after whom I am named—never wrote anything about the ranch except some letters to me, which he meticulously typed on the pale yellow ranch stationery with its old-fashioned lettering and a finger pointing to the telephone number. These I have kept, neatly bound with vinyl covers. They provide a record of those years. If not for them, and what I write here, there would be no record of what went on there. It would be as if it had never been.

How much of life is like that! Now the cabin, the barn, the doghouse, the playhouse, the corral and the tack house, all are burned and gone, as if they had never been. I am glad my father did not live to experience the fire. It would have hurt him terribly, to see all that he had lived for almost 20 years suddenly gone. After he moved, he and I made periodic visits; and despite some changes, all seemed remarkably the same. The first thing that hit me was the old, familiar smell.

A fellow named Steven Moffit lived there the whole time after my father left. He told me that he still frequently saw bobcats. Who today could imagine living with no other houses around, so close to Los Angeles? The silence, the surf far-off down the canyon on windless nights, the rich smells brought out by the fog, the little porch lamp among the live oak trees in the draw.

All these things I was thinking of as I drove out from Santa Monica on the Pacific Coast Highway, or PCH as it is called in the local jargon. It is crowded now, and built up all along. Gazing at the sea and the outline of the Santa Monica Mountains by moonlight, one might suppose that all is the same as it has always been. But it won't be, not until the last fire has burned every structure to the ground, and the last human has succumbed to the Ebola Virus or some other curse.

The road up Big Rock Canyon was still fairly primitive, and indeed the vague outline of the original road that Old Man McAnany, who sold the ranch to my father, cut himself could still be detected, if you knew where to look. Lining the road all the way were expensive homes—"rich man's estates," my father used to call them derisively. Or at least their remains. Many had burned in the fire, leaving just chimneys and concrete pads amid charred trees. Some survived. The fire had been hit-or-miss, leaping from spot to spot in the Santa Ana winds.

A large sign said the area was closed to all except residents and officials, under the authority of the City of Malibu. But there was no one to stop me, so I progressed over the mesa and down McAnany Way. Several work projects were in progress, to recover from the destruction as quickly as possible. I noted that Olivia Newton-John's place, with its horse barns and other outbuildings, was unscathed, while many houses on the mesa's south side were burned to the ground. The hills in front were utterly black and barren, and looked like the Mojave Desert.

Topping that mesa I remembered the first time I had come, a passenger in my father's cranky old car. It was June of 1951, and I was 14 years old. I had just arrived from Pennsylvania after an adventuresome and tiring three-and-a-half-day journey on the train. My father met me at Union Station in Los Angeles. We drove "surface" to Santa Monica, there being no freeway then. We paused above Santa Monica Canyon, with a spectacular view of mountains and ocean, under a sparkling blue sky. My father said the area was once a rough seaport, with sailor bars and a long pier with tracks and steam engines to carry cargo from the ships. I could not imagine such a sight.

He pointed up the coast where, as the Malibu boosters used to say, "The Mountains Meet the Sea," which they do. He explained that as late as the 1920s there was no road there because the family that owned all of Malibu, the Rindges, refused to allow the state to build roads. They hired armed riders who prevented everybody, including state officials, from entering their property. My father said that as a young man in the 1920s he used to drive up as far as the road went, then get out and walk around looking at those mountains thinking, "That must be wonderful country. What a great place to live." The Rindge family finally lost a lawsuit, and portions of the land were condemned for what was called the Coast Road. Somehow Old McAnany then got up to Big Rock Canyon, I think by a horse trail, and in 1919 bought 120 acres, to which he carved a road.

Selling Big Rock Canyon 30 years later was a small real estate office, where my father met Pierce Sherman, who showed him McAnany's property. Even in those days, 120 acres for $15,000 was something of a bargain. But it was way up on top, three miles up a winding, narrow road, subject to all sorts of slides in the winter. Back then, the people who wanted to live "far from town" meant down by the ocean. There were only a few buildings on our way up. My father told me the names of their occupants: a crippled man who played chess by mail, a buxom woman with a shiny Buick convertible out front, who wrote articles for a local newspaper. A couple of others.

At the top we turned up a rutted, dusty dirt road and over a flat area that my father called Big Rock Mesa, or *Mesa Piedra Gorda* in his Spanish. There were groves of dried-up trees, and the grass was golden-brown. All was dusty and dry, which surprised me, being so close to the ocean. Back then I understood nothing of California's contradictions. We slipped down into a draw, the upper reach of Big Rock Canyon. More oak trees, and then we came to a ramshackle cabin and a 1930s-model car. A small, wiry man was puttering in a pile of junk, and a black dog was on a chain. The man waved without looking up, and the dog barked wildly, straining toward our car.

"That's Old Mac, who sold me this place," my father said. "McAnany. He was born in L.A. in 1870, when most of it was beanfields, and just about 5,000 people. He retired up here in 1919 and built the road up the canyon himself, with a Fresno Scraper. He's quite proud of it. He'll stay on in that cabin as long as he wants. He's a real good old fellow, really knows this country. But as you may notice, he doesn't get rid of *anything*! Whenever I suggest hauling some stuff away, he says, 'I don't know that I'd do that, Lummis, might come in handy someday.' Calls me Lummis, like, 'Say, Lummis.'"

After a slight incline we came to rest under some pleasantly cool oaks, in front of another cabin. It was as primitive-looking as McAnany's, out of plumb and patched with makeshift materials. There was junk all about: corrugated tin, an old sofa, a car up on blocks. I thought it all looked awful. In a flat area in front of the cabin were many green-leaved trees, with a system of rusted pipes laid out for irrigation. My father waved his hand expansively. "The orchard," he said. "There are oranges, lemons, grapefruit, figs, walnuts even." I thought he was kidding.

The car's radiator was steaming. "Usually boils on the way up, it's a pretty fair climb," my father said, getting out. I heard the old man hammering on something up above, and the dog barking. My father stepped on the sagging porch of the house and turned to look at me. I just sat in the car, thinking the whole thing was one of his jokes, that he had found this place and the old man and decided to pretend that this was the ranch he had bought. He had that sort of sense of humor.

When he wrote to me in Pennsylvania and said that he had bought a ranch in California, I had envisioned wide, open country, like the terrain I had seen in cowboy movies. And when he suggested that I come out to live there for the summer, I thought of riding horses across sagebrushed expanses, coming back to a big, old-fashioned log ranchhouse and eating dinner in front of a large stone fireplace. That's what I thought a ranch was, what my father had bought. So this pile of Okie junk was surely a joke. I remained in the car. But when he went to the cabin's door and unlocked it with a key, I began to wonder. He was pushing this joke pretty far. Then he stuck his head out and asked, "Aren't you coming in?" That's when it hit me. This really was the ranch!

I was dismayed, but got out and followed him into the building. It was actually cozy inside, nicely fixed up, if somewhat Spartan. The large main room was tall enough for my six-foot teen-age height, but the rooms tacked on to the side and rear were low-ceilinged and cramped. "Old McAnany, being only five feet tall, constructed these rooms to his own dimension, so they are kind of low," my father explained. "The kitchen is okay, though, part of the original cabin, which was here before McAnany came along. Water comes from a well in the canyon, pumped into a tank on the hillside. Kitchen sink drains onto gravel in the rear. There's no hot water, of course.

"There is an outhouse with a toilet that flushes weakly but gets the job done. But Mac and I dug up the pipes recently, and found that they empty into a system of old orange crates, hardly a septic tank! I asked Mac about this, and he thought for a spell, then remembered: 'I didn't have time to get the septic in, was havin' the Pioneer Society up for a picnic, sorta put this makeshift system in. Guess I forgot about it. That musta been in, say, about nineteen-hundred and thirty-six.'"

The crates would not last much longer, my father said, so we needed to adjust to a conventional outhouse, without plumbing. But don't worry, he said—he had bought some chlorinated lime.

Such was my introduction to the West. Born in New York City, raised in a suburb of Philadelphia, I had enjoyed a normal, even privileged, Eastern boyhood, tainted only by the fact that my parents were divorced, an unusual circumstance in those days. An only child, I went to a good boys prep school, attended dancing classes, and spent summers in a rugged camp in Maine. My concept of the West came from cowboy-movie matinees, my grandparents' "Fighting Indians" photo books, and record albums of The Sons of the Pioneers. I really didn't think about it much.

But in 1949, when I was 12 and my parents had separated, my father decided to return to Southern California, where he had lived for a time in the 1920s. My mother encouraged the move, saying, not kindly, that it would be a better place for him to "be peculiar." Perhaps he had acquired that trait from my grandfather's cousin Charles F. Lummis, who in 1884 when he was 25 years old had walked from Cincinnati to Los Angeles. He went on to become the first city editor of the young Los Angeles Times, and then one of the most celebrated Western writers of his time. Among other accomplishments before his death in 1928, he coined the phrase "See America First."

My parents had met in 1935 in Canada, at St. John, New Brunswick, where they both were actors in a summer theater. Acting was a lifelong interest for my father. In the 1920s he had studied the craft at the Pasadena Playhouse in California. His family, however, thought a more serious profession would be preferable. They inveighed upon him to enroll in the Georgetown School of Foreign Service in Washington, D.C. It was not a good fit. He dropped out, and took his talents into the young medium of radio. He became an announcer in New York City, Camden, New Jersey, and Philadelphia, but kept getting fired for his unbridled urge to cut up on the air. Just when my mother was wondering what sort of a marriage she had gotten herself into, I came along. But I was not enough to hold the union together. Realizing that they were most poorly matched, my parents separated in 1940, and my mother and I moved to her parents' home in suburban Philadelphia. A short while later my parents divorced, and my father left for California.

Not long after he became the latest Lummis to head west, we got vague reports that he had bought "a ranch" and was working as an actor in Western movies. He regularly sent me postcards of romantic and exotic Southern California scenes—orange groves, snowcapped mountains, and buxom blondes hurling beachballs. (And also one from "Reno—The Biggest Little City in the World!") When he invited me out to spend my 14th summer with him, my mother thought it would be a good experience. Neither she nor he nor I had an inkling of where it would lead.

That first summer was mainly hard work, cleaning up the place and fixing things, all under Old McAnany's disapproving gaze. He was gone much of the time, visiting his daughter at a resort in the Sierra Madre. But when he was around he would inspect the piles of stuff that my father had sorted out to be hauled away, shake his head and say, "I don't know, Lummis, I don't think you should get rid of all that. Might come in useful someday." But my father contracted with some Okies from "over the hill," who came and hauled off four truckloads of junk and the old car on blocks. I could only imagine what their place looked like! With each load Old Mac would shake his head. But he didn't say anything more, realizing that my father really did want the stuff gone.

Grudgingly Old Mac developed a growing respect for my father. When the pump for the well in the canyon broke down, which it frequently did, Mac and my father would trudge down there with tools and get it going again. Pretty soon my father could do it by himself, and Mac conceded, "One day you might make it on your own here!" My father had a good laugh over that.

In time Old Mac felt comfortable enough with us to come down and have coffee in the evenings and talk. He was glad that "a sort of pioneering feller" was taking over the old place. We enjoyed listening to his tales of old Los Angeles. He was born in 1870 on a bean farm in what is now West L.A. All bean fields in those days, he said. As a young man he was a schoolteacher, and in 1898 had ridden his "wheel," or bicycle, all the way to Chicago for the World's Fair. "You can imagine it was quite a ride in those days, just dusty trails all the way. Took several weeks, pretty hard on my ass," he laughed, looking back over half a century. I asked if he rode his wheel back. "Hell no!" he snorted. "Put the damn thing on the train. One way was enough. Quite an adventure, though. Folks was most kind all along the way. It's a good country, good people."

One night he came down with tears in his eyes and said he wanted to "talk private" with my father. I left them in the kitchen and took a walk out in the dark quiet night. I could hear the owls calling, and the far-off rumble of surf. I liked the nights at Piedra Gorda. Later my father told me that Mac had been stopped by the California Highway Patrol on the Pacific Coast Highway in his old car, which by this time was caved-in on one side from when he had rolled into a ditch in the fog on the mesa. The state trooper had examined his vision and found it deficient. He told Mac he was too old to drive. He added that he was reporting this fact to the Department of Motor Vehicles.

Mac realized he could not stay on at the ranch any longer. He told my father that in a few weeks he would be moving to a small bungalow that his daughter had rented for him in West Hollywood. He was fighting back tears, my father said. "Been here since nineteen hundred and nineteen, thirty-three years," Old Mac told him. "Built my own road up here, kinda got used to being here..." He trailed off. My father patted the old man on the back, told him he could come back and visit plenty of times. "Nope, don't think so," Mac said. "Hate to leave the old place, but I guess it's that time. It comes, don't it?" Looking at my father, brushing tears from his eyes. Old Mac. The end of a time. It does come.

A few weeks later he was gone. Left the dog on the chain, snarling. My father calmed him enough to unsnap the chain from the collar. "Watch out for him, keep away!" he said. But as soon as he was freed, the dog just turned and licked my father's hand. Spike turned out to be a gentle and faithful friend. The place seemed quiet without Old Mac. No sitting around in the evenings trading tales over coffee. Later that summer we visited Mac in his little bungalow. He was not a happy or cheerful man, not at all. He seemed broken in spirit, with little or nothing to do, to live for. Within a year he was dead.

The road in to the ranch is now officially known as McAnany Way. The county authorities asked my father to suggest a name, and naturally that was the one he chose. And so it remains, and presumably always will. Olivia Newton-John's estate has McAnany Way as its address. I wonder if she knows anything about the name of her road. Probably not. I have photographs, taken with my old Brownie Hawkeye, of the area in 1951, the network of dirt roads across Big Rock Mesa with no houses, just the oak groves. Perhaps some of the residents now living there would be interested in seeing how things used to look. Or perhaps they don't care. When I look at those old pictures I remember the tendrils of fog creeping up the canyon in the evenings, the rich smells that the moisture extracted from the sun-warmed earth.

A female coyote hung out around the ranch. She used to climb up in the trees in the orchard to get at the fruit, particularly the figs. Sometimes my father came back in the afternoons and found the coyote and Spike lying side by side in front of the cabin. He wondered if there might be dark, curly-furred coyotes roaming the hills. He would feed the coyote chicken backs and necks that he brought home. She would almost, but not quite, eat from his hand. He had photographs of her eating in front of him, and up in a fruit tree. Then one day she wasn't there, and never came again.

There were almost a dozen half-wild feral cats around the place, a few tame enough to enter the house. Gradually they began to disappear, no doubt due to depredation by coyotes or the bobcat. We came upon several rattlesnakes near the cabin, fat, sluggish ones that we killed. We sliced one up and fried it, but it was not good—tough and greasy. We probably didn't cook it right. When we found a dead rat in the water tank, my father switched to bottled water for drinking.

Year by year the place became neater and more orderly, and many summers I was there to help with the work. My father painted the cabin an unusual shade—"Uranian blue"—and added Victorian trim. He painted the barn the same color. But we really didn't change things much. Our structures at the end of McAnany Way presented an odd contrast to the elaborate, expensive houses being built on the mesa. We felt more and more in another world down there. One day the county inspector came and told my father that we couldn't "live like this," with hardly any plumbing, an outhouse, and so forth. In the end he let us stay, but insisted that no one else could move in.

From 1949 until 1968 *El Rancho Piedra Gorda* was my father's home. He made a little money by boarding horses there, and picked up some more from his work in the movies. He didn't need very much. More and more with the passage of time, he began getting inquiries about the property. Taxes and assessments were increasingly a burden, and in his 65th year he accepted a generous offer. He was growing tired of the primitive life and the amount of work the place required. He also said he was feeling the dampness of living there, that it was time to move into a regular, modern house. The money from the sale enabled him to build a nice place in Pacific Palisades, and he lived almost two more decades. The ranch years grew further and further away, except in his dreams. Those had been amazing years in "The Malibewe," as Old McAnany pronounced it—from a time when there were no houses at all, to being surrounded by "rich man's estates." We had straddled an era, from McAnany to Newton-John.

My father hauled his furniture and other possessions to the new house. He even transplanted some ivy that grew luxuriantly down toward the outhouse, as a "remembrance." The doghouse he left behind. It had been silent for several years, because Old Spike was gone. My father had come home one day to find the dog standing strangely still and silent, not barking and jumping as usual. As my father got out of his vehicle Spike turned and looked at him, then collapsed. He had been bitten by yet another rattlesnake and had hung on until his master returned. But now he was too old to be "rejuvenated" by the bite. This time he expired. My father was very upset. "He was here before I came," he said. "A better or more faithful animal no man would want. I miss him sorely." He never got another dog. My father was not one to replace things. What was gone was gone.

The same thing can now be said about my father, and my mother. He died in 1988 and she in 1997, both at the age of 84. When the Pacific Palisades house got to be too much for him in his old age, my father moved into the small apartment where he lived out his days. My mother, meanwhile, was residing comfortably, although beset with Alzheimer's disease, in a suburb of Philadelphia, where her family had been prominent. Gone also now is the ranch, wiped clean by the flames.

When I went up there, even the piles of ashes that George Green had mentioned were gone, taken away as required by the authorities. Just a concrete pad remained where the barn had been. Just a smooth pad of dirt where the cabin had stood. The oak trees were charred and blackened. I took some photographs, then poked around at the site of the cabin. I gathered a few nails, some hinges, a few pieces of molten metal—all that was left of the ranch I had first laid eyes on 42 years before, a structure so old that some people people thought it might be the oldest in the Malibu.

Leaving the property, I passed through the gate onto McAnany Way. There I got out and stood for a moment, looking around. It was as though no structures had ever been there. As if there had never been any *El Rancho Piedra Gorda.* As if all those years, all of it, had never been. Standing there, I imagined my father, in the denim clothes he always wore, working around the place. I imagined him coming over the mesa at night and slowing when he saw the porch light of the cabin down below in the fog, saying, "There it is—home. It ain't much, but it's ours."

2

The Road From Gila Bend

The long, dusty and lonely highway heading westward from Gila Bend.

In the summer of 1956, when I was 19, I was returning to Los Angeles from visiting my college roommate in Tucson. I was hitch-hiking, both for adventure and to save money. Which was why I found myself in Gila Bend, Arizona, one hot June day, realizing I was on the road to San Diego and not Los Angeles! What the hell, I thought—I could take a bus up from San Diego. The fellow who gave me a ride into Gila Bend was a good old boy, traveling with his guitar.

There was not much to Gila Bend, a few stores and gas stations, a diner, and the desert stretching away to crumbly mountain ranges. A moonlike landscape. A few dust devils spiraling into the immense sky. The sun moved through a cloudless sky, and a hot wind blew off the sands, and up off the black asphalt. Car after car sped by, without even slowing down. Why didn't I get a ride? Did I look like a serial killer? I wondered where I would be when night came. Still Gila Bend? Only my shadow on the sand reassured me I had not become invisible! I fantasized a sleek convertible driven by a blonde, holding out a cold can of beer, saying, "Where you headed, big boy?" Wasn't that what they said in the movies?

My reveries were pierced by the squeaking of mechanical brakes. An old, beat-up Dodge sedan ground to a stop in front of me. It was pre-World War II, maybe 1939. Inside the car were four men. The one by the right front window said they could give me a ride into Yuma if I could contribute a dollar for gas (32 cents a gallon at that time!). Yuma was 115 miles down the road, and out of Gila Bend, so I agreed, threw my bag in the back and climbed in. As we chugged off, the driver, who said his name was Bill, apologized for charging me, but he said they were all broke.

They were migratory farm workers, back in the days when Anglos still "followed the fields." They all had the leathery, weatherbeaten look of the outdoors, but not of recreationalists. They wore clean but faded work clothes. Bill, who seemed to be in his 40s, was missing a few front teeth, and had not shaved in days. Riding shotgun was a thin man who for some reason was called Heavy, about 45, with a white shirt and a battered felt hat. In the back with me was a jolly, red-faced man of about 60, short and bald, known as Red. The fourth man, also in the back, was John, sharp-faced and about the same age as Bill and Heavy. They all seemed friendly, unthreatening. They said they had met up on a farm near Phoenix and now were on their way to Yuma or the Imperial Valley to look for more work.

The car seemed to be their living quarters, at least temporarily. The back floor was cluttered with old clothes, a cloudy gallon wine jug that held drinking water, a half- empty pot of dried beans, and a small black dog wrapped in a wet towel to ward off the desert heat. I asked where they had gotten the dog. John laughed and said they had "borrowed" him. Heavy brought out a bottle of Tokay, took a hit and passed it around. We all drank, but Bill cautioned that there was a highway patrol car up ahead. The bottle was put away.

Bill apologized again for charging me for a ride. Apparently he felt it was not the right thing to do. I said I did not mind, was glad to help out. I guess they thought I was as broke as they were. Red said he had had $40 the night before, but had gotten drunk and passed out, and then some Indians had stolen his money and his groceries. The men denounced the theft and Indians in general, saying they could not be trusted. John turned to me and said that Red had once been worth a lot of money, and he urged the old man to fill me in on the details. As the car chugged westward across the desert, Red began, reluctantly at first, to talk about being a rich man many years ago.

He said he had owned a large hotel in Canada, and when Prohibition came to the United States he made big profits buying whiskey up there and smuggling it south. His luck ran out, however, and he was caught. He was arrested and extradited from Canada for bootlegging and smuggling, and in the United States he was heavily fined and imprisoned. He left prison a broken and ruined man, back in the '30s. At the peak of his enterprise, he estimated, he was worth about $12 million. It seemed incredible that that old man in worn-out clothes had ever been so wealthy. I wondered if the tale was something he had made up and had now told so many times that it had become his truth. The others expressed no doubt at the story. But then, they had just met Red.

We made frequent stops along the highway, beside irrigation ditches, occasional clusters of palms or palo verde trees, to allow the old car to cool off. There sure was not much shade on the desert! It was extremely hot in the car, and stopping provided scant relief. The air was dry, and the wind blew incessantly. I was fascinated by the desert's stark beauty, its grim desolation and forbidding vastness. I had always enjoyed desert trips with my father, and even appreciated the heat for keeping most people out. My companions, however, saw nothing interesting about the desert at all. To them it was just "one hell of a hot and barren place," something to be traveled through because you had to. They griped constantly about the heat. They had been living with adversity most of their lives, and knew nothing else. There was no way they could romanticize the desert.

Bill pulled off at one of those beat-up desert cafés that used to be along Western highways. He said he was mighty thirsty. The proprietor was standing near the gas pumps as we pulled up. He looked us over, and walked quickly back inside the cafe. As we were piling out he stuck his head out and said, "Sorry, boys, I'm jest closing up," and shut and locked the door. Silently we got back into the car. As Bill drove onto the highway he said, "I reckon that feller didn't want no desert bums as customers." Nodding to me he said, "I was jest fixin' to spend yore dollar on some gas, and buy a six-pack of beer fer the rest of us, that's all." He seemed saddened by the incident. The others seemed accustomed to such things. "Probably thought we was gonna hold him up," one said.

Down the road we encountered a more hospitable establishment. Its owner was a sturdy and rugged desert woman, who was still wary and suspicious, the way she kept watching us. I guess not too many people could be expected to trust men who looked like us. We were taken for bums. Bill got a dollar's worth of gas and some beer. Somebody asked about wine or whiskey. The woman told him that was available 45 miles farther along the road. The men gave a collective mock groan.

Probably because I was so much younger than my companions, the woman drew me aside and said it might be "unwise" to be riding with them. I said I did not think there would be any trouble with drinking. That was not what she meant, she said. If they were wanted by the police, I would be in trouble, too. I saw her point but figured I could talk my way out of any jam. Pretty naive, I guess, but I did not think the men were fugitives. Of course, if I got caught in the middle of a gun battle with the highway patrol, well, that would be another matter. I had invested a dollar in a ride to Yuma, that was all. Just then Bill stuck his head in the door and said he was going "down the road a bit" to get water for the radiator and would wait for me there. Remembering my bag in the back, I gulped my iced tea and ran outside to ride along. The other men were standing in the shade smoking. I just knew my fears were groundless—there was a strong sense of ethics in them.

Later, when we were sitting in the car off the road, under some palo verde trees, John threw an empty can out the window, a common-enough practice among roadside beer drinkers. I was surprised, however, by Bill, who criticized the act and went to retrieve the can, which he put in the back of the car. I could not figure it out. Was Bill saving cans for some purpose? Or did he not like litter? I didn't ask any questions, and the matter seemed unimportant, if curious. Back in the car, beer finished, Bill said, "Let's go a block," as he always did when we started back on the highway.

In the front seat Heavy was rolling a cigarette in a practiced manner. He was the only one of the four who did not seem completely natural and genuine. Outwardly he did not look different from the others. His face was heavily lined and tanned; he wore a clean white shirt, khaki pants, and an old felt hat. Just another desert drifter, the gent on the next stool in a beer joint. But he had a confidential manner that set him apart from his companions, who were open and friendly, eager to talk in their Okie manner. Heavy was different. He seemed intelligent, but there was also a slyness about him that made me uneasy. I commented on his ability to roll a good smoke. He glanced back smiling and said, "That's the kind of thing a man learns in prison." I wondered if Heavy might have some interesting tales to tell. "What kind of experience have you had with prisons?" I asked him.

A while back he had been "a guest" at Leavenworth Federal Prison, he replied. I asked what they sent people to Leavenworth for. Heavy said he had been "accused" of robbing a bank. I was about to suggest "convicted," but thought better of it. I just listened as he laughed and went on to say that he and some other men had held up the First National Bank of Phoenix in 1947 for $109,000—a pretty good haul at that time He said it had taken the cops and the FBI almost four years to catch up with him after one of the other men had been arrested and "talked," but that he never had a chance to spend much of the money.

He did not explain, and I wondered if his loot was buried in the desert somewhere, waiting. It seemed unlikely. Heavy's sentence had been seven years, but he had gotten three off for good behavior. He had been out now for a couple of years.

In Leavenworth, Heavy said, he ran across a well-known crooked cop, a Lt. Shoulders, formerly of the St. Louis police department, who was then a federal prisoner. Shoulders was the officer convicted of stealing the ransom money in the notorious Greenlease kidnapping in 1953. Heavy was working as an orderly in the prison hospital, a job he held because he was a "model prisoner" and smart. Shoulders arrived as a mental patient. In his trial he had claimed mental illness as a defense, and after his conviction and sentencing the authorities decided that perhaps his illness might be cured by electric shock treatments. Heavy laughed recalling how that "crooked cop son of a bitch" decided he was all right after a few sessions. Most cops had a weakness for money, he said.

In the back seat, John interrupted to say that Bill was also an ex-con and had gone to prison for car theft. But John insisted that he was no ex-con, that the longest time he had served was six months in a county jail on a drunk-and-disorderly charge. And of course there was Red's story. I was most interested in Heavy, however. Of the four, he was the only one who seemed like a hardened criminal. The others were just happy-go-lucky hoboes who had had their share of trouble. Heavy was the one who complained most bitterly about the heat and made the most cynical remarks about the world and life. To keep him talking I implied that perhaps I was something of a criminal myself, hinting vaguely at some nefarious activities. What was it like to pull "a big job," I asked Heavy. He said it gave him a feeling of power to walk into a bank holding a gun, looking at all the poor scared sons of bitches, hoping no one would do something foolish, making it necessary to shoot. Heavy's hero was Willie Sutton, because in all his holdups Willie had never shot anyone.

The men asked me where I was headed. I said I planned to hook up with a buddy in California and head down into Old Mexico for some adventure. Heavy said he had not been to Mexico for quite a time, and that on the last visit he had been lucky to escape with his life. He and some companions had been doing some "small-time robbing" in Texas, and when the law got hot on their trail they ducked across the border into Nuevo Laredo to hide out. They paid off a Mexican official to keep their presence unknown to any American lawmen. One day they were sitting in a bar when the Mexican came to warn that American police were crossing the border that afternoon to look for them. He assured them he would not give them away. A short time later another Mexican appeared and demanded money for not telling the gringo sheriffs where they were hiding. An argument developed, then a fight. One of Heavy's companions pulled a knife and stabbed the Mexican. Heavy beat it back across the border into the States without learning if the fellow had been killed. Evidently the second man was sent by the bribed official, who was trying to play both ends against the middle. No one could be trusted in Mexico, Heavy emphasized.

By now Heavy seemed convinced that I had chosen crime as my profession, and that I was looking forward to a life of adventure. Though I had not exactly said so, he thought I had pulled something in Phoenix and was on the lam, that my California friend and I were going to Mexico for some profitable enterprises. The subject of firearms came up, and I said I was quite knowledgeable about guns and was a real good shot. For a man with a gun, he said, it was bad to be itchy on the job, but sometimes it was necessary for personal protection. He kept trying to pin me down about Mexico. I finally admitted that I had no definite plans because I knew nothing about the country. My friend and I just planned to raise some money in San Diego, I said, then go down and look around, talk to people, learn things.

That was not the way to proceed, Heavy said. Mexico was a land of great opportunity, but a man had to know his way around, have the right connections. I asked about the opportunities and got vague answers about narcotics and the disposal of stolen goods, particularly late-model cars. He emphasized that a man must have a specific purpose in going. I said we might be hitchhiking, and he told me I was crazy. "An American on foot doesn't stand a chance in that country," Heavy said. "I've known men who were killed for their shoes down there, hit over the head for their hats. If those bandits killed a man like me, no one would care or do a damned thing about it. With tourists it's different. They try to protect the tourists. The last time an American tourist was killed, there was a big roundup by the army and a bunch of executions. The army's main concern is to keep the bandits and trouble back in the mountains, away from the main highways."

Then Heavy surprised me by asking if he could accompany me and my buddy to Mexico. He suggested it would be valuable to have him along to show us the ropes, that there were deals we could work together to make the trip both interesting and profitable. The first thing was to "get" a late-model sedan in San Diego, he said, preferably a Buick or Cadillac, big, black and shiny. We would drive it down to Mexico City, where it could be sold for a lot of money. Then we would work our way back toward the States, parlaying our cash into ever-larger amounts by engaging in ventures along the way. Just what they would be was unclear, but I assumed they had to do with drugs—a risky business even then, when the major dope traffic was only marijuana.

Heavy was not specific. He said it was important for several men to work as a team in Mexico if there was to be success. He added that it was necessary to bribe officials all the time, and that they charged various prices, depending on the locale and the activity. Finally he said the best way to make a killing was smuggling drugs into the U.S. But he said it was too dangerous for "free-lancers." He knew other ways to make an easy dollar, he said, but did not reveal them. No one in Mexico could be trusted, he stressed again, no matter how much you bribed them, because they always went to the other side for more money. In addition, U.S. federal agents offered rewards for narcotics-traffic information. I pretended to be very interested in Heavy's plans. He gave me an address in Long Beach, and said to get in touch with him there real soon. Thanking him, I said I would. Evidently he did not plan on laboring in the vineyards when he could take two innocents to Mexico and fleece them, if not kill them! As Heavy himself said, a man cannot trust *anyone*.

Nearing Yuma we pulled off alongside a palm-lined irrigation ditch and got out to stretch our legs. John reached down and picked a dime out of the sand. "Hey, Bill," he called, holding it up, "I found me a dime!" "I know," answered Bill. "I seen it. That's why I pulled over." We all laughed, standing around the old car. The desert seemed to stretch endlessly to distant mountains, and I felt that I had been traveling with these men forever. I asked Bill where he was from. "Born in Oklahoma," he said. "But never spent too much time there." I asked if he had gone to school. He smiled a gap-toothed smile, and said, "Well, I went one day for my brother." Somebody chided Bill for being the only one not decently shaved. They all agreed that when they reached the Colorado River they go down along the bank so Bill could take a bath and shave. I was impressed by the strange sense of self-respect these men had, their sense of propriety. John kept apologizing for his worn-out clothes, and said several times that he had some good ones hanging in the car. These consisted of a clean but faded suit and shirt that the Salvation Army might hesitate to accept.

Everyone was kind and gentle with the puppy, petting it and keeping the towel damp. No matter how undesirable these men might be in the eyes of the law and polite society, I realized, they had among themselves a sense of ethics and esprit de corps. They repeatedly talked about how important it was for a man to be able to trust his companions, and how worthless an untrustworthy man was. What little food Red had, he shared with the others. Although uneducated, these men were by no means stupid. They had a native intelligence and wisdom geared to their circumstances. They were prisoners of their syndrome, and would never break out of it. That was their life.

Late in the afternoon we entered the outskirts of Yuma. I asked about the possibility of riding a freight train from there to San Diego. John said there were several a day headed west, and I should have no trouble catching one. He doubted that any railroad detectives would shoot, and said probably the worst that might happen was that I could be thrown in jail for up to 72 hours on a vagrancy or trespassing charge, or just held for "investigation." No big deal! He did not seem to think I would mind being booked, fingerprinted and held in some hot, miserable cell for three days. For these men, apparently, such inconveniences were just part of the routine.

Somebody warned that I would have to be extra careful in the El Centro yard, because Immigration checked the trains there for wetbacks. Heavy said it was important to carry a water bag or non-breakable jug of water, because I might get switched off on a lonely siding in the desert for a day or two. Or I might find myself on a train headed into Mexico. I was told that the Southern Pacific was the most tolerant line to ride, known throughout the Southwest as "the poor man's road." Bill said that the Santa Fee (as he pronounced it) was a son of a bitch, that men had been known to have been shot off its trains. The other roads were somewhere in between.

Hijacking was on the increase, and the railroads were getting uptight. One robber would sit atop a freight car and lower another man down the side to break the seal and padlock. Then at some prearranged spot where the freight slowed on a grade, six men could empty the car in a matter of minutes. Everyone agreed that the railroads had to be tough to protect their freight—but it made things hard for the economy-minded traveling man. Bill said the best ride in the world was in an automobile being shipped by rail. In those days they were shipped unlocked, with the keys in the ignition and some gas in the tank. A man could climb in, say, a new Cadillac and ride across Nevada in winter with the heater on and the radio playing. That was as good as it got!

Yet the last time he had ridden into El Centro, Bill said, a tough old yard bull had caught him, taken his money and then told him to get the hell out of there. The only way out was under the train, which had its engine running and was about to leave. When Bill protested that he could be cut in half, the bull said he didn't give a shit. He leveled his pistol, and Bill scrambled under the car. John commented that a few years back a railroad dick caught him riding into the yards in Phoenix and he had gone to the county jail. Someone else then recalled a cop who used to be in the Phoenix yard, who had a real bad reputation for beating up hoboes and taking their money. But he was not around anymore, because a colored man had taken him out of the picture with a pistol shot one night. All the hoboes knew who the colored man was, but the police did not. It would stay that way. Heavy added that in the Indio, California, yards another bull was due for the same treatment.

All the men had a deeply ingrained contempt for law enforcement officers. They felt that cops were just crooks with badges, hired mercenaries of the Establishment. Heavy especially. He said he had never known an honest cop. Red was particularly bitter about the Los Angeles police force, and he had a big scar on his forehead to remind him why. Some years back, he said, he and a dozen other men were picked up one night in a skid row bar, where they were peacefully drinking beer. They were herded into a van and driven to a remote spot in the rail yards. There the cops shoved them around, took what money they had and let them go. Most of the men were afraid to protest, or lost only a dollar or two and were glad to not be in jail. So they just wandered off.

But Red lost 50 dollars, quite a sum for him, and he was mad. He went right to a telephone and called one of the L.A. newspapers. A few nights later a reporter was down on Main Street posing as a derelict, but with money in his pocket. Sure enough, he was picked up and subjected to the same routine. His money was taken and he was told to shut up or be jailed on a drunk-and-disorderly charge. The reporter meekly shambled away—back to his newspaper! A series of articles and a subsequent investigation identified a gang of crooked cops who were brought to trial. Red was among those who testified. Fourteen cops were fired, and a couple went to jail. Red left town immediately. A few years later he was back, thinking that everything had quieted down. He was wrong. One of the fired cops spotted Red in a bar, and with the help of some buddies gave him the beating of his life. He was in the hospital for several weeks. His big ugly scar was a souvenir.

As Red finished his story we were rolling into the broad streets of Yuma. It was early evening, and I was thinking it might be good to get to San Diego that night. The men were talking about hanging out down by the Colorado River, in a hobo jungle, I imagined. I asked them to drop me off at the bus depot. We said goodbye as if we were all going to meet somewhere in a couple of weeks, a year or two, or at least somewhere down the trail of life. Lying, I told Heavy I would contact him in Long Beach. He looked at me blankly. I realized that I had been a part of a world for a brief afternoon, a world where dreams and plans were spun, but nothing ever came of them. It was just one more dusty road, the hot fields, bottles of Tokay and cold beer, honky-tonks and jukeboxes, vengeful women back in Oklahoma—the things that all the songs were about, and more.

A bus was leaving for San Diego in an hour. Dusk was falling as it pulled out to cross the river into California. From my window I saw the old Dodge pulled into a gas station. The hood was up, and Bill was putting water in the radiator. Red was getting fresh water for the puppy.

3

The Lake Tahoe Summer

Bill Farrell (left) and Dayton at the Dock of Bronson Hot Springs, Lake Tahoe 1956.

first saw Lake Tahoe a little later in the summer of 1956. With a job prospect at a resort hotel, I drove up U.S. 395 from Los Angeles. About 10 p.m. I turned west at Carson City toward the lake, 10 miles away. The road had just two lanes then, and very little traffic. Nearing Spooner Summit I turned down a dirt road into a meadow, to spread my sleeping bag under the ponderosas. Looking at the stars, I heard clanging cowbells somewhere in the mountain night. I woke early under a brilliant sky, and hit the road again. Suddenly the lake spread out below. With snowcapped mountains, deep green forest and the bluest blue I had ever seen, its beauty was breathtaking.

The road to the North Shore passed through tall, clean-smelling sugar pines. The Nevada side of the lake had no houses. Not until the California line was there any development, a cluster of casinos, stores and housing. Just across the border was Bronson Hot Springs, a resort dating from the turn of the century, on secluded grounds with a spec-tacular lakefront setting. There I found my Yale University friend Bill Farrell, who had written that there would be a job opening around the first of August. Sure enough, there was. A busboy had just left. After a brief interview with the dining room "captain"—a strange, aloof, as-cetic man—I became a busboy, with the inference that I would move up to waiter as soon as there was a vacancy. Though the hotel provided the requisite white jackets, I needed to supply my own black pants. I bought some down in Tahoe City.

Back at Bronson, Farrell showed me the bunkhouse for male em-ployees. I found a vacant room for my stuff, then looked around. The place was clean and respectable enough. There were detective and girlie magazines to leaf through, but anything more intellectual you had to provide yourself. Bill introduced me to the other boarders. Some were older Anglos who looked like winos, and gave off the odor of food and grease from the plates they scraped for washing. Several college guys were waiters, and a young drifter named Carl was a janitor. They seemed a decent bunch.

Busing tables was easy, and soon I became a waiter. I enjoyed the job, enjoyed bringing out dishes and presenting them to the guests with great flourish and exaggerated gestures, mimicking the waiters I remembered from fine restaurants in New York, Philadelphia and Los Angeles. My removal routine was just as snappy. The guests were pleased, never suspecting that in a way I was mocking them, making fun of the whole thing. Perhaps all servants play such games. The work was not hard, a couple of hours three times a day. The at-mosphere was pleasant, and in my plentiful time off I gloried in the weather, long warm days of bright blue sky, and cool, pine-scented nights.

The dining room was large and old-fashioned, with a high, raftered ceiling. In those rafters lived some bats, which the hotel management simply could not get rid of. We were admonished to never look up at the bats, lest the guests' attentions be drawn to them. So of course we did look up, when we felt playful, and sure enough, guests would follow our eyes, see a bat and gasp. Yet the bats never bothered anyone, and the guests came to accept their presence as something quaint. Our aloof and dignified captain—he seemed European to me, based on Europeans I had seen in the movies—would always reprimand us, mildly, for such tomfoolery. But even he took it as a joke.

We were assigned to certain tables, where the same people were seated for each meal. The guests were often families who came for a week or longer. So the waiters and guests got to know each other. Most guests tipped us well when they left, with at least one and usually several silver dollars from the casinos. We called it the "silver-dollar handshake," because departing guests would press the heavy coins into our hands. Some guests, however, were cheapskates, who would leave without tipping. We could spot them when they made a point of saying at lunch, "We'll see you at dinner," and we knew they were leaving that afternoon. So in their drinking glasses we served them lake water. It was potable, though rumored to cause mild sickness in some people. How strange to remember that Lake Tahoe was so clean back then that you could drink the water!

Of course the Bronson Hot Springs summer staff formed its own society. Bill Farrell had a thing going with one of two sisters who were waitresses. Coeds at Berkeley, they were daughters of a judge in the Bay Area. Joyce was two years older than Judi and a little bit prettier, but in their own ways both were classic California girls. Joyce was somewhat solitary, but easy to talk to. Judi was good-looking in an athletic way, a sorority girl who always had young men hovering about. The sisters exuded clean-cut energy and good cheer. Being around them was always good.

Bill and Joyce were a handsome pair, he curly-haired, blue-eyed and athletic, she tall, fine-boned and intelligent-looking. They seemed a "golden couple" destined for all the good things in life. The test would come in autumn, with Bill returning East to college and Joyce remaining in California to finish at Berkeley. Summer romances rarely survive such separation. But none of that mattered in the passing days at Bronson Hot Springs. Bill and Joyce spent all their free time together, and I was often a "third," perhaps because I had the only car. Judi wasn't interested in me. I was not a Berkeley frat type, and apparently Yale did not impress her. So Bill and Joyce and I would head off in the afternoons to the pristine Nevada side and hike through the sugar pines to a wide sandy beach with a sweeping view of the snow-clad mountains to the southwest. In the California parlance of the day, the place was called "Bitchin' Beach." I preferred Mark Twain's description of the same view: "The Fairest Sight the Earth Affords."

Late-night picnics down by the lake, with steaks and other food ordered up by the girls for non-existent guests, were frequent occasions. On other nights we would drive down to the South Shore, which was even then considered tacky, but lively. Often these trips were suggested by the assistant chef, a lonely older man who had a secure year-round job at the Bronson and the Arizona Inn in Tucson, under the same ownership. He had a lot of money and little to spend it on. He liked to gamble, if woodenly and unenthusiastically. As he had no car, we went in mine. He would give me $5 for gas, and $10 each to Bill, Joyce and me, saying, "Have fun, kids." While he gambled and drank, we pocketed the money and watched. He seemed to win consistently, but with little pleasure; and as his dollars and chips piled up, he would generously throw some our way. These expeditions were not much fun for us, but they did add to our earnings, which was helpful.

One afternoon Bill asked to borrow my car for a special date with Joyce. He knew I was protective of the car, with its new dark green paint job and souped-up engine, and would not be enthusiastic. But I agreed, with the admonishment, "Just be careful." Yet standing on the balcony of the bunkhouse as dusk fell, I spotted my car creeping through the woods, down a narrow road toward the lake. I cringed, imagining rough pine boughs scratching its sides. I accosted Bill the next day, and he admitted feeling guilty. But the few scratches on the car all buffed out easily.

While Bill and Joyce grew ever more in love, I did not connect with any particular girl. None was really available, as everyone was pretty much paired off by the time I joined the staff. So I spent a fair amount of time with Bonnie, a hard-looking blonde from North Dakota. She was not a college girl, was a few years older than I, and was fairly attractive, in a truck-stop-waitress way. Carl called her "the ice princess." She did not have the cheerful All-American look of Joyce and Judi. Bonnie knew I had gone to Mexico that summer, and wanted to hear all about it, because she was thinking of going herself. So I told her of my adventures down there, and she listened. Sometimes she and I and Bill and Joyce walked at night to Crystal Bay, to listen to music, gamble with quarters and enjoy the free drinks that Bonnie's waitress friends brought. But we were not an integrated group. Bill and Joyce were completely absorbed in each other, and after Bonnie had heard all I had to say about Mexico there didn't seem to be much else for us to talk about.

Frequently in Crystal Bay I saw the Bronson's owner, Mr. Steuben, gambling and drinking heavily. I tried to avoid his gaze but was unsuccessful, because on mornings after when I served him breakfast (I was assigned to the Steuben table) he would ask, sourly, "How'd you do last night?" "I did okay," I'd say. He'd grunt and say, "That's better than I did," then lapse into silence as the rest of his family came to the table. There were two daughters. Amy was about 19, tall and serious. Kit was 16 and quite flirtatious, always in very short shorts. Farrell had warned me about Kit: "Your predecessor was fired on account of hanging out with her. You better just ignore her or you're outta here!" Reluctantly I heeded his message, although Kit was a TICKET!

Back in the bunkhouse, I was getting to know the other men. The college guys were nice enough, I guess, but I felt overly familiar with their type. Carl, meanwhile, was turning out to be a wise-ass. But the old winos were fascinating. They had been hoboes, fruit-pickers, all sorts of things. They would work the hotels in the summer, then drift down to Sacramento to spend the winter on skid row. A few "squatted" in old miners' shacks along the American River and panned for gold.

They said they could get about an ounce a week—$32 at that time, enough to keep them in rice and beans, and, of course, wine. One night one of them woke me up after midnight. He said he was having a heart attack, and offered me $25 to drive him up the road to Truckee. I did, but he wasn't having any heart attack. He just wanted out of there. After he left, nobody ever said a word.

Shortly before Bill was to go back East, a tragedy struck. His older cousin, whom he adored and was a Marine Corps pilot, was killed in a flying accident in the Pacific. Bill was despondent for days, alone with Joyce. I lounged about the bunkhouse reading old Westerns, and when the front desk wanted someone to drive guests in the hotel station wagon to the train in Truckee or the airport in Reno, both scenic and pleasant drives, I always volunteered. I enjoyed the extra pay, the tips, and the chance to see the country. The other guys were enjoying the last days with their girls.

Then August drifted into Labor Day, and all the college students were gone. Bill and Joyce, Judi, the Steuben sisters—all gone. I was not going back to school that year, so I decided to stay until the hotel closed for the winter, early in October. Just me, Bonnie, Carl, a couple of older waiters, and a few of the wino dishwashers—only we remained. After Labor Day there were far fewer guests, but many of those who did come were friendly older couples who tipped quite well. None of that "We'll see you at dinner" stuff. None of them got lake water in their glasses. These older guests were nice, dignified people. Their "silver-dollar handshakes" were most satisfying.

Carl the janitor got more and more out-of-control, drinking and carrying on. He would dance with his mop, singing "This mop here be my be-bop mop." I thought he was pretty funny, but clearly he did not give a shit about his job anymore. It was time for him to drift on, and one day he was gone. We were told that he had been let go. The winos took over the cleaning, for a little extra pay. Everything was winding down. We were just a skeleton crew, and I fit in. The winos and older waiters accepted me because I did not seem to be one of the elite workers, the ones going back to college They took me for a regular working man. I did not disabuse them of that notion.

Bonnie and I still spent time together, but nothing like a romance ever developed, nothing physical. She might have been willing, but I'll never know, because I never tried anything—too shy, or not interested for some reason. She was older and from a different background, and I was not entirely comfortable around her. I liked her, but had no desire to be more than a casual friend. The Bronson closed for the season on Oct. 10. Before it did, Bonnie and I went to several closing parties at the casinos down the road in gaudy Stateline. They were good parties, too, for all the food had to be used up. It is hard now to remember that everything at Tahoe used to close for the winter.

As I was getting ready to leave, one of the older waiters asked me for a ride to Yosemite National Park, where he had a winter job in another hotel. Wayne was a hayseed from Indiana, about 30, with thinning sandy hair and glasses. He offered to buy all the gas needed to get to Yosemite. I said okay, but I wanted to take the long way around, north from Tahoe along California Highway 49, through the Mother Lode Country of the 1849 Gold Rush. Wayne said that was fine, he just needed to get to Yosemite, didn't have to be there right away. I left Tahoe with about 150 silver dollars and a fair amount of folding money. Bronson had been good to me financially.

Early on a bright clear fall day we headed north from Truckee through ponderosa forests. Wayne was wearing a red-and-white small-checked shirt and blue pants. He showed no interest in the countryside, the history of the Gold Rush, or anything else. He was not an interesting companion, but I didn't care. I wanted to see that Mother Lode Country. At Sierra City we picked up Route 49 and began to descend from the Sierra Nevada's thick forests into deep, twisting canyons. In one of them was the picturesque town of Downieville, with old-timers sitting out on benches. I remembered that the winos had said that some of the best gold panning was around Downieville. I wondered if I would ever be back to give it a try. The road on to Nevada City was narrow and twisty, with logging trucks laboring up grades, then speeding down. The driving was slow and tedious. This trip was going to take longer than I had thought. Wayne mostly slept.

After Auburn the road got better, breaking out of the rugged highland to run straight through the oak and digger-pine foothills. The lower elevations were quite warm, with heat that lingered in the twilight. South of Placerville seemed remote and forgotten country, with sleepy towns unchanged for a hundred years. Darkness overtook us near Jackson, and around Sonora a full moon flooded the night. I drove in silence through the silver emptiness, which was so bright that I turned off the headlights. I could see the road perfectly, and there was no traffic. Wayne had been sleeping again, and when he woke up he panicked. "Turn on the lights, you fool!" he shouted. "You'll kill us both!" I obliged him, but said I could see just fine. He just shook his head.

We came to the north entrance of Yosemite on Route 128. The hour was late, and no one was at the park office. We drove by without paying, and soon entered a magnificent grove of towering redwoods. I suggested that we stop there to sleep, and go on to the hotel in the morning. Wayne agreed. I parked under some huge trees. Wayne opted to sleep in the car. I spread my sleeping bag on the forest floor and gazed at the stars through redwood boughs. In the hushed night I heard a faint breeze way up in the treetops. Small slivers of moonlight penetrated here and there. It was a magical scene, one I'll never forget. Crunched up in the car, Wayne was oblivious to it all. I fell asleep thinking of people I had worked with and drawn close to, and would never see again.

Early the next morning I drove Wayne to the hotel, where he left with barely a grunt, no suggestion of breakfast or anything. He was as glad to be rid of me as I was to be of him. I explored Yosemite, then headed down into the dusty heat of the San Joaquin Valley, toward Los Angeles and my father's hardscrabble ranch in Malibu. I arrived in a terrible heat wave—110 degrees and no trace of wind. My father was glad to see me. We got a bite to eat at Canfield's Big Rock Cafe, then went back up to the ranch, where we sat on the porch awaiting the cooling ocean breezes. But they never came. The heat wave was predicted to last several days, so my father suggested that we drive down and sleep on Zuma Beach. Thousands of others had the same idea, and there was quite a mob. It was orderly, though, and nobody got robbed or mugged, as would be the case today. After the heat broke I hung around the ranch another week, then left on the long drive back East.

The following summer a friend and I passed through Lake Tahoe, and went to Bronson Hot Springs. Just a few of the people I knew were there, the older ones. Bonnie was not among them. They said there were empty rooms at the bunkhouse if we wanted to stay a spell. That we did, while I showed my friend my old haunts. But of course none of it was the same. It all looked familiar, but didn't seem to mean anything. After a few days we moved on, up into the Northwest.

In the summer of 1958 Bill and I ran into Amy Steuben outside the American Express office in Paris. Our meeting was rather stiff. She remembered Bill, but not me. We chatted a few minutes, but did not have much to say, other than on the subject of the Bronson resort. And even that seemed to bore her. I don't think she had much interest in her family's former employees. Sometime later my college roommate, who was from Tucson and had worked at the Arizona Inn, told me more about the Steuben family. The old man's drinking and gambling had almost cost them their hotels. But not quite, because Mrs. Steuben was tough enough to take hold. And the serious Amy and the flirtatious Kit—yes, he had tales of them, too. Juicy ones, mostly about Kit!

Over the years, Bill and I talked often about Bronson. We remembered one guest in particular, a bronzed, lean, capable-looking man whose wife and children were at the hotel for the whole summer. He came on weekends and often took a canoe far out on the lake by himself, a chancy thing to do because of the strong winds and sudden storms. But he handled the canoe expertly. He was a partner in a hip advertising agency in San Francisco, and was from an old San Francisco family. He was about 40. He and Bill got along well, and spent a lot of time talking. He was impressed that Bill was attending Yale School of Design, one of the best. "Anytime you want to come to work in San Francisco, just give me a call." Bill told me much later that he had considered that offer very seriously, thinking of dropping out of Yale and going to work in San Francisco with that hip firm, to be near Joyce. "How different my life would have been," he said.

Instead Bill moved on to become a designer in New York, and Joyce remained in the Bay Area. The golden couple of the summer of

1956 remained paired only in memory. Six years later, living in San Francisco, I looked through the telephone book. A Joyce Barnes was listed, and also a Stanley Barnes, a federal judge. I assumed it was the Joyce I knew, and the judge was her father. I wondered why such a fine-looking woman had remained single. But I didn't call. No Judi Barnes was listed. I imagine she married one of those fraternity boys and lived happily ever after.

I never see or hear from Bill Farrell anymore. He has had much tragedy in his life, and probably has blocked out many sad memories. But I'm sure he would remember that summer, as I do. The others? Who knows? Most people don't dwell on the past, or see it very clearly.

4

Hell's Canyon—The Deepest Gorge

Narrow dirt mountain roads lead one to some of the West's most
wonderful un-discovered places—i.e. Hell's Canyon.

Rolling south in my truck on U. S. 95 from Coeur d'Alene in northern Idaho, I was making good time until I hit the twisting stretch between Lewiston and McCall. But that was where I needed to slow down anyway. Somewhere to the west in that raw, mountainous country was North America's deepest river gorge,

Hell's Canyon, and I was determined to find it. Though fully half a mile deeper than the Grand Canyon, Hell's Canyon was little known back then, in the mid-1950s, and it was certainly well hidden away from the casual motorist. So I poked along the highway looking for some sort of road, any road, heading west, which might give me a view down into the canyon. Fortunately, there was almost no other traffic on the highway. Not in those days.

Finally I came upon a dirt road angling west off the highway just south of where the Salmon River flowed in from the east. It seemed my best—and only—bet. Up, up, up I wandered on this road, pushing through a bunch of cows not eager to share the space. Finally the road dead-ended at a lookout tower. From this spot the land just kept falling away to the west, layer after layer after layer. From the tower top, I suppose I was indeed peering into Hells Canyon, technically speaking. But it was not what I had envisioned. I could not see anywhere near to the bottom of it, could not see the Snake River that had cut it, nor could I see stark vertical walls rising 7,900 feet.

Instead Hell's Canyon was lost in the endless falling away of the mountains I was standing on, which seemed not so much mountains as a vast jagged landscape with a level horizon and no distinct peaks. It was amazing country, rugged, impenetrable and mysterious. I guess I should have felt disappointed, but somehow I could not muster that feeling. The sky was an amazing clear blue, the air hot and dry, and distant landforms were blurred in a haze. The gorge was only a suggestion of something incredibly deep, hidden in the middle of it all. Hell's Canyon was not an easy place to see, and perhaps it was better that way. Things too easy to see are often not properly appreciated.

This visit to Hell's Canyon, my first, took place almost half a century ago. I discovered later that the most spectacular view of the canyon reachable by vehicle is from the Oregon side (the gorge forms the state line between Idaho and Oregon for about 100 miles), a place called Hat Point. I found it 27 miles up a rough road when I went there some years back. I spent the night, and the next morning watched the sun rise over the Seven Devils, a rugged collection of peaks on the Idaho side. I'm glad I got there when I did. In 1975 the U. S. government designated

652,488 acres as the Hell's Canyon National Recreation Area. Today the former wilderness is dotted with campgrounds; paved roads lead to Hat Point and numerous other overlooks; and a parade of rafts, kayaks and even jet boats zips through the canyon six months of the year—all in the service of "industrial tourism," which inexorably is disrupting the dignity and purity of that land and its people.

Yes, I'm glad I first found Hell's Canyon in the 1950s. My explorations had used up the better part of the afternoon by the time I got back to U.S. 95, which was no less twisty as it kept heading south. I grew tired of wrestling the truck around all the curves, so a small café tucked up against a mountainside came as welcome relief. Considering the lack of traffic, I was not surprised to find myself its only customer. I got to talking with the owner, a rugged-looking fellow in his 50s, with a tired manner about him. He had retired after 30 years in the Navy and had engaged in a number of enterprises in Southern California, all of which bored him and "thinned out" his savings. He had always hankered for life out in the "Real West," someplace remote and unpopulated. Then the American Automobile Association named Idaho the least likely vacation destination among all 48 states. That was why he came. What he failed to take into consideration, however, was that such a remote and unpopulated setting was not conducive to good business opportunities. Now he was stuck with a groovy little cafe in a beautiful, remote setting—and no customers.

He loved the Idaho country and loved being away from all the bullshit down in California, but it just was not working out. There were very few local residents, and those who stopped in just lingered over cups of coffee. The infrequent tourists on the highway seemed in a hurry to get someplace civilized and did not stop. So he realized he had once again picked the wrong thing. Damned café just wasn't working out. He was going to give it up after the fall hunting season. The problem, he said, was that the people up there always did things "ass-backwards." Must be the influence of the Salmon River, he claimed. I did not understand the connection, so he explained.

"They calls it 'The River of No Return,' because there can't be but one-way trips on it, seeing as how the current is so swift and the banks so steep and everything. But there's a hell of a lot of people do take that trip, in rubber rafts with guides, for fishing and hunting, and all sorts of sport, sightseeing even. It's a hard trip, but them with money and guides and all can afford it." He had figured that those moneyed folks would stop in his cafe for big meals after their time on the river. His place was quite near the take-out point. But, he admitted, he had figured wrong.

During that summer, he said, the only people who had come down the river and stopped in his café had been four wild-eyed, half-starved college boys who had spent several weeks struggling down the canyon on foot, half-swimming, half-hiking. Those boys were just damned fools, he said, but having accomplished the near-impossible, they were mighty pleased with themselves. They had hitched down from the spot where the Salmon River meets the highway, and their ride had dropped them off at the café. Tired and hungry, each of them ate three big cheeseburgers and a mountain of french fries and drank about a dozen Cokes, then caught a ride with a sheep truck headed to Boise.

The fellow shook his head, remembering. Why in the hell, he asked, would those kids want to spend so much time struggling along those canyon walls when even the old-time trappers made boats to float down in, it was so difficult to travel on foot? Why the hell did people today go out of their way to make things difficult? I did not try to explain that we were entering a new era of leisure, in which more and more people would be seeking "experiences" because they were bored with the drone-like existences they were caught up in—that as the challenge went out of daily living in the West, and hazards and difficulty diminished, people would seek thrills to fill the vacuum. I just listened to the fellow's complaints, thinking that it would indeed get to a man, sitting all day in that lonely cafe, looking out the window, and waiting for customers who never came.

Then a fellow did enter the café, a local rancher, lean and leathery in the classic Western style. And just as the owner had reported, all he ordered was a cup of coffee. He nodded at me pleasantly, and started telling about digging postholes all afternoon from the back of his truck, "up and down them damned hills where a man cain't hardly stand up straight." His rig had damned near turned over, he said, and would have rolled "all the way down into the durned river" if it had. "What the hell kinda country is this," he asked, "where there ain't hardly a flat spot nowhere?" He chuckled to himself and sipped his coffee.

"If you don't like this country here, how come you don't pull out for somewheres else?" the café owner said. "Plenty of level land in Idaho." The rancher just laughed. "Oh, hell, man's entitled to a little bitchin' after a long day's work. I was born here and I ain't leavin'. It ain't all that bad." He turned to see if I agreed. I nodded. The café owner poured himself a cup of coffee, stared out the window into the fading light of the canyon. He sighed. "Well, that ain't something I aim to do, is stay. I ain't made enough this summer to pay fer this here cup of coffee."

I rolled on down the highway into flatter and more timbered country. It was well after dark when I registered at the old Lumbermen's Hotel in McCall. The smell of burning sawdust hung in the warm, still air, and a certain sense of despair hung in the hotel lobby among the old-timers sitting there. They too did not have much to do, it seemed.

5

A Night in the Big Sur

Dayton hiking above Big Sur, c. 1962

In the summer of 1960 I was driving leisurely down the California coast. One evening I camped on Nacimiento Summit, the ridge above the Big Sur, where the dirt road crosses the mountains. Climbing up I met no one, in those days before Big Sur became an extension of the San Francisco neurosis. At the top, wonderful warm air was pushing west from the interior valleys, and over the ocean was a layer of white fog. I pulled into the deserted primitive campground at dusk, got set up, then just sat around, smoking a seegar and listening to birdcalls in the warm twilight.

I made a small fire and cooked supper. When the fire died down I took a walk along the ridge. A bright moon illuminated the fog, and I heard the surf crashing far below. I remembered another time, when I stayed at Lucia, near Big Sur, and a cute waitress told me, "God, I love this place—I wish I never had to leave!" I understood what she meant. My walk was in complete silence. So I was surprised upon returning to the campground to find another vehicle there.

Someone had pulled in at the far end, which I took as a sign of consideration for my privacy. The vehicle was an ancient truck, from the '30s perhaps, a flatbed, loaded down with all sorts of equipment. Just exactly what, I could not tell. A Coleman lantern hung from a nail in a tree, and a man was busying himself with the gear. He was an older guy, with a big gray beard. He took no notice of me, so I smoked another cigar and finished my coffee. After a bit I wandered over to the spring to brush my teeth. The fellow spied me and called out, "Come on over and jaw fer a spell. I'm jest fixin' some supper." He seemed friendly, so I got another cigar and joined him.

He was frying meat and potatoes, and turned out to be a real talkative old boy. A large round man, he wore bib overalls and his face showed exposure to the elements. We exchanged names and shook hands. His was huge and rough, the real hand of a workingman, not some North Beach *perfumado*. He was in his late 60s, 70s even, but looked fit and capable. From the old truck and all its strange equipment I concluded that he was a tinkerer. An Okie trait.

He said he had a ranch over in the Central Valley, but was mostly retired from serious farming. With a lot of time on his hands, he liked to come over to the coast to get in some fishing. He said he had worked real hard for many years and had built up a large balance of "my own damned time." He said he had always been his own man. "If a man cain't live doin' what he wants," he asked, "then what's the point?" I said I could not agree more, but many people never seemed to find that freedom. "Then they are no damned better than ants!" he exploded. "A man kin always git along bein' free. They jest ain't willin' to take the risks or pay the price, that's all." He was getting agitated. I remained quiet until he settled down.

We got to talking about wandering around the country, being free and seeing all kinds of people. He said he had traveled quite a bit before the War, as a hobo during the Great Depression. "Oh, Lordy," he said, "them was times that challenged a man's ability to survive, they shorely did. But I always worked to put some money in my pocket—a hobo ain't afraid of honest work to earn a few dollars. Not like a bum, who don't and won't work." Most of his travels had been in the Midwest and South Central states, so again I assumed he was an Okie. He sure sounded like one, of the independent, capable type that flooded California in the '30s.

As we sat by his fire, him finishing his meat and potatoes and me smoking a Marsh Wheeling, he recalled the time he and some other fellows found what they thought was a real good place to spend the night, a large, untended warehouse with lots of soft sawdust spread around to lie on. The weather was warm, but he said he had never spent a colder, more uncomfortable or worse night in all his life. When morning came they found that they had picked an icehouse, and the sawdust covered large blocks of ice.

He forked a big potato and laughed out of the side of his mouth. Chewing on the potato, he said that just about all his traveling in those days had been on freight trains, that during the Depression that was the best way to get around, and every train was crowded with men. No one bothered them as long as nobody tampered with locked boxcars or any freight. It was an understood thing, he said. "Sidecar Pullman was the only way to travel, never did have a bit of trouble. It's all different today, with so many automobiles and all."

He cut up the last piece of meat on his tin plate. I looked at the equipment in the truck, wondering what it was. He followed my gaze. "I got me a big old surplus rubber raft," he said. I spotted it, buried under other stuff. He said he liked to float along the coast in the raft, with a long cable attached to rocks on the shore. When he was ready to come in at night, he would winch himself to shore.

The subject of the automobile really got him going. He said that there were "too damned many machines," and they were clogging and polluting everything. He conceded that they were a practical way of getting around, especially in rural areas, and observed that both he and I had used one to get to that private spot. Yes, automobiles enabled people to cover great distances, he said, but even before the coming of "the machine," people managed to cover great distances as well. I thought of the poet Robinson Jeffers, who loved the Big Sur and who said, "the slower you go, the more you have been there."

I did not burden my acquaintance with this bit of wisdom, but the old man seemed to already understand the concept. Before automobiles, he said, people had a better appreciation of the land, because of the hardship of their travel. Now with all the modern distractions, folks were no longer dependent upon or interested in the land. We agreed that automobiles did have advantages, but that too many of them pretty much defeated their purpose.

But motorcycles—they were different! He owned a big Harley-Davidson, which he liked to push up around 100 mph on the flat and empty San Joaquin Valley roads. Remember, this fellow was close to 70! He hated traffic jams. The airplane definitely had an advantage there, being up in the sky and all. He had thought of attaching wings to his cycle, so that when he came to a traffic jam or a town he could just extend them and fly right over the obstruction! He chuckled over that.

All this time he had not asked me one thing about myself—where I was from, or headed, or anything. I figured he was just an old guy who liked to talk, and might go on all night. And frankly, I thought I had my own story to tell. So as he was launching into another yarn I got up and said I was tired and was turning in. He grunted amiably, and gathered his dishes for washing.

Lying in my sleeping bag, curled up under the stars in the deep and still Big Sur night, I pictured a motorcycle with wings, gliding high in the sky over the wide San Joaquin Valley, over the orange groves, toward the white crest of the distant Sierra. It was a pleasant way to fall asleep. The next morning, eating a banana and drinking coffee, I saw him fiddling with his equipment. I wondered if he would rather be floating or flying this day. I needed to hit the road. Leaving the campground, I leaned out the window and called "Happy landings!" He grinned and waved.

6

Dr. Avis and the Desert

Doctor Avis and his Volkswagen bus, with the Black Rock Desert
stretching away behind him, under lowering skies.

The Black Rock Desert of Nevada was something I had never heard of before going there with Dr. Avis in his new Volkswagen bus in June of 1963. I had heard, however, of the Surprise Valley of northeastern California, where that state borders Oregon and Nevada. A college friend had worked there one summer on a ranch with an "Eagleville" address, which had a nice ring to it. He described the area as remote and unspoiled, out of the California mainstream, with a traditional lifestyle still tied to the land. Ever since, I had wanted to get up there. So when the good Doctor acquired his vehicle and announced he was ready for a trip somewhere, I had an itinerary in mind.

He agreed, although this type of travel would be something new for him. Like most Californians, he was bound up in urban life and fast lanes. Thus one June day we found ourselves rolling north through the wide Sacramento Valley under lowering gray skies, unusual for that time of year. The Doctor drove his new bus tentatively, his hands gripping the wheel, his eyes fixed rigidly ahead. He was not exactly a relaxed driver. He glanced over at me and asked, "Does this trip have any eventual destination point, or are we just going to roam around aimlessly?"

I had spoken of the Surprise Valley in vague terms, not knowing the area. The Doctor suggested that we might want to see a bit of Oregon and Nevada as well. "Why don't we swing over there after we've seen the valley?" he said. "Just pick some destination. Not too far, just someplace east of the California line." My map showed northwestern Nevada as a vast empty space. In a big blank area called the Black Rock Desert, however, one spot did catch my eye, a tiny town called Sulphur. I loved the businesslike name. "Sulphur! That's where we'll go," I said. The Doctor grunted. "What's that near?" he asked. "Just west of Jungo," I replied. He laughed.

We left Interstate 5 at Redding and climbed through grazing country interspersed with stands of ponderosa pine. Sporadic rain showers broke out, and fresh snow was on the mountains. Very little civilization lined the 150-mile road to Alturas, the seat of Modoc County, at that time one of only three Republican strongholds in California. Conservative country, with an economy based on ranching and logging, pursuits dating from the last century. Passing through it made me feel good, in spite of the deteriorating weather. Yet the Doctor was driving rather grimly, I thought. Was he having second thoughts about heading out into remote and primitive territory, so far from the bars and coffeehouses of San Francisco's North Beach, where he felt at home? He was the one who had said that he wanted to get "into the Real West." Was he now experiencing the sense of unease that he said came over him in situations where he felt he was losing control? We kept climbing higher. "There's not many too people up here," the Doctor noted tensely.

Dr. Avis was neither a doctor nor an Avis. His real name was Lionel Alves, but my grandmother never could pronounce it right. Her version was "Avis," and it became his nickname. His friends added the "Doctor," as in Doctor Johnson and Boswell, because of his vast historical knowledge and total recall of it. We had gone to Yale together. Of Portuguese extraction and a New England upbringing, he had landed in San Francisco after serving in the Army. Now he lived in North Beach and was a graduate student at San Francisco State College. His bohemian look included a beard.

In Alturas we bought beer and canned food. The place had a frontier feel, more like Wyoming than California. Numerous cowboy hats were in evidence, and the citizens looked both rugged and wary. The rain and clouds increased as we pushed over the Warner Mountains toward Cedarville. We saw two antelope by the road, and farther on was an old boy struggling to get his horse into a trailer hooked to a pickup. The Doctor did not seem inspired by either of these sights, or the winding mountain road with almost no traffic. Stretching out before us as we descended into Cedarville was an expanse of green stretching north and south—the Surprise Valley, named by emigrants amazed to find such lush country after hundreds of miles of barren Nevada desert.

Cedarville was not much, just a crossroads with a few stores and a post office. We turned south toward that night's destination, the fabled Eagleville. The rain and impending darkness prevented me from properly appreciating this valley I had so long wanted to see. I remembered my college friend, Mike MacKenzie, and his summer here in 1955. He had enjoyed his job, the fellows he worked with, the folks who owned the ranch—all of it, immensely. At summer's end he took his earnings 200 miles to Reno and bought a used Harley. Reno was the "big city" for Surprise Valley.

From the backcountry road I saw prosperous-looking ranches off to the sides, and the Warner Mountains rising into clouds. Darkness was falling, and the Doctor expressed concern about what might, or might not, be waiting for us in Eagleville. I didn't share his unease, for I knew we had something to eat and drink, and could sleep in the bus if the rain continued. We cracked a couple of beers as we rolled into the town, which was indeed small. Very small. The only thing open seemed to be a combination store and bar. We pulled up in front and sat there, drinking our beer with the rain drumming on the van's roof. Now that we had reached Eagleville, we both were experiencing a letdown. The reality of the place was not what I had pictured.

"Well, we're here: Eagleville," I said with forced cheer. "This is it!" The Doctor did not smile. "I bet you're the only man in Eagleville with a beard," I said. He laughed then. Beards were rare in those days, especially in rural areas. My father was always being taken for an old prospector or miner because of his. After a while, there was nothing to do but go into the establishment where we were parked. There were no other vehicles, and hardly anybody inside. At back in the bar an old woman was busying herself. In the front a worn couch faced a TV set, which was struggling with a lot of static. And on that couch sat a burly man with a wool shirt and . . . a big dark BEARD! He glanced up as we entered, nodded and went back to the TV. The Doctor elbowed me and said I owed him a beer.

We sat at the bar and ordered beers. The woman brought them but showed no interest in us, except when, after his second one, the Doctor belched. Then she shook her head sadly, evidently at the breach of decorum. Feeling unwelcome after that, we took our drinks to the couch. There was plenty of room, but the man scooted over, saying, "Have a seat, boys. Name's Urban." We gave ours and shook hands. The fellow then resumed his TV watching, without asking us anything. I figured that itinerant ranch hands often passed through, and we were taken for some of these. During a commercial break Urban mentioned modestly that he was the "Injun wrastlin' champ o' these parts" and wondered, not challengingly, if I might want to take him on. Of course not! He was a huge man and was welcome to remain champ, as far as I was concerned.

A few beers later I asked Urban where we might park for the night without disturbing folks. He said there was a dirt road two miles south of town, going into the mountains. "Anywhere back in there, no one will bother you boys atall," he said. He showed no surprise that we'd be sleeping in our rig. We thanked him, took our leave, and set forth in a persistent rain into the darkness to find a spot to pass the night. A little way up the road Urban had mentioned we came to a flat place under some ponderosas. There we sat in the bus and finished the beer. Tipsy by now, Dr. Avis chuckled, "Only man in Eagleville with a beard, eh?" We went to sleep listening to rain on the roof.

The next morning was gray and cool, but not raining. We staggered out of the van about dawn, drank some juice and shared a can of fruit. Then we went back to Eagleville, which we saw consisted of a post office, the establishment we had been in the previous night, a few houses—and that was it! Retracing our route northward through the valley, we could see more than we had the previous evening. Indeed, the ranches were substantial and the area pristine. A lot of snow falls in the Warner Range, from moisture blown off the Pacific; and when it melts it runs down into the valley, creating a belt of rolling grassland about 50 miles long. The moisture stays in the valley through most of the summer. But just east of the mountains, the Nevada desert begins abruptly.

Many of the ranches remained in the families of early homesteaders from the 1870s, and the area seemed to be in something of a time warp. Near Cedarville we came upon some fellows on horseback driving a bunch of cattle south along the road. We parked the bus while they moved the herd along. The cowboys smiled and waved—in 1963 strangers were not yet cause for suspicion. If you were in that country it was presumed that you had some business there. Passing through the valley's northernmost town, Fort Bidwell, Dr. Avis observed, "There is not a single person to be seen here, no one out and about doing anything. I know people live here—but where are they?" I suggested they were still in their houses having breakfast, early that it was. And watching us pass.

North of the valley the road turned to dirt and climbed into low timbered ranges. It was a disaster! First mud, then snow. We got bogged down, but managed to turn around after both the Doctor and I got muddy surveying the situation. We went back the way we had come, back to Alturas and then north to Lakeview, Oregon, a frontier lumber town. We drove past marshes and wide, flat, shallow lakes teeming with waterfowl. The land had a different, northern feel, and I thought it quite arbitrary for this region to be included in California. It had nothing to with L.A., or even San Francisco. No, this country was oriented north, and should have been part of Oregon. I later learned that the people living there thought so, too.

It was still early when we reached Lakeville, where we stopped for coffee and gas. Lakeville seemed a pleasant and very American town, if in the middle of nowhere. I always wonder about places like that—who is the rich man in town, who the prettiest girl, what are the scandals? East of Lakeville was range and timber, with isolated ranches. We passed a combination store and gas station, with a sign that said "No gas for 100 miles," and headed into volcanic, rimrock desert terrain. The road had been paved for only a couple of years, so the land was virtually uninhabited, dipping down from Oregon into the high plains of northwestern Nevada—the Charles Sheldon Antelope Refuge, where "the largest free-ranging herds of wild antelope in the country" roamed the lonely vistas. Here and there we passed water from the recent rains, but most of the country was volcanic dryness, forbidding and empty. I sensed the Doctor's unease as we slipped into it.

Our plan was to turn north at Denio, Nevada, on dirt roads to Steens Mountain, Oregon. From there we would swing east through Oregon high desert, drop down into Nevada again, and navigate to our destination of Sulphur, out there all by itself, in the middle of the Black Rock Desert. Denio was just a small collection of weathered buildings, the kind of place described by the old Nevada newspaperman who said, "A mining camp lies, like a tin can, wherever it has been thrown." It had a gas station, and because we were heading into desolate country we filled up the bus. To the silent fellow pumping gas Dr. Avis asked casually, "How's the road up to Steens Mountain?" The guy looked up without saying anything. But "What sort of damn-fool question is that?" was written all over his face. Then he said, laconically, "Ain't been no one down here from up there in two, three days." As if that explained everything—which it certainly did. Impassable.

The Doctor and I realized that a change of plan was called for. Paying for the gas, he asked if there was a place to get lunch. The fellow pointed at an old wooden building and said, "They's probably set up at the long table, noon meal." Inside was indeed a long table, seating about a dozen men, waiting to eat. A cheerful, heavyset woman greeted us. "Sit right down, boys. It's two-fifty apiece." Thus we found ourselves digging into a hearty meat-and-potatoes communal lunch with those serious-looking workingmen—working at what, I did not know. They ate in silence. Lunch ended with canned fruit and coffee. Everyone paid the woman and filed out. The men drove off in trucks, this way and that. Denio was clearly a busy place, but we were only passing through.

Gazing into dark desert under dark skies, Dr. Avis and I discussed our options, of which there seemed to be only one—south to Winnemucca on pavement, and wait for a change in the weather. The Doctor's relief was palpable. After 100 more miles through vast and desolate country we reached town about 4 in the afternoon. We had a look about, but there was not much to see. A small downtown section and a few third-rate casinos along the highway. It was too early for dinner, and we were still full from our good workingman's meal, so we decided to while away some time within the confines of "Candy's Club." Quite a few others had made the same decision. The place was well patronized by the "professional drinkers" one encounters in desert country. We hoisted ourselves onto barstools and looked around. No bartender was in evidence, but pretty soon a man got up from a table where a card game was in progress and came behind the bar to confront us.

We ordered a beer apiece. The fellow returned and put two bottles each in front of us. We commented that we had only ordered one. "Y'all ain't come in here for jest one beer each, so here's yore second," he said patiently. "I'm playing cards over to there and don't care to get up too much. Okay?" We saw his logic, and yes, had not come in for just one beer. To our left we heard one man tell another "Sure, I'll fly you up to Quinn River Crossing, but not until the weather clears. You ain't in no hurry. I ain't flyin' until the weather clears. Have another drink." To our right were three fellows. Two appeared to be cowhands, perhaps in their 30s, who were mightily drunk. The third was an older fellow with a white beard and very blue eyes. He sat steadily on his stool.

As the Doctor and I were settling in, one cowhand toppled off his stool and lay inert on the floor under the bar. The other lurched up, leaned on the bar and nudged his fallen companion with the toe of his boot, saying, "Come on, Buck, on yore feet. Git on yore damned feet!" Buck rolled around down there, groping for his hat. Evidently he had no intention of getting up until his hat was back on his head. Finally this was accomplished, and Buck staggered to his feet. He stood there swaying. His partner sat down again at the bar. We noticed that the bearded man had moved Buck's glass of red wine over next to his own. Buck stood unsteadily for a few moments, then weaved toward the door of the bar and was out. The two remaining men sat silently, sipping their wine. I found it unusual for them to be drinking wine and not beer, but who knows? Perhaps they had cultivated a taste for wine in the South of France. Or more likely, the San Joaquin Valley.

The bartender appeared with two more beers each. We nodded and he uncapped them, accepting our money. A short time later the remaining cowhand decided he had had enough, and staggered off to join Buck somewhere. He had a problem, though. He crashed against the wall several feet to the left of the door. Some men called out, "To yore right, Tom. To yore right." Tom went hand over hand until he came to the door. Some mild cheers went up, and Tom stumbled out. When we turned back from watching this episode we saw that the stern bearded man had moved Tom's glass of red wine over next to the two others in front of him. Now he had three to get him through the afternoon. He glanced over at us, smiled and nodded, very much in control.

Darkness had fallen when we left the bar. At the end of the street a freight train was hurtling through, fast, maybe 80 mph. We heard the clang-clang of the crossing bell long after the train was gone, loud in the evening stillness. Both of us were feeling that "sadness for no reason" that often comes with drinks and dusk in the desert. Passed out on the sidewalk was one of the cowboys. Dr. Avis said, "Now, I know that those stalwart gents, backbones of the West, come to a place like Candy's and carry on like that only once or twice a year. You know, being out on the range and all, well, it does things to a man. But I am sure that those two you could count on, and if I ever get my big spread up here, there would be no one other than Buck and Tom that I'd want to run it for me."

"It don't mean a hoot that Buck fell on the floor and Tom couldn't find the door!" the Doctor continued, warming to his joke. "Nope, two finer men cannot be found in all of the great state of Neevada!" We laughed, then reeled down to the casino on the corner to try our luck with the coupons we had gotten with our gas upon entering town. These free bets quickly disappeared, but we did okay with our meal coupons. It was getting on toward 10 when we drove out of town and onto a dirt road leading into the desert. The threat of rain seemed gone, so I spread my sleeping bag among the pungent sagebrush, leaving the bus to the Doctor. The desert was perfectly quiet.

At dawn I was awakened by the sounds of a vehicle door opening and closing, then low voices. Rising in my bag I saw a pickup truck facing our bus, and a rancher standing by the window asking Dr. Avis to move so he could get by. The Doctor was muttering apologies, and the rancher was saying, "Don't matter, man has to sleep somewhere." The bus was moved and the rancher waved goodbye. In town we got a big breakfast at a third-rate casino. Those gambling places always have cheap food to lure the public in, so why not take advantage of them? Then we found the dirt road west toward Sulphur, through endless sands.

The road was pretty good, with pools of water here and there. Rain had not fallen for a day or so, but the skies were still gray and the air cool. The road paralleled the railroad tracks, the Western Pacific/Union Pacific line we had noted in Winnemucca. We had bordered the western and northern part of that dark, empty part of Nevada on solid pavement. Now we were headed into the heart of it on a road that made locals shake their heads, as if we were heading across the Sahara. Sulphur was about 60 miles away, and 50 miles beyond was a place called Gerlach, both along the railroad. Rabbithole Spring was just to the south. Nothing else was out there.

As we progressed west, the rolling desert flattened into huge vistas with mountain ranges barely visible miles away. A few dust devils wandered across the emptiness. A feeling of isolation settled over us. "We've seen some big country," I said, "but this is really big!" And surreally gray and grim. The Doctor nervously agreed. After 40 miles of passable road we came to the community of Jungo—or former community, I should say, because it was deserted. "My God, this looks like a movie set!" Dr. Avis exclaimed. And indeed it did, with the big wooden Jungo Hotel facing the tracks, and a few faded wooden shacks nearby. It was a place left over from another time, and forgotten. (I wish I had photographed the hotel, for it and the nearby shacks subsequently burned. Now nothing is left on the site.)

After Jungo the road deteriorated. More water and mud. We questioned the advisability of continuing. The map showed a dirt road running south from Sulphur through Rabbithole Spring and connecting eventually with a pavement near the town of Lovelock on U.S. 50. The route encompassed a hundred miles of desert on unpredictable roads. The Doctor's apprehension was obvious. I tried to sound confident, but in truth I was getting nervous myself. We pushed on.

Sulphur was just a collection of abandoned shacks and buildings left behind by a mining operation. Pits had been gouged out of the hillsides, and near the tracks were yellow piles of what we took to be sulphur. But any activity was far in the past. No road led either west or south, and we drove around looking for the way out. A little bit to the west we found two men consulting a map on the hood of a substantial, mud-splattered four-wheel-drive pickup. They identified themselves as government geologists. They were not sure about the road to the south. "We just sort of felt our way in," one said. Consulting their USGS topographical map, they pointed to a wash and said the road should be in that direction. We bade them farewell, and I directed the Doctor to head up the wash. "You sure this is a road?" he asked shakily. "Absolutely!" I assured him. But as the bus groaned up the rough and muddy wash, I was having doubts. It did not look very much like a road.

We crested a low hill and descended onto what resembled a real road—covered by a large mudhole at the bottom of the hill. Crouched tensely over the wheel, Dr. Avis shuddered to a stop. "Can't go through that," he said. "We'll have to back up." But in reverse the wheels just spun in the mud. I said we would just have to get up speed and blast through the damned mudhole. Reluctantly the Doctor agreed. There was no alternative. We began down the hill, but the Doctor's caution was not building up enough speed. We plunged into the mudhole and made it only halfway across. As we bogged to a stop the bus settled into the muck. The Doctor lowered his head and pounded the steering wheel with his fists. "Shit, shit, shit!" he said in defeat. "Come on, Doctor!" I shouted. "Where is your pioneer spirit?" He replied weakly, "I don't have any. I wouldn't have made it."

But our situation did not seem critical. From the hilltop we had noticed a shack with a battered four-wheel-drive pickup next to it. Whoever lived there could pull us out. Sure enough, a weathered man emerged, beer bottle in hand, and stared at us. I sloshed over to him. "Hell," he said, "it ain't that deep, and it's got a solid bottom. Jest back up a ways and make another run at it. You'll git through." He made no offer to tow us out. I explained the plan to the dismayed Doctor. I pushed the van in front, and Dr. Avis roared the engine—and came out of the mudhole and partway up the hill. I told him to really give it some power, to keep traction all the way through. He nodded grimly. I kept my distance as the bus came flying down, slithering from side to side—much too fast this time, I thought. As he hit the mudhole the Doctor's eyes were wide and his knuckles white. In a huge spray of mud and water, the bus fairly hydroplaned across, and rolled to a stop on dry land.

Shaken, Dr. Avis got out. I congratulated him and said indeed he did have pioneer spirit, among the finest I had ever seen. Somehow this did not elevate his spirits. The ominous qualities of the great desert, with all its dangers and unknowns, were taking their toll on the Doctor, who was undoubtedly now wishing he was in some crowded North Beach coffeehouse with a bunch of intellectuals rattling on about John Crowe Ransom, or Ginsberg and Kerouac. But—we were at Rabbithole Spring, not stuck, and not out of gas.

The weathered fellow waved for us to come over. Three small children in ragged coats hovered around his legs, in a scene out of the Great Depression. "I knowed y'all wouldn' have no trouble gittin' through that, " the man said. He looked us over. Both the Doctor and I were covered with mud, from extricating the bus several times, and were worn out from too much drinking and too little sleep. "I know what it's like, wandering from place to place lookin' fer work," the fellow said. "Come on an' have a beer." He figured he had us pegged. Why else would we be wandering through that country, if not looking for work at ranches or mines? As we sipped the cool ones, the children proudly showed us the scorpions they had caught and put in Mason Jars. They wanted to sell them to us for a dollar apiece. Having no need for scorpions, we declined.

South of Rabbithole Spring the weather began to improve. In the west, where we were headed, there was even a hint of blue. Virginia City, outside Reno, was our destination, but not likely that night, late in the afternoon as it was. I was driving. Exhausted from his struggles, the Doctor was sleeping in the back. He said he had had enough of back roads and desert country, that it all was depressing him. He needed to be around people, things happening, the morning paper and news— things non-existent in the purity of the desert. Dr. Avis had tired of purity. The Real West was not for him. In the vibrancy of the city—that was where he belonged. Not in this endless sand.

We finally reached the paved road. It was perfectly flat and there was no headwind, but I could not get the bus above 45 mph. It had always cruised easily at 65 or more. Something was wrong! The frightful racing of the engine at the mudhole must have damaged the valves. The engine was simply not generating enough power. It was running okay, but I could not push the brand-new VW above 45. Well, nothing to do but roll along. I decided not to trouble the Doctor with this development. Let the man have his rest. Rekindle his pioneer spirit. He slept on in the darkness as I neared the town of Dayton—my namesake, I was amused to think. I decided we should bunk down there, and go on to Virginia City in the morning. When the Doctor stirred, he agreed. He had reached the point where all he cared about was getting back to civilization.

Dayton was a semi-ghost town where much of the Clark Gable-Marilyn Monroe movie "The Misfits" was filmed. We parked behind an abandoned church, leaning startlingly to one side, and kept from toppling over by three sturdy cables. If only that could be done with some men I knew, I thought—put cables on them to keep them from falling! Over canned food we discussed our situation. Dr. Avis, my father and I had been in Virginia City the previous September, when some Hell's Angels came roaring into town. One biker wanted to trade for the Doctor's Aussie hat, with one side pinned up. The offer was declined, jovially. For the Doctor it was a good memory, so he wanted to go back to Virginia City. For this evening, however, we went to "Gene's Last Chance Bar," where some fellows were talking about "a gold strike down by Rawhide." The Doctor was amazed: "It's goddamned 1963 and these guys are talking about gold strikes like it's 1863!"

Next morning the bus simply would not make the hill up to Virginia City. Dr. Avis was driving when the vehicle came to a halt halfway up. I had to inform him that I thought the valves had been damaged by the racing at the mudhole. It was just one more disaster for the poor Doctor, who had no idea what to do. We finally slipped downhill to Reno for repairs. We hoped to get the vehicle back that afternoon, and prayed that the cost would not be exorbitant. We were low on funds, and went looking for someplace that would cash a check. First we tried the office of a prominent physician, the uncle of someone the Doctor knew in San Francisco. But he was out of town, and his secretary refused to help two alkali-encrusted strangers. At the Bank of Nevada we got the same reception. I realized it would be the same all over town. In that pre-ATM era, people were suspicious of drifters trying to cash out-of-state checks. I asked to speak to the bank manager.

This personage eyed the Doctor and me apprehensively as I described our predicament. No doubt he had heard all sorts of "car problem" stories masking gambling losses. He was shaking his head, prefatory to saying no, when I asked him to call the Bank of California in San Francisco and speak to vice president Charlie Thomas. I said I would gladly pay for the call. The man agreed and dialed. He reached Charlie and began to explain the situation. Then his tone changed. "Yes, yes, of course," he said, and I knew things were going to be all right. The manager exchanged a few pleasantries with Charlie, who had been my father's banker in Santa Monica. Then all smiles, the man endorsed my check and said it "had been a pleasure." My bluejeans had sprouted pinstripes!

Cash in hand, we took the bus to a Volkswagen shop for repairs, then got something to eat and strolled around downtown Reno. Except for the casinos on Virginia Street, it was a nice Western town, enhanced by the Truckee River running down the middle. In a city park we rested and waited. Several sleeping men seemed to have had the same idea. But I was pretty sure they had no vehicle and were waiting for . . . nothing! A police car pulled up, and two cops meandered through, tapping the men's feet with nightsticks. "No sleeping in city parks," the cops said. "Get going!" I felt they were infringing on the men's constitutional rights, and told Dr. Avis that I was going to feign sleep, and when jostled make a big fuss. The Doctor grew worried. "No, no! Don't create any hassles," he said. "We'll end up in jail and have to get your friend the bank manager to get us out. Let's just get some coffee, pick up the van and go on to Virginia City. Okay?" I laughed and acquiesced. I had never really intended to stir up trouble.

The bus seemed to run fine, and we made it to Virginia City by early evening. The place looked the same—how was it going to change? There were always rumors of mining coming back, but nothing ever happened. There were some tourists in summer, and not much the rest of the year. We walked down the main street. Honkytonk music was coming out of one place, but the rest was quiet. Old Badwater Bill, whom we remembered from our previous visit, had gone home for the evening, since there were no tourists to pay for taking his picture with his burro Gravel Gertie, loaded down with prospecting equipment. Last year my father had been mightily impressed with Badwater Bill. They passed a few words—one old-timer to another—and afterward my father pronounced Bill "the real thing," not some phony.

The Bucket of Blood saloon seemed the most lively, so we went in. Last year I was sitting on the rear deck when the full moon come up out of Six Mile Canyon, like a giant 50-dollar gold piece. The saloon was hopping—and at the bar was Badwater Bill! People kept buying him drinks in return for a few moments of conversation. He wore a green vest made from a roulette table. It added color to his long gray beard, silver hair and big hat. I shook his gnarled hand, and we talked. He said he had worked in Bay Area shipyards during the war, but had spent most of his life in the desert, prospecting and working for ranches. He said he had hundreds of stories collected from the Indians and was looking for somebody to help write them all down. I suggested the state university at Reno, or even Berkeley. We kept talking until the Doctor said he was ready for dinner.

From our table we saw that Badwater Bill had joined a party of tourists and had a big steak in front of him, along with his drinks. "You know, Old Bill has a real good thing going," the Doctor said. "He stands around in the street all day with that fucking burro, and people pay him a dollar or two to take his picture, of them with him and little Bubba on the burro, to show the folks back home. Then he goes to the bar and never has to pay for a drink, and now somebody has bought him dinner. Yeah, the old guy has a good thing." I agreed, but wondered about the winter, non-tourist season. (Later I heard that a San Francisco social-ite had brought Bill to the city to stand with his burro outside a Pacific Heights mansion and greet the guests, for an enormous fee I hope, plus bed and board for them both.)

We slept outside town, on the ruins of a gold-processing mill. When we rose the next morning the Doctor cocked his head and said, "Listen, I hear a sound seldom heard these days but quite common a hundred years ago." Below us rose a slow, rhythmic clanging. The source was Badwater Bill leading Gravel Gertie, loaded down with gear, toward Virginia Street for another day of pictures and dollars. A man has to make hay in the sunshine.

We left Virginia City and headed over the Sierra into Mother Lode country. I thought the Doctor's spirits would improve in that pleas-ant area. We could fetch up at the old Jackson Hotel in the town of that name, clean up and act civilized. He thought it a splendid plan. We crossed the Sierra on California Highway 88, just opened for the season, with roadside snow piled five feet high at the summit. We descended through spring, then early summer. Jackson was quite warm, and its atmosphere definitely civilized. We cleaned up, ate, and drove to the nearby town of Sutter Creek. The architecture there had a time-warp atmosphere, illuminated by old incandescent streetlights.

In the beer garden where we settled, locals were dancing and drinking. Saturday night in Sutter Creek. The band was a simple affair: guitar, old piano and a washtub thumper. Close to the bar was a large table of men who might in the South be called rednecks. The most ebullient was a heavyset fellow in overalls, who kept everyone else laughing. As I returned from the bar with two beers, the big man caught my arm and said, "Why don't y'all set here with us ole boys and have yore beer?" I said I was with a friend and nodded toward Dr. Avis, obscure in the dimness. Still, his beard and beret were visible—a bit exotic, perhaps, for Sutter Creek. I assumed he did not want to get involved with a bunch of good old boys, so I said my friend did not talk much. The man just laughed and said, "Go git him. He don't have to talk. He kin jest set here an' drink." It was impossible to refuse.

I explained the situation to the Doctor, who reluctantly came over. The heavyset man introduced himself as Ellis. The others smiled and nodded. There were many empty bottles, and all the fellows were in a good mood. "What you think of our little Okie stomp?" Ellis asked. We said it was mighty fine, that we had been out in northern Nevada and it sure was nice to be back among friendly folks. Ellis signaled to the bartender. Someone asked what we were doing in Nevada. "Oh, jest mindin' our own business," I replied. He apologized: "I wasn't tryin' to pry. Minding your own business, damned good thing to do."

Another fellow asked what the price of hay per ton was these days over in Nevada. The Doctor glanced at me, wondering how I was going to handle that one, knowing I did not know the price of hay from the price of beryllium. Before I could answer, someone piped up, "About $18 a ton, ain't it?" No, I said. "With all that rain we been havin', it's a bit higher." They nodded. More stories, more beer. The men lost their curiosity about us, and we were just two more good old boys out on a Saturday night in Sutter CRICK.

In San Francisco the next day, the fog was thick and cold. I shivered as the Doctor dropped me off at my apartment on Larkin Street. Over the next few years I read quite a bit about the Black Rock Desert, the pioneer Lassen-Applegate Cutoff that brought emigrants heading to Oregon across that barren *alkali playa,* to Double Boiling Hot Springs, where they found only poison water. I read the diaries of J. Goldsborough Bruff, whose account and drawings give the most complete picture of that desolate region in 1849. I read George R. Stewart's historical novel "Sheeprock," set out there, and other things that made me want to get back and have a real good look around. It was mysterious, forbidding country—wild and unspoiled. And dangerous.

When the Doctor and I related our journey to friends in North Beach, they had no idea of where or what we were talking about. To them, getting up to Mendocino or the Gold Country was a big adventure. They could not relate to Rabbithole Spring, Sulphur and Jungo, or what it might be like, wandering from place to place looking for work. When they crossed the country, it was without holes in their shoes or alkali mud on their clothes. They could not comprehend ragged desert kids who kept scorpions in Mason Jars, trying to sell them for a dollar.

7

A Tale of North Beach

Through the swinging doors of Vesuvio Dayton passed many times!

W hen I hear a certain piece of music on the radio, here in my casita in Santa Fe, I remember that it was the theme song of a semiclassical station I used to listen to on a tinny radio in my small apartment in San Francisco in 1961. It was a nice two-room place that I had "inherited" from a friend going into the Army, which I had just gotten out of. About all I had learned in the Corps of Engineers was how to blow up things, a skill that was then not very marketable in the civilian world. I was supposed to also inherit my friend's job, delivering paperback books in the Bay Area, but that didn't work out. The boss suggested that I seek something "more permanent." So I was left adrift in the City by the Bay, with just a few vague introductions and this small apartment.

One afternoon in October, rain began to fall, lightly at first then heavily, in gales blowing in off the Pacific. Toward evening I retreated to the apartment, with some Rainier Ale from the Princess Pat store on the corner. The rain was dripping into the light well, and the classical melody was playing on the radio. I had no job, and did quite a bit of reading in the apartment, which was furnished with just a mattress and crate in the bedroom, and a kitchen arrangement made from some boards and Chinese crates I hauled up from Grant Avenue. Spartan but adequate—barely.

I baked loaves of bread of my own recipe, brewed tea, and ate baked potatoes. Once in a while, on a splurge, I had a plate of tomato beef chow mein with curry down in Chinatown, at the basement restaurant Woy Loy Goey. As the October rain fell on that Friday evening I found myself wondering what was happening to me. Here I was in San Francisco, 24 years old, with no job and no friends. My own apartment, yes, as I had dreamed, but somehow this particular one was not quite what I had envisioned. It was in an undistinguished if convenient neighborhood, near Polk and Sacramento, above a mortuary. At least it was quiet. Where was I headed, and why? No answer. I guess I had sunk into an existentialist funk. That was what I had been educated for, wasn't it?

Fueled on the ale, I ventured forth from the apartment and made my way through the rain over Nob Hill and down to North Beach. My friend and I had gone there a couple of weeks earlier, and across an alley from the City Lights Bookstore a certain bar had caught my attention. Vesuvio, as it was named, was lively, with much coming and going of the "beatniks" of that era. And regular folks, too, workingmen and intellectuals. In the 1940s Vesuvio was an Italian hangout, and a decade later it attracted Kerouac and his crowd for the large and cheap glasses of wine, in an unpretentious atmosphere. The place had a reputation, and I was drawn to it as a moth to flame.

I remember pausing outside in the drizzle, then pushing through the swinging doors—"For the first of many times!"—as Dr. Avis later liked to remind me. The place was always crowded. Draft beer was 30 cents a glass. One could circulate, glass in hand, and join various conversations. Everybody seemed to know everyone else. After my first few visits the bartender, Bruce, started nodding to me when I entered. One night my leather jacket was stolen from a chair while I was in the men's room. Bruce said he knew what it looked like, would keep his eyes peeled, and let me know if he spotted it. "You're a regular," he explained. I had never heard of or thought of myself in such a way, but my Friday nights' attendance had evidently earned me the designation.

I found it easy to talk with people in that establishment, and learned the meaning of the old phrase "He spent the evening drinking with a circle of new friends." I did indeed meet people there who became friends, and are to this day—the ones who are still alive. At least three of my friends died violently, or "went down," as they say on the streets. Once when my father was visiting San Francisco I took him to Vesuvio (never Vesuvio's!) for a Guinness Stout. He looked around with interest and amusement, and after one drink we went on our way. The next day he cautioned me against spending too much time in such "philosopher's clubs." He felt that many of the patrons he'd observed had made an attempt at life and given up. I did not inform him that many of them had simply given up, *without* making any attempt. Above the bar he had noticed a sign: "Avoid the Christmas Rush—Drink Early!" He didn't think such an attitude put one on a productive path.

On a recent visit to San Francisco, strolling around North Beach one afternoon, I needed to find a bathroom. I entered Vesuvio, noting a sign by the door that said the restrooms were for customers only, and made my way through the familiar bar. There were just a few patrons, aging hippies—beatniks even—with long gray hair and beards. I smiled. They seemed to be from Central Casting. I descended the stairs to the men's room, as I had done hundreds of times before. The rubber and metal treads felt and sounded just as I recalled. I went into the stall to take a leak, remembering that above the toilet in the '60s had been a small printed paper that read, "Carleton Burgess, Homosex," with a telephone number. I always wondered why anyone would go to the trouble of having such a thing printed, then pasting it in men's rooms. Now, of course, realizing the need and compulsion of such individuals, we recognize that he was indeed advanced. I also spotted graffiti that had been on the wall since my era, particularly some words now mostly erased, leaving only ". . . long to" above ". . . eration." It originally had said: "We all belong to the suicide generation."

Coming back up those stairs I remembered what a terrible clatter used to result when old Frank would "throw himself" down them, a not-infrequent Friday-night event. Frank was a strange figure in bib overalls and a beret, who appeared mostly on Fridays with a sketch pad, and then drank wine all night, mumbled to himself, and drew pictures, most of which he crumpled or tore up. Some he even chewed up. He always sat at the end of the bar toward the stairs to the men's room, and several times a night he would lurch up and launch himself down them with a loud clatter. He was never hurt, and I don't know exactly what he did, but it certainly made a lot of noise and startled those who were not regulars. Frank, it was said, was actually a San Jose electrician who came to North Beach on weekends "to get crazy." Whether that was true I never knew. (Dr. Avis says he has a real treasure from those days: one of Frank's drawings! He had retrieved it from under the bar one night and smoothed it out for a souvenir. Who else remembers Frank today?)

As I emerged from the stairs the bartender asked me what I would have. "Nothing," I said. He looked at me like I was some tourist—which I guess I was, in a way—and said the restrooms were for customers only. I looked at him and said in a loud voice, "I've spent at least $10,000 in this place over the years, so I think I have the right to take a leak. Okay?" He shrugged and went back to drying glasses. A couple of the aging hippies looked up and smiled. "Ten thousand, huh?" they seemed to be thinking. "Wonder how much I've spent?" I pushed through the wood-and-glass doors into the bright afternoon, something

I had almost never done before—most of my exits had been at 2 a.m. closings, when the black cat would stick its head out from the balcony and meow.

There are so many stories that I could tell about Vesuvio that an entire volume would be needed. No doubt I spent more time in that establishment than was good for me. But I did meet a lot of interesting people and had quite a few adventures, not all of them distinguished. My father was generally right about the patrons. (Just as he was when one time in my apartment I tuned in a '60s rock stations. He listened to a few songs, then commented, "I know what they're trying to do with this music: They're trying to get people to give up!") Vesuvio today has remarkably the same atmosphere as it did back then. More Asians come in, and fewer blacks. I don't know anybody there anymore, but I do recognize them as younger versions of myself, or people I knew.

One person I remember vividly. In the early '60s an interesting old-timer showed up in North Beach, as did various people who stood out from the crowd. This fellow was about 70, had a long white beard, and wore a cowboy hat. Naturally, he became known around the bars and coffeehouses as "Cowboy." He had the wise, good-humored and weather-beaten look of a prophet, which gave him instant entry into the scene. He carried three or four worn notebooks wrapped with large rubber bands, and he often recited from these at poetry readings. I heard him several times, but was not very impressed with his work, except that it had a sincere feel for the times, people and events he wrote about—all years in the past, in Montana, Idaho, the Northwest, where he was from. What brought him to San Francisco I did not know. Perhaps a desire to be in the literary scene.

He appeared often at Vesuvio on weekends, and settled in at one of the tables back from the bar. He'd order an Anchor Steam beer, with his bundle of worn notebooks on the table, and allow people to sit down and gather around him. Which they quickly did, since he was a colorful old fellow. To the mostly young people who frequented his table he would say, "Cowboy, jest call me Cowboy." It certainly suited him. Everybody liked the old guy. I often joined his table, and listened as he bought rounds of drinks and spun tales of the old days up in "the North

Country," about logging camps, cattle drives, mines, mills and smelters—and all the characters he lived and worked with back then. He was a good storyteller, with his gravelly voice and wise look. He was the real thing, not some fussy professor at San Francisco State droning on about the Gold Rush and other events he had only read about. No, Cowboy had lived the things he spoke of, had known the people. He talked up socialism a lot, the old-fashioned idealistic workingman's socialism, and the young people ate it up. When he mentioned Big Bill Haywood in one tale there were blank looks. I said, "Western Federation of Miners," sort of to myself. Cowboy shot me a glance, then went on.

I eventually noticed that he had a plastic covering over his left hand, which he kept mostly beneath the table. When he realized I had seen it, he said quietly to me, "Veterans Hospital—that's why I'm in Frisco." I didn't catch the rest of the explanation, which was short, mumbled and swallowed up in the roar of the bar. He turned to some new people and began to talk about the "old days up north, the Hard Country, back at the time of the First War. You kids wouldn't know nothin' about any of that, workin' 10 hours fer a couple of dollars. Hell, there was one great son-of-a-bitch of an uproar about gittin' an eight-hour day. Men died fer that! Nope, you kids wouldn't know nothin' 'bout them things. Country's gone soft, too rich." And on in that vein. It was his element.

One night he started in on how men stuck together in those conditions, unions and socialism, all that. He got sentimental as he told about what great friends he had in those days, "up in the Hard Country." He then got quiet, staring into his beer. "Cowboy, you have friends here," an innocent-looking young girl said softly. "We're your friends." Very sincere. He looked up, agitated. "No! You ain't friends like I had in them days," he said. "They were real friends. The men I worked with, the women who tended us when it got bad. You kids is okay, but you ain't friends like I had back in them days, my real friends who are gone now. All my old, good friends are dead! I've outlived them all, dammit! I never thought I'd be the last!"

There was a shocked silence as Cowboy stared off into some unknowable distance. Then he looked around, picked up his drink and smiled. "You kids are good people." He called for another round. He looked at me—I was older than the others by a few years—and said quietly, "You know, don't you, pardner? You know what I mean." I thought I knew, and nodded slowly. He reached out his right hand and gave my arm a squeeze. I nodded again, and he smiled sadly. Then he turned to the waitress bringing the drinks. He paid for them all, waving away offers to chip in. He put a large tip on the girl's tray. He took a big sip from his glass of Anchor Steam, wiped his mouth and beard with the back of his hand, and began another tale, about the early days, the Hard Country.

I got up to go to the men's room, thinking of old Frank and the racket he made when he "launched" himself down those stairs. And of Whitey, "the Easter Bonnet Bandit," an old seaman who drank in Vesuvio and earned that nickname for some escapade I've now forgotten. (I'll have to ask Dr. Avis—he remembers all that stuff.) The men's room was congested. During the wait I read the graffiti covering the walls. When I got back, Cowboy's table was empty, and there was a commotion out by the front door. I asked a guy at the bar what happened. He said, "It's Cowboy. He suddenly rushed out and tried to throw himself in front of a bus. I think he's hurt."

I pushed through the bar to the door. A crowd had gathered, and Cowboy was lying crumpled in the street in front of a stopped bus, not moving. Some people were worriedly tending to him. A police car pulled up, lights flashing in the fog. And then an ambulance. After a quick examination, Cowboy was loaded into the ambulance. Someone gave a paramedic the battered hat that he wore. The man looked at it, then placed it in the ambulance. The doors closed, and with siren and flashing lights the ambulance sped off into the San Francisco night.

It all seemed unreal—I couldn't believe it had actually happened. I went back into the bar. People were talking seriously. I returned to the table we had occupied. My beer was still there. Coming up from the men's room I had noticed on the table the worn notebooks that Cowboy always had with him—the ones with those heartfelt poems about his life and friends. Now they were gone. I looked around on the floor. Nothing! Someone had taken the books. Why? For what? It bothered me. I finished my beer at the bar. The young people at the table, Cowboy's "friends," all had left. Cowboy too was gone, without saying goodbye. I felt he would not be coming back.

I walked home in the fog, over the Broadway Tunnel. Twenty minutes back to the apartment. In bed by 2:30 a.m., into a fitful sleep, thinking of the old fellow in the bar, of mines, mills, smelters, logging camps, up north, in the Hard Country. And of loneliness, of old and fine friends, all gone. I never did see Cowboy again. There was nothing in the paper about the incident. As far as I know, he never again appeared in North Beach. No one seemed to know anything. Had he died that night? Or been badly hurt, and taken to the Veterans Hospital? Sent back to the North Country? What had happened to the notebooks? Nobody talked about Cowboy anymore. He was gone, into the abyss of history, which is large enough to hold us all. The man who had outlived all his friends, as one man always must.

PART II

THE HIGH COUNTRY

High Country Singing

Remember the songs of snow
in the Colorado winters?
There was almost always wind
blowing from the north?
The snow never fell silently
straight down to collect
in an orderly fashion.
Songs, too, of thunderstorms,
violent and impressive,
regularly on summer afternoons
until the dryness of September.
Songs of winter night stillness,
below-zero crisp snow-crunch cold,
coyotes running lightly on frozen crust
And songs of the bar, Western bands,
that music from old-time religious songs,
someone's rural, Southern roots,
now it's cowboy hats bobbing
in a honkytonk.
There were also songs
in the high empty grass country
on nights when there was no wind
and the power of the stars
electrified the unpolluted sky
while we sat drinking beer,
the two of us, miles from anyone;
those songs all blew away
in a violent wind years ago.
I hear them drifting occasionally
in lonely places, around rocks
or trees, in various winds or
the twanging of a country band
in a remote Montana bar,
bits and pieces of those songs
blowing in the Western wind.

8

The Museum at the End of the World

Lonely and cold in winter, The District Museum presided over deserted
Bennett Avenue in Cripple Creek.

Saturday night in the winter of 1972, Cripple Creek, Colorado, 9,500 feet high on the western slope of the Pike's Peak massif. Bennett Avenue, the lonely main street, deserted. No car or person moving. Ribbons of snow snaking up the empty street in the wind. Dark, abandoned buildings. Metal signs creaking in the wind. A few pickups and cars resting outside the Cottage Inn bar, the only open, lighted place in town. Ghostly music issuing from inside, competing with the wind. Shorty and Gene, on accordion and drums—the kind of music heard at high school dances in the 1950s, because the people of Cripple Creek were still caught in that time warp 20 years later.

I stood alone in the street, listening to the sounds, letting the scene sink in. It was unique, ghostly, unreal, like life in another world. Yes, another world, a world I was getting to know.

Earlier that year there had been a "street dance" over in Victor, an old mining town six miles south of Cripple Creek and slightly higher at 9,700 feet. Dr. Avis and I went to it. Victor was even more a ghost town than Cripple Creek, but in July of 1972 the street dance was supposed to provide some life. Unfortunately, a drizzling mist enshrouded Victor the night of the dance. Even so, Shorty and Gene were playing their accordion and drums on the back of an old flatbed truck outside Zeke's Place, Victor's lone nightspot. Two couples were dancing, strangely, and three or four other people were standing around, drinking from beer bottles.

The mist was diffused by purplish streetlights, which gave the abandoned and crumbling buildings nearby a mysterious look. The dispirited dancing couples moved mechanically, in jerking motions. The beer-drinking bystanders were immobile. As we drove up, Dr. Avis said, "Stop! I want to let this scene sink in. It's not a sight of this world!" No, it wasn't. As I was learning, it was from another world.

The road from Cripple Creek to Victor runs along the edge of the mountains. Dr. Avis had been staring out into the vast darkness to the west. "There's not a single light anywhere out there!" he marveled. The darkness was indeed vast. Victor was at the end of the road, in the middle of nowhere. Just 250 people lived there, amid the ruins of a once-much-larger town, but few of them were in evidence on the night of the street dance. Zeke's Place was the social center of Victor. It was run by Ohrt Yaeger, a solid, short, bald, mustachioed old fellow who wore a gun and hated hippies—he would run them out of his bar. Zeke's Place always stayed open until 2 a.m., often without customers, because Ohrt Yaeger believed it should be ready for any miner in need of a drink. Of course, the mines had been closed for years. Nobody worked the mines anymore.

In 1972 I went to Colorado, to assume the position of director of the Cripple Creek District Museum, a local establishment celebrating the fabulous mining history of that community, which by then had dwindled almost into a ghost town, yet one with a steady stream of tourists. Actually, I was hired as curator, but my first official act was to elevate myself to director. The fellows who hung out at the local hardware store, Doc's, never quite understood the term curator. It just wasn't part of their vocabulary. I was in the hardware store a lot, and they knew I was doing the maintenance tasks they had formerly been called upon to perform for the old ladies who ran the museum. One day one of them said, "Dayton, you ain't the *cur-a-tor* up there, you're the caretaker, ain't you?" Now, that was a term that made sense to them, and so I agreed. "Caretaker," I nodded. "Yep, that's what I am." After that, they accepted me as a regular guy, a workingman, which was the only thing a decent fellow could be. But officially, I called myself the director.

I guess I qualified for that title. After going back to school and graduating from San Francisco State College with a master's degree in history and creative writing, I had worked four years as associate curator of history at the Oakland Museum, across the Bay from San Francisco. By 1972, however, I was burned out with the bureaucracy and politics of such a large institution. It seemed to me that a smaller Western museum would be different and rewarding; and I started looking around. I was pleased to get three job offers. My lack of proficiency in Spanish ultimately ruled out Santa Fe. The other choices were Yuma, Arizona, and Cripple Creek, Colorado. I chose high and cold over low and hot.

The job in Cripple Creek had been advertised in Museum News, a trade journal. I got in touch and was asked to come for an interview with Dorothy Mackin, who chaired the museum board. So in March of 1972 I made my first visit to Cripple Creek, accompanied by my friend Deborah Bristow, an artist from San Francisco. The day was raw, and Deborah declared the ride up to the town "lonely and barren." "Where is this place?" she asked. "At the end of the world?" When we finally got there, Deborah was not impressed. The town was wind-blown, desolate and empty. Abandoned and ruined buildings lined the streets. We met

Dorothy Mackin at her office across the street from the once-grand Imperial Hotel, which she ran as a melodrama theater in the summer, but which was now closed for winter. Dorothy was obviously a take-charge person. After a few opening civilities she and I got down to business, and Deborah went out to look around.

Driving back to Colorado Springs in the cold dusk, Deborah and I compared notes on the day. She had stopped in the local bar, which she reported had a somewhat peculiar name for a rough-and-tumble mining town. "It's called the Cottage Inn," she said, "like some Princeton eating club." There were only a few patrons, she said, and they all looked so "depressed" that she did not stay for a drink. Most of Cripple Creek's functioning stores were closed for the winter, but Deborah had found an open shop "run by a tough old broad," selling Indian jewelry of surprisingly high quality. "She must have good contacts with the Indians," Deborah said—and that was as close to a compliment as anything she had to say about Cripple Creek.

She asked me how the interview had gone. I felt it had gone well, and told Deborah I would not be surprised if I got an offer to direct the museum. We had visited it that afternoon, after Dorothy and I had talked. Located at the east end of town in an old railroad depot, the Cripple Creek museum was run by the usual kindly old ladies, and on that bleak afternoon it was devoid of visitors. I did not tell the ladies that I had applied for the job of curator. Deborah found the place "pretty dull," but I rather liked it, with its emphasis on gold mining, which had long interested me. I also felt the challenge of improving the museum. Already I was getting some ideas.

Deborah asked if I would accept the job if offered. I said I was concerned about the isolation, but that, yes, I probably would. "God, Dayton, I can't imagine you in that place!" she said. I laughed and said it just might be interesting, and certainly different. For a few years, anyway. "It's your life," she muttered. Then she added: "If you do go to work there, watch out for that woman, Dorothy what's-her-name? I think she might be a dangerous person. Yeah, I'd watch out for her." The expected offer came, and when summer returned to Cripple Creek I was there, in charge of the museum.

Although only 458 people inhabited Cripple Creek year-round, the town was actually a major tourist attraction, and the museum a serious enterprise. Located 110 miles from Denver and just 50 miles from Colorado Springs, Cripple Creek was in the heart of the Rocky Mountain West, and was one of the most picturesque ghost towns anywhere. Thousands of visitors passed through it each year, most of them in summer, due to the extreme cold of the winter months. The Imperial Hotel's melodrama had been up and running since shortly after World War II, and was a notable success, featured in several magazines and newspapers. Each summer Cripple Creek enjoyed a measurable economic surge from tourism. But it was nothing compared to the town's glory days.

At the turn of the 20th century, Cripple Creek was known as the world's greatest gold camp. A cowboy named Bob Womack first discovered the precious metal in 1890, and the town boomed to life almost overnight. Although virtually wiped out by two disastrous fires in 1896, Cripple Creek rebuilt immediately, and by 1900 was the third-largest city in Colorado. Some estimates put its population at 16,000, but the official figure from the 1900 census was 10,147—undoubtedly low. In that year some 500 mines in the Cripple Creek District, employing some 8,000 miners, yielded gold worth more than $18 million. And back in those days, $18 million was worth something. Like many fabulous Western boom towns, Cripple Creek flourished in every way, with eight newspapers—five of them daily—two grand opera houses, and a notorious "tenderloin district," with numerous brothels, saloons and casinos. It even had its own stock exchange, where gold shares were vigorously traded.

Nor did the railroads bypass Cripple Creek, despite the tortuous mountain terrain. By century's end three different lines served the city, with as many as 58 passenger trains a day. In addition, two electric interurban systems ran trolley cars between Cripple Creek and other mining towns of the District. But the march of time, plus nature, plus a changing world, took a quick and dramatic toll on the gold camp. By 1903 Cripple Creek was the focus of a long-drawn-out labor war, with the Western Federation of Miners pitted against the owners. The Colorado National Guard was called out to maintain order. Then many of the mines flooded, necessitating the costly draining of the entire District. At the outbreak of World War I, 150 mines were operating. When Armistice Day came, only 40 were still going. Cycles of boom and bust followed, including a flush period during the Great Depression. World War II, however, shut down production once again. After the war, the number of open mines could be counted on the fingers of one hand. The gold market continued to dwindle, and in 1949 the last rail line coming to Cripple Creek, the Midland Terminal, closed. Yet by then tourism was rising as the town's hope for survival; and just four years later, in 1953, the old Midland depot reopened as the Cripple Creek District Museum.

Reflecting Cripple Creek's former prosperity, the depot was a handsome three-story building divided by a stairway, with a total of 12 large rooms, including separate waiting rooms for male and female passengers—the ladies had little tolerance for cigar smoke and spitting. These rooms were now filled with an interesting but ragtag collection of many things: tools and clothes and other artifacts from the underground world of the mines; an extensive photo collection depicting Cripple Creek's history, above and below the ground; old newspaper front pages and articles, framed and mounted on the walls; everyday bric-a-brac from bygone days, ranging from toys to kitchen utensils to canned goods to books; mementos of both World Wars; stuffed animals of the region; statues, busts and other displays of famous and prominent citizens; samples of gold, gold ore and other minerals; and living quarters elaborately re-created with authentic turn-of-the-century furniture and furnishings, complete with mannequins attired in period costumes. It really was an interesting collection, as visitors confirmed again and again.

The museum charged no admission, but it was nevertheless a major component of the tourist allure of Cripple Creek, and thus an essential part of the local economy. I considered my position there to be a legitimate career move, if not a very prominent one. My salary—or "stipend," as I liked to call it—was not much, just $600 a month. But living in Cripple Creek was about as cheap as it gets. Dorothy Mackin arranged for me to live in one of the town's old shacks, for a rent of $40 a month. My only other expenses, just about, were food, heat, gas for my truck, and from time to time a piece of clothing to replace one that had worn out. And, of course, drinks at the Cottage Inn.

I took my job at the Cripple Creek District Museum quite seriously, and threw myself into it. A unique feature that I quickly established was a working assay office, in a separate building, where we determined the content and quality of the gold ore that still was abundant in the area, although not in sufficient richness to make mining an economically feasible proposition at that point. To run the assay office I hired one Michael Vann Moore, or "Old Mr. Moore," as I liked to call him. For some reason I have always been inclined to nicknames, and have bestowed them upon many of the people whose paths crossed mine. Sometimes Old Mr. Moore grumbled about his, saying that it might raise questions among the ladies, with whom he definitely had a way. In truth, Old Mr. Moore was still in his 30s back then in Cripple Creek, and he needn't have worried. With his twinkling eyes and neat salt-and-pepper beard, he was often told he resembled the country singer Kenny Rogers—which was plenty good for the local and visiting Darlas, as he called them.

Mike was a Texan, with a degree in sociology from Sul Ross State College in Alpine. About the only sociology he ever practiced, however, was during a stint as a prison guard at the main unit of the notorious Huntsville penitentiary of the Texas Corrections Department. More than anything else, Mike was a good old boy, in the mold of his father and two uncles, Buck, Bubba and Sonny. Nevertheless, Mike had grown up saying he would rather be from Montana than Texas; and in time he did move to Montana, with his then wife. From there they drifted south to Colorado, and went their separate ways. In Cripple Creek Mike lived simply and cheaply, as did we all, in the old, ramshackle structures left over from the town's heyday. Somewhere along the line he had picked up a knowledge of geology and minerals, which proved invaluable in the assay office, even if Mike did from time to time tend to get surly with the public—though never with the Kansas Darlas.

Old Mr. Moore was just one of the offbeat characters who peopled my decade in Cripple Creek. There was a never-ending stream of them.

I don't know what drew them there. Was it the town's strange name? Its faded glory? Its legend as a place where fortunes in gold could be made overnight? Its tentative but stubborn hold on life? It was, after all, a "ghost town." Was it the altitude, the scenery? Through the years the oddballs just kept coming, and I did my best to get along with as many of them as possible.

My penchant for nicknames helped. With fellows I was a little leery of, I developed the mock-formal habit of addressing them by the title "Mr.", followed by their first name—as in "Mr. Jeffrey," "Mr. James," etc. They responded in kind, calling me "Mr. Dayton." It was all friendly enough, but kept us at just about the right distance from each other. This social device proved so handy that I used it later on in other places, with other oddballs. I also kept "cash box money" on hand at the museum to bail these characters out of jail after their not-infrequent scrapes with the local law. They appreciated that, and I had very few problems with them.

The slow pace of life in Cripple Creek ultimately proved quite agreeable to me, although not at first. My first winter there was the loneliest time I had ever known. The museum opened only on weekends during the cold months, and had only a trickle of visitors. I still felt an obligation, however, to work on it every day, just as in summer. The town's few year-round residents were slow to take to newcomers, which I was still considered after only one season there. The bitter cold did nothing to raise my spirits. But I gritted it out, through one year, then two, then three. Slowly but surely I was making a few friends, becoming somewhat accepted in the local society, such as it was. But I remained aloof from it, and some of its members remained suspicious of me.

Then in the fourth year I had an inspiration that made things much better. It was a case of finally seeing the obvious: that the kindly old ladies were perfectly capable of presiding over the museum's curtailed winter hours, leaving me free to travel to other places, other climes. When I proposed this to board president Mackin, she was surprisingly amenable. After that, each winter found me on the road, often seeking out the West's most remote places. Maybe that was why I stayed in Cripple Creek 10 years. There must have been some reason.

9

A Gun Pointed at My Head

Guns played a significant, and sometimes unfortunate,
role in the Cripple Creek psyche.

At times I have walked the mean streets of some of America's "baddest" cities. I was even stabbed once. But I never had a gun pointed at me until I got to Cripple Creek.

The incident was caused by ill will toward me on the part of the town's mayor, Bill Robinson, who had decided to dislike me before I even arrived in town. As with many things in Cripple Creek, the roots of this situation traced to Dorothy Mackin, impresaria/owner of the Imperial Hotel and board president of the Cripple Creek District Museum, who had hired me to become its first professional curator. When I accepted the position, however, I had no idea of the complex and entangled social scene that had developed in this almost-abandoned mountain town of 458 year-round residents.

In Cripple Creek all roads led to Dorothy Mackin—or so she thought. Just after World War II Dorothy married Wayne Mackin, a Colorado native and distinguished veteran of the Army's famed 10th Mountain Division, which fought the war on skis in the snow. They returned to Colorado to seek an old mining town with a grand hotel suitable for Dorothy's great love, melodrama. Aspen had already been claimed by Mrs. Walter Paepcke, wife of the boss of American Can Company in Chicago. Dorothy was not going to play second fiddle to anyone, so she chose Cripple Creek, with its once-eminent hotel, the Imperial, which in 1946 then was down at the heels, like the rest of the town.

Dorothy recruited a bunch of intellectuals and wealthy patrons, whose goal was to establish a cultural scenario, with the Imperial Hotel at its center. The Cripple Creek District Museum, which opened in 1953, was part of this movement. But there was still quite a tough mining crowd hanging on in the town after the war, and they did not take to the invasion of the la-de-da outsiders, whom they saw as "a bunch of fruits" In turn, the cultural immigrants disliked the "townies" and kept pretty much to themselves at the Imperial, where the melodrama quickly became a great success. Even in this strange and tiny community, the social lines were clearly drawn.

So when Mayor Robinson, who was publisher of the local weekly newspaper, heard that Dorothy Mackin had hired a stranger to run the museum, which had always been managed by local women, he suspected the worst. He was among those who considered the hotel crowd "fruity," and he did not want that element to also take over the museum, on whose board his wife served. Things got only worse when he was given a press release to run in his paper, the Cripple Creek Gold Rush (which had the odd motto "Attempting Business in Teller County" painted on its plate-glass window). When he saw that the new director was from San Francisco and was a man, well, that did it. What sort of man would be running a museum? That was women's work, like libraries. Thus before I even got to Cripple Creek, its mayor had formed a decidedly negative impression of me.

I first met the mayor at a party given by board president Mackin to introduce me to the town's so-called leading residents. I was dressed in a wool shirt and jeans, though others of the guests were more formal. The mayor was a short, stocky, red-faced guy with glasses and a buzz cut. He looked at my six-foot-two-inch frame and said in a gravelly voice, "So you're the new museum fella? I figured he would be a pint-sized fairy in a pin-striped suit." I had the definite feeling that he had been practicing that line, perhaps in front of a mirror. I also had the feeling that he was not a very nice man. I replied stonily, "I am sorry to disappoint you, Mr. Mayor." He snorted and said, "I hope you get on okay in this town" and turned away. I wondered what he meant by that remark.

"Don't mind Bill," Dorothy Mackin said. "He likes to shoot his mouth off. He thinks he runs this town, but he doesn't." I was realizing that she thought she did. Later in the evening I heard the mayor, well into his cups, declare, "The only good Injun is a dead Injun." I was astonished, and commented loudly, "That's certainly an intelligent attitude." The mayor whirled and glared at me. "I can see that this fella and I are going to get along real good," he said with finality. The party broke up shortly afterward.

Dorothy was fond of saying of the local "rednecks"—and I quote— "There is nothing wrong with this town that a few funerals wouldn't fix." She wanted *her* crowd to take over. I was hired to be another jewel in her tiara. She went around referring to me as a "Yale man," which made me uncomfortable. So did a remark from the local doctor: "You'll like this town—no Jews or niggers." I wondered what I had stepped into. To make things worse, the small, rundown shack that Dorothy had arranged for me to rent was owned by the Imperial's piano player, one of the fruitiest of the "fruits," and in local eyes I was tarred by that same brush. I realized that to survive I was going to have to get along with the townies. I had to separate myself from the crowd at the hotel. But how?

That summer in my free time, which wasn't much, I hung out with an attractive, outgoing young woman named Lori Nelson, from Pittsburgh. She had been in Cripple Creek for more than a year, knew everybody and was well liked. She said she was putting in good words for me around town. "Even to the mayor?" I asked. "Sure," she said. "He likes me." But then Lori went back to Pennsylvania to study law. I had only a couple of other friends in town, so I foresaw a long, lonely winter. The Cottage Inn became a home away from home. But I had to watch what I said in there, and never felt comfortable.

One bitterly cold January night, when the heater in my shack was not keeping up, I wandered down to the Cottage Inn about 10 o'clock. Though it was a Friday, just the regulars were there, and only a few of them. They looked up as I entered; but seeing who it was they went back to their drinks, morosely. At the back of the room sat the mayor, red-faced and wreathed in cigar smoke, at a table with his cronies. Many empty glasses and bottles were on the table. I felt the mayor's hostile gaze as I walked to the bar.

The bartender, Howard, slid a Coors to me. Howard had brought his wife and children to Cripple Creek from Dallas, to live in "a man's town where the kids won't be raised by a bunch of queers." His wife, however, saw quickly that a great mistake had been made, and took herself and the children back to Dallas, leaving Howard behind. He was in a downward spiral, the usual kind to be found in Cripple Creek, and was bartending part-time to survive—which he did not do for long. One night, roaring drunk, he heaved a cinder block through the plate-glass window of one of the stores on Bennett Avenue. No one, not even he, knew why. He was arrested, jailed and fined, and left town shortly afterward, in the middle of the night, leaving debts. A Cripple Creek syndrome.

Howard was a friendly enough fellow, however, and on this night we were chatting about nothing when I heard a loud shout behind me. "Hey, Mr. Museum, get yore ass over here! I have something to say to yah!" Howard rolled his eyes. I finished my beer and walked over to the mayor's table. "Yes, Mr. Mayor?" He looked up at me and bellowed, "What's this bullshit about charging admission to the goddamned museum? It's always been free. Goddamn admission's gonna keep people away. You trying to hurt this town?"

Going over the museum's books that summer, I had seen that the place was not on solid financial footing. I felt that a small admission, 50 cents, would provide enough extra income to ensure my small salary and allow for some improvements—which was why I was there. "Half a dollar is not going to keep anyone away, Mr. Mayor," I said, adding that the museum board members, including his wife, had unanimously approved. I also reminded him that he was not on the board, and that as an independent institution the museum could do as it pleased. That really got to him.

He glowered, then asked, "What's the day today, boy?" Boy? Things were not going well. I wondered why he needed to be reminded of the date. I told him, "Today is the 23rd of January, Mr. Mayor." I knew he did not like my repeated use of "Mr. Mayor." He realized I was mocking him. "You're goddamn right it's the 23rd of January, and the next 23rd of January you ain't gonna be in this town, 'cause I'm gonna run yore ass outta here!" Everybody in the bar was staring.

"No one is going to run my ass out of this town, Mr. Mayor," I replied. "I have a job to do, and when I leave Cripple Creek it will be on a date of my choosing." There was silence. Then the mayor exploded. "You smart-ass son of a bitch!" he roared, lurching up drunkenly and taking a swing at me. Luckily the table was between us, and he missed. Glasses and bottles went flying, that classic barroom-fight sound. The mayor's cronies restrained him. I heard Howard yelling for me to get back to the bar. I walked over and he slid another Coors my way. "On the house," he said. "Don't let Robinson get to you. He's just drunk and ornery, mad at the world." I drank a few more beers and mulled over the incident until closing time. I stepped out into the bitter-cold night—and was confronted by a man with a gun, which he pointed directly at my forehead.

I recognized the man as Frank, a Texan who attempted to sell real estate at the so-called Country Club Estates west of town. He and that enterprise were rumored to be fraudulent, selling the same lots over and over again to out-of-town buyers. "What the hell is this, Frank?" was all I could think to say. "It's a .38 and it's loaded," he said. "Don't fuck with the mayor. He's a friend of mine."

So Frank had been in the bar, had overheard the incident, and decided to stage a little tableau to impress the mayor and his pals. Big man! I was not particularly scared. I knew he did not intend to shoot me. He was just showing off. Nor did I believe that the mayor was his friend. Very few people thought much of Frank. But he did have my attention. Then I saw the sheriff's car coming up Bennett Avenue to check on the bar at closing time, as he did each night. "Here comes Sheriff Carlson," I said. "Best put that toy away before he catches you with it." Frank glared at me, gave my forehead a nudge with the pistol, then walked to his truck, opened the door and threw the gun on the seat. A few of the bar patrons had come out, but I had no idea how much, if anything, they had seen of this incident. Frank leaned against his truck, scowling at me. I shook my head in disgust, went to my truck and drove home. I did not sleep well that night.

The next day the sheriff drove up to the museum. I walked to his car to see what he wanted. "Hear there was a little episode outside the bar last night," he drawled. I replied that it was nothing much. "Oh, I heard all about it," he went on. "I know that boy from Texas, he don't belong in this town. I'll be keeping an eye on him." "Might not be a bad idea," I replied. "Be careful, Dayton," he advised me, then drove off. I got along with Sheriff Gus Carlson. He was a good man, of the old school. He was a friend of Lori Nelson. I guess she had put in a good word for me.

I had no more problems with the mayor. I heard he felt he had made a fool of himself, all over 50 cents. Well, he had. I pretty much kept out of his way, and it seemed he was keeping out of mine. When he ran for re-election, I even voted for him, with the notion that civic ineptitude was perhaps a good preservation agent. When he won his race, I sent a congratulatory note and a box of his favorite Dutch Masters cigars. A few days later he came up to me in the bar, all smiles and puffing on a cigar, clapped me on the back and bought me a beer. "Dalton," he said in his gravelly voice—people in Cripple Creek had trouble getting my name right—"we may not think alike, but we can drink alike, eh?" I had the feeling he had been rehearsing that one, too. "Sure," I said. "You got that right, Mr. Mayor." He clapped me on the back again. "I've heard good things about the museum," he said, "'specially that assay office you all has started." Assaying, it seemed, was man's work in his eyes. So the mayor and I, if not friends, had reached a "rapprochement"—a word I would not want to be caught using in Cripple Creek.

The situation with Frank remained tense. Though married, he was always in the bar, drinking heavily in the winter, hitting on tourist women in the summer. He was not well liked. "That poor son of a bitch," said my friend Justis James from Victor, summing up Frank, "couldn't find his dick if he had a string tied to it." Whenever I went to the Cottage Inn—which I did far more often than was good for me, but there was not much else to do in Cripple Creek—Frank glared at me. He never stopped. I figured it was probably going to lead to another incident, and it did.

One night I was shooting pool with Sheila, a young woman from New York I had hired to run the museum's art gallery. Frank kept bothering her, saying things she did not like, asking her to go for a ride with him. I told him to knock it off. He reacted by shoving me. There was a scuffle and some shouting. Suddenly standing one on each side of me were Al Delaney, a hard-drinking, tough former miner, and Ed Rudd, a strapping Okie neighbor I had only nodded at. These fellows were often in the bar but never had much to say to me. Now they seemed to be taking my side. Delaney said, "Frank, don't be messing with Dalson—he's one of us. This ain't Texas." I could hardly believe my ears. Frank backed off and left the bar. Sheila and I went to sit with Delaney and Rudd, and, as I like to say, "we spent the evening drinking with a circle of new friends."

The friendships grew. When my mother came for a visit, about 1974, I took her to the Cottage Inn for the Saturday night dance. Gene and Shorty on drums and accordion. She was intrigued, all the more so when Al Delaney asked her to dance, which she did. Then he asked her again, and again. He told her he thought she was my sister. My mother knew how to handle Delaney, he of the Irish "divilishness," the John Wayne good looks and the whiskey charm. I told him later that she thought he was the most attractive man in Cripple Creek. He liked that a lot. Ed Rudd and I also talked quite a bit in our back yards, which adjoined. We spoke of guns and trucks, the Denver Broncos. Once he asked me what I thought of the women in Cripple Creek. "Well, Ed," I said, "it's sort of like rooting through a second-hand bin." He laughed loudly. "You sure got that right!" I was on my way to being a regular guy.

Frank bought himself a big, used Harley-Davidson Hawg motor-cycle, which in summer he parked outside the Cottage Inn, where it would be right there to impress some Kansas Darla. He was all puffed up in this role, and did not notice that the locals were snickering at him. He was too focused on the Texas and Midwestern gals who had come to Cripple Creek because they had heard that the men there were "built like drill steel." We all did our best to keep that rumor alive.

One summer evening Terry Jones and John Jaccard, two fellows I had hired for casual jobs at the museum, came to the assay office to cook up some steaks on a "miners' barbecue grill" we had rigged up. All of a sudden Frank came roaring up Bennett Avenue on his Hawg and shot around the corner up toward Tenderfoot Pass. Hanging on for dear life behind him was some Darla. "That son of a bitch is going pretty darn fast!" exclaimed John. Terry added, "Frank's been in the bar all afternoon. I bet he's loaded. Not good." We went back to our steaks. About 10 minutes later the ambulance came screaming up the avenue and out of town, followed by two sheriff's cars. Not good.

We finished our steaks with curiosity about what had happened. Something bad. That much we knew. Terry went down to the bar to find out. I had to clean the museum, and John had to do the same at the assay office. An hour later Terry came back, looking somber. "Frank hit the guardrail on Tenderfoot with that bike. The girl sailed about 50 feet, busted up, but will be okay, they say. But Frank tore his leg off. He bought the farm."

Long after I had left Cripple Creek I heard that Mayor Robinson, then ex-mayor, was in ill health and had to move to the lower altitude of Canõn City on the Arkansas River. He did like to come up, however, from time to time to visit the small mining town where he had been chief executive for so many years. The advent of gambling in Cripple Creek, which came in 1991 after a voters' referendum approving it, confused him, I was told. With more than a dozen casinos on all sides, he seemed to not realize he was in Cripple Creek. On one of my visits up there, not too long ago, I ran into him and his wife on Bennett Avenue. She greeted me warmly. "Howdy, Mr. Mayor," I said, but the shuffling ex-mayor did not seem to recognize me, did not seem to know who I was.

10

Mr. Jeffrey's Secret

My primitive shack in Cripple Creek, where Mr. Jeffrey
sought refuge one cold and snowy night.

On a cold October night, with new snow on the ground, my
friend Ted Roberts and I pulled up to my shack in Cripple
Creek. Winter comes early to the high country. Ted was visiting from sunny California, and Cripple Creek both amused
and distressed him. He could never understand what I was doing there.
We had been down in Colorado Springs, and got home about midnight,
in cold fog and light snow. I turned off the truck and sat for a moment

looking at the bright window of my house, which in that small mountain town I never locked. "I don't remember leaving the lights on," I said. Then we heard music. "And I'm *damned sure* I did not leave the radio on!"

Ted and I exchanged glances, realizing that someone was in the shack. We weren't worried, only puzzled. I flung the door open—and there on the faded couch was Mr. Jeffrey, drinking one of my beers. Several empty cans sat in front of him. His face was battered and swollen. He looked at us drunkenly. "Ah was in a fight, Mr. Dayton," he said, lurching to his feet. "Down at the bar. Ah was in a fight. But I won, I shorely did." That struck me as doubtful. I had seen him in numerous scuffles in the bar, and never once had he prevailed over those rednecks.

Mr. Jeffrey was a country boy from the Florida Panhandle, a real hayseed, but not a tough one. Ted and I got beers from the fridge and sat down to hear tonight's tale. But Mr. Jeffrey was mumbling drunkenly, not making sense. Why he had wandered up to my place instead of to his room above the Home Café I did not know. I just wanted him out and on his way. Ted volunteered to walk him back downtown. They left in the cold fog. I was relieved to be rid of Mr. Jeffrey. I did not think there was any danger in the man, but the idea of him getting too comfortable in my house gave me a creepy feeling. I wanted to maintain a certain distance from Mr. Jeffrey. That's why I never asked him what his last name was. I really did not even want to know.

Ted returned with a tale of woe. He said it had been an ordeal. Mr. Jeffrey kept slipping on the ice and falling down. Again and again Ted had to get him back up on his feet, only to have him stagger off in the fog, rambling incoherently, about being threatened with "dayaith." Mr. Jeffrey was intent on returning to the bar, and insisted that Ted accompany him. There they had a couple of drinks, the redneck boys staring—wondering who Mr. Jeffrey's hulking "friend" was, but not wanting to find out. Finally Ted got Mr. Jeffrey to his room, or the stairs to it, and came back. "What an experience!" he said. "How do people get so totally fucked up in Cripple Creek?" I replied that they were fucked up before they got here—Mr. Jeffrey certainly was—"but this place doesn't help." Ted just shook his head. 'No," he said, "it sure doesn't!"

Mr. Jeffrey had shown up one summer day, a young Florida cracker who made his way to our small mountain town for a fresh start. There were many who looked to Cripple Creek as a place of new beginnings, mostly to find out that it was a place of bad endings. It was the image of the West, I suppose, that drew people like Mr. Jeffrey, a tradition of men with no last names. Men with dreams, of being or doing anything they wanted. But dreams have a way of not coming true, and whatever visions poor Mr. Jeffrey had for himself certainly never came close to materializing.

He invested some money in a small novelty shop in a warren of stores in a downtown building called The Mall. His shop sold tricks, puzzles and childish "joke kits," along with silver dollars and old Life magazines, stuff like that. Preferring the bar, he didn't spend much time in his shop; but when he was there he never sold much—or any-thing. "Ah made 50 cents today, Mr. Dayton," he once told me. It was pathetic. But he seemed to have enough money to rent a room and endlessly buy drinks. In spite of the time he passed in the bar, Mr. Jef-frey was not accepted by the locals. There was something about him they did not take to. His sly country-boy manner, the little derby hat he wore, or just his general appearance. The Confederate flag on his white Ford van didn't help. The local fellows beat him at pool and took his money, mocked him behind his back and sometimes to his face, and punched him out more than a few times. The women mostly ignored his advances, or mocked him in the cruel way that women do when they have the upper hand.

Despite his various setbacks, Mr. Jeffrey insisted to Mr. Moore and me, in one of our few conversations with him, "Ah'm a man—I'll make it out here!" But there was something in his past that cast a dark shadow. Trouble in the past—yes, there was trouble in his past. Some-thing back in Florida that had caused him to leave home and family, who now evidently supplied meager funds to keep him gone. Once Mr. Jeffrey's father came to visit. A Southerner but not a dirt farmer, he had a pained look, as though he knew that things were not going well for his son and would come to no good end. Apparently seeing me as someone in a position of authority, the father asked, "How's Jeffrey been gittin' on?" the way he might ask the police chief or the sheriff. I mumbled something noncommittal. It was sad. He seemed like a nice man, worried about his boy.

One day when Mr. Jeffrey and I were shooting pool he mentioned that something "terrible" had happened back in Florida. It seemed he was anxious to unburden himself of this tale, but it did not happen. Instead he started joking about memories of summer Bible Camp, and the "laying on of hands"—that is, feeling up young girls behind the cabins in the Southern piney woods. How much he knew about such things I could only imagine. I saw Mr. Jeffrey make a fool of himself many times. Yet I always talked to him in the bar, as did Mike Moore. We were about the only ones who gave him the time of day. I think he sort of looked up to me, an older guy with a position in the community and respect among the people who put him down. To me he was just another flawed human being, with a story behind the simpleton role he played. I accepted him for what he was.

Then one night the story came out. Mr. Moore was trying to charm two tourist women at the bar, and was not paying attention as Mr. Jeffrey, half-drunk as usual, began to talk of the Florida Panhandle. "Oh, it was awful, Mr. Dayton, it was something truly terrible," he moaned. "Yes, Ah had been drinkin'. Ah'd had a few, an' Ah was drivin' my hotrod, openin' her up on one o' them long straight, empty roads through the sawgrass that we have in the Panhandle. An' this colored family pulled out, from behind a canebrake, right in front of me. Ah barely saw them, didn't have no time to even hit the brake. Smashed them broadside. Oh, Lordy, it was awful. A bunch of 'em died, they was a family. Ah was busted up, in the hospital. They charged me with manslaughter and DWI. It wasn't my fault, Mr. Dayton, they pulled right in front of me." He collapsed onto the bar.

I gathered that he had spent time in jail, and then his family had given him a stake to get a fresh start somewhere out West. But his fresh start in Cripple Creek was just another dead end. As Mr. Jeffrey slowly pulled himself back together, Mr. Moore joined us with his tourist women, and ordered shots of tequila all around. "This is fun,"

Mike laughed, unconvincingly. He was not much of a drinking man. The women were briefly amused with these manly rituals, but then gave up on us as just a bunch of drunks in a nowhere, forgotten old mining town in the mountains—which was, at that moment, true. They drifted away, leaving their shot glasses untouched. So Mr. Moore and I polished them off, too. Even so, we never gained on Mr. Jeffrey's head start.

By closing time he was mightily drunk. In fact, he fell off his stool onto the floor and just lay there. Mr. Moore and I ignored him. Then Sheriff Carlson, who liked to check things out at night's end, entered and saw Mr. Jeffrey on the floor. "What's that man doing there?" he asked. Someone answered, "Jest dronk, Sheriff, that's all." With disgust Gus looked at the inert form. "That boy ain't nothin' but a drunk," he said. "Some of you fellas haul him out to the patrol car. I'm gonna let him sleep it off in the jail. Feed him coffee in the morning an' suggest he don't belong in this town." A couple of rednecks hauled Mr. Jeffrey like a sack of potatoes out to the patrol car and heaved him in. Off he went. The country boys all laughed, the women snickered. The sheriff was a pretty good guy, but did not tolerate men who could not hold their liquor.

Shortly after that incident Mr. Jeffrey closed his joke shop and left town, without saying goodbye to anyone. We heard that he had taken a room in Colorado Springs, and once or twice that winter I ran into him in the Royal Tavern in Manitou Springs, where the cog railway up Pike's Peak is based. He still had his white van with its Confederate flag, and still was getting, I presumed, his stipend from the family. He said he was "maintaining." Soon I lost all track of Mr. Jeffrey.

Years later, when I was living in Santa Rosa, California, one day a letter from Mr. Jeffrey arrived out of the blue. He must have gotten my address from somebody in Cripple Creek. He was writing from Florida, from a box number in some town. It had the ring of some kind of institution. He said he was "doing well," and was ready to come out West again and "start over." Where did I recommend? No place, really, but I wrote back suggesting towns like Prescott, Arizona, or even smaller ones—Bisbee, Arizona, or Taos, New Mexico, places where strangers could fit in if they kept clean. "Don't go to California!" I emphasized.

There would be nothing but everlasting trouble for him in the complicated and dangerous Golden State, where the machinery works around the clock grinding up the likes of Mr. Jeffrey. I never heard from, or of, him again.

But I did gain one more piece of information from Mr. Jeffrey's letter: his last name. It was Dinkins—he wrote it in the return address. Probably had to. Just out of habit these days,when I am in a motel room I pull out the telephone directory and look up Dinkins. Each time I do, I think of Bible Camp, and the "laying on of hands." Once, in Palestine, Texas, I found a listing for a Jeffrey Dinkins. Another Jeffrey Dinkins, I assumed, without bothering to pick up the phone to test my theory. It's probably a sort of Southern name. I imagine the state of Florida has a record of it.

11

Jimmy and Archie and Rosie, and Paul America

I ask you not to judge me, as we have just met on the streets of Cripple Creek.

When I arrived in Cripple Creek, quite a few characters were still around from the 1920s and '30s—"the old days," as anything before World War II was considered. I even met one man who was there before 1900. Most of these guys were pretty forgettable, aged and worn-out relics from days gone by. Among them was the short and wrinkled Little Jimmy Sterrett. I never would have guessed that he had ever been anything but a genial hanger-on in bars and pool halls, the places where I saw him. So the story of his former career came as quite a surprise.

Little Jimmy had been in the area all his life. In his late 70s, he was locally famed as the oldest man alive born in Cripple Creek. With his pleasant wife Gracie he could often be found in the Cottage Inn, drinking beer and playing pool. Fuzzily. One time I introduced my friend Dr. Avis to him, saying that the Doctor, who was teaching at the state university in Laramie, was from Wyoming. That sparked a memory in Jimmy, of being mustered out of the Army after World War I in Themopolis, Wyoming. Somehow he got the impression that he and the Doctor had mustered out together, and for a time afterward Jimmy was telling everybody that his old Army buddy had come to visit him. Old Jimmy was just a fixture, and I never paid him no special mind, as they say.

In time Little Jimmy died. Not until then did I learn that after his Army days, he had worked for Bert Bergstrom, the "Big Swede." Bergstrom—who was still alive, in his 80s, and living nearby in Woodland Park—had the reputation of running all the rackets in the District in the '20s and '30s: gambling, slot machines, liquor, all of it. The Big Swede had been a real tough guy. He would have had to be tough to wield such power in the mining camps of that time. So if Jimmy Sterrett had worked for Bergstrom, well, he too must have been a pretty tough little guy to earn his pay.

And apparently he was, judging from the story that Mr. Moore passed along to me from some of the old-timers in Victor. On a cold winter evening in the mid-1930s, after Prohibition had been repealed and the saloons in Cripple Creek had been reopened, Jimmy Sterrett came into one of them just before dark. He stepped up to the bar and had a shot of whiskey. It was a Friday night, and the place was full of miners. Jimmy turned and said, "Boys, step outside for a moment, won't ya? There's something out there ya oughta see." He strode out the door, and, their curiosity piqued, the miners filed out behind him. Standing at the driver's door of a pickup truck, Jimmy pointed to the bed. The men looked, and there in the fading light they saw a man all trussed up with barbed wire. He looked cold and about dead—perhaps was, some later thought.

The man was not anyone they knew, a stranger, so they just stood and stared. In a voice loud for a little man, Jimmy announced: "Take a good look, boys, 'cause you ain't gonna see this fellow again. He stole from the Swede!" Then Jimmy got in the truck and drove off. Silently the men returned to the bar and their drinks, some shaking their heads. The man, whoever he was, was definitely "not going to be seen again." That much they DID know! That could mean a number of things, but in those days—and even up until recently—it often meant that someone went down a deep, abandoned mineshaft, and indeed was never seen again. Or maybe the man was taken down Ute Pass and left somewhere, and told to never show his face in the District again. Nobody knew, and nobody was going to be asking. A message had been delivered by Little Jimmy Sterrett!

Perhaps until now, only three of us alive today could have told the story of Archie Smith and Rosie Ashby, which took place in Victor in the first decade of the 20th century. That would be me, Old Mr. Moore and John Jaccard. We learned about it by reading more than 20 years ago an old Teller County Court criminal transcript, some 120 pages long, which was stored at the Cripple Creek District Museum during my time there. This transcript is now buried among the papers later given by the museum to the Penrose Library in Colorado Springs, where probably no one else will ever run across it again. No verdict was attached to the transcript, so Mr. Moore went up to the courthouse in search of the outcome. He was successful—but we'll save that for later.

The principals in the case are no doubt dead, although Rosie, who was 12 at the time of the trial, could have lived until recently. And there still could be some relatives who are aware of the story, though I imagine it was not much talked about, as it was an unsavory episode, the sort of thing that gets erased from a family's thoughts. Yet the episode did happen.

The story, which is now beginning to fade even in my own memory, goes something like this: Archie Smith was an itinerant cowboy from western Colorado, in his late 20s. He had inherited a small ranch near Grand Junction, a property that had some promise but nothing that a man in his position could make a living from. So, like many young, single men at that time, he fetched up in the mining town of Victor, where his sister, brother-in-law and their 12-year-old daughter Rosie lived. He found work in the mines and boarded with his relatives, a not-uncommon arrangement. And while living in that house he helped his niece with her homework, or so he said. Apparently, as the court transcript indicates, and as Archie was so charged, he "helped" the young girl well beyond the parameters of simple schoolwork. Rosie's parents charged Archie with statutory rape, then as now a criminal offense carrying a penitentiary term upon conviction. As a result of these charges a trial was held, which attracted considerable attention in the community.

Each day the courtroom was crowded. The lawyers pontificated in ungrammatical language and loosely construed legal terminology, and the judge frequently pounded his gavel to suppress snickers and outright laughter from the public. How seriously the matter was taken is difficult to determine from the transcript, but certainly the charge was serious. Archie must have experienced considerable unease with the possibility of prison hanging over him, quite enough to unsettle the mind of a rambling country boy.

As the trial progressed, certain things emerged. Rosie was presented as a temptress, "a little vixen," rather than a sweet and innocent schoolgirl. This portrait was developed by the defense attorney, who also projected, with equal effectiveness, the impression that Archie was not too smart and had been "taken advantage of." There was no specific testimony about sexual activity. It was only alluded to, in keeping with the sensibilities of those times. Also, the sister and brother-in-law came across as mean-spirited, manipulative and grasping people, with little affection for Archie.

The ranch he had inherited seemed to be of great interest to them, and they seemed to be trying to get it. There were intimations that Archie had been offered a deal: If he would sign over the ranch, the charge would be dropped, the matter forgotten. But Archie considered the ranch his future ace in the hole, and would not give it up, in spite of the predicament he was in. We may speculate that Archie felt fairly confident of beating the charge, or that even if convicted he wanted to hold on to that ranch for his future livelihood, after he served his time.

Anyway, the trial lasted several days, much to the amusement and entertainment of the spectators, and perhaps also the jury, which in those days would have been all-male—and, in Victor, comprised of hard-bitten miners and similar types. As I said, the transcript ran 120 pages, and made for good reading, not only for the salacious nature of the case, the colorful language of the judge and attorneys (whose command of the law seemed limited), but also for insight into the life and times of early-20th-century Victor. For a more accurate rendering of the tale I am telling here, I tried to locate the transcript once again, after it was shipped to Colorado Springs. But it had vanished into the mass of papers I mentioned earlier, and my efforts failed.

I do remember that the trial ended vaguely, in what we today would call "reasonable doubt." All three of us who read the transcript got the feeling that "something" had been going on between Archie and his schoolgirl niece, between the susceptible, not-too-bright young bachelor and the little temptress—but exactly what it was remained unclear. My guess was that those old guys on the jury were not about to send Archie down to the pen in Cañon City for a transgression such as this. But as I have said, no verdict was attached. So Mike went to the courthouse to look for it. He returned with a grin, saying, "Not guilty, boys, not guilty"—perhaps echoing what had been announced loudly in the saloons of Victor long ago.

What happened to Archie, Rosie and the family, we don't know. They disappeared into history. There must have been a lot of bitterness, and perhaps Archie left town. In my mind's eye I see a simple frame house, see Rosie now, sitting by the fire playing with her cat, her schoolbooks open on the floor, her dress slightly unbuttoned, and Archie staring at her with a strange, longing expression. In that house in Victor, Colorado, in the early years of a raw, new century.

And now you, too, know the story—as much of it as ever will be known.

◇◇◇

Late one summer morning in 1976, as I was running museum's assay office, a strange character wandered in. Not at all the usual tourist, he was a man in his early 30s, disheveled and disoriented-looking, in a long dark overcoat. In the palms of both hands he was holding a very ordinary-looking rock, a type of fieldstone. He mumbled that he had brought the rock to Cripple Creek from New York City and wanted it assayed, because "it has gold in it."

I examined it and determined immediately that it was certainly not a rock that would contain gold. I told him thusly, saying that an assay would be a waste of time. He seemed perplexed, and insisted he was sure it was "gold-bearing." I explained my conclusion several times, growing more authoritative with each one. Finally he wandered out, carrying his rock. I turned to other people and other matters. Walking home for lunch, I saw him sitting on the bench in front of the Colorado Trading & Transfer Company building next-door, which the museum operated as an art gallery run by Sheila, an energetic young woman from New York. He was holding his head in his hands. The rock was on the bench beside him. "Some kind of a nut," I thought, and walked on. When I returned, he was no longer there.

Later Sheila came into the assay office, saying she had noticed the fellow sitting there dejectedly, had talked to him, had felt pity, and had taken him to her home for a sandwich. And there she learned that this man was Paul America, one of pop artist Andy Warhol's "Superstars." Paul America had been, in fact, one of the more prominent ones. He had starred in Warhol's 1965 film "My Hustler," in which he pretty much played himself—that is, a young, attractive and none-too-bright sexual hustler, selling his favors to both men and women. He was still proud of that film, which received critical praise and was one of the first Warhol movies to make money. Sheila figured, rightly I think, that things for Paul America had been pretty much downhill from there. His 15 minutes of fame had come and gone more than a decade ago.

Somewhere—he was not clear just where—he had acquired his rock, and had been carrying it around the streets of Greenwich Village in Manhattan, talking about its "gold-bearing properties." One of the people he talked to was—amazingly enough—Sheila's ex-husband, Kieran, an habitué of the Village. Kieran, who had visited Cripple Creek the previous year, told Paul America that his former wife worked for a museum in a small Colorado mountain town with an assay office that actually tested for gold. And so, Paul America had hitchhiked, in that disheveled condition, from New York to Cripple Creek to have his rock tested. My analysis had been a terrible disappointment for him.

Sheila was astonished by his tale, and had given him some food and a small amount of money. She said he was now going to hitchhike back to New York. I looked out the assay office window and saw him up the road, just standing there, on the way out of town. I thought that none of the tourists would give such a disreputable-looking character a ride, but an hour or so later he was gone. He left the rock on the bench, accepting, I guess, that it was indeed without gold. What happened to it I don't know. It probably was just hurled into the piles of rock all around.

Not long afterward, I heard that Paul America had committed suicide in New York, destroyed by the excesses of the Warhol circle. I hoped the disappointment of the ill-advised journey to Cripple Creek did not contribute to his demise. For years I forgot about him. But on an evening not long ago, I was reading a book on the life of Frank O'Hara, a New York poet, and on one page the name Paul America jumped out. I paused and remembered. How I wished that in the summer of 1976 I had thought to go out to that bench and retrieve that rock, to display in the museum as a memento of the day when Paul America came to Cripple Creek.

12

The Pine Ridge Reservation

Approaching Pine Ridge, the country was barren and grim.

The winter had been long and cold. Snow was still falling in May. Mr. Moore was getting restless, and I was too. There's a song about "Springtime in the Rockies," but spring was late getting to Cripple Creek's 9,500-foot altitude. So when Mike suggested a trip to South Dakota, I was receptive. All I had seen of that state was Rapid City and the Black Hills. This time we figured to add the Pine Ridge Indian Reservation, the famous Wall Drug Store and the

Badlands, where Mike wanted to hunt fossilized dinosaur bones.

We set out one Friday morning in Mike's old Chevy, under lowering clouds and the remnants of a spring snowstorm. Dropping down from the mountains, we took state highways across the high plains of eastern Colorado. No other cars were on the road—except for a highway patrolman who flashed Mike down for speeding. He had been going 80, but the trooper let him off with a lecture and a warning. Heading north along the Kansas border, we crossed into Nebraska—miles and miles of empty prairie under a cold gray sky. Western Nebraska is one of the least-populated parts of America, with very few towns and only occasional dirt roads leading off to isolated ranches. We passed through grasslands, the Sand Hills, then the Nebraska National Forest, an attractive belt of pines. We saw eagles, antelope, buffalo and, of course, cattle. Good, clean, honest country.

On an endless two-lane blacktop road, we pushed northward. When we stopped for gas, a second negative incident took place. The large glass jar of Mr. Moore's excellent strip-steak chile rolled out of the car and smashed on the pavement. A total loss. We had been counting on that chile to sustain us for a good portion of this short trip. We had other victuals packed, but nothing to compare with Mike's homemade Texas chile.

At the South Dakota line we entered the Pine Ridge Reservation, so called because of, well, ridges and pines. The land was harsh and lonely, but it struck me as appealing. The spring grass was green and thick, nourished by recent moisture. Mike had been to Pine Ridge several times, and warned me against walking around when the ground was wet from rain or melting snow. The soil was a heavy clay or gumbo called caliche, which would build up on your boots to the point where you could hardly walk. He had experienced this while fossil hunting, and did not remember caliche fondly.

The settlements we saw were grim and depressing, just hovels with junk lying about. There were lots of worn basketball hoops with no nets. Basketball is big on the Rez. Mike told me that many of the Sioux Indians living there had sold their allotments to white ranchers, for very little money. Now they felt cheated, and were bitter. We kept passing signs that said, "No driving on rims." I did not know what that meant, but Mike explained that many Indians had cars with worn tires that blew out and went flat. With no spare they just kept driving on the rims, which chewed up the roads. He added that there were lots of accidents, often rollovers, caused by drinking.

As though he had predicted it, we soon came upon just such an accident. A pickup truck was lying on its side by the road, with six people standing around looking dazed but not hurt. A case of beer and some empty cans were on the ground. We pulled up. A young Indian man holding a beer ran up to the car's passenger window. I rolled it down. "Everyone okay?" I asked. "Yeah, yeah," he said, "help's on the way. Hey, can you guys give me a ride to Interior?" That was a town just north of the Rez, maybe 50 miles away and more or less on our route. I looked at Mike. He nodded okay. I unlocked the back door and the Indian climbed in, with his beer.

"Man, this caliche makes my feet heavy," he said, scraping his boots on the door frame. At first I thought he was talking about some kind of dope, then remembered the wet clay. He mumbled something about the wreck being minor, old Spotted Elk kind of drifted off the road. Probably reaching for a beer, I imagined. The man must have noted our Colorado license plate, for he said, "I been down to Colorado lotsa times, to Boulder, teach the university students the Lakota language. My name's Tim Running Antelope." Under his breath, I heard Mike say, "I'll bet."

When we got to Interior Mr. Running Antelope directed us to the bar, a large cinder-block building. "Come on," he said. "I buy you guys a drink." Mr. Moore and I exchanged glances. He smiled, knowing who would be buying the drinks. But what the hell. We followed Mr. Running Antelope inside. For sociological research. We were richly rewarded. Our new friend called for beers, and when they were brought he made no move to pay. We were being watched by the bar's other patrons, all Indians, who obviously knew Mr. Running Antelope. We surmised that the custom was for the white man to pay. Mr. Moore did the honors, and when he did, we were introduced all around. Mike was enjoying this. As with women, he has a way with Indians. I think it is his gentle, nonthreatening manner. He also knows a lot of Indian lore, which helps, too.

I looked around the establishment, which was indeed interesting. We were seated at a narrow bar, and in the back was a large room, probably for dancing. It was crowded with Indians, many drinking out of paper cups. That was odd. Mr. Running Antelope had told us we were going to "Doris and Bob's," but I did not expect that there really were any such personages. I was wrong. There they were, right in front of me. Doris was a perky, blue-eyed blonde, a cowgirl type. She was directing an Indian who was sliding many cases of beer out the drive-up window to customers in pickup trucks and rusting cars. Well, it *was* Friday night, but I doubted that Friday was different than other days on the Rez. Bob was an unsmiling, wiry guy in his 30s, with cold gray eyes (Mr. Moore said later, "prison eyes"). He seemed to be in charge of everything. His cold gray eyes roamed around, especially watching the bartender, a huge Indian about six-feet-six, with very long jet-black hair. He looked like he could handle trouble, which I figured they had plenty of. Within easy reach behind the bar were various instruments to subdue unruly patrons: a leather sap, a pool cue handle, a baseball bat. Along the top of the back bar were quite a few items I took to be pawned: saddles, boots, beaded leather gloves, radios. "Doris and Bob's," Interior, South Dakota.

Mr. Moore bought a second round of drinks, for us and Mr. Running Antelope and for several "cousins." I said we should get going, darkness was falling. Mr. Running Antelope urged us to stay. "Hey, you guys should stick around," he said. "This place really heats up later. There's music, girls, rumbles ..." Rumbles? I had not heard that word in years. Yeah, right. A good rumble was just the thing that Mike and I needed to get caught up in. Two white men in a bar with 200 drunken Indians. That would be a real good dose of "reality." I wondered if that was what the South Dakota tourist bureau emphasized: "Get in touch with the Real Native America at Doris and Bob's Bar in Interior, South Dakota. Music! Girls! Rumbles!" I doubted it.

We told Mr. Running Antelope that we had to go, and over his protestations headed for the door. Just then three Indian girls, perhaps about 20 years old, came bursting in. They were rather pretty, in a tough sort of way, with tight jeans tucked into high cowboy boots. They were in good spirits. They smiled at us, and one of them winked at Mr. Moore. He paused, but we were on our way out—and probably a good thing, too. Girls! That was what usually led to rumbles, wasn't it?

Darkness was settling in, and a cold wind had sprung up. Interior had just a few buildings and no streetlights. It had the feel of a ghost town, far away from anywhere else. I began to feel the sense of desperation engendered by the Rez. But unlike the people living there, we quickly left it behind, heading up the road to Wall, just an hour or so distant. Within a couple of miles we came upon a bar/restaurant that Mr. Moore correctly identified as a "white man's establishment." "I've spent enough time in Indian country that I kin just tell," he said. We had a good dinner, and afterward decided to drive back by Doris and Bob's to see what was happening there. Pickup trucks and old, beat-up cars were parked willy-nilly all around the place, at strange angles as if the drivers just coasted to a halt and jumped out. The bar was packed and overflowing, with groups of Indians standing outside, around cases of beer in pickup truck beds—a cheaper way to drink, no doubt, than being served inside. Some of the Indians had already passed out, and were lying face-down in the mud, a situation that seemed to be of no concern to the others. Sounds of music wafted into the night. The scene was pretty much what we expected, and we wisely did not venture inside. We had no need for either girls or rumbles, and we decided to pass on the music. We drove on to Wall to take a motel.

The next day we toured the famed Wall Drug Store, a big, sprawling establishment that I did not find interesting. It has been in business since before the Great Depression, during which time it made a name for itself by giving free ice water to parched motorists. I'm sure I would have preferred it back then. Today it is a monument to tourism and ticky-tacky, with acres of parking and room after room of the most ridiculous junk. It even has an animated, life-size tyrannosaurus rex, to note the region's fossil beds. We soon were out of there. We made a pass through the Badlands, where Mike found no dinosaur bones. With caliche underfoot and a cold, raw wind, he did not try very hard.

Then we pushed on across the prairie for the Black Hills, stopping for refreshment in Scenic, at a nice little bar where the stools were oil drums topped with saddles. We decided to skip Mount Rushmore, another zoo.

The beautiful Black Hills were sacred to the Indians, and I could understand why. They were promised to the natives forever by the U.S. government, and the place should have been left alone. But gold was discovered there, so the white man rushed in and took over the Black Hills. Treaty after treaty was swept aside. Today the Indians have made some progress toward getting back some small portions of that holy land. They believe that someday they will once again have it all. I hope so. That would be a good thing.

13

Showdown With Dorothy Mackin

Dayton at the District Museum reception desk—with the "ADMISSION—50 ¢"
on the sign, which brought on the wrath of the mayor.

One year stretched into the next in Cripple Creek, and I just kind of settled into my unusual situation there. I did enjoy the winters and the opportunity for travel that they brought. I also enjoyed the summers, and the many compliments that the museum drew from appreciative visitors who liked the improvements I was making. More than anything else, however, I think it was just habit and familiarity that kept me there for a full decade. Yet all things end—and exactly as my friend Deborah had predicted at the start, it was a showdown with the town's *grande dame,* Dorothy Mackin, that resulted in my demise.

Over the years, my relationship with Dorothy had become adversarial, in a low-key manner. Technically speaking, as head of the museum board she was my boss, and I recognized that. But it was not my way to be pushed around by her or anyone else; and it was Dorothy's way to push people around. My resistance was passive rather than overt, and I was careful not to be insubordinate or give her other reasons to fire me. But a low level of tension existed between us at all times. Sooner or later I knew it would erupt.

The long-building crisis came in 1982. That was the year Dorothy hired a lawyer from Kansas to draw a map of the historical boundaries of Cripple Creek, for property-tax purposes and the general valuation of the town's real estate. I did not like this man, nor he me. His name, ironically enough, was Profitt; and as far as I was concerned, he had "shyster" written all over him. When the map project was completed, the boundaries of the historical district were strangely drawn to include Dorothy Mackin's outlying properties, plus the newly built home of lawyer Profitt himself, all clearly outside any area of historical significance. There were tax breaks for structures in the historical district, and being included added enormously to property values. The map amounted to a windfall for both Dorothy and the lawyer. To make matters worse, the project was charged to the museum. I was presented with a bill for $600—an outrageous sum!

I balked, and protested to Dorothy that I did not think the museum should be paying for such a self-serving exercise. She told me curtly, in essence, to shut up and pay the lawyer's bill. I did so, but wrote on the check "For nothing." Evidently this enraged Profitt. He demanded a new check, and threatened to sue if he did not get one. I issued one, as ordered to, coldly, by Dorothy. Then I left with a girlfriend for a Christmas vacation in New York. In my absence, however, Dorothy's machine was grinding me up. Determined to get in touch with me, she called my father in California; and upon learning that I was currently staying at the Yale Club in Manhattan, she tracked me down there.

In a terse telephone conversation she informed me that "the board"—i.e. D. Mackin—thought it would be best for me to "resign." I was disturbed to say the least—her call did nothing for my holiday cheer. I realized, however, that my time in Cripple Creek had run its course, and resisting her was futile. I agreed to resign as requested. I returned and loaded my few belongings in my truck. Then in the midst of a snowstorm I made my departure from Cripple Creek, with a sad sense of relief. Contrary to local custom, I exited in the middle of the day, leaving behind no debts. I heard later that lawyer Profitt had moved to Crested Butte, Colorado, with his fancy Porsche automobile, and had fallen in with a fast and shady crowd there. There were rumors that he had been arrested, disbarred, and even sent to prison, but I never learned if they were true. When those reports reached Cripple Creek, however, Mike Moore notified me that they convinced the good folks there that my protest had been "justified."

My decade running the Cripple Creek District Museum had done little for me financially, nor, as I soon discovered, professionally. But finally, after many dispiriting interviews with marginal institutions in out-of-the-way places, I got lucky. I was hired to become the first director of the Sonoma County Museum in Santa Rosa, California, just 60 miles north of San Francisco. The salary was generous, and the region felt like home.

I know I did not make much of an impression on the museum world during my time in Colorado. But that's all right. Because Cripple Creek rests at an altitude of 9,500 feet, I always liked to say that I had "attained the highest position in my field." Later I was dismayed to learn that two other Colorado towns had museums even higher: Fairplay's at 10,000 feet and Leadville's at 10,200. And now that Cripple Creek's neighboring town of Victor, at 9,700 feet, also has a museum, I have to concede that I reached only the fourth-highest position in my field (although it was third-highest when I occupied it). Still, not bad.

And now, after that lofty digression, how did Cripple Creek get its name?

14

How Cripple Creek Got Its Name

From this grassy bowl meandered a small stream, for which the town
shown was named—"Cripple Creek."

In 1873 the Hayden Survey map of the West Pike's Peak region recorded the name Cripple Creek for the small stream in the area known locally as Pisgah Park, east of a small peak called Mount Pisgah, probably named for the one in the Bible, or more likely the one in North Carolina named for the one in the Bible. Rancher Levi Welty and his sons, who came from Appalachia, had grazed cattle there since 1871, and according to legend had come up with the name Cripple Creek.

The commonly accepted story of how this name came to be is that while building a cabin by the stream, the Weltys endured a series of mishaps, including a runaway log, an accidentally discharged firearm, and a calf falling into the water, all of which resulted in injury to man and beast. Confronted with these events, Levi Welty is said to have exclaimed. "Boys, this here SURE IS some Cripple Creek!" And the name stuck. It surely was given to Hayden's mapmakers when they came in 1872. A colorful story, repeated so often that it found its way into numerous books about Cripple Creek, and so has come down through history as gospel truth, and thus unshakable.

Yet as with many such stories, one wonders. Another version of how the stream was named also bears repeating. Around 1870 there were numerous squatters around Pisgah Park. One of them, a crippled veteran of the Civil War, had a cabin near the stream. People said that if you ran into trouble in that then-wild country you could always find help down by "the cripple's creek." Perhaps. A local historian said he saw an obituary for "the man for whom Cripple Creek was named." But he never showed me a copy. So who knows? The tales do not cancel each other out.

And yet a third version, sketchily noted in a display at the Cripple Creek District Museum, tells the story this way: "According to Horace Bennett, one of the founders of the city, 'An old cow became mired in a bog alongside a stream. In pulling her out, one of her legs was crippled. For years, the cow hobbled over the range, and the cowboys called the stream Cripple Creek because of the accident.'" A variation on this theme can be found in a popular booklet that sells in the museum gift shop and other places around town. Titled "Cripple Creek! The World's Greatest Gold Camp: A Quick History" and written in 1967 by one Leland Feitz, the booklet declares: "The town was incorporated in 1892 and was named Cripple Creek after the stream that meandered through it. The creek had been named earlier by a rancher who had seen a cow fall and cripple herself crossing it."

But now we come to a curious matter. The song "Going Up Cripple

Creek" is commonly supposed to be about the town in Colorado, and is played with great frequency there. But it is clearly a bluegrass tune that most likely has origins in the Appalachian Mountains, not the Rockies. And sure enough, there is a Cripple Creek in the hills of Virginia, in Wythe County, in the southwestern part of that state. The Virginia town would obviously predate its namesake in Colorado.

In 1982 I visited Cripple Creek, Virginia, to learn how that town was named. I wandered into the Appalachian foothills east of Wytheville, the county seat, on narrow roads passing poor little farms. The country was pretty but lonely, and had seen better days. Not sure of my bearings, I hailed a grizzled farmer, who came slowly and somewhat suspiciously down from his porch to see what this stranger wanted. I asked if I was headed toward Cripple Creek. "Cripple Creek?" he repeated. "The fellow who wrote that song lived over yonder," pointing to a distant farm. The town? "Yep, 'bout three miles on up this road, cain't miss it." I could barely understand him, his accent filtered through the tobacco juice running down his chin. Driving away, I saw him staring at my Colorado license plate. "Far piece from home, that one," I imagined him thinking. "Wonder what he wants in Cripple Creek. Ain't none his age left up there no more."

Soon I came to the barest suggestion of a village, a scattering of houses in a small valley, or "hollow" (or more precisely, "holler"), as such places are called there. Somehow I just knew that the song and this town were linked. An old fellow was walking along the road, and I engaged him in conversation, explaining that I was from Cripple Creek, Colorado. "Yep," he said, in the same mountain twang used by his neighbor down the road, "heard of yore place. Some of our boys was in the Army out to Colorado, and went up there. Had a right good time."

He chuckled when I said I was interested in how this particular town got its name. "Well, now," he said, "You'll want to be talkin' to Mr. Dewey Wright, lives in that white house on the hill yonder, knows all the history of this place." I thanked him and headed up yonder hill to Mr. Wright's house. In response to my knock a big man in bib overalls came to the door, a sturdy fellow perhaps in his 70s. "Mr. Dewey Wright?"

I asked. "Leave the mister off, and that's me," he said with a grin. I explained why I was there, and he invited me in. We sat down to talk. The house was plainly furnished but thoroughly comfortable. His wife brought apple pie and coffee.

Dewey Wright was nothing if not talkative. He told me the story of his life, which gave me a feel for the region. He spoke of farming, logging in the mountains, railroad work, chopping ice on the Ohio River and working in coal mines in West Virginia before returning to his hometown, where he had now been postmaster many years. "Our people round here ain't always too friendly to strangers, not always to each other, too," he said. "I got on better with colored people over in West Virginia than I get on with some folks 'round here. But they are good people, just proud and independent. It's poor country now, all the young people gone off. Just us old folks hangin' on."

I finally got him on the subject of how his town got its name. "Well, now, this here's a bog-iron town—know what that is? Settled in the early 1700s, produced bog iron for all of Virginia, made into cannonballs for Washington's army. Now back in the early settlement days an old boy jumped an elk—yep, we used to have elk here in this here holler by the creek—and wounded it, crippled it, you might say, then trailed it to the next holler, where he killed it. That creek over there is called Elk Creek, and this'un here is called Cripple Creek. Now that makes sense, don't it?"

I said it made as much sense as the stories about how Cripple Creek, Colorado, got its name. "Well, that's the way they tell it," he said with some finality. I had more pie and coffee while Dewey Wright said, "If you write all of this up, you tell them that Dewey Wright is a good Christian man with grandchildren and great-grandchildren. You'll tell them that back in Colorado, now, won't you?" I looked at the man's strong and honest face, reflected on his lifetime in and concern for this region, one of America's forgotten backwaters, and told him that indeed I would tell that. He smiled and offered me still more pie and coffee. But I was pretty full by then. I took my leave of Dewey Wright and his wife, and their amiable hospitality. But writing this I remember well my visit. I wonder how it is now in those lonely hollows and foothills, and whether anyone still comes wandering into that tiny town to ask about the name or the song. Cripple Creek, Colorado, has surely fared differently in recent times, with its new gambling palaces, bright lights and throngs of strangers lurching from one establishment to another clutching paper cups of coins. I don't suppose the gaming enthusiasts give a hoot about how the town got its name.

Driving back from Virginia, I had the feeling that somehow the two Cripple Creeks shared some connection other than a name, something more than just a coincidence. But what it was I could not say. Six months later I was reading a book by John McPhee about the Pine Barrens of New Jersey, a pine-and-swamp area that has remained outside the state's mainstream development. The residents, called "Pineys," continue to speak in colonial-era English, McPhee wrote, using terms no longer familiar to the rest of us: "In the vernacular, a low, wet area where the Atlantic white cedars grow is called a cripple. If no cedars grow there, the wet area is called a spong, which is pronounced to rhyme with sung. Some people define spongs and cripples a little differently, saying that water always flows from a cripple but there is water in a spong only after a rain."

Hmmm. This sent me to the dictionary, which under "cripple" had this listing: "Local, U.S: bog, swamp." Obviously a stream flowing from such a bog or swamp would be called a "cripple creek." This probably was a common usage in colonial times, and continued in regions such as the Pine Barrens and Appalachia, where Levi Welty and his family hailed from. So how does this apply to Pisgah Park? Well, in Colorado's Cripple Creek there is (or was, before it was bulldozed over by the gambling mania) a low area where melted snow drained into something as close to a bog as could be found in that country. From this flowed the all-year stream known as Cripple Creek. Now, those early Appalachian folks like the Weltys probably referred to this stream as a cripple creek, in the terminology they had grown up with. And the same thing doubtless held true for the stream in Virginia—just a cripple creek, meaning "flowing from yonder bog." None of this necessarily invalidates the legend of Welty's mishaps and his exclamation. He may have just been giving a double meaning to the term already used. Anyway, that is my interpretation. No doubt there are those who will refuse to consider it, preferring to stay with one of the old, accepted stories.

And still . . . two towns, 2,000 miles apart, worlds apart, one sleeping in the foothills of Appalachia, the other resounding to the strange tunes of gambling, both sharing a common name and a common feature, an all-year stream flowing from a swamp. And somewhere in the mists of time, I am convinced, sit silvery, grizzled figures from both towns, sharing a bottle and laughing in the starlight, saying in their own mountain twangs, "Boys, this here SURE IS some cripple creek!"

PART III

THE DRY COUNTRY

The Lonesome Triangle

These tracks in the wash are new,
some coyotes were running here last night,
small, swift animals Clarence Spangler
calls "desert dogs"—everything
out here hunts or is hunted.
I am wary, too, watching
for sudden movement,
the shadows of eagles
passing overhead,
the silent flight of owls
in the moonlit stillness.
Cold, windy days
are no good for hunting;
they are days of hunger,
of laying up and watching
in the shelter of washes.
This desert is a place
of lean-ness,
of the feathers of ravens
rippling overhead,
of wind drifting through
rabbitbrush like waves
washing through time,
echoing from silent rocks
suggesting that a life
can just as well
be spent here
as anywhere.

15

The Ranch at the End of the World

Vast, empty, and silent desert surrounded the Rocking L Ranch house,
72 miles from the nearest town.

For four years, on and off, I worked as caretaker of a ranch in the Lonesome Triangle of the East Mojave Desert in California, 72 miles (the last 42 on dirt roads) northwest of Needles, at an altitude of almost 5,000 feet. The nearest neighbors were 12 miles away. Snow came in winter, and summer was almost tolerable, with nights that were pleasantly cool. The views were spectacular.

When I arrived at the Rocking L on January 1, 1988, there was no water. I had to fill five-gallon containers at the Cima Store, 22 miles away, where I went on Fridays to collect my mail and talk with Bob Ausmus, the proprietor, who was a wealth of knowledge on the desert and a damned fine person as well. The generator was also non-functioning. I had to take it to Las Vegas to be repaired. But there was propane, which provided heat, light and gas for the kitchen stove. In its simplicity and isolation the ranch was somewhat reminiscent of both *El Rancho Piedra Gorda* and Cripple Creek. Living in those places, I guess, had conditioned me for this stop along the way.

The Rocking L was owned by Bill Lesher, a big, amiable "window Westerner" from the Bay Area. It was not a large place, as ranches go—just three sections, 640 acres each, for a total of 1,920 acres. The core area, where the buildings were, was one of those sections, and was fenced in. "Within the smooth wire" was what we called the core. The ranch was built in the 1930s by some Hollywood guy who had failed in the Great Depression. He ran a few cattle out there and survived. The place had long been abandoned when Lesher bought it in the early 1980s, thinking to turn it into a dude ranch for businessmen. He hired a couple of cowboys to run the place, got some cattle for atmosphere, and had a big party for some people he hoped to turn into clients. But then Lesher had a falling out with the cowboys, fired them, sold the cattle and put his plans on hold. After that, the Rocking L went through a series of caretakers, if they could be called that. They included hippies, bikers and methamphetamine freaks, who were cooking up the stuff out there. That bunch was run out at gunpoint by Lesher, who then hired my artist friend Deborah to take over.

Deborah and I had met back in North Beach, before I went to Colorado. During the time I directed the Sonoma County Museum, after leaving Cripple Creek—a four-year stint of civility, wine-sipping pretense and considerable professional accomplishment—I visited Deborah frequently in nearby San Francisco, where she owned a little Moped business. Twice we went camping in the Black Rock Desert, where Dr. Avis and I had gone. There Deborah fell under the spell of the desert. Out there on the searing playa her artist's eye was overwhelmed by the starkness, the severe forms, the strange colors, the extremes. In

1986 she sold her business to concentrate on her art. She rented a house in Palm Springs, as a base from which to paint the desert. First she ventured into the Joshua Tree National Monument, next the Twentynine Palms region, then the Anza-Borrego wilderness down near the Mexico line. She painted in the sun and wind, and often slept in her little truck.

By the time spring came in 1987, she was ranging far out into the rugged and deserted East Mojave. On the old U.S. Route 66 she discovered the eccentric café in the tiny town of Goffs, and went there often for sustenance and company. She made friends with the owners, Connie and Morris, and with other locals dropping in for relief from the desert loneliness. Forty miles to the north, alongside the tracks of the Union Pacific Railroad, was the town of Cima, population three. There Deborah soon was friendly with storeowner Bob Ausmus and his wife, Irene, who ran the post office, which served the vast surrounding area. The third resident was their granddaughter Rosemary. From the Ausmuses Deborah got the name of Bill Lesher, and the tip that he was looking for someone to watch over the Rocking L. In the summer of 1987 she moved in.

I, in the meantime, was on the road again. Four years had proved just about enough of the refined, postured world of Sonoma County, and I had left my position at the museum. With a heady sense of freedom I was discovering byways I had not found before, and rediscovering places I did not want to forget. With money in the bank and a pent-up supply of wanderlust, I figured I could roam for at least six months before worrying about what to do next. While visiting Victor, Colorado, I learned that Deborah was no longer in Palm Springs, but instead was holed up in some decrepit ranch a hundred miles from nowhere. That caught my attention, and I contacted her. She was painting watercolors and enjoying the solitude, Deborah said, but would be ready to leave at year's end. Maybe I would want to take over for her, she suggested. Well, maybe I would. On New Year's Day 1988 I arrived at the ranch, at a salary of $300 a month, to be the next caretaker.

Life at the Rocking L was pretty spare. Every now and then Lesher would show up, with booze and food, and at other times I was able to coax a few friends into visiting me. Occasionally Deborah would return, for extended painting projects. Otherwise, I had the place to myself. Or almost to myself. Four big cats, semi-feral toms tracing back to previous occupants, also lived there. They were not exactly tame but were friendly enough, following at a distance as I made my daily rounds on foot around the place. I set out dry cat food for them, and they augmented this diet with desert mice and jackrabbits, which from time to time I found dismembered in the barn. I had a battery-powered radio, but it didn't pick up much except at night, when KNX in Los Angeles got through. I did a lot of reading by Coleman lantern.

The ranch house was a 1950s-style cinderblock structure, with big plate-glass windows. It had been built by the son of the first owner. Next to the barn was a trailer, for visitors or whatever. In the barn was evidence of horses and cattle, but none were there in my time. During its long season of neglect the Rocking L had been slipping steadily into ruin. All manner of junk had accumulated, paint was chipping, doors flapped in the wind. Although Lesher had given me no firm instructions, I decided to take my job seriously and do what I could to fix up the grounds. I kept busy, piling up junk for an Okie family to haul away, making repairs, laying pipes and stone walks, raking and generally cleaning the place. In the ample time that was left over, I took long walks and drives in my truck exploring the area.

This is not the life for everyone, but I found it more than tolerable. It was at the ranch that I learned, more or less, to make a paper towel last a week. "That's pathetic," Deborah said when I reported this to her. "Don't tell people things like that. They don't understand." Well, there are some who do. My friend Old Bill was one.

Old Bill Howarth and I also went back a long way. We met at the Vesuvio bar in North Beach. Later we were both graduate students at San Francisco State College, along with half the population of Northern California. Old Bill was born in England just before World War II, in which his father was killed. He came to America as the stepson of an American GI who married his widowed mother. He did most of his growing up in California's Mill Valley, which was then a simple, unpretentious community with lots of redwoods and mountains nearby. There he developed a great love and understanding of the California mountains. As a young man he hiked the entire length of the John Muir Trail, several hundred miles along the spine of the Sierra Nevada.

Old Bill became a teacher of writing at various community colleges in the Sacramento area. He tried marriage for a while, but when that failed he took to spending more and more of his spare time camping in the very highest parts of the High Sierra, sometimes setting up his tent in the dead of winter, then waiting out blizzards inside it before skiing back to civilization. He bought a rustic house in the forested foothills near Auburn, and with his wolf-dog Kiska prowled the high country at every opportunity, avoiding people as much as possible. Old Bill was nothing if not rugged.

Bill came to visit in my first April, while the desert was greening. His vehicle, an ancient Ford Pinto station wagon, broke down 50 miles away and had to be towed to the tiny town of Essex, to a ramshackle truck stop owned by Jack, an Okie right out of Central Casting. Jack thought he could repair the vehicle, and said to check back in a few days. In the meantime, Bill needed a ride to the Rocking L. Jack was glad to oblige, but said he would have to charge. "Dollar a mile," said Jack. "Figure it's about 25 miles up to there." Having no other choice, Bill agreed. Unaware of this development, I spent the late afternoon on my "spy rock" with binoculars, waiting to see Old Bill turn off Black Canyon Road into the ranch, figuring he'd be in by dusk. A thin haze of clouds made dusk come on early that day. As it settled, there was no sign of my friend, no traffic on Black Canyon Road. Never was much, maybe three or four vehicles a day, but today nothing, not even a dust devil. In the last light, just as I was about to give up on Old Bill, figuring he'd gotten lost, I saw a white pickup headed north, like it knew where it was going. It dipped out of sight then reappeared, coming toward the Rocking L.

I headed toward the ranch house to meet the truck. Driving it was Jack, accompanied by Old Bill, looking uncomfortable. He'd been saying something like, "You sure this is the right place? It looks deserted." Jack reassured him that he knew this was the Rocking L and added, "Look, there he is, coming down from those rocks." When Bill saw me, he relaxed and smiled. He and Jack piled all his gear in front of the house. Bill reached into his cooler and pulled out three Rainier Ales, which had become the traditional brew for us. I offered one to Jack, but he said he'd best be headed back, coming on dark. Watching the truck bounce away, we drank ale in the darkening silence. Bill looked at me and said, "I don't know, Dayton, it's kinda lonely out here." We chuckled. Coming from him, that was quite an admission. But lonely it was at the Rocking L.

I got Bill settled into the trailer, then fixed a good dinner. Afterward we turned in for the night. Next morning Bill said the tomcats had kept him awake, growling on the roof. "They'll kill each other," he said with alarm. "No," I told him, "they'll work it out." I knew they would. They were good cats, all related, and basically liked each other. Lately, however, some point of contention had arisen among them. I'd been watching them, and knew which would prevail. There was a lot of hissing and staring, but after a while they all settled back down and got along.

Old Bill seemed to enjoy the ranch—the leisurely breakfasts, coffee on the porch, watching the desert, hawks and eagles hunting, the long walks around the area, exploring in the truck, the good dinners and sitting outside drinking many beers and talking as darkness fell. One evening down at the Goffs cafe we ran into Carl, an artist who had lived many years in the desert. In the course of his conversation Carl said something about a "mandala," the circular Hindu design symbolizing the universe. Bill was turned off by that, was suspicious of that kind of talk. He said to me later that he didn't care to visit Carl at his rock house 18 miles from the ranch, didn't care how interesting the house or the mandala was. Old Bill was mighty rigid about some things.

One afternoon we drove to Carruthers Canyon and hiked up to the old copper mine. "More my type of country, these mountains," Bill said. When we climbed the Mid Hills for a view of the Providence Range, he commented, "Strange-looking mountains, more like Mexico than California." That thought had never occurred to me, but looking at the Providences poking up off the desert I did indeed see the resemblance to Mexico's Sierra Madre, which I had visited 30 years earlier. Old Bill sure knew and loved mountains. Mountains were his element. He would never live in the desert, but at least he could relate to it.

After a few days I drove Old Bill to Essex to check on his vehicle. What a collection of junk Jack had piled up there, a few miles south of the Interstate! Jack loved to carry on about how his junk pile was going to become the biggest truck stop between Barstow and Needles, but I had my doubts. (It's still sitting there now, abandoned, with a crude sign spray-painted on plywood, "ALL FOR $80,000.") A lanky, blank-eyed fellow whom Jack said was his cousin was lounging around. No work seemed to be getting done. Jack said the vehicle would have to be towed to Barstow to be fixed. Bill said he'd go along for the ride, and asked me to come back that afternoon to pick him up. I did, and we had a few more days at the ranch, just hanging out.

Then it was time for Bill to be going. I drove him to Barstow, where his repaired vehicle was waiting. "I understand, Dayton," he said on the way. "You being out there in the middle of nowhere, with the coyotes and the hawks and the eagles and the cats, in the silence and the darkness at night, fixing that old place up. Yep, just you and no bullshit. I understand." I could see that Old Bill did, and I appreciated that. We said goodbye, and I set out on the 125-mile drive back to the Rocking L. Once again it would be just me and the cats, until the next visitors, a few weeks down the line.

16

The Party in the Desert

Dayton and his mother, in the sudden December blizzard at the Rocking L Ranch,
just days before Deborah's big party.

L ife moved slowly at the Rocking L. Deep and quiet are the
rhythms of the desert, and pretty soon I was in synch with
those rhythms. Every Friday I drove over to Cima for mail
and supplies, and there got to know Deborah's friends Bob

and Irene Ausmus. Bob was born and raised on a nearby ranch, and although his chief occupation at this point was that of storekeeper, he still ran cattle on his place. He was a repository of East Mojave desert lore, which he shared with the readers of articles he wrote for the *Las Vegas Sun*. When the weather was warm enough, Bob and I would sit on the bench outside his store and talk for an hour or so. Occasionally tourists would photograph the two of us sitting there—real desert characters, I suppose. One time Bob and Irene came out to the ranch to join Deborah and me for dinner, and I much enjoyed their company.

As months passed I gained the acquaintanceship and the friendship of other hardy residents of that challenging and forbidding region. There weren't many of us, and we all needed occasional socializing to offset the vast and empty solitude of the desert. A dozen miles from the Rocking L was the ranch of Harry and Trudi Tucker, likable folks. Out there all by himself in his primitive Rock House was Carl the artist, whose "mandala" had rubbed Old Bill the wrong way. Jack the Okie had his "truck stop" in Essex. A few people sold real estate, or tried to. Some pumped gas, some served breakfast, lunch and dinner at the Goffs Café. Each had a role to play in the life of the region. Most of us knew each other, but slightly. We respected privacy—otherwise, we would not be in the desert.

An occasional visitor was Deborah. Although the Rocking L had proved too lonely to hold her more than six months as caretaker, she found it perfect as an artist's retreat. In June of 1988, six months after I came to the Rocking L, my father died, in his 84th year. I was glad he had come out to the ranch the year before to visit Deborah, and had bestowed his stamp of approval upon it. No "rich man's estates" in the East Mojave! From June until August I was back in Santa Monica, wrapping up my father's affairs. During that time, Deborah returned to the ranch, to guard it and to paint.

Naturally outgoing in personality, Deborah also had an impressive capacity for solitude—a good mix for an artist, I suppose. Each day she would go out into the desert to paint her big and powerful watercolors; and every time she visited Cima, or Essex, or Goffs, or Kelso, or Twentynine Palms she cultivated her friendships with the people there. In

August I resumed my duties at the Rocking L, and Deborah returned to San Francisco, to put finishing touches on her bold landscapes. Her creative output during her time in the desert had been enormous, and her socializing had been energetic. As the end of the year drew near, both her collection of art and her collection of friends were large. That's when Deborah decided to merge the two—in a big Christmas-season party at the Rocking L, where her watercolors would be presented to the scattered residents of the "Lonesome Triangle," as the area between Barstow, Needles and Las Vegas is called.

Except for Big Bill Lesher's unsuccessful shindig for prospective dude-ranch clients, we were sure the Rocking L had never been the scene of such an ambitious event. That thought only added to our zeal. Deborah sat down and made a list of desert folks she wanted to invite, 40 or so, which would push the capacity of the ranch. Then we both added our own friends who might otherwise never have a reason for coming to the Rocking L. Formal invitations were mailed out. Yes indeed—this was to be an occasion!

As party day drew near, I was dispatched to Los Angeles to bring back honey-baked ham, prodigious supplies of beer and liquor, and delicacies available only in West L.A. and Santa Monica. After returning with them, I made sure the electrical generator was oiled and tuned— Coleman lanterns would not suffice this time. Also by this time we had a reliable water supply, with a functioning well and two large, full water tanks. The grounds were cleaned up and raked. The pathway to the outhouse was lined with stones. Firewood was stockpiled. Deborah's paintings were displayed on every suitable wall space.

It seemed that everyone we invited, plus some, were going to show up. After all, how often did one get to attend an event at the isolated and mysterious Rocking L? Many of the locals had never gone there, and certainly none of the outsiders. The first guests, a few days early, were our friends Ted Roberts, his wife, Janet, and their two young boys, driving down from Berkeley. When they arrived, Deborah was 125 miles away at the Las Vegas airport, picking up her Bay Area friends Carol and Caroline, and my mother.

Yes, my mother was coming to the Rocking L, from Pennsylvania. She had her own special love of the West, and was always up for the next adventure. She first came as a young girl, to visit relatives in Colorado. In 1926, when she was 14, she returned with her parents; and when she stepped out of her railroad car in Cody, Wyoming, a cowboy hanging out at the depot looped his lasso around her. She threw it off, and everybody laughed. Maybe the cowboy was paid to do such things even then—a precursor of the "tourist West" to come. Maybe he was just paying cowboy tribute to a pretty girl. Whatever the case, my mother loved telling that story all her life.

When I sent her photographs of the ranch, she decided that she wanted to see it for herself. The Christmas party provided the perfect occasion. Yet by then her mind was starting to slip, in the early stages of Alzheimer's disease. Deborah realized this at the Las Vegas airport, when my mother's suitcase failed to appear on the baggage carousel. It had been stolen en route, my mother indignantly insisted. Summing up the situation more accurately, Deborah gently took her to a shopping mall, where the missing items were replaced.

By Wednesday night all the sleepover guests were bunked down at the Rocking L. My mother loved the ranch, and her enthusiasm and good cheer kept everyone's spirits high. On Thursday, however, those spirits were put to the test. Without warning a furious little blizzard dropped five inches of snow in Gold Valley. Suddenly we found ourselves in a strange, frozen world, through which driving would be hazardous or even impossible. And the party was on Sunday, just three days away! A flurry of consternation rippled through the people assembled there. I was less concerned than the others. Over the previous winter I had seen several snowstorms, and in my experience they were events of little permanence. Sure enough, on Friday the sun came back out, and by Saturday only traces of the storm remained, in the few spots where there was shade.

Early Sunday afternoon the guests began arriving. They kept coming for hours. From all over the desert they came, from Needles and Baker and Kelso and Twentynine Palms, as well as Cima and Goffs and Essex. From ranches and trailers the guests came, and two of them from a desert mansion. The wealthiest couple in Needles was there, dressed like everybody else, understating the money they had made in real estate, an auto dealership and a hardware store. Also present were members of the Overson family, a serious clan that ran the vast OX Cattle Company. There were artists and mechanics and cowboys and teachers and cooks. And bums.

Bob and Irene Ausmus were there, with their daughter and grand-daughter, little Rosemary. So was Bob Stern, an ex-cop from New York City, who sold real estate sporadically. So was Lois Black, editor of the Baker newspaper. I was intrigued by the couple who ran the Inn at Twentynine Palms, where Deborah often stopped. The wife was as pretty as any socialite, and the husband was the very image of Ernest Hemingway, a fact of which he was not unaware. But they both knew how to relax and fit in.

Some of the Oversons had brought fiddles, banjos and guitars. Soon the sounds of Western swing filled the ranch house. Wafting through also was the occasional smell of marijuana, a presence that made some of the more redneck guests uneasy. They figured out the right solution, however: more shots of bourbon, more bottles of Bud, of which we had laid in what we felt was an inexhaustible supply. One young fellow, whom I learned had long been a wannabe sheriff's deputy in Needles, admired my "ranger's hat." When I told him, for no particu-lar reason and with no particular truth, that it was a souvenir of my "days along the Border," he exclaimed, "I *knowed* you was a lawman!"

Carl, the artist from the Rock House, was holding forth on how there was nothing like being shot through the cheek to grab a man's attention. He knew about it firsthand. A year earlier he had been read-ing by lamp light in his primitive abode when a single shot rang out. A bullet came in through the window, passed through one cheek and lodged in the other side of his mouth. Fortunately it was just a .22. A larger bullet would have done a lot more damage. With no vehicle of his own, Carl had staggered three miles through the snow, holding a towel to his bleeding face, to his nearest neighbor, Bud Smith, who drove him to the hospital in Needles. A week later Carl was back at the Rock House, sipping beer and eating baby food. He had no idea who had shot him or why, and the sheriff showed little interest in investigating the incident. The mystery was never solved. Carl admitted he was nervous about returning home, but he had no place else to go. There had been no further trouble, however, and his reputation and success as a desert painter were growing steadily.

Sometime after midnight, which is indeed late for East Mojave desert folks, the party began to disperse. Everyone leaving assured us that it had been a real swell time, memorable even, and we could tell they meant it. Another indication that a good time was had by all was the absence of leftover food or booze. Our "inexhaustible" supplies had pretty well been cleaned out. We were glad to think that we had brought enjoyment, excitement and merriment to the good people who came to our Christmas party at the Rocking L. We did feel a twinge of regret, however, that Big Bill Lesher had not been among the guests. We wanted him to see the ranch at its finest, and Deborah had urged him to attend. But I think he had run up a few financial problems with some of his desert neighbors, and apparently he felt it best not to show up. Maybe it was just as well.

Our only other regret was that not one of Deborah's watercolors had sold. They were admired no end all night long. But only after the guests were gone did we realize that most of the people at the party did not understand that the paintings were for sale. Art openings were not a standard part of the social scene in the East Mojave desert, and our guests probably thought the paintings were just real nice party decorations.

A few days later my mother was put on her plane in Las Vegas, with firm instructions to the airline personnel to make sure both she and her luggage made all the necessary connections to get back to Philadelphia. Although she lived almost 10 more years, the party at the Rocking L was the last great adventure of her life. I look back and feel glad we made it happen. All too often, we wait too late to do what we mean to do.

I take similar satisfaction in thinking back about the party itself. Within two years the Rocking L was abandoned, the land sold to the BLM and the complex of buildings left rotting in the sun. I hear that the Feds plan to bulldoze the place back down to bare earth when theycan get around to it. And then it will be as if nothing ever existed there—just vacant winds swirling over empty sands where once there was a magical gathering, where the scattered dwellers of the East Mojave were wined and dined and exposed to art. Surely in all the lonely life and times of the Rocking L, that was its finest moment.

17

A Scenario in the East Mojave

Fire-arms, and knowing how to use them, were important
for self-preservation in the lonely desert.

I t is about 7 o'clock of a May evening in the Lonesome Triangle. I am at the Rocking L, walking its northern border, heading east on the little-used dirt road that parallels the fence. Coyotes have been singing and carrying on over in Black Canyon Wash to the east, over toward Wild Horse Mesa. Two golden eagles had been circling high above Gold Valley, where the ranch is nestled, but they have flown home. There was also a slight wind from the southeast earlier. But now the desert is still and quiet. I am walking slowly, savoring the feeling that I know where I am.

"The hour of darkness" Mr. Moore and I liked to call the quiet time when night fell, in the cold time of year when evening came so soon, when we would sit alone—I in the ranch house, he in the trailer—listening on battery radios to the news from the cities. Before turning on the propane lights, before fixing something to eat, before doing any of that. But now in spring, with the desert greening up nicely after good rains, and with daylight lingering on, I am enjoying a long walk around the perimeters of the ranch. There are no snakes yet, but soon the East Mojave green rattlesnakes will be out, and night walking will get dangerous.

Each day at this time I go walking, sometimes just out to the locked gate, about half a mile, with all four cats following me, in their way. But a couple of times a week I take these longer walks, to check the fences and gates, to see if any vehicles have been over the roads, and generally to see what has been going on in this little corner of the world. I carry my binoculars, to watch for late-flying raptors or coyotes, or to just "sweep the country." And I carry a snub-nosed .38 in a holster—"Little Pepé, the Desert Stinger." I don't really think I need a gun, but it provides an extra margin of safety that makes me feel more confident in this lonely land that I now feel is my own.

I walk along the fence line, on the road leading to the petroglyphs in Sand Wash, four or five miles away. I turn back for a moment to check the sunset over the Providence Mountains. There are no clouds, so the sunset is nothing special, just a vibrant desert afterglow. Through it I notice dust rising from a vehicle heading north on Black Canyon Road, rather unusual for this time of evening. I raise the binoculars and spot a light-colored van, moving slowly. Perhaps some tourists—"desert specialists," Mr. Moore and I call them, sarcastically. We don't like to be bothered by people poking around, although we ourselves often go poking around. I watch this van creep along, kicking up dust, and wonder about it. Perhaps someone looking for a place to camp. But why not back at Hole in the Wall campground? It is usually empty this time of year. The van slows down by the sign to Gold

Valley Ranch, and turns in. Now I *am* interested!

In recent times the Gold Valley Ranch, just four miles from the Rocking L, has become our nearest inhabited neighbor. Like the Rocking L, the Gold Valley Ranch had been abandoned for a long time. But now, as at our ranch, a caretaker has been hired to live there. Ed Marquette, a crusty old man with many memories, stretching from California to Montana, is looking after the place. Maybe this van is bringing someone to come see Ed. Yet never before have I seen him have a visitor. Ed is more of a loner than either Mr. Moore or me. And we are not expecting anyone.

The van dips out of sight into the wash, emerges, climbs the hill, and pauses when the gate to Gold Valley Ranch comes into view. I know the driver can see Ed's truck parked at the house. I watch through the binoculars. The van moves on toward the Rocking L, and once again disappears. Whoever is in there cannot see our buildings. So they are "exploring." Or are they? A line of dust marks the van's progress. Now it comes into view again, pausing by the outside gate, which we leave un- locked, as told to by the Bureau of Land Management, to provide "ac- cess to public lands." Now the van is turning onto the north road I am on, heading slowly toward me, about a mile and a half away. I watch through the binoculars, thinking that whoever is in there has probably spotted me. I see one person, the driver—no passengers—a man wear- ing sunglasses, even though it is getting dark now.

He comes on slowly, obviously unsure of where he is heading, perhaps wanting to ask me questions. I am not in the mood for ques- tions. I want this van gone. Perhaps it brings some "desert specialist" looking for the damned petroglyphs, which unfortunately are marked on some of the U.S. Geographical Survey topo maps. As the van ad- vances I move off the road, drop the binoculars from my eyes and let them hang. I get out Little Pepé and tuck it into my right hand, hidden by my leg. You never know out here.

The van draws up. I position myself so that my left shoulder is at the rear of the driver's window. The man takes off his sunglasses. He has to look slightly back at me, but not so much as to make me seem to be acting suspiciously. A bearded man, perhaps in his late 30s, an outdoor type, I suppose. Average-looking. He says, "Hi." Friendly enough. I nod. He continues. "I'm looking for a place to camp. I like this wide-open, empty, desert country." Okay, I think, one of those. It could be me on my wanderings. Except I get set up in a place much earlier. For some reason, standing there with my hidden gun, I decide to put on my "simple" act—that is, act not too smart. I tell the man, stammering a bit for effect, "This here private land, Sir. Public starts yonder, 'bout a mile and a half on, through a gate. It's all public out there, can camp anywhere." The man is watching me, smiling. I don't like his looks. Too smooth. Not a "desert specialist." Something else.

"You get any news out here?" he asks. "Damn radio in this thing conked out on me. Anything interesting happening out there in the world?"

I find this question unusual, but perhaps I am being paranoid. I shake my head, and stammer, "No Sir, I don't git no news out here. Don't care about the world. Coyotes been singing over to Black Canyon Wash. That's all the news I git. Mebbe they know something." He smiles, rather grimly I think, resting his hands on the wheel. I see hard eyes. No, I don't like this man, want him gone, want him out of here. But he seems determined to sit and ask questions. "Say, that ranch I passed just back there. No lights, but I saw a truck. Who's there?"

Why these questions? Now I *am* getting suspicious. I tell him, "Why, that's Mr. Ed there, Ed Marquette. An old cowboy, I think from Montana. He's caretaker there." I am consciously stuttering, thinking it might give me some sort of advantage, if needed. Don't know where I dreamed up this strategy! I ramble on. "He's okay, Mr. Ed is, but a sort of nut case. Takes cocaine, I'm told. I wouldn't know about that, but Mr. Moore said one time he had white powder stuck to his nose—that'd be cocaine, I'm thinking. Or he passed out in the pancake flour. He drinks a bit."

The man seems to smile, looking back toward Gold Valley Ranch. I stammer on, "And he tells wild stories, like how he was a secret agent for the government, got dropped with a Jeep with a machine gun mounted on it into some Ay-rab country, to guard pipelines and kill terrorists. Said he wore a necklace of human ears, said them people was mighty impressed."

The man interrupts my rambling and asks, gesturing toward the Rocking L, "Now, that place over there at the foot of that mountain, anyone there?"

"Oh, yessir," I say, a bit too loudly, "That would be Mr. Moore down there—another nut case. He's in there with a whole bunch of guns and stuff. Says he has barbecue—no, not barbecue, booby traps around that place. He's always prowling around. I think he was in the war or something. He's okay, though. We cook steaks and drink beer down there a lot in the hot weather, but when it gets dark he's like, from the war, on guard, on patrol, something. Can't seem to let go."

"Yeh, probably a vet," the man says. Then he asks, "What about you? Where's your place?"

"I have a camp up by the old line shack," I tell him. "Can't see it from here. It's where the bees are. They buzz a lot, but I'm okay there. The bees, I guess they know me." The man smiles again. Hands no longer on the wheel. Where are they? This has gone on long enough. It's getting dark. I don't like this man's smile, now that I have seen it. Sort of a cruel smile, not a nice smile. I feel my finger tightening on the trigger of Little Pepé, and I begin to move back and away from the van window. If this dude tries to pull something I'll blast him fast. But mostly I want him gone.

The man senses my movement. I say loudly, "Mister, you can camp anywhere beyond that fence, that gate, a mile and a half on. Best get movin', dark's comin' on." No longer stammering, talking forcefully, like a command. The man stiffens. He knows that I was jiving him, that I am ready, perhaps have a gun. People out here often do. "Okay," I hear him say coldly. "Thanks." The van slides off. Just before the lights flick on, when it is 10 yards beyond me, I bring up Little Pepé and draw a bead on the rear window. I don't know if he sees me do it, don't care. I feel like shooting him. I think he might have shot me if he thought he could get away with it. Why? I don't know. But there is something definitely "off" about this guy. I think I will be "on patrol" tonight.

I walk after the van, watch it disappear down the wash and into the low hills toward the gate to the BLM land. I continue to the gate, and see that it has been opened, the van driven through, and the gate closed again. This surprises me, but perhaps this guy has been brought up around ranches and just automatically closes gates, in the country-courtesy way. I wait for an hour in the darkness by the gate. No sounds. How far in there is he? Best place to camp is a flat area about two miles on. Bet he's there. I am not going to find out, though. Best get back to the ranch, and apprise Mr. Moore of this event. I don't like the idea of this man in the area. Will he come for us in the night? Did he believe that stuff about "nut cases"? Why not? That's the type that lives in these god-forsaken places. He may know that. Mike agrees that we should go on patrol, and alert Ed as well. We stay up all night, then drive out next morning beyond the gate, heavily armed, to conduct an investigation, to make sure that dude is out of this country. We find nothing but his tracks.

A couple of weeks later Mr. Moore and I are cooking steaks on the porch of the ranch, watching open-range cattle drift north, then south again. Coyotes singing in the wash don't seem to bother them. Mike looks up from the grill. "You know, that dude in the van you told me about," he says, "when we were on patrol all night?"

"Yeh," I answer, almost knowing what he is going to say.

"Well, I heard on the radio, something about a shoot-out over near Vegas, some guy in a van, wanted for three killings, over in Arizona. Cops wasted his ass. Same guy?"

I nod. "Probably."

Mike grunts, turns a steak. I drink my beer, gaze out across the desert to the Mid Hills. There is no dust rising over Black Canyon Road. No vans moving slowly south. Nothing out there at all. The way I like it. Lonely. Empty. Just us nut cases.

18

Shifting Seasons

Mr. Moore trying to get warm in the kitchen of the Rocking L Ranch.

Yes, I did enjoy the odd life of the Rocking L. Only up to a point, however. It really was not a place for living out my life, or investing my career. And after the glittering Christmas party, everything that followed seemed anticlimactic. About halfway through 1989, my second year, I knew that pretty soon I would need to move on, and leave the ranch in the hands of the next caretaker. But I came to this conclusion reluctantly. Both Deborah and I wanted the Rocking L to remain in the care of someone who would let us visit, make us feel at home. I realized that this job was not for everyone. But I felt I did know somebody who might be just right for it—Mike Vann Moore, "Old Mr. Moore," my eccentric friend from Cripple Creek.

I called Mike from a telephone booth in Needles. He was receptive, but could make only a six-month commitment. A couple of years earlier the old mining town of Victor, near Cripple Creek, had opened its own little museum, and—no doubt due to the experience he had gained working under me—Mike had been hired as its director. The Victor museum, however, was seasonal, open just six months of the year, late spring through early autumn. Mike needed someplace to go during the long, cold winter, and when I suggested the East Mojave desert, he jumped at it. I could tell he envisioned a warm oasis like Palm Springs, and I did not disabuse him of that notion. I felt an obligation to find my own replacement as caretaker of the Rocking L, just as Deborah had found me. Mike's coming would solve the immediate need—and the future, as always, would just have to take care of itself.

By telephone I told Bill Lesher of this development. Then he and Mike talked and made the same deal I had—$300 a month. Thus in October 1989 Old Mr. Moore rolled into the Rocking L, pulling a little trailer and bringing along his two dogs, from whom he was never separated. I was in no great hurry to leave, nor was Mike in a hurry to see me go. For the next several weeks we both resided there, me in the ranch house, Mike in the trailer. Based on the lonely ranch's norm, it amounted to a population explosion. It was a pleasant time for me. Though accustomed to isolation, I enjoyed having company. I even enjoyed Mike's grumbles as he shivered in the increasingly nippy air, wondering what he had gotten himself into.

I figured to hang on at the Rocking L through the holidays, then return to San Francisco and just take it easy for a while. Christmas in the desert that year brought back fond memories of our gala event; but there was no encore at the Rocking L, and nobody else hosted anything that even attempted to match our splendid occasion. Mike and I were, however, invited to a New Year's Eve party over at the Tuckers' ranch, 12 miles away on the other side of Table Mountain. It was a neighborly gesture, and we accepted.

Harry and Trudi had rounded up about a dozen people, most of whom I did not know, and none of whom were known by Mr. Moore. There was food and drink and some desultory talk about this and that, none of it very connected. Harry had cranked up his propane generator, and he entertained and surprised us by playing modern jazz on some kind of electric piano that he had somehow learned to play out there on his remote spread. Or maybe before he got there—in the course of the evening I learned that Harry had been a pioneer of neon lighting in Los Angeles, and had made quite a bundle. When midnight came there was a bit of cheering, and some stranger's wife gave me a chaste kiss. I poked Old Mr. Moore, dozing on the couch, and told him it was time to go.

The moon was bright in the clear, cold desert sky. I popped open a couple of beers as we bounced through the Tuckers' gate and onto the deserted road. "It was nice," Mike summed up the evening. "They're good folks." I agreed, but added that I felt we had somehow not quite fit in, us two loners from the Rocking L. It was just another indication that my sojourn in the East Mojave was drawing to its natural conclusion. We drifted in silence across the moonlit sagebrush toward the ranch. Mike got out to unlock and relock the gate, while alone in the truck I was remembering New Year's scenes of urban revelry, crowded and noisy bars, shouts of strangers, the warm embrace of some sweet Darla.

Old Mr. Moore grunted "Happy New Year" and disappeared into his trailer. I fumbled around the ranch house, got the propane lamp going, and sat down with another beer. Something was wrong, or, more precisely, not quite right. Slowly in the silence the realization settled upon me that the problem was—the silence. The endless silence of the desert. Usually I loved it, far more than most would. But on New Year's Eve?

"Why not?" I said to myself. "Goddammit, why not?" I chugged the beer, got out my Smith & Wesson 9 mm pistol, went outside, and fired two shots into the great black sky. The blasts echoed back from the dark Woods Mountains. From inside the trailer came a startled "What the hell!" from Old Mr. Moore. Standing in the wild darkness I shouted, "It's New Year's Day, Mike! It's a new decade! It's 1990!" There was no reply.

San Francisco was good for a while, a welcome, boisterous contrast to the Rocking L. But soon enough, predictably, I began to miss the desert. Irregular reports from Mike informed me that he was holding his own out there, once he got past the January blizzard that closed the roads and dropped the temperature to 14 degrees—just as he ran out of propane, from neglecting to have the tank filled up for winter. Until then, I think, he had been clinging to his Palm Springs imagery. But the blizzard made a believer out of him. With no way to leave the ranch over the snowbound roads, he hunkered down into survival mode. He retreated from the frigid house into his trailer, where he wrapped himself up in blankets, with both of his dogs tucked in there, too. Their shared body heat got them through, although Mike noted that the inside thermometer fell to 28 degrees.

A more sociable man than I, Mike realized that one season at the Rocking L would be enough for him. So in keeping with the custom, he began looking for someone to take over when he left. On supply runs to Needles, Mike had become acquainted with one Patrick Smith, a 40-something knockabout fellow who made and sold pottery from time to time, and his wife, Willow, a biologist for the Bureau of Land Management. Mike suggested that they become Rocking L caretakers when he returned to Victor in June. They jumped at the offer. The free rent was an inducement, as was the $300 a month, more money than Patrick usually made from selling pottery. An added attraction was that the ranch was a perfect place for Willow to board some semi-wild mustangs that the BLM had rounded up off the range. Bill Lesher was called, and hired them by telephone.

When Mike related this development to me, I agreed that it sounded like a good thing for the Rocking L. The ranch was just sitting out there in the desert, going nowhere, but it had by now become part of my life. I wanted it to be respected and maintained as it waited for whatever its destiny would bring. Its unique mixture of nostalgia and isolation tugged at me strongly. As a matter of fact, I told Old Mr. Moore, I would be coming to see him in May, before he departed for Victor. He could count on it.

19

Failure Writ Large Upon the Man

Mr. Patrick, at the Rocking L Ranch, with dogs and horses.

To welcome Patrick and Willow Smith to the Rocking L, and to bid farewell to Mr. Moore, Bill Lesher threw a party when I got there in May 1991. He came down from San Francisco for it, and treated us to all the booze we cared to drink, which was a lot. Big Bill was in an expansive mood that night, under a piercingly bright full moon. He kept calling me his "foreman," a term I appreciated but felt was more fantasy than reality. After a day of recovery,

Mike hitched his trailer to his truck and set out on the long road back to Victor, and Patrick and Willow moved into the Rocking L. They brought with them his pottery kiln, four big white dogs to add some excitement to the lives of the resident cats, and four mustangs that the BLM had rounded up on the range. I was enjoying my visit, so I decided to hang on for a while after they arrived. We fixed up a little "apartment" in the tack room of the barn for me to throw down my sleeping bag. It was a pretty nice arrangement. My creature-comfort needs have always been rudimentary.

Patrick and Willow were an odd couple, and he was more odd than she. Willow was a quiet and retiring person, and openly acknowledged that she preferred the company of animals to the company of people. I guess that's why she became a biologist. Her husband (and why they ever got married was something I could not readily determine) was a far more garrulous and a far more empty person. "Drifter" was a word that came to mind to describe him. "Loser" was another. Right from the start I established the "Mr. Patrick" and "Mr. Dayton" routine with him, although Willow and I just called each other by our first names. I wanted to keep a certain distance from this man.

With his wide hat, scruffy old wool coat, the butt of a pistol sticking from a pocket, and his slouched demeanor, Mr. Patrick looked every inch a character right out of the Old West. But unlike some men I had known in Cripple Creek who worked hard to affect the image, I realized that Mr. Patrick was not intentionally trying to play this role. He seemed to me like one of those men who had ridden west after the Civil War, hard-eyed, bitter, defeated men, looking for a new life, swearing that never, ever, anywhere would they take any shit from any man, ever again!

That's the way I saw Mr. Patrick, touchy and unstable, full of grandiose plans that never did and never would come to anything. Some things about him didn't add up, but I just let it all go. There was failure in his past and surely more failure in the future. I could see right away that he wouldn't last long at the Rocking L. Nothing seemed to get done there while Willow was off at her job with the BLM. Mr. Patrick's rusty old pickup just sat in the sun, while empty cans of beer accumulated in his truck bed. He spoke of vague plans, old scores to settle—the whole syndrome. Though concerned for the fate of the ranch, I had to accept that it was no longer my responsibility. I had put in my time there, had done my part. But still I cared for the Rocking L, and was worried.

Lying in my sleeping bag one morning, watching the sun illuminate the desert sky, I was suddenly startled to see Mr. Patrick standing in the door of the apartment. In his hand was a steaming cup of coffee, which he put on the chair next to my boots. "Pull yerself together, Mr. Dayton," he said. "We're goin' fer a mornin' ride. Horses are saddled and waitin'." Willow and Mr. Patrick and I had stayed up too late the night before and downed many beers. But now he seemed fresh and eager. When I stepped outside I saw two little mustangs ready to go. Willow was atop a third, riding bareback. Mr. Patrick swung into the saddle of his horse and handed me the reins of mine, a gray stallion I didn't much like the looks of. I suspected some mischief was afoot, a feeling that was not allayed when Mr. Patrick commented, "Hope you're wide awake, Mr. Dayton. He may buck a bit on you." Then he and Willow rode off eastward into the sun.

One of my secret prides is that I feel I get along with animals. I think they know I like them. Twice I have had birds land on my head (well, once on my bare head and once on my hat while it was on my head). In the Nevada desert a big golden eagle landed about five feet away from where I stood, hopped around a bit, stared calmly at me and then flew off. One evening in the Colorado mountains, just as I was finishing a fresh-air dinner, I caught some movement from the corner of my eye. It was a bobcat, not more than 10 feet away. We looked at each other for several minutes. I tossed him some gristle from my steak. He ran off. Next morning the meat was untouched.

Hoping for the best but fearing the worst, I passed a few words with the gray mustang, then climbed on. I made him back up a little way, then go in a complete circle. It seemed he would respond to my commands. With more than a little relief I trotted off after Mr. Patrick and Willow. "Good mornin' fer a ride, ain't it?" said Mr. Patrick, pulling up beside me. "Figure we'll push out to Mabry's Well, see if any water's flowin'. Sound good?" I agreed and we headed on east. Willow galloped her horse in big wide circles around us. She seemed glued to that pony, her long hair flying in the wind, a feather floating in the morning sun. Mr. Patrick was considerably more grounded, with his hand resting on the pistol butt, ready for any real or imagined threat in the peaceful morning. He seemed to be in some sort of trance.

As I had expected, the flow from Mabry's Well had dried up. Only for a brief period after it was built in the 1930s had it really flowed, its now-rusted pipes then plugged into a wet mountainside. The East Mojave was considerably wetter in those days. I suggested we ride a bit farther up the draw to a small watering hole, a spot I called "The Place of Bones," because so many of them, from so many different animals, were scattered about. This was where I had found a big coyote skull, with fur still attached, which now was displayed in front of the ranch house, alongside other smaller skulls from the same place. They made a nice collection, bleaching among the cactuses. At The Place of Bones several wild burro trails converged, and numerous piles of burro shit lay upon the ground. This did not please Willow. She said the BLM was going to relocate the burros out of the area, so that only indigenous species would inhabit the desert. I said that sounded fine with me, but that I did admire the burros' ability to survive, and even thrive.

Looking at the trickle of water coming out from the rocks at The Place of Bones, Mr. Patrick said, "Seems like this oughta dry up in summer." I informed him that it did, "But back in the rocks where all those bushes grow is the real source. Those that know find it, and survive. Lots of secrets in the desert. 'Course there's competition here, and some preys on others. The Place of Bones." Mr. Patrick just grunted. I knew he would not be discovering any secrets of the desert. Seemingly uninterested in my little tour, Willow galloped off toward the ranch. After a moment or two, Mr. Patrick loped after her, not really trying to join her, just wanting to go back. I followed slowly, glad to have the desert to myself. I sensed that Mr. Patrick and Willow would soon be going their separate ways. Just another failure for him looming up. Probably a victory for her.

I took my time, moseying around quite a bit. Back at the ranch Mr. Patrick was pitching hay out for the horses. I unsaddled the little gray and turned him into the corral. He hesitated a moment, then went in for food and water. Mr. Patrick set aside his pitchfork and said, "Come on. Let's get us a cold beer. It's nearly noon." Willow was nowhere in sight. Mr. Patrick and I made our way to the ranch house porch, where he pulled two beers from the ice chest, handed me one, and plopped down into the old stuffed chair that Mr. Moore had found somewhere and lugged to the Rocking L. I sat in one of the wooden folding chairs, left over from a time that only I was still connected to. Many times had I sat in this chair by myself, staring out into the emptiness stretching toward the Mid Hills, thinking, I have all this, and yet it is not mine . . .

Sensing my contemplative mood, Mr. Patrick said, "Best quit that cogitatin' and drink that beer. Too much on the top o' the haid ain't good fer a man. Have another beer, 'cause I got something to tell y'all." I finished my can, got another from the cooler, and waited for whatever revelation Mr. Patrick had for me. He was already working on his fourth beer. His gun in its holster was lying on the little table on the porch, and his hat was hanging on a nail by the door. He looked tired and beaten down. Was it too much drinking for too many days, or worries I knew not of?

"I have a little confession to make, Mr. Dayton," he said. "That little gray mustang almost always bucks. Nothin' too bad. Jumps sideways a bit. But today he was as steady as a toy boat in a bathtub. What'd y'all do to him?" I looked at Mr. Patrick. He was sweating; the white of his forehead was glistening, and drops of perspiration were clustering on his eyebrows. "Willow said it warn't fair, gittin' a hung-over man up on that little bastard. But I just wanted to have a little fun. What'd you do to him, Mr. Dayton?"

I gazed back at this strange, flawed fellow, who came up with stunts like this for no discernible reason. He meant no harm, I supposed, but was certainly harming himself. He had the same purpose as a dust devil wandering across the desert, using itself up, into oblivion. "Waal, Mr. Patrick," I drawled, "I just told him that we were going for a morning ride, and I would be pleased if he didn't buck on me. That's about it." Mr. Patrick took another swig of beer, half of which ran down his chin and onto his shirt. Failure was writ large on the man. Some people just project it.

20

The End of the Rocking L

The Rocking L Ranch, deserted and trashed.

October 1991 found me heading back once again to the Rocking L, on yet another of my great loop tours of the rural West. My base was still San Francisco, and the death of my father had left me with enough of an inheritance to continue living an unstructured life. A man could get accustomed to it, I had found. Turning off Black Canyon Road, I saw Ed Marquette's truck parked outside Gold Valley Ranch, and pulled in to catch up on the local news. The main topic of discussion turned out to be Mr. Patrick.

"That damned hippie's still down there," Ed growled, spitting on the ground for emphasis. A Montana mountain man from the old school, Ed had nothing in common with Mr. Patrick, and had despised him from the start. I was not surprised to learn that Willow had left Mr. Patrick—not for another man, but just to get away from him. Mr. Patrick had stayed on at the ranch, but had let the place go all to hell, Ed said. "Damned if he ain't made a mess of everything. Got all the damned gates locked—you'll have to walk in there to raise him. Watch that he don't shoot you, though. I've heard all sorts of damned shootin' down there. Man's crazed, if you ask me."

I drove on down to the Rocking L. The road was rougher than I remembered it being, seemed like not many vehicles had been in or out. Sure enough, the outer gate was locked, despite the BLM rule that access to public lands must be provided at all times. It seemed that Mr. Patrick's paranoia and unfriendliness outweighed his regard for the law of the open range. I left my truck and walked the mile to the ranch house in a cold wind and the rapidly falling darkness. I could see just one dim light coming from the house. I shouted out, and after a moment Mr. Patrick came to the door, gun in hand. I hoped he would not shoot first and ask questions later. But he recognized me. He drove me back to the gate and unlocked it. I then re-entered this place that I had called home, but did so with a heavy heart. The ranch was all in shambles, in worse condition than ever before. Few traces of my many months of diligent caretaking remained.

It was clear that Mr. Patrick had been drinking, probably non-stop, I figured. Wine bottles and beer cans were strewn all about, as were dirty clothes. There was dog shit on the floor. Mr. Patrick did fix me a plate of beans and rice, however. I ate it in front of the fire, while he rattled off a long list of things that were wrong with the world. Chief among them was Willow—"that bitch"—who now was living somewhere along the Colorado River and would soon be coming to take away the horses and the dogs. When she did, Mr. Patrick said, he would be leaving the ranch, too. No reason to stay. I took my sleeping bag to the apartment in the barn, and fell asleep with a mild case of depression.

The desert sun and the crisp autumn air made the world seem

a little brighter the next morning. Mr. Patrick and I took a ride on the mustangs, which helped to get the blood flowing. After lunch I told Mr. Patrick I figured I'd drive down to Needles to see a couple of people and bring back some supplies. He asked if he could come along. I said sure. Going to the truck I noticed Mr. Patrick's pistol, a hog-leg six-shooter, half-hidden under his ragged jacket. He seemed to be packing that gun all the time now. I asked if he thought he would be needing his pistol in Needles. He mumbled back an incoherent answer, something about that if we were stopped I could say he was just a hitchhiker. I let it go at that. I didn't want to provoke him, and I didn't really think he was dangerous.

At a fork in the road I paused. I usually took the back way into Needles, down through Lanfair Valley and Goffs. Longer but more interesting, with hawks and an occasional coyote. But with Mr. Patrick for company I opted for the shorter route, south on Black Canyon Road. As usual, there were no other vehicles. A few miles out we bounced over the cattle guard that marked the beginning of the open range. I chuckled, recalling Bob Ausmus at the Cima store telling how some city folks had once asked him if "those steel-rail devices set in the roads" were there to clean the mud off tires. We pushed on past the Hole in the Wall fire station, now abandoned for the winter. Visitors had wondered why there was a fire station out there at all. They couldn't imagine that the desert could burn, with all the sand. But there have been some mighty powerful fires leaping from bush to bush across that East Mojave country.

Some 20 miles out near the Colton Hills, halfway to the point where Black Canyon Road picks up pavement for the rest of the way into Needles, we saw a car about 100 feet off the road, apparently stuck in a wide, dry wash. This was not surprising. With some regularity the "desert specialists," as Mike Moore and I called tenderfoot tourists, would drive into those washes, not realizing how soft and sandy they were. What was unusual, however, were the two men standing outside the car. They were black men.

Black men are rare in the desert. I could not recall ever seeing any. Mexicans don't wander around in the desert, either. They know enough to keep to the towns. It was Anglos that you met poking around in the desert—and dangerous ones, too, as often as not. But these two black motorists did not look dangerous at all, just foolish and worried. One was older and one was younger, probably father and son. I stopped the truck, and they gazed at us uncertainly. Mr. Patrick jumped out. "Ya'll got a problem?" he shouted, looking like a redneck and packing a pistol! The black men flinched. This was not what they wanted to see, stranded with a disabled car on that lonely desert.

"Y'all stuck?" Mr. Patrick asked, covering the short distance to where they stood. I followed him. Nervously the young man nodded. The older man just seemed helpless. The son also seemed pissed off, like he had been driving and had made the damn-fool decision to turn into the wash, despite his daddy's warning. Now they were stuck here, with two redneck white men, one of them carrying a gun. But nothing to do but get on with it. However it had happened, here we all were, each with a part to play in this drama.

Mr. Patrick immediately took charge, assuring the men that we would have them back on the road in no time. They relaxed slightly, but did not drop their guard. After studying the situation Mr. Patrick grabbed the shovel that I carry in my truck and started digging around the car's imbedded tires. The men offered to help, but there was nothing for them to do. Soon Mr. Patrick had cut a slope behind both of the rear-wheel-drive tires. Into one of the holes we put a piece of plywood that I happened to have in the truck. Into the other we shoved some old carpeting. In the desert, you learn to use what you have.

While three of us pushed, the young man goosed the gas pedal. Inch by inch the car lurched backward, and suddenly the wheels took purchase on firmer ground. In just a minute or two it was back out on the road, none the worse for this little misadventure. Mr. Patrick was mightily pleased with himself. He had effusively directed the operation, and it had been a success. This was probably the first effective thing he had done in weeks. I did not begrudge him his moment of glory. He needed all of those he could get.

By now the black men realized that we would do them no harm, and they thanked us for our help. Each gave thanks in a different way, however. The old man's manner was old-fashioned, self-deprecating, subservient. He said "sir" a lot to the redneck cowboys who had dug him out. The young man was thankful in a more restrained, sullen and embarrassed way. He seemed uncomfortable to have gotten himself into a predicament that left him beholden to white men's knowledge, abilities and equipment. I wondered, but did not ask, what had brought these men into the desert. Maybe they were tourists, who had drifted down from Las Vegas. More likely the young man was in the military, stationed at one of the numerous installations scattered all through the Mojave.

For just a moment the young man caught my eye, and a flash of communication passed between us. Yes, his father was an old fool, he seemed to acknowledge, and my companion was a young but useful fool. Meanwhile, the two of us were just caught up in the situation, each a bit burdened by the man riding with us. How much better it would have been if he and I had met under positive and neutral circumstances, instead of these. Maybe I was just projecting that message, but that's the way it seemed to me. Still basking in his role, Mr. Patrick had a parting admonition. "Well now, you fellows better take care out here in the desert, y'heah?" he said, with enough of a country-boy inflection to make the old man almost say "Yassuh" and the young man almost roll his eyes.

Nobody got shot in Needles. Mr. Patrick felt real good about himself all the rest of the day, and the next day as well, when we drove over to Nipton, Nevada, to buy him some lottery tickets. He just might spend the winter in Flagstaff, in a tent, Mr. Patrick told me, as we crossed the desert. Or he might go back to the Black Range in southern New Mexico, he said over another dinner of rice and beans. He had liked the Black Range. "Renegade country," he called it. All his plans were unfocused and unrealistic, and I knew that whatever road he took would be a dead end. I saw him driving aimlessly in his battered pickup, turning up somewhere.

Not until a year later did I come back to the Rocking L. Ed Marquette was still hanging on at Gold Valley Ranch. He had heard something about Mr. Patrick being over in Oatman, Arizona, but really didn't know and didn't care, as long as that "damned hippie" was gone from this territory. Bill Lesher had given up on his dream, and was negotiating to sell the ranch to the BLM. He had asked me if I wanted to buy it, at a "big discount," for $175,000. Deborah nudged me to accept, saying the Rocking L could be a retreat for "all of us." I was not sure whom she meant. I considered the proposition. But I realized I did not want to live there full-time, nor hire an endless string of caretakers. Such a hassle. I declined. So Lesher had put the place on the market, for $250,000.

A few prospective buyers came around to look at it. I was there when one of them did, accompanied by a real estate agent. As the fellow gazed across the Rocking L's vast emptiness, I overheard him say, "This would be great for 40-acre lots." I groaned to myself. Not that, not that for this place that was part of my life. I asked Willow if the BLM might want to acquire the Rocking L. She said maybe. So I suggested to Lesher that he contact the Feds. He did, and ultimately sold the Rocking L to them, for his asking price of $250,000. The BLM had no use for the place, except to make it rangeland. But to me, that was a far better alternative than "ranchettes."

From Gold Valley Ranch I drove on over to the Rocking L. The gates were open again, the buildings unlocked. The ranch house had been given a quick once-over by desert vandals who apparently didn't find much to take, nor much need to do any damage. Some photographs of Mr. Patrick and Willow, in happier times, were scattered among the whiskey bottles. I found traces of me, too: a pair of my old boots, a tattered shirt that I had left for Mr. Patrick to wear. Amid the disorder I sat in Old Mr. Moore's stuffed chair on the porch, gazing out toward the peaceful Mid Hills, thanking God that even Mr. Patrick couldn't fuck them up.

I remembered better and more ordered times at the ranch, relaxing on the porch, listening to cattle bawling on the range. I remembered the boss—Big Bill Lesher—rolling with in with steaks and whiskey, and Mike Moore working on his petroglyphs, which he learned how to make look almost as authentic as the ancient Indians'. I remembered Deborah cooking lemon chicken for Bob and Irene Ausmus, and Bob laughing deep into the night, until 1 a.m. I remembered looking at the water pump, and realizing I could not fix it. I remembered the Christmas party, and nine or 10 or maybe even 20 of the guests. I recalled them clearly. But the others—what were their names, what were their names?

21

The Ghosts of Galeyville

John Galey at his home in Neosho, MO.

nly about 650 miles, give or take a hundred, depending on which roads I chose, separated the Rocking L from the former mining town of Bisbee, in the far southeastern corner of Arizona. Bisbee is where my friend Lionel Alves, or Dr. Avis as I call him in my nickname-prone way, went to live when he had had enough of the Bay Area. Thus Bisbee, the seat of big, sprawling Cochise County, became a standard part of my tour during the years in which I watched the Rocking L fade from bright dream into dull memory. Surely I would not find myself within a thousand miles of Dr. Avis without going to visit him, as I did in the fall of 1991.

Bisbee is charming, quaint and sturdy, and vertical to a significant degree, with homes and stores and other structures charging right up the sides of the steep slopes where the town sprang into being when huge deposits of copper were discovered late in the 19th century, just in time for the Electrical Age. Like Cripple Creek, Colorado, Bisbee has a rich history as a mining camp; but now the mines are closed, and, again like Cripple Creek, Bisbee has been drawn into the theme-park mentality of the "New Recreational West." It even attracts refugees from Cripple Creek. Art galleries and bed-and-breakfast inns have proliferated in Bisbee's old buildings, and the formidable outdoor stairways that once were the bane of delivery boys are now the site of an annual "2,000 Steps" uphill climb. Even so, with just 6,500 residents, Bisbee retains its own identity and is still better than most places in the West. I always enjoy my visits there with the good Doctor.

When I went to see him in 1991, however, Bisbee was not my primary destination. A town that no longer existed was. That town was Galeyville, Arizona, first brought to my attention by my old friend John Galey from Neosho, Missouri, on the edge of the Ozark Mountains. In this quiet, very American town of 10,000 people, John lived in his parents' house, a Greek Revival/Victorian place hidden by the trees. He made his living by doing odd jobs, painting signs and selling an occasional artistic painting. In his spare time he worked on a strange outdoor sculpture in his large back yard. He called it *Jardin de Sueños,* Spanish for "Garden of Dreams." It was a network of intricate wooden pillars, between which were carved wooden representations of periods of his family's history. One was of an oil derrick, with the engraved word "Spindletop." Another was of a mine headframe, with a crossed pick and shovel, and the carved word "Galeyville."

John's grandfather, who also bore the name John Galey, was a geologist and mining engineer from Pittsburgh. An early oil wildcatter, he discovered some of the biggest fields in the Southwest. He and his partner founded the Gulf Oil Company in Texas, but sold out to bigger interests while the company was in its infancy. In the 1880s John's grandfather got involved in some Western mining ventures. He prospected in southeastern Arizona, in the Chiracahua Mountain region, and purchased several promising silver prospects. With capital from Pittsburgh he developed a mine and smelter, and a town called Galeyville popped up around them. For a little while the mine and town flourished, and people flocked there for both employment and entertainment.

In its heyday, Galeyville had no fewer than seven saloons. The place was briefly notorious as a hangout for outlaws and rustlers, who amused themselves by shooting at various things, including cigars in miners' mouths and the shoes of tenderfeet. Among the best-known outlaws were Curly Bill Brocius and Johnny Ringo, who moved on to fame, or at least notoriety, a little farther west in Tombstone, where Western legend says they ran afoul of Wyatt Earp and Doc Holliday. But in less than two years Galeyville went from *bonanza,* a Spanish word meaning sudden wealth, to *borrasca,* another Spanish word that literally means a storm or tempest, but in mining terminology means a played-out vein. That is what happened to Galeyville. Attempts to procure ore from new mines did not work out, and the company became insolvent. The town's post office, which opened on Jan. 6, 1881, closed on May 31, 1882. Mr. Galey borrowed money to pay off his debts, and turned to oil exploration. And Galeyville ceased to exist.

As was often the case with suddenly defunct mining camps, people dismantled the abandoned town's buildings to use the materials for structures elsewhere. A vast silence descended on the site, among the oaks and pines on the east side of the Chiracahua Mountains. There were no more mining booms in that country, where the spirits of Geronimo and Cochise still hover over the lonely ranges rising from the Sonoran Desert. The name Galeyville is noted in books about ghost towns in Arizona, but on the site of the town itself, now on private property, only a historical plaque is said to be there.

When I told my Missouri friend John Galey that I was going to be in Bisbee, less than 100 miles from where Galeyville used to stand, he asked if I could go up there and maybe take some photographs. He had never been there himself, but was fascinated by his grandfather's mining exploits. I proposed to Dr. Avis that we make a day-trip out to Galeyville. He agreed, and on a fine spring morning off we drove in my pickup.

Our first stop was the border town of Douglas, 25 miles southeast of Bisbee. Unlike the prettified Bisbee, Douglas is a *real* place, with more than a hint of rawness and even an ominous feel. Its sister city, on the other side of the Mexican border, also has a touch of the sinister about it. Its name is *Agua Prieta*, which means "dark water." We had lunch in the old Gadsden Hotel, a "museum by the side of the road" if ever there was one, with its ornate copper-and-stained-glass dome above the lobby, its bar with cattle brands on the wall, the old Anglo men in white shirts and broad-brimmed hats playing dominoes in the lobby, the old Mexican man waiting at the creaky elevator for the few-and-far-between occasional guests. The Gadsden Hotel was not busy. Tourists these days avoid Douglas, with its "drug-and-border" syndrome. They prefer Bisbee.

From Douglas the road turned north and east through dry, empty country, and followed the tracks of the old El Paso & Arizona Railroad. After about an hour we stopped in the wide-spot-in-the-road town of Rodeo, just over the New Mexico line, for gas and perhaps some information. The pleasant young woman in the combination gas station and country store seemed chipper and modern, alert and energized, despite the isolation and somnolent atmosphere of Rodeo. But when I asked about Galeyville, said my friend's grandfather had founded it and we wanted to have a look, she turned serious.

"Well," she said, "it's up there, all right, but I don't think you want to go poking around. The fellow who owns that property now, I'd have to say he's unhinged—you know, mentally off. He patrols around on a horse with a shotgun. There's been some incidents with the Forest Service. He's shot at people. He's dangerous. I'm afraid somebody's going to get hurt one day. No, I wouldn't mess with that place if I was you."

Her words gave Dr. Avis and me pause, but we pressed on. In the little town of Portal, back now on the Arizona side, we stopped for coffee, and to ask more questions about Galeyville. "Oh, there's nothing up there now, it's just a site, nothing left," said the woman at the register. "I wouldn't go poking around there, though. Fellow owns that property is a dangerous man. No, I don't advise you to go near to that place." By now Dr. Avis had a look of alarm on his face. "That's two of them said the same thing," he muttered, back in the truck. "Some nut up there with guns. Must be something to it. Maybe we had better forget the whole thing." It took some doing, but I persuaded him to at least drive up and take a look from the road.

We headed into the Chiracahua Mountains, climbing through oak country, then turned toward Paradise, a dot on the map. We knew that Galeyville was just a mile or so beyond that point. The road turned to dirt, and on it we passed a crew of Hispanic men doing drainage work for Cochise County. Paradise was nothing but a small cluster of trucks and houses, some occupied, some not. Outside one stood a couple of furtive-looking individuals in camouflage gear. I waved at one of them, a big, burly man, and he nodded slightly. In the rearview mirror I saw him turn to study our license plate. I hoped that New Mexico—and the fact that Dr. Avis and I were wearing cowboy hats—would be okay. We passed through more dry woodland, then into a draw where a small stream flowed alongside the road. To the left was a sign that said "Site of Galeyville," and a fence with a locked gate. A little-used road disappeared into the woods beyond the gate. "Well, this is it!" I announced to the Doctor. "Galeyville! I'm getting out to take a leak."

Dr. Avis looked nervous, but did not try to dissuade me. To tell the truth, I was not all that comfortable myself. I left the engine running, and by the time I came back from the bushes the Doctor was downright agitated. "Let's get out of here!" he said. "Don't take any pictures or anything. I don't like this place!" In his vivid imagination the nut was crouched behind an oak, drawing a bead on us with his shotgun. Maybe he was. Not wanting to let John Galey down, I did take a picture of the sign from the relative safety of the truck cab. Then I noticed a small sign on the gate. "Brooks White," it said. Rising from the ground next to the gate was a lettered stake, indicating an underground telephone cable. "Well, I'll be damned," I said to the Doctor. "Maybe Old Brooks has a telephone. We'll just have to look that up."

"Yeh, yeh, yeh," huffed the Doctor. "But let's get going!" I put the truck in gear and we slipped away from the silent, scary site of Galeyville. In Paradise the same burly, camouflaged man was standing by his truck, but his companion was gone. I did not wave this time, and the man did not nod. He did look mighty suspicious, though. Or was that just my imagination? Dr. Avis was slumped down in his seat, like he was trying to make a smaller target. Not until we passed the road crew again and got back on the pavement did he finally relax. Never one to take a risk, Dr. Avis was a naturally cautious man.

And yet, I thought to myself in the silence that now had descended upon the truck cab, it's odd. Down South of the Border, in Old Mexico, I am the one who gets nervous in awkward situations, while Dr. Avis, who has spent much time down there, is quite at ease. I recalled a time when I and Dr. Avis and his friend Steven were in a bar in Naco, Sonora, just across the border from Bisbee. Steven, who had lived many years in Mexico and spoke the colloquial Border Spanish perfectly, had suggested we stop for a beer or two, but said we should be sure to leave before dark, "because things sometimes get funny in these places." That was almost enough to quench my thirst for beer, but I didn't let on. While the Doctor and I drank our brews in the back of the cantina, Steven was up conversing with the bartender, a big, powerful man who kept looking at me. I figured they were enjoying a joke at my expense. I just hoped it did not lead to trouble. I was ready to go. Finally Steven rejoined us. "The bartender paid you a compliment," he said.

"Yeah, yeah," I replied. "Some gringo joke, no doubt."

"No," Steven said. "He told me, 'Your friend looks like the Sheriff of Tombstone.' They are serious when they say things like that. It really is a compliment." I looked over at the bartender, and he smiled back at me. Well, maybe so. Maybe my big hat and big Pancho Villa mustache and my tall Anglo frame had indeed made a positive impression on the fellow. To him I was *un hombre grande del Norte*—a big, strong, gringo cowboy.

I recalled a time in the St. Elmo Bar in Bisbee, when a heavyset Hispanic man kept buying me beers. "I'm Mendez," he introduced himself. "I'm with Corrections in southern Arizona. But guys like you!" He clapped me on the back. "Guys like YOU! You are the backbone of the

West." I figured he had seen too many cowboy movies. I knew he had had too many beers. But nevertheless, it was an indication of something he felt.

And then there was the sleazy redneck in Bisbee, lounging on the sidewalk outside a tourist-junk shop he evidently owned, who made insulting remarks, low and under his breath, but loud enough to be heard, whenever Dr. Avis walked alone by him. The Doctor would simply walk on, ignoring the slurs. "But when I am with you," Dr. Avis told me, "there isn't a peep out of him. He doesn't even look up." Well, I decided to test the fellow. The next time we passed, I looked at the man and said, "Asshole," hoping for a response. He was silent, eyes averted. I guess I was wanting an excuse to "kick his ass," as the Doctor's usually drunk Apache friend Phillip would advise. That might have gotten me into trouble, but I think the people of Bisbee would understand. "Asshole," I repeated, again drawing no reaction. The man got the message, Dr. Avis reported to me later. The insults ceased immediately. Yes, we all vacillate between courage and fear in one situation or another, I suppose.

With Galeyville now miles behind us the tension in the pickup cab eased. We pushed on up past 8,000 feet, and there we found a new cause for concern. At a deserted campground the Forest Service had posted warning signs about bears, with the message, in large letters, that bears can be DANGEROUS! Well, it's true, and we knew there had been several recent sightings. But it didn't worry Dr. Avis or me nearly as much as the "gun nut" up at Galeyville had.

Nor did the bear warning seem to bother some Anglos we came upon while descending the western slopes of the Chiracahuas. With their funny hats and expensive binoculars they could only be birdwatchers, drawn by the astonishing 300-plus species that nest in or visit the region. We chuckled at these nice-looking, well-educated and sensitive folks, who looked like they had never entered a bar in Mexico and never would, and would probably not survive a riot in the cities where they lived. And yet, even their presence here in this semi-wilderness was a bolder statement than many of their urban friends might ever make. Everyone has his own threshold for "danger."

When we met for lunch the next day, Dr. Avis said he had done some research that morning in the Cochise County Courthouse. "That fellow who owns Galeyville, Brooks White. Sounds like a member of the Merion Cricket Club, doesn't he? Well, he does have a telephone, and it's listed. And my friends at the courthouse all know who he is. He comes in from time to time to file papers, deeds, that sort of stuff. They confirmed that he is some kind of a recluse. According to my friends, this is his story:

"Seems Mr. White was a fireman, in Phoenix, I think, and got burned and disfigured in a fire where something went very wrong and the city was liable. He sued them and got a big settlement, which he used to buy that Galeyville property. They say he is a bitter, angry man, and that he does ride around with a gun and has taken potshots at the Forest Service guys, and maybe at other people, too. Nobody has gotten hurt, as far as my friends know, but they're afraid that someday somebody will. That's about all there is to it. You have to admit, it *was* sort of spooky up there. Tell your friend John he can call or write this man Brooks White if he wants to. But I don't think I'll be looking him up."

I decided not to, either. I did write John and told him what we had found out. He wrote back, thanked us for going up there, and said, "Well, that sounds like all there is to the story." I'm sure he looked no further into it. But I do still wonder about Galeyville. The stories that swirl around it really never end. There is more fiction than fact in them, I'll wager.

One fairly reliable historian reports that Johnny Ringo was seen in the dying town of Galeyville late on the night of July 9, 1882, depressed and drinking heavily. By July 11 he was gone. Then on July 14 he was found slumped against a tree outside town, a .45-caliber Colt in his hand and a gunshot wound in his right temple. He was buried at the spot. Some said it was a suicide, others that Wyatt Earp had tracked him down and killed him. His horse was not at the scene, but was found a couple of weeks later, still saddled.

The stories about Curly Bill Brocius are more colorful and more vague. Known as "Arizona's Most Famous Outlaw" after gunning down Tombstone marshal Fred White, he used several aliases, and now no one knows where he came from or where he went. One story says he committed suicide somewhere. Another says his suicide was faked, that in reality he was a wealthy Easterner, a graduate of Harvard no less, who came west under an assumed name to live the life of an outlaw—rather successfully, it must be said—then returned to Pennsylvania to resume his place in society and head his family's steel business. One story says he discovered fabulous silver mines in Chihuahua.

In moments of imagination I like to picture Curly Bill sitting down with Mr. John Galey, in a frame house under the oak trees in the boom town of Galeyville, a bottle before them, swapping stories about Pennsylvania and people they knew in common back there, before both of them headed west to seek their destinies. I see Curly Bill roaring drunk, shooting out the kitchen lamp and shouting, "I have larceny and homicide in my blood! It's my Celtic heritage!" And Mr. Galey smiling to himself in the darkened kitchen, liking Curly Bill in spite of everything and wondering where it all would lead.

But this is for Mr. Galey's grandson, my friend John from Neosho, Missouri, to sort out, if anyone ever does. Should he undertake that task, I imagine John would get considerable help from the mysterious Brooks White, who, like Curly Bill, seems to have gathered quite a bit of legend around him. Despite the rumors of burnings and shootings, which I now think are probably highly exaggerated if not downright fabrications, I have learned that Brooks White is the author of a most respectable book, about the town site that he owns. "Galeyville, Arizona Territory 1880: Its History and Historic Archaeology" the book is titled. I have acquired a copy. It is a serious work, from a serious man. My guess is that the prickly shooter up there was a caretaker or a squatter, not Brooks White.

Like Curly Bill and old Mr. Galey before them, in the vivid imagery of my mind, John and Brooks could sit under the oaks in the moonlight, drink their drinks, listen to the far-off singing of coyotes and hooting of owls in the Chiricahua Mountains, and trade tales about the invisible town stretching down the hillside at their feet—the fabulous silver town of Galeyville, Arizona, now populated in its entirety by people who are no more.

PART IV

THE LOST COUNTRY

Starting Points

The winds that blow
across the faded map
are not the cold winds
of Colorado mountain winter,
they are not the shriveling
winds of the Black Rock Desert—
they are winds of thought,
blowing from a printed jumble
of things needing arrangement,
order different from the
wrinkled landscape seen
from the airship window.
We must take this map
and lay it out with others,
tracing the winds of thought
inward to their sources,
the starting point of journeys
across strange-colored sage
plains into darkness
always swelling up over
the ever-distant mountains,
journeys of vague purpose
toward spots lifted from
murky currents of thought.
Hidden on the map are
things submerged in time,
points of no return,
layered in among mountains,
the twisting rivers and
widely separated towns,
thick space of one-way travel.
The maps, once full of promise,
carried no warnings.
They were of freedom,
no winds of thought
rippled from them.
Now they are full
of spots never reached,
they rustle in the evening
winds blowing out of darkness.

22

The Trail Leads to Santa Fe

Dayton's *casita* in the South Capitol area of Santa Fe,
one of the last "bargains" in that traditional area.

Downtown Santa Fe has all the integrity of an airline terminal, although it is far more attractive. Does the visitor
realize that the longtime residents have been pushed aside,
and no longer feel welcome in what was once the heart and
soul of the community their ancestors founded almost 400 years ago?
I don't think many visitors are aware of that. No, they see only this
materialistic mirage that has been created for their amusement—for

above all, the tourist must be amused, kept busy, provided with things to buy.

Santa Fe is where I live now, and have since 1992. As with the Rocking L, my friend Deborah led the way. Her artist's love of the desert, combined with her sociable need to live somewhere more populated than the East Mojave, caused her to choose Santa Fe, also in 1992, six months before I came, bringing with her the good cat Zephyr, the last of the ferals from the Rocking L. I, in the meantime, was growing restless in San Francisco. I was not employed there. After my father's estate was settled, I inherited the proceeds from his selling first *El Rancho Piedra Gorda* and then his home in Pacific Palisades. I also had a nest egg of my own, from my time as director of the Sonoma County Museum. I ran some figures and calculated that I did not have to get a job if I did not want to—and I did not want to. But I didn't know what I did want to do.

When I was on the road the answers to these questions seemed not to matter, so I was on the road a lot. But back in the Bay Area, question marks kept arising. In 1992 one of my grand loop tours of the West brought me to Santa Fe, to visit Deborah. She pointed out that a small house just a block from hers, on West Houghton Street in the attractive but unpretentious South Capitol neighborhood, was for sale. It turned out to be a real deal, one of the last in the city's ever-escalating housing market. I bought it on the spot, and thus became a Santa Fean. In the years since then, I have thought a great deal about the town I now call home.

The tourist steps out of his pricey downtown hotel—La Fonda, perhaps, or the Inn of the Anasazi—strolls across the Plaza, and doesn't have an inkling that the handsome, mud-brown, two-story buildings surrounding him are not the real thing. Instead they are "mock adobe," in proper "Santa Fe style." Hiding behind this façade are sturdy, red-brick Victorian structures, erected at the turn of the last century, when Santa Fe, the capital of the United States Territory of New Mexico, was energetically trying to charge ahead into the modern era. Not until an economic downtown in the 1920s did Santa Fe seize upon the idea that tourism would be its salvation, that the old things should be "re-created."

When I eat downtown at the Plaza Café, almost all the other patrons are tourists, many of them studying real-estate brochures. Virtually all the downtown stores are expensive, tony ones for tourists. Santa Fe has 150 art galleries, most of which line Canyon Road cheek by jowl, offering in many cases a most dubious smorgasbord of "Southwestern art." Some tourists come here on a higher level, doing something with the museums and institutes of sociology and anthropology, several of which exist to "study" the Native American. Visitors at that level may indeed realize what has happened here, what they are caught up in. In that case, they might as well relax and enjoy themselves.

Still, we must realize that tourism, modern "industrial tourism"—in a phrase coined by the late maverick writer Edward Abbey—is incompatible with a strong, stable and egalitarian community. Tourism creates a false environment that caters to a constant stream of strangers, while the inhabitants are reduced to what has been called "the new slavery of tourism." If a community has absolutely no other way to earn a living, then tourism must be tolerated as a necessary evil. But certainly it is more desirable to develop a strong local economy that provides good, stable jobs and enables people to retain their independence and character, so that they do not have to sell out to the role of amusing tourists and waiting on them. The saving grace in Santa Fe is that the city is also the state capital of New Mexico. There are more government jobs here, in fact, than tourism jobs. But only a few more. Sometimes it is said that the Santa Fe economy stands on three legs: government, tourism and "everything else."

For the most part, tourism profits accrue to the rich and powerful, who often are outsiders, while locals get the crumbs. They are sold the notion that the endlessly circulating tourism dollar brings good things; and before they realize it, they have traded away their community. This is happening in Santa Fe. Lately the pace of change has been exacerbated by the influx of wealthy persons from California and New York, drawn to Santa Fe because of its romantic aura, beautiful vistas, manageable size and cultural life. The *arrivistes* drive around town in their BMWs, Mercedes and Land Rovers, stirring anger and resentment among locals who have been pushed aside. Much ill will is directed toward the wealthy newcomers.

And I guess I am one of them. Sort of. Not wealthy but comfortable. Nor am I really a newcomer, having moved here in 1992. But it takes a while before you stop being a newcomer in Santa Fe. People who moved here in the 1970s tell me that that was the "golden age," when everybody got along, when the living was easy and cheap. Others say the golden age was the 1950s, or even the 1930s. "Everybody wants to be the last person to move to Santa Fe" is heard often around here, and it's largely true. I wish I had been.

I just try to blend in. The last thing I want to do is flaunt what modest amount of financial comfort I have. Not even back East had that ever appealed to me; and by now I am thoroughly westernized, shaped by the region's bleakest, most isolated country, and drawn, always, to what few remaining authentic places remain. I have nothing against the dependable electricity, heat and water in my Santa Fe house, nor, for that matter, against the city's abundant cultural opportunities. I appreciate these things. But a cool, lonely campsite in the mountains and the endless, open road—I enjoy those things too.

I work hard not to act like the arrogant and insensitive intruders who make so many people in this town seethe. My little house—*mi casita*—is a modest one, although nice enough, in a neighborhood about half Anglo and half Hispanic. My neighbors are quiet people who smile and wave, and are polite and helpful. My appearance, I admit, is knowingly Old West, with blue jeans, work shirt, down vest in the winter, handlebar mustache and always some kind of hat.

My vehicle is a two-seater Ford Ranger pickup, which I don't use much. Most days I walk everywhere I have to go. Santa Fe is a good town for walking, although relatively few do so. I have met a few people walking, but somehow thought there would be more. There are several pleasant routes to choose from. Some go through the eastern foothills and end up on the Plaza, if one so chooses—or not, if one wishes to avoid the tourists and the shops laden with trivia. The shoppers at Wal-Mart on the south side of town reveal another side of Santa Fe, and the contrast could not be greater. At Wal-Mart I found a fine winter cap for $6.95. Something similar would cost $30 or more downtown. The one I found at Wal-Mart serves me just fine.

Occasionally I take the truck and wander off into areas of New Mexico that are not fashionable—the *real* parts of the state, I call them. As much as possible I avoid New Mexico's one large city, Albuquerque. To me it is an incipient Los Angeles, with vast room to spread out over the Western landscape. Like L.A., it is completely automobile-oriented, and like so much of America it is materially well-off without much character.

At night I sit by the fire, read, "work on my papers," as my father used to say, and think about things. Once in a while I go downtown at night, to La Fonda to hear funky Western swing, or to Evangelo's Bar, where the young, shouting crowd reminds me of other places, other times. Mostly, though, I am content to stay home by the fire. The blue skies and whitened mountain peaks are peaceful, timeless. When warm winds blow I'll get restless and search out some hidden Western spots I've marked on my map, still-empty places that need discovering, or returning to.

I never have regretted moving here, and probably will stay. On balance, we are lucky here. Santa Fe is peaceful, and has only 65,000 residents. Some people, accustomed to excitement and energies larger and more complex, find it boring. Still, there is enough sophisticated diversion to, as my father used to say, "keep your spoon in." Occasionally at night I hear sirens, indicating disorder out there. There is a graffiti problem here, and the city has a special squad to come around and paint over it. Some fellows nearby were drinking beer in the street the other day and left cans lying about. I figured to pick them up the next day—no big deal—but when I looked, the cans were gone.

On my first Christmas Eve in Santa Fe I went to the Festival of the Luminarias, joining the crowds walking up Canyon Road amid the streets and buildings decorated with thousands of flickering *farolitos* (candles set in sand inside brown paper bags) and dozens of blazing *luminarias* (bonfires on the ground). It was lovely, and I felt privileged to take part in this northern New Mexico tradition. At midnight on New Year's Eve two loud reports shattered the stillness outside my house. My beer-drinking *compadres* firing a shotgun at the sky, I supposed. It put me in mind of the East Mojave, the Rocking L, and the pistol shots I had lofted into the dark New Year's sky, waking up Old Mr. Moore.

And then, from out of nowhere came a different memory, of an old Army sergeant I once knew, who was at the Chosin Reservoir in South Korea in 1950, when hordes of padded, bugle-blowing Chinese Communists came howling out of the star-bright, 20-below night, firing their World War II Russian submachine guns. The old GI never forgot this devastating defeat, or the torturous retreat that followed. Suddenly I was thinking that if you were stranded out there somewhere, thinking you were about to die, you would dream of seeing the Festival of the Luminarias just one more time, just one more time.

I don't know what made me think of that. Maybe the combination of the holidays, the coldness, the gunshots in the night. I don't know. Yes, Santa Fe has its share of problems, I thought. But those of us who live here are lucky, my friends. Very lucky.

23

Spanish Gold and Silver

Many an old prospector explored the deserts of The Bootheel,
looking for "Catholic treasure."

On an early-summer evening, with thunderstorms building over the Sangre de Cristo Mountains, I was in Evengelo's Bar at the corner of Galisteo and San Francisco streets in Santa Fe, drinking beer with my California friend Ted Roberts. I felt a tap on my shoulder. A stranger was handing me a bottle of Miller Light, which was what I was drinking. He smiled, urging me to accept. I set the bottle on the bar, nodding "Thanks." I studied the man, who perhaps had earned some conversation with this gesture. He was a rugged-looking older guy, maybe in his late 60s. Not exactly the sort that needs to strike up talks with strangers in bars. With him was a much younger, good-looking woman.

He pointed to my hat and said, "I like your hat. You look like a man who knows about the West." I was wearing what some people call "an old miner's hat," the crown shaped into four creases, like some fellows up in the Klondike in 1898 used to wear. I wondered where all this might be leading. "Waal, I know a few things," I said, "but not too much." The man said he was from Chicago and had spent quite a few years in the West looking for lost gold mines. He fixed a look on me and asked, "You know anything about any lost gold? Old mines, buried treasure?"

So he thinks I'm some fucking prospector, I thought, wants to hear tales of "the real thing." Ted was grinning, knowing I am seldom at a loss for a story when the other guy is buying. But somehow I liked the look of this fellow, young girlfriend and all. Whatever he was after, I didn't think he was after bullshit. I told him that all I knew was from the literature on the subject, such as the book about the gold suppos-edly buried on Victorio Peak on the atomic-bomb test range down at White Sands, gold repeatedly looked for but never found. I had heard about things like that.

"You ever have any personal exposure to any of those stories?" he probed.

"Only once," I replied, and told him this tale:

One blustery December evening in 1978 we were camped on the desert in the New Mexico Bootheel, close to the Mexican border, three friends from Cripple Creek, Colorado: me, John Jaccard and Old Mr. Moore. We had just finished a meager dinner when we saw headlights in the distance, approaching us. Nothing to do but stand up, warily, and watch. We were well off the dirt road, hidden in the mesquite, so we thought. Perhaps the Border Patrol wanted to check something.

But it was a battered old pickup that pulled up, with a hunting dog in its bed. The driver was a bearded man in his 30s. Seemed friendly.

"Howdy, fellows," he said. "What y'all doin' down here? Jest like the desert?" We told him that was about it, we were just some old boys coming back from a little vacation in Mexico. Seeing our Colorado license plate, he seemed satisfied. "Kinda cool," he said. "It's usually warmer than this. My ranch is way yonder on the far side of the valley. Three generations we been there." He pointed. Far in the distance was a single faint light. "Wife teaches up at Lordsburg, drives the school bus in and back. Longest route in the state, maybe in the country. Just a few kids here and there."

We relaxed and invited him to have a beer. He accepted, got out of the truck, set his dog loose from the bed, and stood with us by the fire. "I been out chasin' wild pigs," he said. "Peccaries?" I asked. "No," he said, "feral pigs, ones that run off from these ranches years ago. There's a bunch of 'em in this valley. My dog Copper runs 'em 'longside the truck and I drop a weighted canvas over 'em. Got a bunch penned up back at the ranch. Pretty good eatin'."

In the desert silence my friends and I pictured a large wild pig struggling under a weighted canvas. Then the fellow pointed at the tallest mountain to the west, in the Animas Range, still visible against the afterglow. "Catholic treasure up there," he said. "Yep, gold and silver bars stamped with crosses, from the Spanish mines at Santa Rita. They was takin' this stuff down to Old Mexico when the Injuns got after them, chased them up yonder mountain. They buried their stuff in a cave up there so they could travel lighter, crossed down the other side and escaped into Mexico. Died somewhere down in Sonora, never came back. No one else knew about the stuff, I reckon."

We were quiet, wondering. Finally John Jaccard asked, "So how do you know about it?'

"Well," the fellow smiled. "That's what my grandpappy always said. Heard about it from an old guy that one time showed some silver bars over to Hillsboro, with the crosses stamped in them and everything."

"You ever been up there looking for stuff?" John asked. He was getting interested.

"Oh, sure," the fellow said, with a certain finality. "Years back I poked around a bit, then gave up. It's an awful dern rough old mountain. Mebbe the stuff is up there, mebbe it ain't." He smiled some more in the firelight. "Best be getting' on, fellows. Thanks fer the beer. You boys keep yer fire down, there's armed men ridin' out here fer the big outfits, don't take kindly to strangers camped on their land." We said we thought we were on BLM land. "Not on the valley floor, you ain't. If you're worried, git up into them mountains a bit. Mebbe you'll find some treasure." He chuckled getting into his truck. Copper jumped into the bed, and they headed off toward the dim point of light on the other side of the valley. The desert was dark and windless.

The mountain he had pointed to was a lump on the horizon. We stirred the coals of the fire. "Catholic treasure, boys," I said, pointing. "Maybe we oughta look around," said John. "Maybe there is lost treasure up there." "There ain't!" said Old Mr. Moore, with great finality. "Man was jest funnin' us. Heard them stories all my dern life." He stomped off to his sleeping bag. Then John went to his. I stood staring into the dying coals. The desert was still and quiet. I thought of gold and silver bars, thin ones, stamped with old-fashioned crosses, gleaming in the moonlight.

That is the story I told the man. At the conclusion he bought another round of drinks. Giving me my Miller Light, he said, "Maybe there is something up there. You never know." He looked around the crowded bar, then at his young companion. She put her arm around his waist.

Figuring he would want me to tell him the location in payment for the beers, I decided to head him off. "I met a fellow in Taos one time, told him this story," I said. "He wanted to know exactly what mountain I was talking about. Said he had a construction company, could tear that mountain apart. He was agitated—and greedy. I refused to tell him, out of general principle. I like that Bootheel country, don't want strangers poking around looking for treasure."

The man smiled patiently and said, "I have no need or desire to know. This is my last trip West. I have six months to live. Going back to Chicago to die." Then he was out the door. His friend had not said a word. He was lucky to have a woman like that.

24

The Bootheel

Mr. Moore in The Bootheel, the desert behind him stretching south into Old Mexico.

The Bootheel of New Mexico—it's one of my favorite places, despite the act that I hardly ever run into anybody who has been there. Or, more likely, because of that fact.

There are not many people down there, that's for sure. Nor is there much area to the Bootheel, only about 1,500 square miles. Some 50 miles wide and 30 deep, the Bootheel barely makes up one percent of New Mexico's total land mass, which at 121,336 square miles constitutes the nation's fifth-largest state. Running along the Arizona border and dipping down into Old Mexico, the Bootheel is in Hidalgo County, named for a Spanish title of nobility. There are only two or three paved roads in the Bootheel, and not a single community large enough to rate a spot on the map. There are some damn fine desert mountains, though, in the Animas and Alamo Hueco ranges. Black Point in the Coronado National Forest rises 6,457 feet, and both Animas Peak and Big Hatchet Peak top out at more than 8,000. The Continental Divide runs smack down the middle of the Bootheel.

As I told the inquisitive stranger in the Santa Fe bar, I first discovered the Bootheel in 1978, returning with my Cripple Creek friends from an ill-advised and non-beneficial visit to Mexico. We were slogging north on dirt roads in my truck, which this landscape was putting to the test. On the morning after the campfire visit from the pig-hunting desert rat, we did not talk of Catholic treasure. Such yarns are good enough to while away an evening now and then, I guess, but it would take even bigger fools than us to actually go poking around "yonder mountain" in search of bars of Spanish gold and silver, with crosses stamped in them.

The day was warm and cloudless. Four military jets came screaming down the valley at low altitude, a rude intrusion of the modern world. We packed up and headed first north then west on a dirt road that appeared to cross the mountains at a low pass. The road devolved into a streambed more or less, but was passable. John Jaccard was driving my truck, rather roughly, I thought. I told him to take it easy. "What's the matter? It's a truck, ain't it?" he responded. I didn't much care for that reply. "Yeh, it's a truck all right," I told him, "—and it's mine. I reckon I better drive it."

We crept up the streambed in the lowest gear and came to better country at the top of the pass, a wide grazing area with a windmill and water tank, and a few cattle. A primitive road headed into a draw, and on to some ranch buildings in the distance. We had no choice but to take this road, but figured we better have some explanation ready if some cowpoke wanted to know where the hell we were coming from and what we were doing. Cautiously we approached the ranch, coming first to a large barn and some wooden sheds. No one seemed to be about, no vehicles or activity usually associated with a working ranch. Just a few dust devils struggled to get going. This was getting a little odd.

On a rise to the left, as we progressed toward the ranch house, was a large faded utility building. Spray-painted on it, rather recently it looked like, were the names "Brenda, Rhonda, Rhoda." Strange. The place was way too far out in the middle of nowhere for these names to be random graffiti. No, this had to be something about the people who lived here. If anybody still did. At the ranch house, set among large cottonwoods, nothing stirred—no people, horses, vehicles. But the place was not really rundown. If it had been abandoned, it had not been abandoned very long. The ranch-house door was wide open. John wanted to go inside, to look for interesting things to pick up, but Old Mr. Moore dissuaded him. "We don't belong here, son," Mike said. "It ain't our place to be doin' no 'exploring,' as you put it. We best be getting on outta here."

I agreed. There was something spooky about that recently abandoned ranch, something unsettling about those names spray-painted on that building. We drove on, came to a closed but not locked gate, and let ourselves out, closing the gate behind us. On it was a weathered sign saying "Godfrey Ranch" and another sign indicating that the place was "protected" by the New Mexico Cattlemen's Association. John wanted to take the signs for souvenirs, but again Mr. Moore dissuaded him.

About 10 more miles of dirt road led us out to the highway, and about 15 miles later we came upon a small store and gas station out there all by itself, just before the Animas Valley turns from honest ranching country into marginal cotton growing. We thought about going in and inquiring about the Godfrey Ranch, about Brenda, Rhonda and Rhoda. Had they ever gassed up their pickup there, or bought a six-pack of beer? But we decided not to, because—suppose there had been some "incident" out at the Godfrey Ranch, one that still needed solving? Strangers we were, and why attract attention? So we just pushed on north.

But leaving the empty country of the Bootheel we kept wondering about Brenda, Rhonda and Rhoda. Who had painted their names on that weathered building, just before they left the ranch? Were they known as "The Godfrey Girls," celebrated locally before their pappy sold out to some big spread? Old Mr. Moore rather thought so. He had a vivid imagination about things like that, buxom girls at lonely ranches. "Them Godfrey gals has gone wild," he cackled. "They was there all along, perched in them hills, watching us, bare-breasted and bronzed, all kinds of burrs and thistles in their hair. Wanting to capture us and fuck like wildcats. HA!" Yes, Mr. Moore fantasized like that.

But—who *were* Brenda, Rhonda and Rhoda, and what *was* their story?

In January of 1995 Old Mr. Moore and I drifted back into the Bootheel. John Jaccard was not with us this time. I had returned from time to time, but for Mike this was sort of a homecoming party—with most of the entertainment courtesy of the federal government. Mr. Moore and I were driving from Santa Fe to the Bootheel by way of Reserve, the seat of Catron County, one of the West's most reactionary places. At a gas station Mike picked up a flyer about some "good American citizen" being hassled in Catron County by an agency of the "So-Called U. S. Government." All "patriots" were urged to show support for this courageous brother. In Uncle Bill's Bar, labeled "the most redneck bar in New Mexico" by some alternative weekly paper in Albuquerque, were more of those flyers. Just a few men were inside, but Mr. Moore and I fit right in—a couple of "right-thinking" good ole boys, in jeans and cowboy hats, driving a New Mexico vehicle with a ranch brand on the front bumper.

When she brought our beers Mr. Moore asked the barmaid, one of those "thin Darlas" who always seem to work in such places, how the matter referred to in the flyer had worked out. I noticed that his Texas twang had become more pronounced. She said the fellow had got off, that the "government" was just harassing him. "Well," said Mr. Moore, "Ah'm awful dern glad to be hearin' that." A man to our left nodded in agreement.

Mr. Moore went on to allow as to how we were from southern

Colorado, taking a break, checking out some land and all, and maybe might push on down to a border town, Palomas, maybe. "Y'all know, jest git away fer a spell, be our damn selves." The man nodded some more. Why, surely, that's exactly what us ole boys have to do from time to time. Mr. Moore has always been real good at getting along in "white man's country."

We rolled on down to Silver City, about a three-hour roll from Reserve. Mr. Moore liked the looks of the country we were passing through, some of the least-populated in the state, wide and uncrowded, the snow-covered Mogollon Mountains rising to the east, and range land stretching toward Mexico to the south. We took rooms at the Drifter Motel, where I always stay in Silver City, and noticed in the parking lot, as always, pickup trucks with barrels of lubricants, chains, various machines—the vehicles of working men, probably with the big copper mines in the area. This was no "lah-de-da" environment. Silver City is NOT, as some try to pretend, ever going to become another Santa Fe!

With a population of about 11,000 people, an altitude of 5,900 feet, and an institution of higher learning—Western New Mexico University, which my cousin calls a "cowboy college"—Silver City is a right nice place, in my opinion. There is an interesting downtown with the usual old brick buildings, which some folks keep trying to revive into antique shops, galleries, coffeehouses, those sorts of superfluous things. But those places keep closing, while the stores that sell oiled clothing, chainsaws or a good pry-bar stay in business. Mike found Silver City interesting, but not a town he wanted to move to. We had steaks at the Red Roof Restaurant, a place of the people where I have always eaten well, then retired to our rooms.

In the local telephone book I looked up Ed Elbrock's well-digging and windmill service in Animas. On a previous visit I had talked to Mr. Elbrock while he worked on a lonely windmill close to the border. I wanted to know if had heard anything about jaguars crossing into the Bootheel out of Mexico. He laid down his tools and said, "Interesting that you ask about that. There has been some talk. Two incidents that I know of. One rancher down here said that something got after his chickens, and when he come out with a light he seen a big spotted cat jump away into the brush, way too big for a bobcat. Another fellow, he was tracking a mountain lion up in the Peloncillo Mountains, near to the border, a lion that had been bothering his cows. He heard a god-almighty row, and found his dogs all tore up, worse than any lion would do. He reckoned it had to be some cat bigger and stronger than a lion. And that would have to be jaguar. It's possible." The last known jaguar crossed over into southeastern Arizona in 1987, he said, and was promptly shot by some cowpoke.

There was a very rich Mexican rancher, Ed Elbrock went on, one Pedro Varilla (he pronounced the name with two Ls in the Anglo manner), who owned more than a million acres just south of the border, and kept most of it wild, with all sorts of stuff on it. For instance, there was a remnant buffalo herd down there, and occasionally some of those animals wandered into the U.S. and had to be herded back down, since the local ranchers did not want any buffalo on their range. It seemed entirely possible that jaguars were hiding out on that place too, Mr. Elbrock suggested. He seemed well informed, and was happy to spend time talking with an interested stranger. After a while we shook hands, and I drove off.

I knew that the old Gray Ranch, some 325,000 acres, had been sold to the Nature Conservancy and was being managed by something called the Animas Foundation as an "ecological working ranch." This made the local ranchers nervous. In the phone book I looked up the Gray Ranch, and found listings for the headquarters and numerous"camps," which were small ranches bought and absorbed into the big ranch. One listing was for a "Godfrey Camp," undoubtedly the former Godfrey Ranch that Mike, John and I had stumbled onto in 1978. I remembered that strange deserted ranch house, the three names spray-painted on one of the buildings: "Brenda, Rhonda, Rhoda." I considered ringing up Godfrey Camp and asking all sorts of questions, but decided against bothering some old boy or his wife.

Early the next morning the workingmen set out for their jobs, amid much noise and exhaust. I raised Mr. Moore and we went to the nearby café for a big breakfast. Again there was nothing effete about Silver City. The fellows in the café were miners, cowboys and some who looked like retired Texans, large men in white shirts and gray Stetson hats, plus a few guys who looked like things were not going well for them. In San Francisco they would have been homeless, huddling in doorways or under bridges. But in Silver City, I guess, it is easier to get by.

With full and satisfied stomachs Mr. Moore and I headed down for the Bootheel. The mild January day held a hint of clouds. South of Silver City, the land begins to look like Mexico, wild and forbidding, with strange, isolated mountain ranges rising in the distance out of the flat, immense desert. Not like any other place in the United States. I wanted to show Mike an old mining area I had discovered the year before. South of Interstate 10 we followed a poorly maintained two-lane road to the former railroad town of Hachita, which means "Little Hatchet." But now the rails were all pulled up, and there was not much reason for its existence. The only reminder of the railroad was a large water tank with a spout for steam engines, stark against the desert sky.

About 10 miles south of Hachita we headed into desert on a dirt road and soon came to the old mines. There were some posted claims, some decrepit buildings and piles of ore. I parked the Blazer in a wash, more or less out of sight. Realizing that in this remote country, so close to the border, we might meet unexpected persons, we both each strapped on handguns, the 9 mm Smith & Wesson for me, the .38-caliber "Little Pepé, the Desert Stinger" for Mike. I swept the area with binoculars, seeing nothing but stark, empty desert. Mr. Moore collected a few ore samples while I explored a bit on foot. The road headed east toward the border, but seemed to peter out. I saw no habitations or roads to the south. Nothing but a few dust devils. Probably drug and people-smuggling country. I had not wanted, the year before, to camp out down here. On this day too I felt a sense of unease. So we just took some photographs and headed back to the paved road.

Approaching it, I saw a Border Patrol vehicle going south. It suddenly stopped, backed up and turned into our road. We were in perfectly clear view, so we just continued toward the vehicle, waiting for us, about half a mile from the pavement. When we got there we stopped. A middle-aged Hispanic Border Patrolman got out and stood alongside the Blazer, staring in. "Hello," he said, then asked Mr. Moore, "Is there some reason why you are wearing a handgun, Sir?" The tip of the holster was showing beneath Mike's jacket. He chuckled and said, "Well, I'm too old to throw punches." The patrolman did not laugh.

He asked what we had been doing "out there." Just showing my friend the old mining area, I replied. "Well, that's a hot spot in there," he said, with no explanation. I knew he was referring to drugs, and told him so. "Who are you working for?" was his response. It struck me as an odd question. "No one," I said. He asked for identification. I provided my driver's license, which was California, and the registration for the Blazer, which was Santa Fe. Writing all this down he asked, "You're out of California, but the vehicle is out of Santa Fe?" It didn't strike me as all that strange, but he seemed puzzled, and asked again, "Who you working for?" Again I told him, "No one." This was beginning to annoy me.

I asked about the condition of the road running south to the border. He answered that he was new here and didn't know. He was pleasant, but seemed quite nervous. Now that he had stopped us, he seemed anxious to be on his way. In the rear of the Blazer were two odd-shaped plastic containers, in which Mr. Moore was transporting his dogs, who were with us on the trip. The patrolman must have seen these boxes, but did not even ask about them, much less inspect them. It was really kind of hard to know what the patrolman wanted to do.

Suddenly he blurted out, "We knew you were in there, and were looking for you." Maybe so, maybe not. Maybe the movement of our vehicle had been picked up by one of the tethered "spy balloons" that the Border Patrol was using these days. But I doubted it. I happened to know that the nearest balloon was 100 miles away, near El Paso. I think the guy had just seen us and wanted to investigate. However, it sure wasn't much of an investigation. The patrolman concluded the encounter with some light banter. I thought of complimenting his "handling of the contact," but decided not to complicate things. Soon Mike and I were back on our way, glad to be rolling again, and already chuckling about the incident.

On Highway 81 we pushed on south toward the outpost at Antelope Wells, "America's Loneliest Border Crossing," at the far southern tip of the Bootheel. I had been there once before and remembered that an airplane had been parked next to the U.S. Customs office. We were just about the only vehicle on the road, but we did meet a pickup hauling a horse trailer and a bunch of cowboys. Partway down we diverted onto a dirt road that went in on the north side of the Hachita Mountains, a game refuge for desert bighorn sheep. But pretty soon we came to a muddy area that made further progress on that dubious road inadvisable. So we retreated to the paved road, which soon degenerated into a construction zone, with crews working to take the asphalt all the way to the border. I much preferred the dirt trail we had followed in 1978, when we camped in the mesquite and had the whole place to ourselves.

The last section of road before the border, running through a grassy valley, was not yet paved. What few side roads there were came with unfriendly signs warning of "armed patrols." Much of the land down there now belonged to either the experimental Gray Ranch, which had been closed to public travel, or to the huge Phelps Dodge Corporation, whose now-closed copper smelter dominated the Playa Valley to the north. The prevailing feeling in that desolate part of the state was that "Copper Works for New Mexico!" There was a decidedly lower regard for "eco-ranches," where good old boys could no longer even go hunting.

The American side of the Antelope Wells border crossing consisted of a couple of suburban-style bungalows, a garage, a guardhouse with barrier lowered, and a dirt airstrip where small planes could land. The Mexican side, with a blue pickup lying on its side, presented somewhat the same scene, except for more disorder and no airstrip. We pulled up to the American office, got out, stretched, and looked around. The sky had become completely overcast but the air was not at all cold. I figured it very seldom got cold down there. Might even have provided a welcome change when it did. Even after my time at Rocking L Ranch, the place struck me as lonely and depressing. I wondered what being stationed there was like.

In the office were two middle-aged U. S. Customs officers. Both were talkative and friendly, and seemed glad to have visitors. They wore dark-blue jumpsuit uniforms and were packing firearms. One was reading a book, "None Dare Call It Conspiracy," which he urged us to read, "to know what's going on in this country." My father had also discovered this alarmist right-wing tome, and I was familiar with it. I told the officer, and he was pleased.

They expressed little interest in Mexico, spoke no Spanish, and had little contact with their *compadre* on other side, whom I had read had been at his post since the late 1940s and had the longest tenure of any public official in Mexico. Oh, they said, he was a good fellow and they visited him from time to time, but I had the feeling it was not often. They seemed to like it down there. No pressures. One was married, the other not, and I guess the routine was not too troubling. I asked about the airplane I had seen on my previous visit. They said it came now and then, never knew when. The non-reader, a heavyset fellow, was only too happy to pose for photographs, "frisking" Mr. Moore in a very professional manner.

Our encounter with the Border Patrolman amused these boys. They did not know that particular one, so I guess he was indeed new to the area. When we ventured that perhaps he thought we were dope smugglers, they both guffawed. They had been in this business for more than 20 years, they said, "and you fellows are so far from the profile that it's almost funny." One of them suggested that Mike's pistol probably made the fellow think we were with another federal agency, and that was why he kept asking, "Who do you work for?"

Back under the Red Roof in Silver City that night for another good steak and more beers, Old Mr. Moore and I reflected upon our long-delayed return to the Bootheel, 17 years after we first found it. Except for a little more pavement and a lot more smuggling, very little about the implacable, majestic countryside was different, we agreed. Then Mike capped off the trip with this observation: "Just about all our amusement this time around has been provided by the U.S. Government." I couldn't dispute him on that.

25

New Mexico's Las Vegas

Dayton and "tall Darla" with Tom Mix (Serge Darrigrand) at
Rails and Trails Day in Las Vegas, New Mexico.

On a bright June day Deborah and I drove over to Las Vegas, New Mexico, for the last day of the "Santa Fe Trail and Rail" celebration. The 60-mile ride reminded us that New Mexico is still a largely vacant state, even this close to its capital city. "Las Vegas" means "the meadows," and the name is appropriate. The southernmost tip of the Rocky Mountain chain ends at Las Vegas, and the Great Plains begin. Or coming from the east, I guess, Las Vegas is where the Great Plains end and the Rockies begin.

Anyway, Las Vegas is an old mercantile and railroad town, once the busiest in the state. In the old days it was a stop on the Santa Fe Trail; and then when a railroad replaced the Trail, Las Vegas was situated perfectly to capitalize on progress. The trains could not get over the mountains, so the tracks were laid through flat country. Las Vegas became the New Mexico hub of operations for the Atchison, Topeka & Santa Fe Railroad (despite that colorful, romantic and musically famous name, Santa Fe itself was served by just a spur line). From Las Vegas the tracks pushed on through the lowlands to Albuquerque, which in the 20th century surpassed Santa Fe as the state's biggest city.

Many railroad executives from the AT&SF were stationed in Las Vegas, and most of them came from the East or Midwest. They did not relate to New Mexico's native mud architecture, and wanted to live in houses like the ones they remembered back home. The tracks made it easy for bricks, lumber, glass and other building materials to be shipped to Las Vegas, and the railroad paid the freight. As a result, a large residential section of the city looks like it came right out of Illinois or Ohio. Ringing Las Vegas, however, are poor adobe settlements that seem to have been shipped north from Mexico. As I said, it's an interesting town. For a while in the 1970s, I am told, it was known as the "heroin capital of America," and when that "industry" took a downturn, Las Vegas started sliding deeper into poverty. "I have to tell you, it's depressing over there," my neighbor Mr. Martinez says.

But I like Las Vegas. Most of its 15,000 inhabitants just go about their business, which, of course, is what most of the world does. Nobody in Las Vegas is putting on airs, which too many people are doing in "Santa Fake." I enjoy looking at the grand houses, and the Victorian downtown—honest-to-goodness Victorian, the way it was built, not mock adobe like Santa Fe. Las Vegas has its own plaza, on which the Plaza Hotel has been restored to its glory days. The stores on the plaza are for locals, not tourists. Anyone seeking tourist wares must go to Bridge Street, where some shops sell those useless things. But tourists in Las Vegas are in short supply, so those stores do not do well.

The plaza, in its peacefulness, is a very real place, a quality to be savored. Late one autumn afternoon I sat on a bench there for more than an hour. A breeze rustled the changing cottonwoods. The atmosphere was quiet and contemplative. Gathered were a few teen-agers, who seemed just ordinary young people, unlike the punks who make the Plaza in Santa Fe unappealing to me. The kids talked a little while, then drifted off. For the next several minutes the plaza was deserted, except for pickup trucks and low-riders passing by, and an occasional stroller heading home. Two men in cowboy hats emerged from the Victory Bar and unsteadily made their way to the Plaza Hotel, probably for a few more. I followed them. Inside were local folk, modestly dressed, discussing matters of local interest. Except for the hats, it could have been almost anywhere in America.

The average tourist, I suppose, would find this boring. To appreciate simple reality is no longer possible for most folks. They need an extravaganza, a theme park. They have been media-manipulated into this mentality, which holds them in its sway to extract the maximum profit. Obviously there is no profit to be made from people sitting contemplatively in the plaza of New Mexico's Las Vegas. For me, however, an hour of simple reality there is a precious antidote to the atmosphere of Santa Fe's Plaza.

The huge old Harvey House hotel, La Castañeda, over by the rail yard, still stands, boarded up except for one small bar. That area was where the Trail and Rail fair was taking place on the day Deborah and I drove over. Promotion had not been enthusiastic, and attendance was sparse. No effete Santa Feans, just working-class Las Vegans, mainly Hispanic. The petting zoo for children consisted of a mongrel dog and a small pig. The crafts were odd and primitive, and sales were anything but brisk. The atmosphere was small-town 1950s.

We arrived just in time for a show by legendary silent-movie cowboy star "Tom Mix," or rather an individual dressed up like Tom Mix. It all seemed appropriate, for as best as I could recall, the 1950s was just about the era when Tom Mix passed from the American scene. But now on this day in Las Vegas, New Mexico, he had come back. The impersonator put "Tony the Wonder Horse" through some uninspired tricks. The announcer, an Anglo in a cowboy hat, stumbled along, out of synch. His words did not match what was happening. The little performance ended with horse and rider slumped to embody "Trail's End," a Western cliché familiar to just about everybody. Polite applause followed the show. Tom Mix led the horse over to a pickup truck with a camper, with a Michigan license plate. That seemed about right, Deborah observed.

I pulled out my camera. "Go on," I said to Deborah. "Pose with Tom Mix." She refused, so I took some shots of him with a tall Darla in tight jeans and a cowboy hat. He seemed to like having his picture taken. Part of the show, I guess. The Darla walked off, and Tom prepared to get the horse into the trailer. He asked me to open the "escape door," so he could get out after leading the horse in. This done, we stood and talked. He was a paunchy man, perhaps in his late 40s, with the dark good looks of the real Tom Mix, who died in an automobile crash in 1940. He had an American flag crudely sewn to his shirt. The whole outfit, including the enormous hat, was beige, with silver ornaments. Deborah found it admirable, especially his boots, which he said had been made for him by Paul Bond of Nogales, Arizona, modeled on the exact boots that Tom Mix wore.

His name was Serge Darrigrand. He spoke with an accent, which I took to be Eastern European. He was friendly, because we were interested in Tom Mix and there was no one else around. Deborah photographed me with "Tom," then agreed to pose with him herself. He said that in September he would be at the Tom Mix Days in Dewey, Oklahoma, where Tom had been a marshal before going to California. (Tom was born in Pennsylvania.) While in Oklahoma, Serge also would appear at the Guthrie Road Celebration, to give his presentation and tell the kids to make something of themselves.

He had a video of segments of Tom Mix movies to show in the ballroom of the partly renovated Casteñada Hotel, and he invited us in to watch. With us and Serge in the room was an old man by the TV, there to preside over the videos, and one other fellow. Serge gave a detailed commentary on Mix's career, which had been fabulous before the talkies came along. Tom had starred in more than 300 films, and in his heyday was making $10,000 a week. Obviously Serge was knowledgeable, and had talked to everyone left who ever knew Mix. His hero was important to this Eastern European man whose life consisted of going to second-and third-rate small-town celebrations, imitating Tom Mix and putting his horse through the routine ending with "Trail's End."

We watched the video, which went on and on, with more to come that Serge was intent on having us see. I went the men's room, and when I came back I knew Deborah wanted out, that she had tired of Tom Mix. "Deborah, Leroy's here," I said. "He wants to see you." She said "What?" then caught on. Serge seemed hurt as we departed, leaving him with an audience of just one. "We'll have to catch the rest of it in September, in Guthrie or Dewey," I said. "You can," said Deborah, after we left. "I've seen enough."

We walked away from the depot. Some electric trains were set up in an empty building, one of many near the rail yard. In another part of town we went to a coffee shop run by a friendly Texan. We were his only customers. Deborah had a soda concoction, of which the fellow was quite proud, saying that his syrup was imported from some faraway place, Seattle, perhaps. But what does Seattle have to do with Las Vegas, New Mexico? The store was filled with poor art and useless crafts. I did not think it likely that the Texan was going to make it. I expect that on a future visit I will find him gone and the building vacant.

Such is the way of things in Las Vegas. Bridge Street, where the coffee shop was, is one of the purest scenes of its type. The reason is the arrested state of the buildings—and no people or business, always the best "preservation agent." I remembered the motto that Mr. Moore and I had cooked up in Victor, Colorado: "The price of purity is poverty."

Back in my quiet casita in Santa Fe that night, I could not get "Tom Mix" out of my mind. The hurt way he looked when Deborah and I left the video presentation. He knew that we had had enough, that we had exhausted our limited interest in his hero. He had seen it many times before. I imagined what it must be like to be on the road, sleeping at fairgrounds in small towns. An aging, paunchy Tom Mix, still, perhaps, marginally attractive to women like that no-longer-young tall Darla in the tight jeans and cowboy hat. Perhaps he had something arranged with her later, there in Las Vegas, New Mexico.

Was there still some magic in Tom Mix, as presented by Serge

Darrigrand, he of the Eastern European accent and a vast supply of lore? Over drinks and steaks in small towns of the West, before returning to his wife in Michigan for the winter? How American it seemed, living the life of this long-dead cowboy who acted in silent movies so many years ago. Going around to second- and third-rate county fairs, ending each performance with "Trail's End."Polite applause. "Be good, boys and girls, respect your parents, and go out there into the world and make something of yourselves. Just like Tom Mix did. Never lied, never cheated, treated women with respect."

I picture him driving down a lonely highway, perhaps in Kansas or Oklahoma, a two-lane blacktop stretching into prairie vastness, in that pickup with the camper, "Bar/TM Ranch—Tom Mix" emblazoned on the bumper, pulling the horse trailer, headed to another little celebration, to be Tom Mix once again, for a few hours. I pull up to pass, look over. He is grimly determined at the wheel, under the big cowboy hat. He seems tired and vaguely dispirited. He looks over as I slowly pull ahead. He doesn't remember me from Las Vegas—just another damned Okie in a truck.

But seeing me staring at him, he perhaps senses that I know the name Tom Mix, can dredge up something about the man from the lost memory of another America. He smiles and raises his left arm from the steering wheel, thumb up. I wave back, then accelerate past, leaving him and his rig behind, ever smaller against the prairie sky. Serge Darrigrand, from some darkened Eastern European village, growing up on silent movies. Dreams of the American West. Cowboys! Tom Mix! And now, after so many years, he *is* Tom Mix! Headed to another small town, for $500, perhaps less. "Be good, boys and girls. Tom Mix is counting on you." Trail's End. Lost America.

I imagine inner-city rappers confronting Serge Darrigrand somewhere on an empty prairie. "Who the shit give a fuck about Tom Mix?" one says. "Some old, fat mother-fucking white man in a big honky hat. Doing dumb tricks on his horse in the middle of nowhere. Fuck motherfucking Tom Mix! I kick his ass for breakfast!" Serge faces this outburst with tired resignation. Then he draws his old, decorated .44, slowly takes aim and drills that smart-ass loudmouth right through the big pile of hair that decorates his head, leaving a tiny groove in his scalp. The asshole puts his hand to his head, then slowly sinks down backward, wide-eyed. Not physically injured, just shocked and astonished. "Sheet!" he exclaims. "Why the mother-fucker do me like that? What I do to him?"

His friends laugh: "Dude cool. Rasheed dissed the man. Dude popped a cap through his 'do. Right on!" Tom Mix blows gunsmoke from the barrel of the pistol, replaces it in his hand-tooled holster, mounts Tony, looks around and smiles grimly. Then he wheels the Wonder Horse around and rides off into the green, everlasting hills of Oklahoma, into the mists of time, into lost America.

26

Life Goes On in Santa Fe

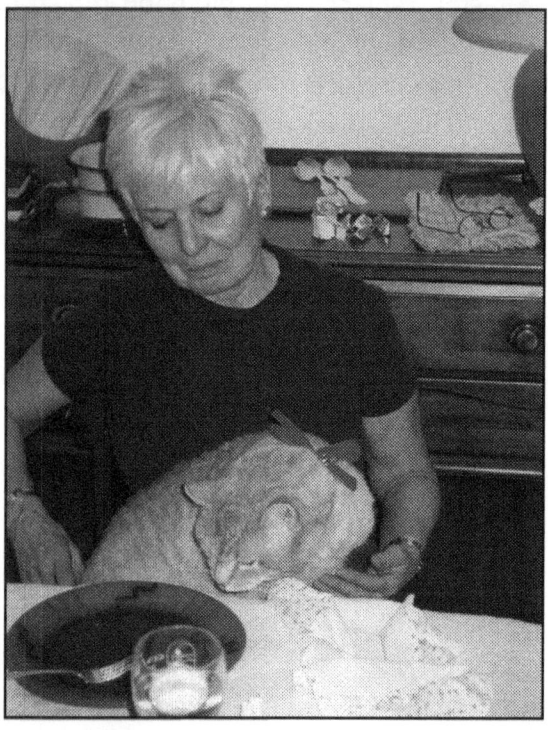

Deborah and Zephyr, at home in her *casita* in Santa Fe.

What has been going on in Santa Fe will continue, and I don't know that anything can be done about it. But some folks keep trying. Yes, they do.

A rally was held on the Plaza to protest the planned expansion of the local ski area, which is interpreted by many as another sellout to the powers of tourism. It was a decidedly liberal affair, and at its heart elitist. Nevertheless, I lent my support to the effort, signing a petition and listening to a speech or two. A recurring theme was that this issue had brought together all three of northern New Mexico's cultures: Hispanic, Anglo and Native American. That was basically true, although at the rally were very few Hispanic or Native American faces. The crowd was about 95 percent Anglo, with an aging hippie/spiritual element much in evidence. The sleek rich Anglos were not. Perhaps this sort of thing is beneath them, or maybe it's that they like to ski, and can afford to.

There was also a recent seminar on how to deal with "whiteness." It was based on unease and guilt. I have neither, so I did not attend.

Santa Fe has been peaceful, slumbering under clear blue skies in the vestiges of Indian summer. But soon the cold weather will come. I have purchased a good load of wood, on a swing through a village north of Santa Fe, and the price and nature of the transaction were both most satisfactory. In town, I would have paid considerably more. In town the price of a cord of wood has been rigged artificially high. It is a way that the locals make the Anglos pay. And pay they do, having seemingly unending funds from sources that somehow seem both obscure and possibly corrupt. The pickup trucks full of wood, and before them the wagons, winding out of the mountains have been a tradition for hundreds of years; but now the rules and regulations of firewood gathering are irritating those who consider it their due. So is the rising pitch and whine of Anglo intellectuals who want cattle and sheep off public lands. Hispanos have, from the beginning, taken their animals into the mountains for summer grazing. Now they are told that this practice should cease, so that Winthrop and Heather can cavort in a pristine setting in their Land's End outfits. Heaven forbid that they should come upon a stump, or the droppings of a cow.

My neighbor Antonio greets me cheerily on the street and asks if I would like a drink. He has a reputation as a bum, and that is perhaps why we get along. I find him pleasant enough, and his conspiratorial greeting I find comforting. He calls me his "favorite focking cowboy!"

It makes me think he feels I am some sort of kindred spirit. The Anglo women in the neighborhood are afraid of him. The Hispanic women are not. He is related to most of them.

My Hispanic neighbor from a nearby house is a native of northern New Mexico, but he feels that the rising tide of Anglo prosperity is a good thing, that it lifts the locals along with everyone else. He calls himself a "Spaniard." People such as he look down upon Mestizos with heavy Indian blood, as is done in South America. People like my neighbor also disparage Hispanic activists. (¡No soy Chicano!) They are proud Americans, and look with unease upon the increasing agitation about La Raza, the "Nation of Aztlan," all that. They also view the increasing hordes from south of the border with alarm, for they do not want the conditions of Mexico replicated here.

In northern New Mexico the residents of small Hispanic villages have banded together to resist the programs of the elitist outsiders who, they feel, are more concerned about spotted owls than they are about people. The environmentalist groups also profess their concern for the traditional villagers, and support their continued access to the old ways of surviving: small-scale logging, grazing, firewood gathering. The environmentlists' concern, however, seems to get lost somewhere in the rhetoric and suspicions of Los Ricos.

Many Anglo people in Santa Fe have no reason for being here other than their desire to be so. They have no roots in the community, no ties or involvement with the local society, few business reasons. Their links are mostly artificial, yet they have usurped the established culture. Often the Anglo attitude toward the Hispanic culture is patronizing. They really do not like Hispanic people and the reality of their lives. They overcome this by sanitizing these realities, thus making those realities acceptable.

For example, the Anglos do not relate to "primitive Catholicism," although they do romanticize it. Try to imagine a bunch of rich Mexicans in New England, eating codfish and baked beans, walking around in tweed jackets and Shetland sweaters, building saltbox houses all over the place, and going wild buying, selling and collecting Massachusetts antiques for huge amounts of money. Mexican craftsmen in Vermont, setting up shops, turning out replicas of old weathervanes, dolls and so forth. Wealthy Mexicans building quaint little churches in New Hampshire "for the locals." Suppose the "most New England" parts of New England were those contrived by rich Mexicans, who established cultural foundations to study and maintain these traditions. This would all be rather odd, now, wouldn't it? And also rather annoying and insulting to the native inhabitants, to say the least.

The scene in northern New Mexico is not exactly like this. But close. I'm sure there are, and always have been, many happy, fulfilled lives in the landscape, even though outsiders may find it primitive and lonely. Before I moved here I thought of the Indian pueblos as smoky, dark, gloomy, cold and uncomfortable places, with people huddled about fires difficult to keep going. I still think of them that way. Perhaps the inhabitants experience spiritual enlightenment that I can only imagine. But maybe they long for the warmth of a new day, dreaming of spring, when they can escape the confines of those cold and gloomy structures—which indeed have now become the inspiration of the million-dollar mansions dominating the hills above Santa Fe, erected by rich Anglos who found a different enlightenment, ushered in by the indulgent capitalism of the 1980s.

All these themes came together in a crescendo of irony, or humor, or something, in the making of the 1988 movie "The Milagro Beanfield War," produced and directed by Robert Redford, and based on the book by John Nichols. Redford is a Westerner and a Hollywood heavyweight well known for his socially conscious involvement in preserving the environment, supporting liberal causes, things like that. Nichols is an Easterner who moved to Taos, New Mexico, in the early 1970s and within a few years was more in tune with the pace and flavor, and the underlying tensions, of life in northern New Mexico than many people who are born here ever become. His book was a masterful effort to pull all of this together. It teemed with traditional Hispanic villagers, arrogant and wealthy Anglos, water rights, do-gooder environmentalists, social workers, cops and all the rest.

In writing his book, Nichols was honoring the life here, as well as poking good-natured humor at it. In choosing to film the story, Redford was guided by the same motivations. To maximize the economic benefit to northern New Mexico, he decided to shoot the movie on location, in a suitable northern village that would resemble the fictional one in the novel. He found just what he was looking for 25 miles north of Santa Fe, in the hamlet called Chimayo.

More than 300 years old, almost as ancient as Santa Fe itself, Chimayo has a large central plaza totally surrounded by massive adobe walls, behind which all the villagers could retreat during not-infrequent Indian attacks. The plaza was still there, but long ago had fallen into decay and ruin. Only a few buildings in it were still occupied, the thick walls had caved in at several points, and the courtyard was overgrown with weeds and sagebrush. It was a faded relic, but quite a picturesque one; and as soon as Redford saw it, he envisioned the perfect setting for his movie.

So he made Chimayo a proposal: If the village would let him film "Milagro Beanfield War" there, he would fully restore the plaza to its former glory, entirely at his expense, and then would leave the renovation behind, for future use by the locals. This touched off a huge local debate and several village meetings, at which the pros and cons were fervently discussed. One faction thought Redford's plan was wonderful. Not only would the historical aspect of the village be regained at no local cost, the re-created plaza would also become a new tourist attraction, to go with the weaving shops and the Rancho de Chimayo restaurant that already drew outside dollars into the community. Yet that was precisely the worst fear of the opposing faction. Observing the relentless transformation of Santa Fe, many Chimayo residents were dead-set against Disneyfying their own rural village. At a showdown meeting the villagers overwhelmingly rejected Redford's offer. His movie was filmed in a nearby town, which he did not make over. If only the same sentiment had prevailed in Santa Fe, 30 years ago. Or back in the 1920s.

◇◇◇

On a fine, clear, breezy day Deborah and I went to an organic farm near Abiquiu, where the artist Georgia O'Keeffe had her home. She is dead now, and her house has become a shrine, attracting a steady stream of the faithful, which the local people do not appreciate. It was enough having the strange *gringa* in their simple village for so many years. Now these often-disrespectful curiosity seekers is a legacy they do not want.

Then the other night Deborah took me to a dinner party given by some of her "spiritual" friends. Now she is upset with me. I tried to explain that I was alienated and bored by the atmosphere, all the talk of yoga and gurus. She countered that this was no excuse for tapping my fingers, gazing at the ceiling, going outside "for some fresh air." She is right: I was rude. I did offend her friends, and for this I am sorry. I just cannot be around such people. Something about them sets me off. I should not have gone.

The "spiritualism" of Santa Fe both repels and interests me, because of what I see as its neurotic quality. What has happened to these people to make them this way? Is it liberal guilt, overeducation, oversensitivity, dissatisfaction or a combination of all of the above? What does it all mean? Is it simply harmless, or does it indicate some serious fracture and the ultimate disintegration of society? Whatever, this stuff annoys me—which may reveal more about me than I want to reveal, or even realize. I should lighten up on Santa Fe. After all, I live here. When I go on like this, Deborah's eyes glaze over.

My father came to Santa Fe in the 1950s, working on some movie that was filmed here. Not long ago, going through his file of letters, I ran across his impressions of the town. "A small city built out of mud," he wrote. "Everything small-scale, low doorways and ceilings, the inhabitants short, dusty plains stretching to the southern and western horizons." He might have been describing a scene from Peru. I wish it were still like that.

◇◇◇

Today I went to a liquor store to buy some beer. It has been hot lately. Ahead in line was a heavyset Indian, perhaps in his 40s, with dark glasses and a long braid of black hair. He bought four six-packs, which the clerk stacked in two paper bags The Indian picked them up, then lurched backward into the man behind him. "Hey, sorry, bro," the Indian said, jovially. The man nodded agreeably. The Indian seemed like a nice fellow, but one who had already "gotten started." As he left he said loudly, to no one in particular, "The ladies are waiting, the ladies are waiting." An imaginary party? Or perhaps some ladies were waiting. The guy had bought much more beer than one man ought to drink. But you never know.

A couple of minutes later the Indian was back. "Have you seen my briefcase?" he asked the Hispanic girls behind a counter. "Not here," one answered, smiling at the other in a way that struck me as condescending. Both of them seemed to be amused. Why? The Indian went to the beer department and asked the Hispanic clerk, "Have you seen my briefcase?" The clerk shook his head. "Sure haven't." He too seemed to find the episode entertaining. I was leaving with my purchase. The Indian walked out behind me into the parking lot. As I climbed into my truck he was walking back and forth, confused and quite upset, looking for his briefcase. I wondered what was in it. I wondered if there was a briefcase.

I also wondered why the clerks in the store found him so amusing. He seemed a nice man, a fun-loving man. "The ladies are waiting." He was also a customer, whose money was as good as anybody else's. But instead of showing concern for his predicament and offering to help, they just casually dismissed him, as though it were a laughing matter. Was he a familiar figure to them, a bumbling alcoholic who vexed them frequently, looking for non-existent briefcases? Or did they just feel superior to him? What was it that made them smile?

In my rear-view mirror he was still wandering around the lot, searching, not happy at all. Suddenly I felt depressed. I felt a sadness—for all the lost briefcases of the world, for all the things that get lost, never to be seen again in our lives. Whether he knew it or not, this poor fellow had lost much more than a briefcase. He had pretty much lost it all.

◇◇◇

There is just something fundamentally wrong with Santa Fe! What it is was spelled out succinctly in a letter-to-the-editor in the local newspaper. "I was born in Santa Fe," said the writer, one Lake Strongheart McTighe. The name made me wonder: Was he an Anglo, a Native

American, a wannabe? "I grew up on the West Side. I have lived and worked here for most of my life. I am a part of this community, but I cannot afford to live here. The city of Santa Fe is increasingly becoming a city segregated along racial and economic lines. The working poor of this community are being pushed out by unchecked gentrification and the city's refusal to follow the guidelines contained in the General Plan with regard to affordable housing and infill development.

"Santa Fe is turning into a playground for the rich, the white and the famous. The lack of affordable housing, both for renters and owners, is a very real crisis that is affecting the heart and soul of our community. What kind of city do we want to live in—a vacation town full of beautiful, big and empty houses for the rich or a city full of homes owned by the people who live, work and die here? I know the kind of city I want to live in: a real city, a city with a government that cares for its citizens."

Well-said, Mr. Lake Strongheart McTighe. The Santa Fe community is ever more profoundly divided, geographically, culturally and economically. I am always aware that at certain restaurants, certain stores, certain "cultural events," there are *never* any Hispanos. Yet on the streets it is possible to spot several of the new Mercedes-Benz sports utility vehicles, costing $120,000 and driven by Anglos. It is precisely this type of arrogance and wastefulness, I am convinced, that is destroying the town.

This attitude has been imported from California, in just the recent past. People here used to make jokes about the Texans, for their loudness, their accents, their boorishness, their flashy ways with money. "If God had wanted Texans to ski, He would have given them mountains," a frequently seen bumper sticker said. But the jokes were actually affectionate. The thing about the Texans was that they came here in summer to escape the lowland heat, came here in winter to ski, made a lot of noise, dropped a lot of their money, then went back home, leaving the town to the locals for most of the year. The Californians came to stay.

With their computers and wealth and frequent-flyer programs and ostentatious ways, the Californians discovered that they could live here while still raking in bucks on the Coast. And once they redefined Santa Fe as a place to occupy rather than visit, they set about to convert it into the California they had escaped. They bring their $100,000 vehicles—BMWs, Land Rovers, Mercedes-Benzes—and parade them downtown as though it were Rodeo Drive in Beverly Hills. They line the mountaintops and ridges with 12,000-square-foot mansions, as though they were still in Pacific Palisades. They eat $80 lunches and $150 dinners in fancy restaurants that could never make it on the native trade. They push the price of real estate beyond the means of state employees. They set an example that tells the youth of this community that money is everything. Confronted with the invasion of the "Californicators," longtime residents are positively nostalgic about "our Texans." I expect a to see a bumper sticker saying, "Bring back the Texans!"

As you can tell, I have developed really negative feelings about California, as a place just simply gone wrong. I am sorry to see California's influence taking hold so much in Santa Fe, but I realize that this is just a natural extension of the Golden State, particularly in its death throes. As the British explorer Sir Richard Francis Burton noted in the 19th century, "The allure of beautiful places always carries the seeds of destruction." That is what happened to California, and now, I fear, that is what is happening to Santa Fe.

When I first went to California in the early 1950s, to stay with my father at *El Rancho Piedra Gorda*, things seemed pretty normal to me there. But probably even then, normality was just an illusion. After all, California had already endured the Gold Rush, the Okie migration, earthquakes and Hollywood, among other aberrations. I remember, in fact, once being at a party where my father's old-time Angeleno friends all agreed that "L.A. used to be such a wonderful place—before World War II!" In my naïve youth, however, I did not see that California was on a disaster course, something that any fool must now acknowledge. Look at what has happened to the children of the people who prospered there, children who can never be satisfied, never. Look at the never-ending hordes of newcomers, from Asia and Latin America, so full of voracious hope. They all want so much, the rich *and* the poor! More than they can ever get.

And the impressionable young, in the grip of the media vulture, are promised euphoria and fulfillment that could not be delivered in the paradise of any religion. There is just not that much to deliver anymore. If there ever was. Even during the Gold Rush there was only so much, and most people were left staring into emptiness. In 1865 Captain Sutter, on whose land the rush began in 1849, packed up what few belongings he had left and fled "The Accursed Land of Gold" to live out his days in the German community of Lititz, Pennsylvania. Like the beautiful, long-legged blonde dream girl who proves elusive and unattainable, the "golden girl" of California was first corrupted by her pursuers and then became a bitch who made life hell for everyone.

These days California fills me with an extreme sense of unease and distaste. It's a place of corrupt lifestyles, dangerous extremes, narcissism and self-indulgence. When asked why he was leaving, the English poet Louis Simpson replied, "Why should I want to stay in a place where everyone is eternally 17?" Then there is the huge destructive growth, and the influx of alien cultures and people of unsure sexual orientation. Los Angeles is a nightmare, its inhabitants wandering in a wasteland of materialism and social disorder, many of them just hanging out, drones of the entertainment syndrome. In the year 2030, when Los Angeles is projected to have an Anglo population of just 14 percent, what sort of place will it be then? Will it be like today's Tijuana, or worse?

Some years ago in San Francisco I was walking on Nob Hill when a sudden, intense rain shower sent me scurrying for cover, which I found under the awning of one of the opulent apartments buildings in that area. I was quickly joined by a jovial Chinese-American mailman, who seemed eager to talk. "You live in San Francisco?" he asked. I replied that I did. "I live in Vallejo," he said. "Not so many Chinese out there." The distinction struck me as a bit peculiar.

"What's your country?" he asked. I told him I was an American. "Yes, yes," he said."But what country did your people come from?" I told him England and France. "How long have your people been in this country?" he continued. My people have been here since the earliest settlements, I replied, Plymouth Rock and all that. He smiled broadly, and mumbled "Very good, very good . . ." The rain was letting up, and he prepared to wheel his cart out from under the awning and continue on his rounds. He gave me a long, slow look, then asked, "How come you let us take over your country?"

I was taken aback, and stuttered something about things not being exactly like that, even if the view from San Francisco might be a bit skewed. But he was on his way, with a friendly wave, leaving me to ponder his question, and his thinking. I recalled a remark made by the late Premier Deng of China, when asked by a Western journalist, "Mr. Premier, if by some magical process the Chinese people achieved complete freedom to move to wherever they chose, how many do you think would go to America?" Deng smiled. "Maybe a billion," he said.

I doubt that I will ever go to California again, even to visit friends, except maybe to the East Mojave, which I do not consider as being in the same state. Nor do some of the other residents of the East Mojave. I remember a third-generation rancher, Howard Blair, with a handshake like a vise. Once he told me, "Out here in the East Mojave, afore World War II, we were proud to be part of California. These days I'm plum ashamed of it. Now we consider ourselves more affixed to Nevada, if ya'll understand what I mean."

I have developed such a negativity to California that I don't want to have anything to do with it anymore. One day up in Tonopah, Nevada, I got to talking with an old boy in a café. The subject of California came up. The fellow was a native of that state, but had fled. He sighed and said, "Those folks over there have thrown away a paradise." Before long, I am afraid, we might be saying the same thing about Santa Fe. If so, we'll largely have ourselves to blame. And in the end, will it be said of the entire United States that "those folks threw away a paradise"?

◇◇◇

Deborah and I go out often in Santa Fe. On Friday evenings you might find us at art openings, usually on Canyon Road. Art openings are places to see and be seen. They are populated by willowy women, ineffectual men and occasionally (very) an angry-looking Hispano or Native American. One year we went to the Mountain Man Rendezvous and Buffalo Roast in the courtyard of the Palace of the Governors, on the Plaza.

Among the attendees was a heavyset, older, red-faced couple, dressed in identical buckskin outfits, he bearded, with a giant mountain-man knife in a sheath across his back. No one was talking to them, and I sensed suppressed mirth among some other attendees. My analysis? New to Santa Fe, rich, and seeking to "fit in." There were no Hispanos at the Rendezvous.

At a luncheon honoring recipients of the annual New Mexico Arts Commission award I sat next to a young woman born and raised in Santa Fe. She said she was glad to see all these new, interesting people here, because when she was growing up the place was dull and boring. On the other hand, there have been articles in the newspaper about prominent people leaving Santa Fe because it is no longer the town they enjoyed 20 or 30 years ago. So around and around it goes. But one thing is sure—the natives are restless.

Deborah likes Santa Fe "fine, just the way it is." The hotels and boutiques do not bother her, although once she did remark that Santa Fe draws too many tourists. She calls the Hispanic resentment "their problem." They should not worry about what the Anglos are up to, she says. Deborah is focused on her own agenda. She does not spend much time dwelling upon Santa Fe's societal issues. I do.

27

My Famous Relative

Dayton presenting to the President of the Historical Society
of Southern California at El Alisal, a painting of C.F. Lummis and his
daughter Turbese, with a Mission sacristan, done by his father.

In 2001 a new biography of my most famous distant relative, my
grandfather's cousin, was published. Written by Mark Thompson, the book was titled "American Character: The Curious Life of
Charles Fletcher Lummis and the Rediscovery of the Southwest."
I read it, and think that a little of his blood might have filtered down
to me.

Lummis was born in New England in 1859, and grew up there. He came west from Ohio in 1884, covering 3,507 miles on foot, to take a job at the three-year-old Los Angeles Times. During a spectacular career he made a name for himself as a crusading journalist, author of almost two dozen books, editor of the influential political and literary magazine *Out West,* amateur anthropologist, photographer, poet, preserver of Spanish missions, Indian-and Hispanic-rights activist and tireless promoter of the Southwest. He was the first city editor of the *Los Angeles Times,* the first Los Angeles city librarian, and the founder of that city's Southwest Museum. His name was recognized nationwide, and he was one of the best-known Westerners of his time. Today he has been largely forgotten; but the new book "rescues him from undeserved obscurity," said a review in *Library Journal.*

According to Thompson, Charles F. Lummis saw in the Southwest a "promise of a far more exalted existence, rooted in the ancient rhythms of the earth." Yet, Thompson notes, "in 1905, before burgeoning cities had spread across the plains and paved roads filled with automobiles had covered the old trails," Lummis felt the region's bright promise was already extinguished. In a lament for the passing of an era, he wrote:

"When I first stumbled upon the Southwest, more than twenty years ago, it was different. The stark peaks, the bewitched valleys were as now. As now, except that the Old Life had not yet fled from them. Across those incredible acclivities, where distance loses itself and the eye is a liar, the pronghorn antelope still drifted, like a ghostly scud of great thistle-down, five hundred in a band. In the peaks, the *cimarron* still played ladder with the precipices; in the pineries, the grizzly shambled snuffling; and in green *rincones* where valley and foothill come together, and a spring issues of their union, there were lonely adobes, with a curl of friendly smoke from their potsherd chimneys—gray, flat little homes, bald without, but within warm and vocal of the Old Times when people sang because they Felt Like It.

"Today the antelopes are gone, the *cimarrones* have yielded up their wonderful coiled horns to adorn the walls of those who didn't kill them, the grizzlies are rugs for persons who couldn't shoot a flock of barns flying low, and the songs are almost as near extinction." I certainly identify with those words.

During my early years with my father in California, he hardly mentioned Charles F. Lummis, despite the fact that both of them had lived in Los Angeles in the 1920s. I do not know the reason why the name never came up. I first learned in depth about Lummis in the 1960s, when I attended a Western History Association conference and was asked, "Do you know that some guy is here imitating a relative of yours?" Thus I became acquainted with Dudley Gordon, a longtime Los Angeles City College professor who evidently had devoted his career to the study of the life and work of C. F. Lummis, eventually writing an earlier biography, "Crusader in Corduroy," which is now out of print. The title referred to the unique corduroy suits that Lummis almost always wore, with a colorful sash around his waist and an oversized sombrero on his head. Apparently Gordon had gotten hold of one of those suits, or more likely had one made, and wore it at occasions like the history conference. With this outfit, longish hair, neat mustache and a cigar, Gordon was virtually a double of Lummis. Some of the other historians thought this a bit much, and looked upon Gordon as something of a lightweight—as if their own studies of how many arrows stuck into General Custer amounted to anything momentous.

Because I was a Lummis, Dudley Gordon was drawn to me. I found him to be a charming and intriguing fellow, his peculiar fixation on my relative notwithstanding. We got to be friends, and whenever I was in Los Angeles we got together. I introduced him to my father, and soon the three of us were having lunches, followed by ritual tours of the Lummis home, *El Alisal*. A handsome stone structure built by Lummis with river stones in Arroyo Seco, halfway between Los Angeles and Pasadena, *El Alisal* by that time was a state historical monument and the home of the Historical Society of Southern California. Through Gordon my father at last became interested in Lummis and his career, and began to collect first editions of Lummis books from antiquarian bookstores. Reading these books, my father formed a picture of an individual whose energies and accomplishments he greatly admired, but with whom he would have neither gotten along with nor liked. Too aggressive and boastful.

My father and I also got to know, through Gordon, Lummis's son Keith, who lived in San Francisco and had had a colorful career of his own as a Secret Service agent. Keith was full of stories, many about his father, and was planning a large, comprehensive book about C.F. He eventually got it done, and it came out some time ago. Whenever my father visited me in San Francisco, Keith entertained the two of us in royal fashion. I began to feel a personal connectedness with Charles F. Lummis—his rebelliousness, his unorthodoxy, the breadth of his enthusiasm, his immersion in the Spanish culture and settlement of the Southwest, for which the king of Spain bestowed upon him a special decoration.

Though Lummis lived in Los Angeles, his writings made it clear that his favorite place was New Mexico, which I too now call home. He resided for a while in the Isleta Indian Pueblo south of Albuquerque, befriended New Mexico's aristocratic Chaves family, went on digs with the famed archaeologist Adolph Bandelier (for whom a national monument is named in northern New Mexico), and lovingly described the state in his book "The Land of Poco Tiempo," which means the land where time moves slowly.

Whenever I hear the phrase "See America First," I reflect that Lummis was the one who fashioned it. And today I cannot help reflecting that perhaps Lummis might feel that the tourism he helped promote has gone rather too far. While Lummis was in some ways a sort of "first hippie," his accomplishments were too vast and impressive for any bohemian dilettante. As biographer Thompson describes him, Lummis was "a popularizer more than a ground-breaking scholar. His eccentric behavior and ostentatious outfits were really the mark of a savvy salesman, but also a form of personal protest against silly prejudices toward people who are different, which was at the root of the racism and xenophobia that Lummis spent his life fighting." One of the true pioneers of the old Southwest, he died in 1928. Though his legacy now has faded, there remain devotees who still honor it, especially in New Mexico and Los Angeles.

For a while, Dudley Gordon would invite my father to meetings of the Lummis Society, a collection of elderly Angelenos who had known the writer in the early years of the 20th century. "Dear souls, like Dudley," my father described them. "They reflect the honor and decency of an earlier period, the best of old Los Angeles. They are fragments of a forgotten world." Shortly afterward, the Lummis Society suspended its meetings, and gradually faded away. Dudley Gordon died in his 80s, a gentleman all his life. One would hope the Historical Society of Southern California keeps his name alive and recognizes his devotion to Charles F. Lummis, who understood the Southwest better than any other man of his time, and perhaps after. In Santa Fe an elderly Hispanic historian once asked me about my name. When I confirmed the connection he nodded and said, "Lummis was the first Anglo to pay any serious attention to our culture."

28

On the Road Again

Victor, Colorado, has been called by the Smithsonian Institution "perhaps the best preserved of any mining town"—shown here virtually deserted in the winter.

Warm winds were blowing in Santa Fe, and I was getting restless. So of course I hit the road, in the summer of 1994. By this time in my life, however, I was driving off in search of old things more than new. Standing in the shadows at the margin of my world were so many people I had called friends, and with whom I wished to remain connected. Yet so many had slipped away, or I had set them loose. I needed to hold on tighter.

Occasionally while rooting through my desk I come across an old address book from the '60s in San Francisco. I gaze at the names and try to connect faces and events, often with poignant success. I wonder about the girls from North Beach—hot tickets then, but now just ordinary women in late middle age. And the beatnik characters—did they survive their marginal existences? With French poet Francois Villon I lament: "Oh, where are those I danced with in my long-gone youth?"

My travels that summer included the Jarbidge (that's right, no "r") Mountains of north-central Nevada, some of the last unexploited country in the West, although more and more people are discovering it now that it has been designated "wilderness." You've got to love the irony. On the way I passed through the honest Nevada town of Ely, in an area of defunct copper mines. Ely has seen better days, but remains rather unspoiled and pure. It's not a neo-Western town that people are rushing into. My adage from Victor, Colorado—"The price of purity is poverty"—seems to apply to Ely and nearby McGill. These places are not really poor, but their non-boomtown atmosphere makes for a normal, non-recreational environment—at the opposite end of the scale from Las Vegas, Nevada, which I consider Hell on Earth. A lot of older folks, I guess, have spent their lives in these parts, have been through boom and bust, and are now just sticking around.

After lunch in a plain but adequate café in Ely I headed toward a suitably isolated place to spend a couple of nights, sleeping in my truck. I had one in mind, a spot I had used several times, hidden in some of Nevada's countless mountains. The road up passed just one hardscrabble ranch. Soon I reached a ridge with a sweeping view to the north, and snowcapped mountains behind. I pulled up in the familiar flat place I knew, and assembled my tarp. Here I figured to lounge around, do some reading and fiddle with my equipment, before meeting Old Bill Howarth and his wolf dog in the Jarbidge Range.

The next morning I heard the rattling of a vehicle coming up the grade. Walking out, I saw it was an old white pickup, hauling a traditional sheepherder's wagon. It disappeared down a draw, and about an hour later re-emerged, without the wagon. I walked to the road and hailed the driver, who looked at me with what I took to be great suspicion. He was a swarthy man with a mustache. With him in the cab was another fellow; and a boy of about 10, wearing a cowboy hat, rode in the truck bed. I told the driver that I was camped "up yonder" for a few days, that I always liked to inform a man when I was in his territory. He got suddenly friendly, said he really appreciated that. Most strangers, he said, gave him a hard time about running stock on public lands, stuff like that. Like he was a criminal. Some even gave him the finger. No wonder he was wary.

My courtesy surprised him, he said. Well, I told him, I had been around ranching and had the highest respect for ranchers—most of them, that is. He smiled. He and his companion and the boy had been setting up a camp for a fellow who would soon be bringing sheep over the divide, he said. Suddenly he pointed and said, "There he is now, comin' over to check on the camp." Sure enough, I saw a man on horseback making good time down the ridge, two sheep dogs running alongside. I told the driver that I came to this spot because I did not like people much. "Well, then," he laughed, "I got a job fer you. I need another herder." I shook my head. "Nope, too old for that," I said. "The hell," he replied. "Elizar made it to 92 over to Colorado, and Domingo is still goin' at 89."

In the Jarbidge I met up with Bill and the good dog Kiska. And, of course, some Rainier Ales. We poked around those peaks and some even more isolated ones to the east. On the day of parting we drove south to the town of Tonopah, a good departure point for heading back east and west. Not wanting to patronize a chain restaurant, we landed in a small café, run by the owner. The proprietor was a small, wiry man with a bit of a Spanish accent. He had run this café for 27 years, he said. He asked where I was from. When I said New Mexico, his eyes lit up. "Me too," he said. "From over near Mora. You know that country?" I told him I did indeed, a rugged area on the plains 40 miles north of our own Las Vegas. He was most pleased. As a boy he had cut hay on the big Salman Ranch, he said, for a dollar a day. He added that he still owned 80 acres over there, and was going back someday.

His grandfather was Jewish, he said, and his mother's people were Spanish. I said I knew about the Jews of Mora and neighboring San

Miguel County. They had come with the Santa Fe Railroad to be merchants. He obviously enjoyed talking with me. Very few people from New Mexico stopped at his place, he said. Yet all during this conversation, Old Bill remained silent. The proprietor assumed that Bill was also a New Mexican, and told some other diners, "These fellows are from my home state, New Mexico!" For some reason, however, this did not go down well with Bill. Getting up to check on Kiska in the car, he growled, "I'm from California." By way of apologizing to the assembled folks, I said, paraphrasing Doctor Johnson on Boswell's Scottish lineage, "But he cannot help it."

When Bill pushed off to California, I headed for Colorado. Utah was in between. I like to take my time getting across Utah, like to poke around, like to stop at little cafes and roadside spots. I like the people who work in such places. I had several meals at the Red Rock Café in Hanksville, near the Henry Mountains, because of its pretty, sweet Mormon waitress, Diane. She seemed to like me, too. "You goin' to be in for lunch tomorrow?" she asked me, on the day that I was leaving. When I told her no she looked sad and said, "I'm sorry, I was just getting used to you." That reaches a man.

At Mom's Café in Salina, I had the Daily Special, chicken-fried steak and mashed potatoes, smothered in rich gravy, a sort of salad before. Honest food, at an honest price. When I paid for it, the cashier, a sensible-looking middle-aged woman, put my change on the counter, some coins and a few worn dollar bills. By habit I began to smooth out the corners of one of the bills. The cashier snatched up the others, and started smoothing them herself. "Jest habit," I said. "One of my earliest memories is my daddy smoothin' out the dollars afore puttin' 'em in his billfold."

"Was he a banker?" she asked. "Lordy, no," I said. "He was just a man who liked things neat and tidy." "Well," she said, smiling, "I kin understand that." She handed me the rest of my dollars, now all smooth. I thanked her and put the neatened bills in my wallet. I couldn't tell what she thought of me, if anything at all, but at least we had had a human exchange. If she watched me as I left, she would have seen me get into my dusty pickup, a new Ford Ranger with a tarp in its bed for sleeping.

A traveling man, maybe she thought, an outdoor man. Lord knows she had seen plenty of them.

That sort of minor personal encounter is why I stop at these little cafeś instead of chain restaurants. Makes a man feel like a human being, a person. Driving off I recalled another place in another state—Darlene's Café, in Dillon, Montana. Darlene, the owner—blond, Nordic, who had put some German items on the menu—brought me second helpings, unbidden, after I polished off the first. "You look like a man's been on short rations for a while," she said. As a matter of fact, I had, and was glad to get the seconds.

For the past week I had been on the lonely 147-mile dirt road that runs through Idaho just north of the Salmon River, in the upper central part of the state. By this time I was good and tired of my own camp cooking. On the previous evening I had camped just below the 7,264-foot Chief Joseph Pass on the Montana side of the border, where Lewis and Clark crossed the mountains. At the place where I pulled over for the night, I found, oddly, a frilly pair of women's panties stuck on a sagebrush, fluttering in the wind.

Just before dusk a pickup with a young couple in it drove up to my quiet and hidden spot. They had a ranch near Dillon, and had a case of beer in the truck bed. We drank and talked. He told of hearing wolves while hunting elk in that wild country. She was interested in why I was "wandering" and camping alone. "I have some girlfriends in Dillon might like to meet you," she said. Wanting to get a "wandering fellow" tied down, I guess. She wrote something on a scrap of paper and handed it to me. "Call us over to Dillon," she said. "You might get on with some of my friends. They's all good gals." We had another beer, and we all felt it moving through us. The fellow and I pissed loudly into some bushes in front of his truck, while she relieved herself more discreetly behind it. Then they left, leaving me in the dark, silent mountains.

I saw by a sign the next morning that the place where I was camped was called Sacajawea Spring. The spot that the gal had moistened behind the truck was still damp, and that got me to reflecting upon our encounter. Those "good gals" in Dillon were just waiting around for "a good man" to show up, it seemed. I wondered what was wrong with the local bubbas. In Dillon later that day, I looked at the crumpled piece of paper with the young ranch wife's telephone number on it. For a moment I considered ringing her up, and maybe meeting her friends. It might lead to something—you never know. But then I wadded up the scrap and tossed it into a trash bin, not really knowing why. I guess I was afraid of some-thing. But what? I entered Darlene's for lunch. After bringing my seconds, she lingered by the table, smiling. I smiled back. She was sort of attractive, if no spring chicken. But I had to move on. 'A-movin' on is what it's all about, it seems sometimes. Climbing into my truck, I saw Darlene staring out the window at me. In Dillon, Montana. In memory. Several years ago.

I fetched up in Victor, where I slept in Old Mr. Moore's house. He prefers to sleep in his trailer, with his dogs. There was a third man also bunking on the property: "Mr. James," who slept in his battered old car. Mr. James was a semi-literate Southern hillbilly who was sure that he had been a lawman Out West in a previous life, and had come to Colorado to relive that life. In his current life, however, he was a vagrant, a drifter. For a while he had hung out in Colorado Springs; but the sheriff there got tired of having him around, and told him to push on, maybe to Victor. When Mike Moore found him he was sleeping in the forest outside town. Naturally Mr. Moore took him in.

When I arrived, Mr. James was anxiously awaiting each day's mail, which sooner or later would bring a correspondence course on how to become a private investigator. He had seen an ad for it in *True Detective* magazine, and with Mike's help had filled out the form and sent it in, along with a money order. Without coming out and saying so, I dropped hints that I just might be involved in law enforcement myself. It was what I had done with the deputy-wannabe at the Christmas party at the Rocking L, and now it had the same effect. Mr. James was duly impressed. Once he completed the course, Mr. James excitedly assured me, he would be "certified," with a badge and everything! "Then I'm gonna do some real investigatin', Mr. Dayton. I'll put you on a BIG case."

Ah, yes, where else would I get to associate with genuine American marginal characters like this? I rummaged through my things and found a golden bullet and badge that I had acquired when I was museum director in Cripple Creek. The bullet was made of authentic area gold, which we retained from our tests at the assay office. Once I had gathered enough of it, I had a local jeweler shape it into a .44-.40 bullet, like one for a Western revolver of that caliber, and inscribe onto its casing the words *Los Hermanos de la Bala de Oro*—"Brothers of the Golden Bullet." Mike Moore had one just like it. We were the "Brothers."

The badge was not official, but resembled one of a Teller County deputy sheriff. I wanted it to assert my authority over people littering the museum parking lot and other minor miscreants, just to make my job a little easier. Before ordering it I had checked with Sheriff Gus Carlson, who said, "I reckon so, Dayton, as long as you don't pull nothin' funny." Gus and I did get along. When I showed these items to Mr. James, he was wide-eyed. "Oh, Mr. Dayton," he said. "I'd surely like to have somethin' like that!" Mike was listening, but did not bother to bring out his own bullet. "You don't jest git somethin' like that," he told Mr. James solemnly. "You gotta earn it—and it don't come easy. Now, Mr. Dayton has been working on some real hard cases lately, come here to Victor to relax. So don't you be botherin' him too much."

The days in Victor were uncomplicated. Each morning I would walk "downtown" to the Victor Museum, at the center of this 250-person community. There I would sip coffee, read the Colorado Springs paper, and watch the comings and goings of the town. From time to time someone would wander into the museum, pay the $1 admission, and spend a few minutes in the past. Mr. Moore's arrangement was that the museum kept the first five dollars of each day's revenue, then he, as director, got to keep the rest. "I've had seven people in here today, made myself $2," Mike would grumble on slow days. Other days were better. On one of them Mike showed me the guest book, in which some old boy from Texas had scrawled, "Best museum I has saw—better than the Smithsonian!" High praise indeed for a collection of old butter urns, photographs and mining gear.

Each noon I would cross the street and take lunch at the café run by a cranky old fellow. "Now dammit, my name ain't Dudley," I had to tell him more than once. "It's Dayton, so don't you be callin' me Dudley no more, y'hear!" Where were Darlene and Diane when I needed them? After lunch I would sit on a sidewalk bench and shoot the shit with whoever came by—Clifton Bradley, Charley Frizzell, Miriam Birmingham, whoever. Or if it rained, a frequent afternoon event, I would go to the little gun shop run by old Gus Conley, and listen to him and his cronies relive the Depression and World War II.

When the sun came out after the rain, which it usually did, Mr. James might suggest we go target shooting. "Ah got some bullets on credit from Gus." We would drive a mile south of town and shoot at beer cans in an old gravel pit. Mr. James had a 9 mm pistol (not to mention a police-band radio in his car), and as a would-be lawman was a pretty good shot. On days when he was hot, he got real pleased with himself. He was the "meanest, fastest and baddest gun in Colorado," he told me. If "anything" happened to him, he said, Mr. Moore was going to put his gun in the museum, along with his hat and saddle. I told him it would probably start a cult. He got all excited thinking about that.

When we got back to town, Victor Avenue was usually deserted except for a dog or two wandering aimlessly. At Mr. Moore's house we would drink beer and cook up some spaghetti. The conversation was not on a real high level. Mr. James would talk about how many cans he had hit that afternoon, while Mike groused, "It ain't been a good day for me. They's all gamblin' over at Cripple Creek, ain't interested in Victor." Then Mike would take his dogs to the trailer and go to bed early, Mr. James would go to his car and fall asleep with his hand on the butt of his 9 mm, his ears on his police radio. I would sit up and read, or listen to talk shows out of Denver. Not a bad life—for a week or two. A welcome change from the pretensions of Santa Fe. Just between you and me, all those rich people and their cultural doings "ain't nothing but diamonds on a dog's ass."

29

Back East in Pennsylvania

The small farmhouse in Pennsylvania, to which Dayton occasionally retreats.
Jack Gallagher rents and "caretakes" there.

In August of 1994 I flew back East from Colorado Springs, to my mother's home in the quiet, leafy Philadelphia suburb known as St. David's. It was like entering a different world. The traffic on the roads outside the airport was overwhelming, astonishing, in stark contrast to Victor. The weather was god-almighty hot, and the humidity left me drenched with sweat. And the greenery! Folks who live in the desert West and become accustomed to its vast, arid expanses talk of experiencing a "green-out" when visiting lusher places. They feel a vague sense of disorientation, unease, when the dominant color, in all directions, as far as the eye can see, is green. Sometimes several days are needed to adjust. But what the heck, I said to myself. Sudden change is good for a man.

I went to make sure that my mother was being well cared for, while the insidious Alzheimer's disease continued its slow but inexorable march through her mind. To my relief, she seemed to be holding her own in the mid-stages of the illness. The live-in caretaker, a young black woman named Chrissy Allen, was competent and also nice. The house was clean and well organized, and my mother's spirits were high, perhaps lifted because I was there. She wanted to talk, and though she often could not remember what she had done the day before, her memories of her childhood were vivid and abundant. Such is Alzheimer's. She rambled on about growing up in Strafford, Pennsylvania, in the 1920s, and remembered things about her parents and grandparents. Her stories were so interesting that I got a tape recorder to preserve them.

Her father, Paul Lewis, was born in 1882, in the upstate Pennsylvania coal-and-lumber town of New Millport. His father was a blacksmith, and a Civil War veteran. The family was relatively prosperous by the standards of the time, certainly when compared with the nearby coal-company hamlets, which did not even have names, but were merely called "Number 10" or "Number 8." The houses were grim company-owned shacks that the miners had to rent, just as they were forced to buy their supplies at the company store, a system that kept them always in debt. Almost all the miners were poor Eastern European immigrants, who did not even know where they were on the American continent, having been shipped straight from Ellis Island to the coal regions on special trains chartered by the companies. Perhaps they were grateful for their jobs and their hovels. They barely survived, always hoping for a better life for their children, The American Dream.

When the price of coal fell, as it often did in the turbulent economic climate of the latter years of the 19th century, the companies simply closed the mines until it rose again. The men were thrown out of work, and although they were allowed to remain in the houses, credit was often cut off at the company store. Those times were desperate for the miners and their families, and the mothers were forced to beg for food from residents of older, more settled communities. My mother's father had told her of gaunt women, wearing babushkas and carrying pale, coughing children, holding out baskets and pails for scraps and morsels, pleading silently with their eyes, because they spoke no English. His mother always placed a few eggs or some canned food in those baskets. The women thanked her by crossing themselves in the Slavic Catholic way. When her son, my grandfather, asked her to explain what was happening, she hushed him, saying, "We always help those in need."

Paul Lewis never forgot those grim scenes from his childhood, my mother said. They helped explain why he became a lifelong Democrat, remaining one even after he attained affluence in the Philadelphia area, where he became a successful businessman, as creative director of N. W. Ayer, the nation's largest advertising firm. He and his family led a comfortable, even privileged life in the pleasant suburb of Strafford, with a big house, a Packard automobile, a maid, membership in the Merion Golf Club and other trappings of affluence. Remembering those women in babushkas and the malnourished children in their ragged arms, my grandfather vowed that he and his family would never be poor, my mother said. He often wondered what became of those people—whether their grandchildren were now prosperous insurance men, car dealers and storeowners, and their own sons football players for Penn State, all voting Republican, of course.

Listening to her, I recalled once driving to New Millport. A raw coal-and-lumber town it no longer is, just a quiet village of a few dozen houses. There would have been some stores in the old days, and my great-grandfather's blacksmithing shop. The coal mines are long gone, and with them the shanty towns. The area had been aggressively strip-mined, but an admirable reclamation program had covered the ravaged hills with Scotch pine and birch, good only for game and hunting, I was told. I found a large Lutheran church, and across from it the graveyard where my grandfather's parents are buried. The home they lived in still stands, about a hundred yards down the road, a solid wood frame house, under big trees with enough of a yard for chickens and a vegetable garden in the back. The house where my grandfather was born, on March 17, 1882.

My mother had another story to tell, about her grandfather and the church bell. A church in New Millport had burned down, leaving only the bell amid the ashes. When they cooled off, the young men of the town gathered and issued a challenge to see who could lift the bell off the ground. None could, until my great-grandfather, Ralsten Lewis, the blacksmith and Civil War veteran, came along. He grasped the bell, strained, and raised it several inches off the ground. From then on he was known as "the strongest man in town." A few years later, those strong blacksmith's hands pressed a one-way railroad ticket to Philadelphia into his son's hands, for an education and a better life than a small coal-and-lumber town could provide. The boy kissed his mother, shook his father's rough right hand, and said he would love and honor them always. He did, and now my mother was honoring him and them too, keeping their memories alive even as she faded away.

During the days back in Pennsylvania, I took drives to places that once were familiar to me, but now were fading in my own memory. I visited my friend Hoffman in western Chester County, where he was growing older on what was left of his ancestral farm. He took me on a tour of the Amish country, on back roads. We talked with an old harness maker, and bought fresh vegetables. On the way back we stopped at a tavern. The other patrons were rough-looking country boys. "They all know me," Hoffman said. "Their fathers knew my father. We belong here." Then we returned to the old schoolhouse in the rock quarry, which Hoffman had made into a home for himself and his teen-age son, Preston. Hoffman's wife, tired of the farm life and the winters, had left him, and soon Preston would be going, too. But Hoffman would stay. He knew where he belonged.

On another day I drove to the Jersey shore, to see the ocean. From the Walt Whitman Bridge I studied the old Navy Yard, soon to close and wipe out 8,000 good jobs. Heading for the Pine Barrens I passed through endless Jersey suburbs, in a constant swarm of traffic, much of it headed to the casinos of Atlantic City. It sadly put me in mind of Cripple Creek, which also had been swallowed up by gambling. But the Barrens were much as I remembered them—old wooden houses, swamps, trees, "piney shacks," white sandy soil. A pocket of the past. The boardwalk in Ocean City also looked like it had in the 1950s, when I went there as a boy, to ogle girls in swimming suits. The boarding-houses with the bright striped awnings were still there, and the tacky shops and amusement arcades. Yet the roads leading to Ocean City were wall-to-wall clutter.

Each night a thick, moist darkness descended upon my mother's house, there among all those trees. I would go out and stand in it, and listen to the shrill cicadas. If I placed myself just right I could not see a single light, just blackness. I closed my eyes and imagined the dark, brooding Henry Mountains of Utah, the moonlit playa of the Black Rock Desert, quiet star-bright nights at the Rocking L. The call of the West. Sometimes the skies opened with rain, and I fell asleep listening to it patter on the shingle roof.

Chrissy liked talking with me, and I liked talking with her. I told her about the ranch in the East Mojave, about the museum in Cripple Creek, about Victor and Old Mr. Moore and Mr. James, the poor boy from Mississippi who could not read or write and slept in his car. "Is he a white man?" she asked, puzzled. I showed her a picture of Mr. James, proudly posing with his gun. "He's a good-looking man," she said. "And he lives like that?" I said he was better off sleeping in his car in Victor than sleeping under a bridge somewhere else. Chrissy said she had to agree with that. But still she wondered about Mr. James.

One time Chrissy asked me if I believed in mixed marriages. I said it's a free country and people can do what they want. Then she asked about the children from such marriages. "Now that's a different matter," I said. "Yes," she replied, "those types of marriages produce children that don't know what they are, black or white. It ain't fair to them. I don't believe in no mixed marriages." Chrissy spoke "black English," which surprised me because her mother did not, and had taken pains to "elevate" her children beyond that linguistic level. Yet for some reason Chrissy talked like an inner-city black.

Chrissy wanted to introduce me to her boyfriend Clarence, who came by one night to take her dancing in "Philly." He was a handsome, muscular, intelligent-looking black man, slightly shorter than Chrissy, who was all decked out for dancing and looking quite pretty. "Chrissy has told me that you has written a book," said Clarence, carefully articulating his words but fumbling them a bit anyway. "That's right," I said. "A book of poems. The title is 'High Lonesome.' I'll get you one." I brought a copy down from my room and gave it to Clarence.

"It's yours," I said. He smiled and studied my picture on the back cover, in jeans, work shirt, bandanna, turquoise belt buckle, boots and hat. "Lookin' good, cowboy," he said. I doubted that Clarence had read much poetry, especially about the West, but I hoped the book would reach him. The next day Chrissy asked what I thought of her "little friend." "He seems," I said, "like a real good man."

A few days later I was back in Colorado, back into my other world. All was the same there. Mr. James sleeping in his car, and shooting beer cans in the afternoons. Mr. Moore reporting a slight upturn of visitors to the museum. I got a haircut for $5, and one night treated Mike and Mr. James to $4 steak dinners at a casino in Cripple Creek. The price, a locals' discount, was right, but the place put me sadly in mind of Atlantic City. The high point of the evening came when the waitress (whose name was Dharma, not Darla) told Mr. James that he looked "just like a real old-time Western sheriff." That pleased him no end, in his all-black outfit, with a badge on his chest and "silver" pieces running down his legs. "Honey, this is the outfit I wore when they give me that prize at Victor Gold Rush Days," he proudly responded. Sure enough, Mr. James had in his possession a trophy declaring him " The Man Who Best Upholds the Tradition of the Old West." Mike Moore had arranged the whole thing, but we never let on to Mr. James.

The next day found me in my truck headed for Santa Fe. The road I chose led to Saguache, Colorado, a town between mountain ranges, untouched by tourism. I had a reason for going there. Years before, I had bought at the Denver Art Museum a piece of traditional Hispanic art, a *colcha,* a framed woven scene, of a Western-looking adobe house. A note on the back explained that the image was of "my grandparents' old house in Saguache, Colorado." It was signed by the artist, one Nettie Quintana. I hoped to find the house and photograph it. Someone at the courthouse directed me to the home of a Mrs. Lujan, who, I was assured, "knows everything about Saguache." And indeed she did know the house and its story.

The house was no longer standing, she said. The people next-door had bought it and bulldozed it down. Mrs. Lujan had known Nettie Quintana, and confirmed that the house had belonged to her grandparents many years ago. Then another family lived there, only to suffer a double murder within its walls. "This boy come looking for his girlfriend in a rage, killed her and her mother," Mrs. Lujan said. "It was a terrible thing in this little town. Just about the worst thing I can remember. After that, Nettie lived there for a while. But she was not a good house-keeper, and the place became a wreck. Then Nettie and her daughters moved to Alamosa, and the house just sat there empty. It began to fall apart. When those people bought it, all they did was knock it down. Guess they just got tired of looking at it." Mrs. Lujan was fascinated that I owned a *colcha* of the house, which I showed her. She said she remembered when the Hispanic women in Saguache made things like that.

My little house in Santa Fe was in fine shape when I arrived. I had rented it to the Santa Fe Opera, and the income from that had financed all my summer travels, with some left over. The cleaning service had been there just hours before I got back. Everything sparkled. The toilet paper was even folded into a point, something I had not seen before. I decided to walk downtown for supplies. Setting out, I passed my al-coholic neighbor Gilbert and his disreputable cronies, drinking beer in his yard. I waved at them and they waved back. The *desesperado* (the hopeless one), as they called me, was home.

That evening in my *casita* I reflected on the concept of home. My mother was playing out her days in hers, which long ago had also been mine and to some degree still was, I supposed. Her father had passed on from his nice home in Strafford, just as his father, "the strongest man in New Millport," had long since passed on from his. Chrissy was hoping to build a home with Clarence, full of all-black children, who would know exactly what they were and be proud of it. Meanwhile in Victor, the home of Mr. James, who had a trophy proving he was the Man Who Best Upholds the Tradition of the Old West, was a car. In Saguache, the home pictured in the *colcha* on my wall was there no more. Both life and death had unfolded inside it, but now its woven image was all that remained. Down the street from where I sat musing, poor drunken Gilbert and his brother shared an old, rundown former store that they called home. Yet some of Gilbert's drinking buddies had no home at all, and slept most nights in the yard.

And I? I was fortunate. After all the years, I had my *casita,* where I probably would stay. *El Rancho Piedra Gorda* was gone. The Rocking L was gone. My father was gone, and before long my mother would also be gone. But I had found a home in Santa Fe. Yes, I was lucky. But perhaps not so lucky as my friend Hoffman, who could say: "They all know me. Their fathers knew my father. We belong here."

30

Eastern Oregon—The Last Refuge

Old Bill at camp, East Eagle Creek in the Wallowa Mountains of Eastern Oregon. He is not exactly a "minimalist"—except when on a weeks long back-packing trip.

Santa Fe in summer attracts too many tourists and weirdos, and I was getting that restless feeling. So on the 7th of July in 1995 I started up the road, heading, in a roundabout way, to the Wallowa Mountains of eastern Oregon, to rendezvous with Old Bill. Wanting to avoid as many people as possible, I planned a north-west route.

The trail north from Santa Fe goes along the Chama River, good clean country settled by Hispanic pioneers three centuries ago. Crossing into Colorado it passes through nice mountain land, with some of the few working ranches left in the state—which cynics now refer to as "100,000 square miles of 40-acre lots." My goal for the first night was the mountain country above Monticello, Utah, where I was familiar with some aspen groves that hide a man and leave him alone with his thoughts. Even the fullest moon barely peeks through the canopy of leaves. I was relieved to find my private spot unoccupied.

Relaxing with a beer, I watched a pickup truck carrying several Indians approach. A young fellow got out, pointed to a certain tree, and asked shyly where they might find more of that type. He said they needed its branches for a peyote ceremony. Why a Native American would ask a white man this question puzzled me, but then I realized that my green Ford Ranger probably made them think I was with *La Floresta,* the Forest Service.

The tree was a lowland species, although I did not know its name. I said he would find none farther up, but would perhaps have luck down below, where there was more sun. They thanked me and were off. Trying to go to sleep that night I heard what sounded like low "boombox" thuds sifting through the trees. At first I was annoyed by such insensitive tourists, but then I realized it was the Indians' drums. That made everything okay.

As I drifted toward sleep, the rhythmic thumping took on the sound of a rolling railroad car. Half-forgotten images from long ago seeped into my mind. One was of a young, blond Czech woman who was in my compartment on a train from Venice to Vienna. We shared no common language, and struggled to communicate with bits and pieces of various languages, smiles and a certain suggestion of closeness. I learned that an aunt would be meeting her in Vienna, and thought that in other circumstances things might be "different." The drums beat on. Suddenly I was remembering a young American girl I had kissed in Venice, in a moment of sudden attraction, gone as quickly as it came.

I recalled the time when Deborah was asked to dance by an older, solemn French farmer at a country festival in the Dordogne. They had danced woodenly, he saying nothing until the music stopped, then only a polite "*Merci, Madame.*" And the shop in a small French town, also in the Dordogne, where we had stopped for wine, bread and cheese. The proprietor, a jolly, rotund man in a white apron, came out from behind his counter to grasp Deborah and whirl her around. *"Elle est tres jolie!"* he said. His wife gave me that helpless Gallic shrug, as if to say, "He is impossible, does this all the time." Images of Europe, so very, very far removed from my solitary American West campsite.

These images from the past disturbed me vaguely. The time is coming, I reflected, when the past will have more meaning than whatever future there still might be. The drums beat on. Finally sleep blurred my sense of unease. I awoke fresh and rested.

I got on Interstate 70 to make time through Utah into Nevada. At Salinas, after a lunch at Mom's Cafe, I diverted onto U.S. 50, known as "The Loneliest Highway in America." That has a nice ring, but it just ain't true anymore. The slogan has been too effective. It has lured travelers. Certainly western Utah remains one of the most deserted parts of the country, one that does not attract "desert specialists." But in recent years, I have noted with regret, Highway 50 does have an increase in traffic—probably caused by people wanting to experience its "loneliness." I guess I am one, though I got there before they did. For the current title of "loneliest highway," I nominate U.S. 6 between Tonopah and Ely, Nevada—167 miles of no habitation, one place to buy gas, few vehicles and endless vistas of barren mountains. But back to Highway 50. After a vast desert valley, the high mountains of the young Great Basin National Park came into view. I hear that the park service is disappointed with the number of visitors since it was elevated from a national monument to a full-fledged park in 1986. I have mixed feelings.

Arriving about 4 p.m., I wandered up a rough dirt road to an isolated spot I had found on an earlier trip, along Siegel Creek. Even in national forests, I don't use campgrounds. When I sleep out I want to be totally alone. I set up the tarp over my truck, and retreated into my shelter. At about 6 I heard some stamping too loud to be either deer or elk. I went out to look. Six wild horses exploded up the hill to the east. Blowing and staring at me, the stallion waited until his harem was gone before following them. At dusk three large birds, which I took for great horned owls, flew silently overhead. They seemed agitated. I ducked under my tarp. A great horned owl can do quite a bit of damage to a man's head. After a while they were gone, and I reemerged. For a long time I peered into the absolutely black night.

Next day I drove through the Ruby Valley, as honest ranching country as can be found in the West. But Elko was another matter. A mini-city riding the crest of gambling and a mining boom, it had big new houses thrown all over the hillsides and dubious-looking characters walking the streets. I resupplied and pushed on, toward Boise. In the Humboldt National Forest, still in Nevada, I made camp. Sitting on my tailgate with a beer, I watched a mud-covered Chevy Blazer make its way to me. It held a portly, middle-aged deputy from the Elko County Sheriff's Department. "Howdy," he said, looking at my New Mexico license plate. "You just traveling' through here?" Yes, I told him, on my way to Oregon. "You have any identification?" he asked. I handed over my driver's license. He examined it and radioed in its number. "The reason I'm checkin'," he said affably while awaiting a response, "is we've had some cattle rustlin' along the Idaho border. Some of J. R. Simplot's cows done disappeared. And a calf got butchered. Can't be havin' that—Mr. Simplot owns half the state of Nevada."

I knew the name—who doesn't in the West? "And most of the state of Idaho," I replied, thinking of the man's $2.8-billion-dollar empire of cattle, agriculture, aviation and god-knows-what else. He laughed. "Well, Deputy," I said, "no blood on my hands." His radio squawked. My license was current, with no record or warrants. He gave it back. After he left I mused upon being interrogated for suspicion of cattle rustling. If anything could make me feel like part of the Old West, that would be it. The next morning I was stopped for some highway construction by an attractive Indian woman on the crew. I was the only one on the road. We chatted, and I asked her about the portly deputy. "That's old Galen," she laughed. "He's been here a long time." Without too much respect, I surmised.

Pushing into Idaho I crossed a long, empty stretch down toward the irrigated fields that line the Bruneau River. In the town of Bruneau I had lunch at the café that bears the same name. Local folks sat at a couple of tables, and another was occupied by solid, short-haired ranch kids, who looked like they were putting in a good day's work. Lots of Mormons live in southern Idaho, and the work ethic runs strong among the young people. These kids did not have bolts through their noses! Then on along the river to the point where it flows into the Snake. Quite a lot of water flows through that desert, all of it put to good use. The name J. R. Simplot was much in evidence on trucks and buildings.

On through Boise and then Ontario, the first town in Oregon after Idaho. I left the Snake River at a point appropriately called Farewell Bend, where the stream begins to curve down into what will become Hell's Canyon. It was lonely high sage country, where sheep do well. Just an occasional ranch, and those abandoned buildings seen frequently in eastern Oregon, where the boom expected in the early years of the last century petered out. I remembered this landscape from my first trips to the Northwest in the 1950s. There was no tourism in those days—just people going about their daily lives, making a living, people rooted in a sense of place, who knew who they were and what they were about. People with character. Without character, people are nothing. So many today just don't have it.

In their small, clean towns, which looked like they have been frozen in the 1950s, the people of eastern Oregon still had character. I had heard of a fellow from Portland going around saying, "It's time to hang up your saws and saddles, boys, and send for espresso machines. Your new role is to serve the urban tourist." But the folks there didn't appreciate that kind of talk, and one old boy replied: "Seems to me that under that state of things your wife and daughters end up being waitresses for them rich folks, your son drives a plastic stagecoach made in Korea, full of foreigners loaded down with cameras, and they'd want me to tell tall tales about all sorts of bullshit that never happened. Well, pardner, that sort of life don't appeal to me, so I'll jest hang out on the range and starve with the rest of the boys, an' be free." Eastern Oregon and its people—the best of what's left of the West. Character!

I pulled into Baker, or Baker City, as it is once again called, a community of 15,000 souls. I had visited it numerous times and remembered it as a gem of a place, with a real downtown, where the merchants waved as you walked down the street, and the Blue & White

Café, where your 10-cent cup of coffee would be topped off repeatedly. Baker was also a place where a man could get an honest drink in a number of authentic old-time saloons. In the second one I sampled, I got to talking with a wiry, outdoorsy, middle-aged woman who seemed to have already had a few. But she was nice and not bad-looking, and she told me that Eagle Creek was running at flood stage, too high for fishing. After a while her son came along to make sure she got home safely. He turned out to be a mountain man and a taxidermist to boot, and a durned nice fellow. As they left he looked back at me, winked, and said, "She's single, too!" How flattering to think I might be accepted into that rugged, outdoor family.

The next day was cool and overcast. Rain had come in the night. Further dampening things was the fact that the Blue & White Café was not open. "Closed for the winter" said a sign on the door—but this was July! So Baker City and the rest of us had lost another of America's fine institutions. I was saddened, but could not say I was surprised. It was not part of a huge national chain, with prefabricated food. (Someone confirmed to me later that the Blue & White Café never reopened.)

In the local museum was a "Leo Adler Room," honoring the town's leading citizen. The woman running the place told me about him. Still alive and then in his 80s, he had come to Baker as a boy in the 1920s and prospered in the news business. He was a great baseball fan and once chartered a private railroad car to take a bunch of Baker people to Chicago for the World Series. He never married, and as old age came upon him, he began sharing his wealth with the town. There was a Leo Adler Playing Field and a Leo Adler Swimming Pool, and he had contributed to just about everything else as well. Right up until it "closed for the winter," he had met his cronies every morning at the Blue & White Café. Completing her presentation, the woman said, "He's a Jew, you know." As if that explained everything. Maybe it did explain why he never found a wife in Baker City. I thought of Mr. Adler, all those years in Baker, trying to fit in but never quite achieving the easy camaraderie achieved by the other men. Leo Adler, "Mr. Baker."

East of Baker the Wallowa Mountains road climbed through dry hills with occasional ranches, then through timber in the higher reaches. No tourism there, just tough people making a living in a rough land. The road grew narrower and passed a small settlement of deserted shacks. A sign said the place was named, oddly, Lily White. On one of our previous visits the settlement had been occupied, but Old Bill, fearing it was a white supremacist camp, refused to ask anyone there for directions. I thought the name was more innocent. In the clouds and drizzle, Lily White reminded me of logging camps in I had seen in Maine, in summers as a boy. The smell of dampness, pine and fir, the thick air and the dull gray light through the conifers, the murmur of a stream in the near distance—yes, it reminded me of Maine, so many years ago.

I dropped down into Eagle Creek Canyon, then up East Eagle Creek, heading for the campsite where Bill and I were to rendezvous. Several times before had we met there, each time all by ourselves. I wondered if someone else would be there this time. Each year more and more people find their way into even the remotest places of the West. A few deserted cabins, left from logging and mining operations of years gone by, dotted the road. At the end of it I examined the Forest Service bulletin board where people leave notices. A few soggy scraps of paper showed that we were not the only humans aware of the spot. But no note from Bill. Nor was anyone else at the spot. It seemed that he and I had won once again. Bill had said he would arrive on the 11th, the 12th or the 13th. I had chosen the 12th, but he was not there yet. No matter. I was prepared to wait another day.

I made my way to the place Bill and I had used before, alongside East Eagle Creek. The stream was loud, startlingly so. That old gal had been right when she said it was at flood stage, much too high for fishing. Anyone foolish enough to try to cross it, I felt sure, would perish. Rain began to pelt down. Thunder boomed in the distance. I was surprised I could hear it over the water's roar. This must be a hell of a storm, I thought. Under a big spruce I put up my tarp, getting only moderately wet. In my shelter I was warm and dry. The only sounds, almost deafening, were the rain and the creek. A locomotive could have charged up the canyon and I would not have heard it. All of it made me drowsy. In the wet afternoon I drifted off to sleep, in comfort and contentment.

About 6 o'clock I was wakened by the sound of barking. It was Kiska, Old Bill's wolf dog. And there was Bill, just agrinnin' and extending a Rainier Ale. We got his tarp up over the fireplace in a hurry. The rain was really coming down. Bill said he had passed through a violent storm on the way into the canyon—the thunder I had heard —and had worried about me, sitting it out by the creek. Bill put up his tent, and we started a fire with wet wood, which eventually burned, and reflected upon all the water that had flowed downstream in the six months since last we met, in the Sierra Nevada foothills. We went to bed at 11:30, with rain beating down and the stream roaring.

Deep in that rugged canyon south of the Wallowa Range we stayed five days, wild, peaceful and free. Then I left, and Bill stayed on a little while. He told me later that in the roaring of the stream in my absence, he imagined he heard "voices in the night."

31

'You Can't Take It Seriously'

A dinner party at Deborah's *casita*, definitely a light-hearted mood, with all eyes on Zephyr, nothing "taken seriously."

Friends ask why I spend so much time in Victor, Colorado. There are several reasons. I know people there. The summer climate is invigorating. The mountain scenery is inspiring. I have a house to myself. The small-town atmosphere is quaint. I can sit on the sidewalk benches, or retreat to Gus's gun store if it rains. I don't spend much money there. Colorado Springs, where I have friends and relatives, is nearby. And Victor is far removed from mainstream, contemporary America. Enough?

Victor is quite a contrast to my other life in Santa Fe. When I show pictures of Victor to my Santa Fe friends they are amused, and often astonished. When I compare Victor to the pretensions of Santa Fe, I feel a bit cleaner. That is not a bad thing. Victor may not be as pure as eastern Oregon, of which it is said, "If you have a ring in your nose there, you are going to be sold at a cattle auction!" But I know I couldn't live in eastern Oregon.

The drive south from Victor to Santa Fe passes through honest, agricultural country in the San Luis Valley of Colorado, then through high, barren sage plains—grazing country—in northern New Mexico. But beginning in Española, 26 miles north of Santa Fe, different signs appear: Bumper stickers saying FREE TIBET! and ANIMALS HAVE RIGHTS! Expensive suburban utility vehicles driven by sleek blond women—*las blanquillas*—or older men with silver ponytails. Weird costumes of every description. Wheezing VW vans with odd totems hanging from the rear-view mirrors. The symbols of Santa Fe: rich exhibitionists, unreconstructed hippies, wannabe artists amid the real ones.

Mr. Moore came down to visit me. "What do you think of Santa Fe?" I asked at one point. "Well," he said, after an afternoon of watching "types" parade past the upscale Galisteo News coffeehouse, "you can't take it seriously." I felt it was an excellent observation. I do take Santa Fe seriously, and so allow it to offend me. If you don't care about a place, it can't get to you. If one could just take everything with mild amusement, as Mike does, and live with the good and the bad—that's the way to do it. Accept Santa Fe as a place of unusual dimensions, sheltering many local and tourists types, a place of pleasant ambience with serious flaws, set in an inspiring locale in a state still largely free of the California decay that sends so many people this way.

There is still very much of the West in New Mexico, especially in the rural areas that make up most of the state. Not the imagined West as represented in the sad, pseudo-Western costumes flaunted around Santa Fe by fools, but the real thing. Well, Mr. Moore, from his vantage point in isolated Victor, provided valuable insight. I shall try to reflect upon it when my thoughts about Santa Fe grow too harsh and critical. Take Santa Fe as it is, he advised, and don't take it seriously. Just disconnect. Wise counsel.

The locals, however, have a harder time disconnecting from the wealthy Anglos in funny clothes, because they know that these types have taken over the town. The locals resist, but often in crude and ineffective ways. One day as I was walking across Paseo de Peralta, a spindly Anglo was crossing toward me. Then a "low-slung car" (a media euphemism to indicate a low-rider) inched into the intersection, forcing the man to move out of its way. In the car were four young Hispanic men, who shouted at this fellow, "Fucking queer! Get out of Santa Fe! This is our town! You don't belong here, *cabroń*!"

That last word is a supremely Spanish insult. It literally means "goat," but as an insult it can mean anything the hurler wants it to. In origin it meant a man who has been cuckolded (and thus wears the horns of a goat), but now it often means a goat with its balls cut off—perhaps a variation of the same theme. The fellow in the intersection got the drift, and scurried on without looking back. The young men in the car looked at me, laughed and pointed at the fading "*cabroń*," as if they knew I would share their feelings. At a glance they saw me as the kind of Anglo they respect, a tough cowboy who gets things done. With my Western clothes and big mustache I am more or less accepted by Hispanic men in low-slung cars and pickup trucks. It does make life easier around here.

On another occasion I was walking along Palace Avenue not far from the Plaza, a short distance behind a young man with shorts, sandals and a ponytail. A passing car held young Hispanos. They glared back at the fellow, drove on, and seemingly were gone. But up ahead somewhere they turned around, and slowly returned. I did not even notice them, but suddenly the man in front of me jumped away from the curb and said, "Shit!" I asked what was wrong. "They threw Coke on me, the bastards!" he said, in a European accent. Each summer seems to bring more and more assaults on tourists, and robbery. Local officials and the Chamber of Commerce fear that the word will get out; but nothing seems to prevent Santa Fe from remaining one of the nation's Top 10 travel destinations.

Though I grumble, only half-jokingly, that Santa Fe would be a fine place if it weren't for all the damn people, I must confess that even I take advantage of tourism, renting out *mi casita* for a pretty nice price when I leave on one of my tours. For as long as I've been here, and long before that as well, the town has had an ambivalence about tourism, a real love-hate relationship. This was summed up to me one day by a Hispanic acquaintance, who put it this way: "Fuck the women and steal the men's wallets." Yes, they do like those *blanquillas*! But very little else about the tourists.

I attended a conference about the impact of tourism on Santa Fe. Amid the usual comments on how much money it brings in and how many jobs are created, some bitter longtime residents were saying different things. "You people have destroyed our culture," said Mr. Valentine Valdez. "My city is being turned into a prostitute," said someone else. "I was born and raised in Santa Fe, but I don't feel I belong here anymore," said a woman who runs her own business. What a sad thing to say about her hometown. There are ethnic overtones, of course. Many tourists are rich Anglos, who push aside the locals. Most owners of the facilities that cater to the tourists are also rich Anglos. The locals get minimum-wage jobs, creating a vast sense of unease. Instead of saving the town, tourism may well be destroying it.

Someone coming here in the 1950s would have seen a real community. The shops around the Plaza then catered to the needs of locals, who were most of the people on the streets, at the lunch counters and cafés, or just taking their ease on a Plaza bench. Santa Fe back then had the essence of what a community is all about. But today that essence has been replaced by a tourist-oriented syndrome—something neither normal nor natural, something fake. The city also seems to be the lesbian capital of America, a predominately Anglo phenomenon that many Hispanos do not understand or appreciate. Then there are the men and women in peculiar, flamboyant costumes, perhaps inspired by Santa Fe's artistic reputation. Again, this is something that rubs many Hispanos wrong. It all adds up to a growing Anglo takeover, and a growing bitterness among longtime residents. To make matters even worse, the Anglos seem to be acting with a growing insensitivity.

One afternoon I saw a group of tourists gathered at one corner of the Plaza. An "event" seemed to be taking place. Drawing near, I saw an agitated, hard-eyed Indian man in a large black cowboy hat, directing heated words at a cluster of tourists, children and adults. I couldn't make out what he was saying, but he obviously was angry. With a great look of disgust he faced the tourists, who seemed bewildered, clamped his left hand in the crook of his raised right arm, and gave them all the finger. Then he pushed through them and headed angrily west on San Francisco Street.

I was walking that way, just behind him. "Hey, man," I called out. "Some shit, eh?" He whirled to regard me, but evidently finding me neither a tourist nor a jerk, said, "Hey, bro, those assholes think they can say dumb things, take my picture, things like that, just because I'm an Indian. Fuck 'em! I'm a person just like they are." I didn't ask for details, but it was easy to imagine what the tourists had done. "Hey, chief! Will you pose for a picture with the kids here? Bill, Suzie, this is a real Indian!" Like an oddity. He did not like it a bit, and I did not blame him.

Walking beside him, I said, "Man, don't let it bother you. They are just ignorant people, don't belong here, don't understand anything. I don't like them either." We walked on, him shaking his head, still mad. He was a strong-looking man, his face grim under the huge black hat, which was probably what had attracted the tourists. "They piss me off," he snarled. "I'm getting the hell out of here," presumably meaning Santa Fe. "Man, there's plenty of empty country out there where you don't have to deal with this sort of shit," I replied. He smiled for the first time and said, "You got it, bro." At the corner of Galisteo Street we parted. He stuck out his hand, saying, "Right on, bro." I knew it would be the "brothers' handshake," which ends with the tapping of fists and a raised clinched fist. My neighbor Antonio had taught it to me.

The Indian continued west on San Francisco Street, and as I walked on toward my house I mused upon the encounter. The insensitivity of the tourists was indeed infuriating. Occasionally up at Cripple

Creek they wanted to photograph me or my old, bearded father when he came to visit, thinking we were "the real thing." One time in Victor I spotted a man surreptitiously videotaping me from a van. I walked over and said, "You are lucky I don't take that fucking toy away from you." I was mad and he knew it.

So I knew exactly how that Indian felt. I was glad that he saw me as "a man of the people," and not just another ignorant, insulting tormenter. I was glad he felt he could unburden himself with me. It made me feel that I fit into Santa Fe the way it ought to be, the best part of Santa Fe. Nor was that the first time I was perceived in such a manner.

Walking downtown one windy afternoon, taking a shortcut across a state office parking lot, I was hailed by an Indian-looking man seated in an old sedan. "You're a country fellow, aren't you?" he asked. I was dressed as usual: jeans flannel shirt, down vest and cowboy hat. Not a tourist! "Well, you might say that," I answered, walking over to see what he wanted. He held out a small hand-painted rock for me to inspect, a crude rustic scene of snowy mountains and an adobe building. "I'm not buying anything," I said. "Have no extra money for that." The man smiled generously and extended the rock once again. "I'm not selling it," he said. "I'm giving it. I want you to have it."

Seeing that he was sincere, I took it. "Well, thanks," was all I could think to say. He smiled, said "God bless you," and drove off. On his rear bumper was a faded sticker saying, "Jesus loves you." An Indian man and a painted rock. I put the rock in my vest pocket, not wanting to carry it in my hand all over town. The Indian saw me do that, and swung his car around at the end of the parking lot. He pulled back near me and called out: "Careful. It's fresh. I just painted it, waiting here for my wife." I nodded in response, and removed the rock from my pocket. It rested comfortably in my hand. Carrying it to the library and then back to my *casita* would be no problem. The man waved, and was gone.

At the library the rock waited by my chair with my hat and sunglasses as I sat and read the papers. Leaving the library I ran into Mr. Dandi, a local character I enjoyed chatting with. I told him about the

Indian man and the painted rock. "A good sign?" I asked. "A good sign," Mr. Dandi replied, turning to make some remark to a passing tourist woman, who smiled back. He does that sort of thing. I carried the rock back to the *casita,* thinking about where I would place it, this small, crude scene of snowy mountains, pine trees and an adobe house. Not over the fireplace. Already too crowded there. The kitchen, yes, the kitchen, on the shelf above the stove. And there it went.

I am glad that tourists ask me for directions, glad that older Hispanic men wave at me from their pickups, glad that Indians see me as "a country fellow," if not exactly one of them. That's not bad for Santa Fe. It beats getting Coke thrown on you.

32

When the West Leaves the West

Perhaps the now suburbanizing and "recreational" West will
someday look like this. . .

During my isolated years in Cripple Creek I would go from time to time to Denver, for a little big-city life. I had relatives there, and some familiarity with the place. Denver in those days was still sort of a "cowtown"—an image it wanted to shed, but which clung. It impressed me as having many of the drawbacks of a city but few of the advantages. The people on the streets had a rustic look and were not fashionably dressed. Not that there was anything inherently wrong with that—Denverites were mostly Coloradans born and bred, with a special character. My mother's cousin Bob was that sort. I liked the way he punctuated his conversation by saying "Ahh, shoot."

In those days the restaurants in Denver were solid and plain, except for the fabled Brown Palace. I think it was writer Brooks Atkinson who called the Brown Palace "an oasis of civilization between Chicago and San Francisco." It indeed was that, back then. Now Denver sure has changed. It has grown up into a cosmopolitan city. Its people are very much part of the modern world. There are lots of yuppies making vast amounts of money. Radio station KOA has long since given up the farm-and-ranch reports at noon. Even the yearly Western National Stock Show, which used to be just about the biggest thing in Denver, seems a lesser event. Many of the restaurants now are as elegant and pretentious as elsewhere. No longer are the patrons treated as bumpkins, as I once was at the Brown Palace, when I ordered a curry dish and the waiter began to explain what it was, as though I had ordered something unfamiliar by mistake.

Traffic helicopters and major league sports teams now complement the city. Gang problems are widespread, the underside of urban life. Yes, Denver has come a long way from "The Queen City of the Plains." A cowboy hat today in the Brown Palace would most likely be smirked at—even the Texas oilmen dress in Brooks Brothers suits these days. It all may be for the better, but the old Denver and the Coloradans that grew out of the 19th-century experience are just about gone.

Colorado Springs, too, has changed, from an individualistic town to Anywhere USA—with a goodly portion of right-wing Christianity mixed in. In my time in Cripple Creek, in the mid-1970s, I remember one of my runs to Colorado Springs. Pike's Peak had a dusting of new snow, the air was clean and fresh, and I reflected that this was a nice place indeed. With mountains and plains and plenty of space, it was very Western. But returning to Colorado Springs not long ago, I felt something nagging me as I drove into town.

The fall afternoon was warm. Walking downtown, I decided to get a dish of ice cream at Michelle's, an old-time store with high-school girls in striped uniforms. It was just the sort of thing I always liked about "The Springs." I took my ice cream and sat at a table on the sidewalk. People passing by seemed congenial and civilized, not at all pretentious. A smattering of Colorado College students added just the right mixture of youth and exuberance. It was all relaxing and pleasant. But back in my truck, headed over Ute Pass—"up the mountain," as Cripple Creek folks used to say—the nagging sensation returned. Something about Colorado Springs, nice as it was, was different.

Then it hit me: In spite of the same mountains and plains, Colorado Springs was no longer "Western." It was just another city, with the same people one would see elsewhere in America. No men in Western hats downtown, no influence of farm or ranch. All the stuff I remembered was gone, had slipped away. Bronco's restaurant, on the eastern edge of town, had been a place where rustics from the plains stopped for breakfast, supper or just coffee, on their way to and from "town." Gone! Torn down and replaced by some chain thing catering to cookie-cutter people. Shopping malls and suburban houses spread east and north, as far as the eye could see. The city's downtown was struggling to stay alive. It was no longer the vital core I remembered.

My nagging thought reverberated: Colorado Springs was no longer *Western*! I could see all the rest of the state being drawn along the same path, away from its roots and essence. Yes, the West was being suburbanized. I remembered the maxim that if one thing were taken away and not replaced with something of value, what was left was a vacuum, which would fill with decay. I did not think that what was being taken from Colorado was being replaced with anything of value.

Toward Cripple Creek the aspens were at the height of their glory. The stream of tourists coming to view this yearly spectacle was now called "The Fall Foliage Industry," an offshoot of the general "Tourist Industry." So very many Coloradoans had been reduced to "dancing like monkeys for tourists"—certainly the people of Cripple Creek, where gambling casinos had transformed the once-rugged, once-haunted town into a theme park. I wondered what the ultimate value would be.

I thought of the historic yearly fall migration south on the branch of the Denver & Rio Grande railroad called the "Chile Line," down through the San Luis Valley into northern New Mexico and eventually Santa Fe, of Hispanic men with bedrolls coming back from summers on the sheep ranges of Montana, Wyoming—and Colorado. It was one of the things that gave Colorado its special character, its "Westernness." Suburban-ized Colorado was not nearly such an interesting place, I reflected, with people glued to the TV, becoming drones of the media. No, that sort of thing did not, to my way of thinking, produce character, which is ulti-mately what defines a people.

It struck me that America was producing a society of people pret-ty much like cats—beings simply looking for something to eat, a warm place to sleep, someone to procreate with, a little amusement, and not much else. No sense of past or future, no heritage or cultural tradi-tions. Just here. Like cats! A society of people like cats! Deborah, who has civilized the once-feral Zephyr, has warned me against such top-ics. She says people do understand, do not want to think or talk about such things. "Try to control your mind, Dayton," she says. "And your mouth."

33

The Southwest—Land of Contrast

Shape, color, shadow, emptiness and deep mystery combine with long
human history to form the Southwest.

The great American Southwest is a vast land of intense contrast. Of silence and sweeping vistas, great multicolored clouds, "walking rain" drifting across mesas and arroyos. And of wind—dry cold, or hot churning, out of places with strange forms and hidden twistings. Dust devils whirling out of nowhere, dancing across the desert and suddenly there no more. Always the unexpected cottonwoods bursting into color in shadowy, wrinkled canyons, aspens high up on cloud-mottled slopes—gold blazing against gray-green, or the intense clarity and blueness of a sky unlike the sky anywhere else. Mountain ranges fading away into tawny deserts, the horizon ridged in heat-distorted slow-moving afternoons of *poco tiempo.*

Sudden deep canyons, cut strangely into red and ochre rock, rock baked by the sun, where things disappear, taken by the wind, to be no more seen in this world. Things that are suddenly no more, but then reappear elsewhere in different forms: A raven, starkly black against snow. Eyes glittering just beyond the circle of firelight. A puma hunting quietly on the forested edge of Escudilla Mountain. Reflections from the evening light fading westward across Arizona. Little shadows jumping into darkness across the Painted Desert, suddenly gone. Things happening at the edge of Spirit Country, pots and pans flying in a circle around the campfire. Strange talk of "Catholic treasure hidden up there on Animas Peak." The dry smell of ponderosas in the sun. The brittle sound of sand drifting across the polished smoothness of slickrock. And emptiness beyond imagination, a loneliness, even a sense of loss at times, a strangeness rising like a sudden wind from nowhere. Sometimes perfume and a woman singing in Spanish far-off in the immense darkness. A slowly turning windmill in the Bootheel country near the border, and a faded sign reading "HIGH LONESOME"—someone has been here who *knows*!

These are impressions not part of the "tourist" Southwest, not found in the guidebooks. They are from a hidden Southwest, away from the pulse and glitter of the new cities and popular attractions, beyond the slick photographs and romantic interpretations that are everywhere. They are elements, perhaps not individually unique, that suggest an essence found in the writings of "mystical" authors who peer deeply into the "real Southwest." These elements, obvious as the rocks and plants on the landscape, are hints of a path into a Southwest that is multilayered and fractured, like the land itself, broken into complexities and contradictions that cannot be explained in rational terms. The real essence of the Southwest must be *felt*, experienced like wind and rain, or flown through, mysteriously, in a way not known to anything that flies.

The real Southwest is not experienced standing with a crowd of Japanese, German or any other tourists, all clicking their cameras at the mighty vistas of the Grand Canyon while sightseeing flights of bleary-eyed gamblers from Las Vegas buzz overhead. It is not to be found in any of the obvious and publicized attractions that people go to because they don't know any better. Of course, everyone must start somewhere, with a map and a guidebook, but eventually a few find other maps—special maps that are neither printed nor easily read. For these few, the tourist information is put aside, dispensed with. New signs are followed: coyotes sniffing the wind after a storm has rumbled through the high country; the rustle of aspen leaves in a sudden wind, the shades of rock as the sun slides across the sky, or the long shadows of silence filling the arroyos at dusk.

The true Southwest has no fixed or defined boundaries; one comes into the region in stages, through an awareness of certain changes. Suddenly, one is affected by a certain quality of light ("*luz especial*"), by adobe buildings, by piñon smoke hanging in the fall or winter air, by red-walled rock formations and canyons, by the sounds of Spanish, Navajo, Hopi and other languages spoken softly, by the blueness of deserts at dusk, by wind rising in the cool ponderosas, bringing at times *una tristeza para no razón*—a sadness for no reason. One is suddenly aware of being in, and a part of, a special region. It is more a feeling, a sense, than a matter of physically being there.

The process of entering the Southwest, then, is not quite so simple as stepping off an airplane, or negotiating an automobile along a stretch of highway. Nor can the Southwest be exported, as trendy stores and restaurants are now attempting to do. The popularity of the so-called "Santa Fe Style" is a superficial layer that has been peeled off the Southwest and blown into a parody, the appropriation of one group's culture by another. The true things, the things that matter, cannot be reduced to commercial enterprise. They remain hidden, disguised. The Southwestern architecture, design, cuisine and so forth that are being currently bandied about are illusions, things casting shadows to confuse and divert—remember the sly trickster, Coyote?

José Concho loading piñon into his truck in the fall coolness on

Canillon Mountain is absorbed into the scene around him. He is simply a part of it, as his father and grandfather were. He feels no need to photograph or paint any of it. That sort of thing is for *los otros*—the others.

Toward Mexico the land and sky begin to change. The washed-out haze of the Sonoran Desert predominates, the sky displays new cloud patterns across the far mountain ranges of Sonora and Chihuahua, a flattening of distance looking south into different, older cultures. The early people spread across the Southwest following water and arable land, the rivers and streams that cut deep into the rock and formed hidden places. These people built their stone dwellings, their strange little cities that flourished and then were mysteriously abandoned. Today ruins and spirits remain, and winds whisper in these empty places with no answers. Contemporary pueblos and villages survive, settlements of duality, caught between two worlds, carefully preserving their secrets from those not of "the culture," who seek to understand things that are not theirs to know.

Again, strange shadows obscure reality. The modern world nibbles at these cultures, creating a certain confusion, an unease, always just beneath the surface of things in the Southwest. At times this tension creates incidents not easily reconciled, and people are not happy with the way things are going. There are things to be understood from the land, from the wind and the sky, which cannot provide easy answers for the today's impatient people. The Southwest is a land that requires patience, a slow understanding of how things come together over a period of time that cannot be measured as people now divide the movements of the sun and moon. Some feel that the earth is a nurturing thing and should not be torn up and depleted for short-term gain. The *anciano* comes into the assay office with some samples that show *pocito de oro*, but will not say where they came from. His grandson lies on the car hood outside, bored with this "foolishness", but the *anciano* knows that there is some gold to be drawn upon when the need arises. Not much perhaps, but enough.

There is an openness and an emptiness about the Southwest, often with a sense of loneliness that forces one's vision and energy inward, away from the vastness of sky and land that makes one seem insignificant. Amid this vastness the grids of many Southwestern cities are rapidly expanding—Albuquerque, Phoenix, Tucson—bringing a new world of change and opportunity (of sorts) to the region. A "New Southwest" some would say, full of the lure and promise of a more prosperous world, at least in material terms, which certainly appeals to people who have been poor all their lives. But the burgeoning cities bring change that cannot be reversed, at least not in the foreseeable course of things. There are those who observe, rightly, that when too many people come to the Southwest it will no longer be anything more than just a geographical region. The search for what once was will be just the turning of pages in books, looking at pictures and having "weekend adventures" that seek to suggest what once was, or what might have been.

It is possible that somewhere in the future, winds will blow across open desert where once these cities stood, and the skies will be clear once again. Even now, as great water projects make more growth possible, we are told of coyotes creeping at night through the suburbs of these great cities. There are those who say these coyotes know something that we don't, that they are laughing at our cities and our cleverness. One remembers the words of Ishi, the California Indian who was the last of his people, when asked by his "benefactors" to comment on the civilization that he had been introduced to. "You are like clever children," Ishi said, "who do not understand."

He meant this not unkindly; it was just a simple observation. The Southwest, then, is a matter of understanding, of balance among diversity. It is not of cleverness, not of "heaping up." To be of the Southwest is to understand the slow rhythm of hammer blows coming from a cottonwood grove on a ripe fall afternoon in New Mexico It is to be able to answer without speaking the question *¿Que busca, Senor?* What are you looking for, Sir? Ultimately one no longer feels the need for words or pictures about the Southwest, when these things are only the outer layers, the diversions from the essence. Still, one must start somewhere, like crossing Raton Pass in a rainstorm, a point where the stern, ordered symmetry of the Midwest is left behind, where the land begins to look and feel different, where new energies flow from different sources.

There are scholars and artists of the Southwest, distinguished writers and self-proclaimed experts on the region, all of whom have something of value to offer those who seek knowledge and understanding. But the true seeker must be like a sponge, squeezed dry of all formalism and structured notions, ready to absorb those things that are special, unique, obscure even—a few rocks, some bone, the wavy lines of distance, long flat hours of silence. Then a certain understanding creeps across the mind. Most people are too hurried, too preoccupied with the obvious, too distracted by those things that have commercial value in today's world, to wander quietly; or to sit for hours watching shadows and clouds, listening to winds; or to explore mountains and rivers that are not as maps show them. These experiences, without name or definition, begin to shape a comprehension beyond words, photographs, paintings, maps, artifacts or architecture—beyond any of those things, which are merely points of entry.

A very few achieve an understanding that signifies a special journey into the Southwest, with no beginning or end. At this point words lose their meaning, maps no longer have relevance, and the Southwest is not just a matter of geography, culture or history. It is something that can no longer be written about or spoken of, painted or photographed or interpreted. It becomes as one's innermost being, a jumble of fragments that mysteriously come together and have meaning, and then vanish—perhaps an illusion that Coyote, the sly trickster, has formed out of wind and *la luz especial*.

It is at this point that we become a part of the Southwest, that we are absorbed into the rocks baked by the sun, into those fall afternoons of blazing cottonwoods, when we find ourselves casting shadows on adobe walls that are no longer strange to us. It is this understanding that challenges our way with words, that makes it difficult to explain a *loco moon* struggling to rise over Truchas Peak, filling the electric arroyos with a chalky whiteness, with *un silencio sin significado*.

34

A West No Longer Relevant?

For some, the West is a long, lonely and hot old dusty road,
where a man is always "amovin' on. . ."

O n a train rolling across western Nebraska in 1929, my
grandfather Paul Lewis wrote a letter to his young daughter
Dorothy, who was to become my mother. He and a group
of other high executives from the Philadelphia advertising

agency N. W. Ayer, some accompanied by their wives, were on their way to the West Coast, to develop some big accounts there. Their transcontinental journey started in Philadelphia, on the Pennsylvania Railroad. In Chicago they changed to the Union Pacific line, on a route that would pass through Omaha on the way to the coast. The luxury train they were riding was named the San Francisco Overland Limited.

My grandfather's letter, perhaps written at a linen-covered table in the club car, with a whiskey-and-soda in front of him, was dated 4 March 1929. It was on Union Pacific stationery. Night had fallen. "Now the ground is completely covered with snow, a white prairie on which the lights from our car windows make a yellow streak," he wrote his daughter. "I have been wondering about the little ranch houses we can see—what people are in them, what thoughts or ambitions they have. Do they look at this train and wonder about us? Of course they do. Hildegarde has been pitying them. I am not so sure. I think it is possible to be happy even in a sod hut on the Nebraska prairie. Anything except to have an envious heart."

Paul Lewis had great imagination. He could see beginnings in those lonely ranch houses, different lives, taking shape and form. Possibilities, not endings. Promise. I think he would be pleased to know that more than seven decades after he sent those thoughts to his daughter in Strafford, Pennsylvania, I, his grandson whom he then could not picture, would be studying his words, reflecting upon their meaning, and agreeing with them.

Once we get into a thing it is often hard to find a way out. This book, for example. For me it started with a train trip west from Pennsylvania in 1951. Or did it? Maybe it started 22 years earlier, on a train trip west from Pennsylvania taken by my grandfather. More likely it started with a train trip west taken by my father, in 1924. I feel that my life journey has been unplanned. But it definitely has been a journey. Many, many journeys.

I take airplanes now. I fly back east frequently these days, to stay for a month or two at the small suburban Pennsylvania "farm house" I inherited from my mother. My tenant in the room over the room in the garage, 70-something-year-old Jack Gallagher, keeps things tidy for me. He drives a courtesy van for people getting their cars fixed at the local Ford dealership. Jack meets me at the airport, and joshes me in his Irish manner about giving him "enough notice to get the girls out of the house."

While there I wander old familiar haunts, visit with Hoffman at his farm and see a few other old friends. I go into Philadelphia, a city that my grandfather always said "was good to" him. I explore around, catch some foreign films that do not get to Santa Fe, have lunch at some of the good new restaurants. I sometimes reflect upon how my life might have been if I had not gone west. I come up with no comprehensible scenarios. Then the old restlessness sets in. I fly back to New Mexico and Santa Fe, with all its many defects.

My trips now are shorter ones, not so far from Santa Fe. To Chaco Canyon in northwestern New Mexico, or Canyon de Chelly in northeastern Arizona. Up to Victor to see Old Mr. Moore. Or down through Silver City, the Bootheel, then over the Geronimo Trail to Bisbee. There I stay at the Copper Queen Hotel and drink at the St. Elmo Bar, remembering. Local old-timers and characters come over to join me. I still seem to fit in. I recall trudging up Tombstone Canyon late at night from the bar to Dr. Avis's house. Dr. Avis is no longer there, having returned to his own place of origin, Connecticut. Though the old incandescent streetlights I enjoyed in Bisbee have been replaced by garish mercury-vapor ones, still the shadow of me and my cowboy hat is cast upon the walls.

In my *casita* in Santa Fe, I wonder how to end this book. I realize that it has of itself been quietly sliding to its own end. Well, that's all right. There comes a time of reflection. One often finds a man sitting alone at a Western bar. "Jest thinkin' 'bout things," he might say, and prefer to be alone. Well, I think about a lot of things these days. I am not quite an aging crank wandering the streets of Santa Fe in a bad mood, complaining about everything and everyone. But Deborah tells me, only half-joking I think, "Dayton, you seem dangerously close to that."

◇◇◇

In the last year of my father's life, 1988, I drove over from the

Rocking L Ranch in the East Mojave to visit him in Santa Monica. He was alert and active, and asked all about the ranch, which he had seen, and the cats. One afternoon we walked on the old Santa Monica pier, which was being rebuilt. Toward the end of the structure a tall, lanky fellow in logger's boots was pounding long spikes into the planks. He seemed the "sort of Gary Cooper type" that my father admired. We stopped to watch. The man paused and looked up. Seeing my elderly, bearded father, he smiled. "Hey, old-timer, " he said pleasantly. "Bet you've seen some things—some of the lost things!" My father nodded.

During the years before he became an old-timer, my father was perceived in a different way. A Los Angeles fellow whom I knew slightly was very impressed by my father's bearded, dignified and interesting appearance. "Your father could be a *great* con man," this fellow said. I wondered about that observation. What kind of thinking did such a remark indicate? L.A. jive? My father was an eccentric, to be sure, but never a con man. I too am somewhat peculiar, I suppose, but not a con man. I realize, however, that like my father, I have indeed seen some of the lost things. That role keeps creeping up on me.

On my last visit to Santa Monica, several years after my father's death, I drove up the crowded Pacific Coast Highway to have lunch at the old Malibu Inn, across the road from the pier. For me, it was a sentimental journey. The place dated from the early 1930s, and was a longtime favorite with movie people. Long rows of photographs of Hollywood characters who had patronized the restaurant lined the walls. My father and I occasionally ate there in the 1950s, when we came down from the ranch. Over the years the Malibu Inn had gone through a long period of neglect, but recently had been taken over by new owners, who restored it to its former condition and pointed with pride at the photographs, many of which were not identified by name.

I introduced myself to the young, athletic-looking proprietors, and told them I used to come there, almost 50 years ago. They were pleased, and gladly showed me around. As they did, I spotted two photographs of my father. In one he wore a cowboy hat, in the other a homburg. I asked them if they could identify that particular gent. They could not. They were surprised and mildly impressed when I told them he was my father, a bit player in many movies. I said I would send them a "bio" of him, an offer they quickly accepted. They were trying to gather information for all the faces on the wall, they said, because diners often asked who those people were. Now one more was known.

A one-paragraph biography of my father is on the Internet these days. The entry calls him "one of those actors whose face everyone remembers but whose name everyone forgets." Even that assessment is exaggerated, I feel, although the Internet blurb goes on to list 45 movies in my father's "filmography." Some are quite well known—"Elmer Gantry," "Spartacus," "The Caine Mutiny," "How to Marry a Millionaire," "High Society," etc. Yet my father never enjoyed movie work. He did it just to bring in money to support the ranch. One of his few featured roles came in his final film, the eminently forgettable "Moonfire" in 1970. In it he plays an evil Mexican land baron who strangely speaks with a German accent. One of his co-stars is boxer Sonny Liston.

Now he is gone, this bearded chap. This face on the wall. This old actor. The Captain. The proud owner of *El Rancho Piedra Gorda*. My father . . .

Well, I am sitting here tonight, finishing this up at my desk. From time to time I look up at a painting I had restored in Pennsylvania and then shipped out here, where I think it belongs. It is of an old-time cowboy sitting tall on his horse, watching a longhorn cattle drive. It was done in the 1920s by a Montana cowboy who taught himself to paint. No, not Charlie Russell—he was earlier—but by an old boy named B. U. K. Ulreich, as best I can read his signature. I don't think he ever amounted to much as an artist, but this painting is good. It works! At least for me. My grandfather acquired it for N. W. Ayer, and now it has passed on to me and come to Santa Fe. It is an honest painting, about something that the artist understood. It speaks of a West full of pride and purpose, a West perhaps no longer relevant.

Looking at it I can sense the dust, and the bawling, the creak of leather as the man shifts in his saddle, watching the cattle pass. Not some piss-ant intellectual who cannot get through the day without a cappuccino or a caffe latte, who is all fucked up worrying about the fate of the Earth. No! This painting is a reminder of the West in which things got done, which paved the way for the *perfumados* lolling about places like Santa Fe. I look at this image with pleasure. Not a "spiritual experience," just simple understanding.

Ruminating in my chair, I realize that this "changing West" is losing its appeal for me. I reflect upon how so many people, Anglo newcomers, are intent on changing Santa Fe into some "imitation Europe," with cafés, galleries and fancy restaurants. It sure isn't what it used to be, nor are most places in the West. I remember the old boy in western Colorado who said, "I am tired of these Denver and Boulder-based environmentalists coming around and telling me how to preserve the environment. Hell, for the last 50 years I've been trying to *survive* the damned environment!" I knew what he meant.

Now it all seems just fun and games. And we know that fun and games do not produce character. No, fun and games are just an offshoot of what my father used to call "the croissant culture"—a bunch of people hanging out and living off each other. There is a limit to that, he said. Yes, I see a chapter closing in the American West. I am glad to have been part of it, before it went away. I am pleased to have been able to stand in the many places I have stood throughout the West. I am pleased even if these experiences cannot be transformed into anything that makes me important in the scheme of things.

No, they were just solitary experiences, but they make life worthwhile. To have been there, to have lived it. Yet all the experiences of life are never enough, just as all the rivers run into the sea, and the sea is never full. We are always 'a-movin' on, toward an unknown end, but we can at least write down some of the highlights of the journey, and hope that somewhere someone understands, or cares.

◇◇◇

I remember Old Mr. Moore telling me how he would sit on the porch of the Rocking L ranch house, watching the open-range cattle from East Mojave ranches drift north, then south again, listening to their bawling. An occasional dust devil would draw his eyes up into the immense blue nothing of desert sky. And when evening fell, the coyotes would commence singing out there in the emptiness between the ranch and the Mid Hills, behind which the sun had sunk and over which float- ed the dull, low throbbing of diesel engines as a Union Pacific freight train made the long climb up Cima Grade. Yes, I thought, I knew those things too. We had all that land to ourselves, but it wasn't ours.

Only the memories are ours—we hold on to the events of our past only in memory. They existed in reality for only a moment, then were gone, like the winds that blew on that fierce night at the Rocking L in 1991, when Mike and I heard on my tinny radio that country-music great Webb Pierce had "gone down" from cancer. In tribute, the Truck- ers Network played a long string of his songs. I listened alone for a while, then shut the radio off and just listened to the wind, as it tore roofing paper off the barn and rattled loose pieces of the ranch house. Nothing by man is forever, I mused. Often the East Mojave winds had lulled me to sleep, but this night they made me feel uneasy and alone, mortal. In the wind were voices, faces, scenes, memories. Everything dies, but maybe memories die last. After the wind has died.

For a few long moments, the older man stood in the soft incan- descent glow of the streetlights. He was confused, wondering about the five U.S. hundred-dollar bills on that table. He had almost picked them up. Perhaps he should have. He had not liked that slick fellow from Los Angeles. Nothing good from that place these days. But—no! He had not touched those bills, and now he was glad he had not.

He stood next to his truck, there in Old Bisbee, and savored a sweet, warm wind that had come suddenly out of the south, out of Old Mexico, he imagined. He remembered the tales his grandfather had told about adventures in that country, raven-haired girls laughing and singing after the clattering, out-of-control battles that Pancho Villa fought against "Los Perfumados," the rivers of tequila trying to wash away the awful stink of blood. His own adventures in Mexico had been somewhat colorful, but not like that. When he turned to climb into his truck, he permitted himself a grim smile as his eyes fell on his shadow on the wall behind him. His cowboy hat seemed distortedly large, the whole image of someone else, not him, not him at all.

He got into his truck, started it, and drove out of town. He thought he was headed north, where rain fell and the land was green, where he was from. Wasn't that what he had told that weaselly fellow from L.A. in the bar? Didn't matter. He just drove, with a vague sense of unease. He used to drive west, there was always something pulling him west. He had wandered all over the West for years, but now it seemed like the West was all used up for him, or perhaps the West that he had known had quietly slipped away, had become a suburbanized, recreational theme-park sort of West, where people looked at him strangely or asked to take his picture. He punched a cassette into his tape deck. Waylon Jennings, "Ain't No God in Mexico"—"Down in Matamoras, being busted by The Man..." He laughed at that. A strange sense of justice in Old Mexico.

He drove into a sudden desert cloudburst, thunder and lightning, sheets of blinding rain. He pulled off the deserted road to wait for the storm to pass. He had sat out many a desert squall in his day, and he remembered the rich desert smell that came afterward, the familiar mesquite aroma. Sitting there he smelled it, and for some reason tears welled up in his eyes. Just that "sadness for no reason" that in the old days came on with dusk in the Great Basin West. Fellows recognized that a man has things in his past that he doesn't talk about, things that bring on the sadness.

The storm drifted off to the east. He rolled the window down and sat a little longer, enjoying the damp desert smell and the memories it stirred. Suddenly he was troubled, by a strange, recurring thought that had come to him in recent days: "I don't know if I am entering into a nightmare or emerging from one." What the hell does that mean? he wondered. He started the truck and drove on, into the night. He had no destination. He had never had one.